MIKE,

If they don't show you
none before you leave
make sure they fear
and respect you!

MIKE.

WE KNOW YOUR NAME

WE KNOW YOUR NAME

Finding the truth is powerful ... but at what cost?

ERIK FOGE

Deeds Publishing | Athens

Published by Deeds Publishing in Athens, GA
www.deedspublishing.com

Printed in The United States of America

Cover design by Mark Babcock.

ISBN 978-1-950794-43-0

Books are available in quantity for promotional or premium use. For information, email info@deedspublishing.com.

First Edition, 2021

10 9 8 7 6 5 4 3 2 1

This book is dedicated to those in the CIA and other government agencies who gave their lives in the service of their country.

CONTENTS

"Everything I write has a precedent in truth."

— Ian Fleming

This is a work of fiction. Names, characters, government agencies, places, projects, events, and incidents either are the products of the author's imagination or used in a fictitious manner. Any resemblance to actual persons, living or dead, or actual events is purely coincidental.

PROLOGUE

The Unexpected, But The Small Things Matter

"In the adrenaline rush of a high-stress situation, you tend to miss details. But it's the little things that make all the difference."

—*Burn Notice*, episode "End Run",
voiceover of Michael Weston

ORLANDO, FLORIDA

June 1990: It was two weeks after their high school graduation. Best friends Erik and Jacques were spending their time doing landscaping at Jacques' house. They had met nearly a year ago at a basketball game. Neither of them knew much about sports, but their friendship blossomed quickly. Jacques admired Erik because Erik knew a lot about history, especially European history, mainly because his family was directly involved in many current historical events. He was impressed with Erik's library, which he had begun at age thirteen. Because of his vast historical knowledge, Erik often corrected his history teachers and helped his few friends on history reports.

Outside school, both had similar interests. One was the United States Navy, specifically nuclear submarines. Erik spent most of his spare time reading and researching every kind of document published on the subject. Even better were the conversations he had with Jacques' father, who was one of four Fleet Master Chiefs in the world and served as the eyes and ears of the admiral of the United States Navy Sixth Fleet.

While Erik and Jacques were finishing their landscaping work, Jacques' father came home and told Erik to go home, get his suit, and overnight bag to spend the night. He told Erik that he had already gotten permission from his parents. Over dinner, Erik studied the master chief's mannerisms. He was impressed by his appearance, as well as his alertness and decisiveness. Erik couldn't contain his curiosity. He took a deep breath and peered down the table into the cold and untelling eyes of the master chief. "Master Chief, may I ask why I am staying the night and why I need my suit?"

In his authoritarian military tone, he replied, "You and Jacques are going to meet some individuals tomorrow morning." He took a sip of his tea and added, "And after supper, you boys are going to help clear the table and clean up the kitchen. Then go to bed because you are getting up early."

Jacques knew never to question his father when he had

that tone; however, though Erik was aware of the tone, he probed further. "May I ask who?" The stare from the master chief compared with Medusa's when she turned a man into stone. "No, you may not."

The next morning Jacques and Erik were awakened by the bedroom door abruptly opening and the order to shower, get their suits on, and be downstairs in thirty minutes. As they descended the stairs, Jacques' dad, in his Dress Blue uniform, was waiting. Once in the car, they headed to the Orlando Naval Training Center (NTC), and once inside, Jacques' dad parked in front of an unmarked building. Inside, they went to a desk, signed in, were given visitor IDs, and went to the second floor. Erik was told to sit in a chair and wait while Jacques went with his father. Curious, Erik took note of his surroundings: polished vinyl composition tile floor reflecting the fluorescent lights in the ceiling and matte gray walls. It was not a friendly environment. However, most government buildings were not designed by interior decorators from Architectural Design. His thoughts ran wild, wondering where he was and why he was there.

Erik had never been in trouble with the law or hacked into any websites. He was an average student in school, and he had earned the rank of Eagle Scout, the highest rank in the Boy Scouts of America and earned by only one percent of scouts. One thing Erik was certain, whoever he was meeting knew everything about him and Erik had to decide how he was going to introduce himself. His concentration was broken by the sound of hard rubber heels on an ombudsman's dress shoes echoing down the hallway and magnifying as he drew closer. Then the noise stopped.

"Erik, follow me," the ombudsman said in a neutral tone.

There was no sign of Jacques. When Erik was escorted down the hallway, out of the corner of his eye, he saw Jacques being led to another room. Erik took several deep breaths to calm his nerves and straightened his posture. As a Boy Scout, he knew there was no substitute for lateral thinking. For the most part, Erik could plan as he went, hope for the best, and roll with the punches. However, this time, there would be no improvisation, and he wouldn't know where the punches would be coming from.

They came to a solid wooden door. It was opened, and Erik stepped in. There in front of him was a tall admiral, and alongside him was the Fleet Master Chief, an intelligence officer, and other individuals. All of them were in their Dress Blue uniforms. The room was cold, but the faces staring at him were colder. The ombudsman closed the door. The admiral was holding and looking at a folder. He motioned Erik to take a seat.

Little did Erik know, the folder contained a dossier about him, and provided every aspect of his life to the smallest detail. He realized then that his visit here was far more than an opportunity to meet an admiral. But Erik did not know that yet. The admiral showed no emotion as he skimmed several highlights that had piqued his interest. One thing that had caught his attention was that Erik was able to speak German and Russian fluently. He had learned German because his father was German, and he learned Russian in four years of high school classes. The admiral was going to put that to the test.

Also, the case study indicated that Erik was honest and trustworthy, with integrity, and a single-mindedness that could see, plan, organize, and work tirelessly to achieve goals. For example, as his Eagle Scout project, he had selected a tree survey of a sizable section of the city of Winter Park. It was an enormous undertaking. That and other information showed Erik to be a hard worker capable of assuming roles and responsibilities in areas others might avoid. Besides, the one trait that pleased the admiral was that Erik was more concerned with the cause than with himself and his ego.

"What makes you different?"

"I have my way of doing things, getting information, and figuring things out, which is different from most. I also don't give up."

The admiral adjusted his glasses, flipped through pages of the dossier, and put Erik up to his first test. "Что вы знаете о Alpha атомной подводной лодки класса? What do you know about the Alpha Class Submarine?"

To show he was different from others, Erik chose to answer in Russian. He took a deep breath, dug deep in his memory, cleared his throat, and spoke in a perfect Russian dialect and inflection.

"It was known as Project 705, which started in 1974 at Admiralty yard, in Leningrad." His eyes focused on all those individuals at the table as he continued. "I believe there was another location, but I am not certain where it was." The admiral nodded his head and gestured him to continue. "The Alpha class was a fast attack sub and assigned to the Northern Fleet. Alpha class subs had a displacement of 2,300 tons on the surface and 3,200 tons submerged."

Though his expression remained neutral, the admiral was pleased that Erik could speak Russian fluently, as indicated in the file.

"Do you care to repeat yourself?" the non-Russian speaking intelligence officer asked somewhat angrily. Erik repeated it calmly and objectively, but this time in English. "Anyone can find that information. An amateur could tell us this, Admiral," the intelligence officer said absently, without interest, as he stared at the admiral.

A trait the admiral noted about Erik, from reading observation notes, was that Erik could gather information about people by studying their body language and the tone in their voices. However, Erik was able to go even further by penetrating below the surface, getting into other people's heads, and figuring out what made them tick.

Erik quickly went on the defensive. "That is correct, and I know you will say an amateur will say the speed submerged is approximately 40 knots, which was published in an official Russian publication and Jane's Fighting Ships; however, the real speed, which is classified, is approximately 60 knots. Also, both publications say the crush depth is 600 meters, but we know that it is over 1300 meters."

Erik was stubborn but always respected the chain of command. As a high schooler, he had no real experience with a chain of command a possible mistake when dealing with individuals who only answer to the president of the United States. He was not the most intimidating of individuals, but he was not weak—far from it. People were always trying to put him down, and that is why he was determined and perseverant in everything. Thus, when it came to situations like this, Erik always managed to prove them wrong.

His eyes filled with rage, the intelligence officer demanded through his teeth, "Where did you get your information?" He paused and looked at others around the table as though wondering if others were going to add anything.

"I just read books and publications, sir." That was correct; however, he also knew where to look.

The admiral raised his hand and leaned forward. "The Chief was right about you." He looked to his right and then back at Erik. "You just read books and publications…hmmm," he said with an undertone of doubt and suspicion, but he did respect Erik's resourcefulness.

"Furthermore," Erik added coyly, "It helps to be in the right place at the right time."

"Who do you know in the navy besides the Chief?"

"No one, sir."

A grin came over the admiral's face as he rubbed his chin. "I would like you to work for me."

Erik gripped his knees, looked around the table, and back at the admiral. For ten seconds, give or take a few, he xviii | Erik Foge

stared silently. Then his voice and face got eager. "What would I be doing?"

"You will be a junior analyst."

"Do I have time to think about it?"

He looked at his watch. "You have thirty seconds to make up your mind."

"Sir?"

"Twenty seconds."

"Sir, I would like to inform you I am planning to go to college."

"Yes. I know more about you than you do. What is your major? Ten seconds!"

"History." It was clear the admiral was not going to move the conversation forward until Erik answered his question.

"Five seconds."

Erik took a deep breath. "I accept."

The admiral nodded and stated. "I'm Admiral Bonesteiner, and I control the Sixth Fleet. Outside these walls, you don't exist, nor will there be any record of you working for me." Erik nodded. "You will not repeat anything you see or hear. Understood?"

"Yes, sir." Erik replied. He suddenly found himself working in some aspect of naval intelligence, and he wouldn't have any protection from the U.S. Government. That was because Erik was a NOC (non-official cover), and NOCs are expendable. He also knew that outside the small group of people in this room, he had to assume that everyone was a potential enemy or threat. So, in short, he should trust no one.

"Welcome." The admiral's voice was different from before. It was softer and almost friendly as if he welcomed Erik into his inner circle. Little did Erik know that his talents in research, resourcefulness, and reading-people skills would soon be put to a much greater test—a test of dark, secretive, and even deadly proportions.

1. TRANSFORMATION TO ANOTHER PLACE

"As a spy, you get used to people having whispered conversations about you. It's a little like being in high school. But, when people are whispering about you in algebra, they're a lot less likely to try and kill you afterward."

—*Burn Notice,* episode "Mind Games," voiceover of Michael Weston

ORLANDO, FLORIDA

August 1997: Seven years later. It was a warm, clear, fall day, with a slight breeze tickling the branches of the trees, as a young first-year history teacher walked from his classroom to his car. His name was Erik Függer. He was physically unremarkable and below the average height for his age group. However, he had broad shoulders and a medium build. His skin was lintel-brown colored from the sun. A clean-shaven face, with a hawk-like nose, firm lips, a ridged jaw, and short, dark brown hair brushed in place.

As Erik reached his car, he suddenly felt a presence behind him. The same hair-raising feeling he got when someone was following him. A sense left behind when he was learning the ropes as a junior analyst while attending college. He arranged his keys between his fingers and used his car's window reflection to see who was there. Hovering over Erik was a familiar face from his past, Admiral Bonesteiner, unrecognizable in civilian clothes.

"Good to see you again, Erik. How are you?"

"I am alive, Admiral. How are things in Washington?"

"Busy as always. But not with the navy." Erik raised his eyebrows and motioned, he was intrigued to know more, as the admiral positioned himself by the passenger side of Erik's car. Erik unlocked the doors, and they both got in. Erik hadn't been aware that after he had left Bonesteiner the first time, he was being watched.

"Why are you here?" Erik said boldly.

"You." Bonesteiner was there to offer Erik a job where his personality, aptitudes, interests, likes, and strengths would be honed and used for the greater good. He was about to be placed in an organization that would allow him to use his skills where they would thrive and flourish.

"I don't think I've pissed anyone off recently."

Bonesteiner shook his head. "You did tend to do that when you worked for me."

"Does he still hate my guts?" Erik was referring to the intelligence officer who had asked how he got the information on the Alfa.

"What do you think? However, that's not why I am here," the admiral stated as his eyes met Erik's. "I am asking you for your service."

"Like last time?"

He shook his head affirmatively. "In a way, but this time you will not be working for the navy."

"Who then?"

Bonesteiner handed Erik an envelope and got out of the car. Erik jumped out after him.

"Sir, you do realize I cannot just leave Edgewater; I am under a county contract."

Bonesteiner strolled to his car, totally ignoring Erik. He climbed into a dark tinted, four-door sedan and proceeded to the parking lot exit. He stopped beside Erik and lowered his window, "Not anymore."

Then Bonesteiner quickly left with Erik in his thoughts. Erik stared at the envelope, pondered what was inside and then opened it. He took a glance at it and realized he had just been recruited. The letter read:

Recruitment and Retention Center
Washington, DC 20505

Erik Függer
9208 Bergamot Street
Orlando, FL 32817

Dear Mr. Függer,

This letter is to confirm an invitation to your information session on 2 December 1997, from 8:30 a.m. to 12:30 p.m. at our headquarters. Please do not make specific inquiries of airport staff or anyone regarding this event. There will be an individual waiting who will approach you once you get off the plane.

Bring this letter and a government-issued photo ID (driver's license or passport) to be presented at sign in. I ask that you tell as few people as possible about your attendance at the session. You will be required to sign a non-disclosure agreement. Business attire is recommended.

Applicants often ask what they can do to better prepare for the interview. A portion of your meeting will consist of a discussion of foreign affairs and current events that are of interest to U.S. policymakers. In addition, we expect applicants to be familiar with the history and literature of our profession. There are many books published about our work. I strongly encourage you to read as much as you can about foreign affairs and our profession. Since you will be arriving by plane, please give us a call once you have made your lodging arrangements as we need a phone number to keep in contact with you during your stay in the Washington, DC area.

We are looking forward to meeting you personally at the briefing. If you have further questions, please feel free to contact the executive secretary Julie at 1-800 336-3850.

Sincerely,
Director of Human Recourses

2. THE NAMES OF THOSE NEVER HERE

"For you see, the world is governed by very different personages from what is imagined by those who are not behind the scenes."

—Benjamin Disraeli

CIA HEADQUARTERS, LANGLEY, VIRGINIA

2 December 1997: The driver proceeded down Route 123 until he reached the George Washington Parkway and veered right. Erik was in the back seat of a four-door sedan that had dark tinted windows.

While his always watchful blue eyes observed, Erik made mental notes of his surroundings. Still thinking ahead by nature, he was busy contemplating what the meeting would be like and what questions he would ask. Erik's pride in and love of his country made it hard to contain his enthusiasm as he saw the entrance to CIA Headquarters. The driver glanced in the rear-view mirror and instructed Erik to pull out his ID and the letter he had received from the admiral.

In the grassy areas in front of the entrance, there were several signs giving warnings for all those not authorized to turn around or suffer consequences that could mean being stopped by deadly force. There was a solid concrete structure that looked like the tollbooth on an interstate highway. Uniformed security officers, with high caliber assault weapons, eyed every vehicle approaching the entrance and were ready to stop anyone trying to penetrate the perimeter. Pulling into CIA HQ, if you were already an employee, you would veer left where a security officer would wand your badge before entering. However, Erik's driver knew where he was going and turned right to the visitor center. He parked in a parking spot, immediately retrieved Erik's belongings, and both headed to the entrance. Once inside, the driver motioned him to the desk, and then he left.

There was a man behind a counter with a stern interrogative look as Erik approached him. "Can I help you?" a deep, commanding voice asked.

Handing the letter and his ID to the security officer, Erik stated, "My name is Erik Függer, and I have an appointment with Admiral Bonesteiner."

"Take a seat."

A man barged through the doors, looked to be in his mid to late forties. His Roman nose held his polished gold-plated classic aviator glasses with smoke-gray scratch-resistant lenses. He moved toward the desk. The security officer passed over Erik's ID and letter, then pointed in Erik's direction.

"Erik Függer..." Erik had a moment of confusion and

lifted his head to follow the sound of the voice and approaching footsteps. He saw a man walking toward him.

The smoke-gray scratch-resistant lenses shielded the man's mirthful crinkles surrounding his grayish-green eyes, which had to look down nearly five inches to meet Erik's eye level. His thick black hair showed hints of grey in a flattop-style haircut accenting his egg-shaped face and round, firm chin. His trimmed mustache resembled the wings of a bird above firm lips. He was remarkably muscular and compact like a pit bull, with massive oarsman's shoulders. His charcoal-colored suit went well with his pale complexion. He smiled as Erik placed his duffle bag down, stepped forward, and extended his hand.

"Erik Függer?"

Erik nodded and grinned back. "Yes."

"Paul McLaughlin, but you can call me Paul. I'm one of the section chiefs." He motioned back to the desk, where Erik was given a visitor's badge. Mike and Erik took a stroll to Mike's car, and once inside, Mike started to study Erik. Erik had an inner feeling; this could be Mike's favorite part to see if an individual will shut up and enjoy the view or be an egghead who wanted to talk it away.

CIA Headquarters was on 258 acres. The lush and thick Langley Forest surrounded the structures, and they were designed to keep prying eyes from looking in. Uniformed security officers roamed the parking lot to help those who were lost or needed directions. Mike knew where he was going and parked his car. He immediately retrieved Erik's belongings and both headed to the entrance of the Original Headquarters Building (OHB). Erik noticed several security officers in suits with their radios visible, and the bulges on their upper left or right chests made it clear they were armed.

Before reaching the entrance, Erik paused to admire the impressive seven-story off-white building, with windows that had a hint of green. As he would learn later, that was to prevent electronic surveillance. Once inside, he glanced down to the floor of the lobby entrance at the CIA emblem, a sixteen-foot-diameter inlaid granite seal with its three focal features: the American bald eagle, a symbol of strength and alertness; the shield, a symbol of defense; and a sixteen-point compass rose, representing intelligence from around the world that converges at a central point.

Then Erik proceeded down the walkway, his eyes, like sponges, absorbing everything he saw, causing him to mouth "Wow" to himself. Paul motioned Erik to follow him to the security desk, and, once there, Paul turned to one of the security officers and instructed him to take Erik's belongings. Then they went through the turnstiles after Paul punched in a seven-digit security code. Erik watched closely. They went up a flight of stairs where they took a right and a sharp left to the elevators. The elevator doors closed, and they ascended toward the seventh floor.

"Is this your first time at Langley?" Erik nodded. Paul asked, "How do you know the admiral?"

"I met him after I graduated from high school."

The elevator came to a halt, and they exited. They walked down the waves (hallways) where the corners had hubcap-like mirrors to prevent collisions at the blind intersections. Erik saw through Paul's apparent attempt to test him to see if he would divulge any information. So, he was vague with his answers. Those they passed kept to themselves, and if they were walking with someone, their voices were just above a whisper. Erik thought, everyone is working on the security of the country, yet no one or no department knows what any other one is working on. Eventually, they came to Executive Row, which had its private corridor and a rug, which led to an office where the admiral was waiting for Erik. It was the office of the Deputy Director of Intelligence. Paul opened the door, and they entered. The lobby was very spacious with eggshell-white walls, royal blue carpet, and a window directly behind the secretary. She glanced at them while she was typing and acknowledged their presence. Then she picked up the phone and informed the director.

As he stepped through the door of the director's office, Erik saw a familiar face, Admiral Bonesteiner. His spacious office, with white eggshell walls and royal blue carpet, took up the entire right corner of the top floor overlooking the tree-filled Langley Forest. Framed artwork of naval vessels and aircraft covered the walls. Also framed were photographs of Bonesteiner's military past and certificates and awards of merit he had earned throughout his career.

In front of the window was a large oversized mahogany desk, covered with neatly organized piles of classified folders, color-coded by classification. Bookcases filled with books and scale models of military aircraft and naval vessels were strategically located throughout the office. A mahogany coffee table, surrounded by four leather lounge chairs, occupied the center of the room. Bonesteiner was in civilian clothes and leaped from his chair, with a smile on his face, and his hand extended.

"Erik, it's great to see you again. How are you?"

"I'm alive, sir."

"I see you still say that," said Bonesteiner, to which Erik nodded.

Admiral Baldric Bonesteiner, nearly forty years Erik's senior, was showing his age by his salt and pepper hair and the wrinkles around his soft but watchful eyes that were screened behind titanium framed spectacles. It would not matter if he were standing or sitting; the admiral, Erik still remembered from the first day he met him, at age 19, had an intimidating presence and demeanor that made people uncomfortable. When he spoke, his tone was unaffected by pressure or authority. That calm, but firm, tone had been learned while Baldric had served at the height of the Cold War, thirty years in the Navy. His entire career was in the Office of Naval Intelligence (ONI), which he had begun as a cryptology officer who broke many of the Soviet submarine codes. This ability enabled him to rise through the ranks quickly. After he retired from the Navy, the CIA approached him and offered him the position of Deputy Director of Intelligence, which he was still holding.

"You met Senior Section Chief Paul McLaughlin."

Paul was born into a privileged family. His father was a U.S. Senator who structured and planned his son's life.

After high school, Paul had attended the U.S. Military Academy at West Point and had graduated with honors. From there, he was commissioned as a second lieutenant in the Army. After completing Infantry Officers Basic Course (IOBC), he was accepted in Ranger School. Upon graduation, Paul was hoping to go to Vietnam to see combat. However, the Vietnam War was over, but he was given a choice where he would be station. Germany was his choice, considering that if the Soviet Union did attack Western Europe, he would be in the thick of battle. That never came. Therefore, he focused on military intelligence and made a name for himself. His father had other plans for his son. What most people didn't know was that his father had influenced and persuaded individuals, both in the Pentagon and CIA, to help Paul get those positions. Thus, he had served his entire military career behind a desk, and this continued in the agency.

Paul lived in a world of facts and concrete needs. At work, he was continually scanning his environment to make sure that everything was running smoothly and systematically. Paul honored traditions and laws and had a clear set of standards and beliefs. He also expected the same of others, especially at work, and had no patience for or understanding of individuals who did not value these systems. Paul appreciated competence, structure, and efficiency and liked to see quick results. He had a take-charge personality and a clear vision of the way things should be. He was self-confident and aggressive at work. Paul was talented at devising systems, action plans, and at seeing what steps were needed to complete a specific task. He was demanding and critical because he had such firmly held beliefs, and he was likely to express himself without reserve if someone wasn't meeting his standards.

Bonesteiner glanced to his right and gestured with a nod toward another man in the room. "This is Chief of Station Alan James."

Alan stepped from behind Bonesteiner as he extended his hand to shake Erik's. Alan also had to peer down to meet Erik's eyes. "The admiral has told me a lot about you, and thank you for your patriotism."

"You're welcome."

Alan was in his mid to late forties. He had dark, sunken, relaxed eyes with a hawk-like nose. Alan's lips were firm, but they seemed always to create a frown. His thinning black hair made it easy to keep a military regulation haircut, which accented his rectangular-shaped face and a broad chin. He had a remarkable muscular definition with his broad shoulders. Alan was a Navy SEAL, and he had the ideal physique for one.

Alan was a military brat whose father had been a U.S. Navy fighter pilot and was MIA in Vietnam in 1968. Alan joined the US Navy after graduating from high school. After boot camp, Alan was accepted into the Navy SEAL program to find his father. During his twenty years in the Navy, he moved up the ranks and retired with the rank of commander. He was divorced from his wife because his military service meant he was rarely home. Nonetheless, he felt fulfilled when he could help change something that he felt needed to change. When he served on CIA teams, Alan was an unconventional thinker able to develop new, cutting-edge approaches, enjoy challenging the status quo, and motivate others to think differently.

The admiral motioned Erik to take a seat in one of the leather lounge chairs around the mahogany coffee table. Paul poured coffee for everyone and then took his position by the admiral.

"You know why you are here?" Bonesteiner directed his question toward Erik.

"No, sir."

Paul jumped into the conversation, with his tone changing to professional intelligence senior section chief. "The admiral told me about what you did when you worked for him. Why do you want to work for the CIA?"

"I'm loyal, have a strong sense of duty to my country, and I can process logical thought, and manage extroverted relationships. Also, I have insights. Aside from seeing the way things ought to be, I follow through with my ideas using willpower, conviction, and planning on complicated projects until they're completed. I also can read other people's thoughts and figure out what makes them tick."

As Erik paused, taking a moment to look at everyone directly in their eyes, Paul leaned forward. "Is that so?"

Erik quickly studied everyone's facial expressions and began with Paul. "You think that you don't believe me." Erik paused and continued. "You are about to say, 'No, I'm not.'" Erik then looked at Alan. "You are impressed and wonder if it's a one-time occurrence." Last, Erik peered at Bonesteiner. "The admiral is wondering what you are going to say when I am not in this room." Then he focused on Paul again and stated, "I am very ambitious and want to make big changes in the world; thus, I believe one person can make a difference."

Paul attempted to emphasize his point persuasively. "This isn't like the James Bond movies. We in the agency work as a team. I'm sure you have heard the phrase, 'There is no I in team.'"

"That's true, but there is an M and an E," Erik nodded. "I know there are success stories of individuals who have made a difference in the Honor Book. Some of their names are known, and some aren't. Also, they are represented by a star on the Memorial Wall. Above the stars, it says, 'In honor of those members of the Central Intelligence Agency who gave their lives in the service of their country.' For example, on the other side of the spectrum, there is Chief Warrant Officer John Walker." (Paul gave an inquisitive glare, as Bonesteiner nodded, his eyes filled with rage.) "He alone, with his son, greatly increased their technical advantage in the silent service of the Soviet Union."

Paul leaned back, adjusted his spectacles, and took sips of coffee between his words, "What makes you stand out from all the other candidates?"

"I feel that I'm more qualified than others because of seven years of experience with the Navy and because I can analyze and pick up on things quicker than most." Paul signaled for Erik to continue. "Your seven-digit to proceed at the turnstile was one-nine-two-one-three-five zero. I'm not done, Paul …" Paul squinted and drank more of his coffee, as Bonesteiner leaned back as if he were watching a sporting event. "I know you were in the Armed Forces by the style of your spectacles." Pointing at Paul's mug, he continued, "To be more precise, you were an Army Ranger." Bonesteiner raised his hand to let Erik finish. "R-L-T-W, I believe that stands for Rangers Lead the Way. Last, your rank was a major from the golden oak leaf." Erik pointed to Paul's mug that had both of those things. "If I am allowed to work as an analyst, I can apply these skills when I meet people, and I feel confident that with my qualifications and experience, I could do that and more for the CIA."

"Well, not everything will come that easy," Paul replied with an elaborate gesture, as he adjusted himself in his seat.

"Paul, I would agree with you; however, as a civilian, Erik could see things with a different perspective than someone in the Special Forces," Alan added.

"Well done, Erik," Bonesteiner interjected as he peered into Erik's eyes and read his mind. "You are eager to know why you are here." Erik nodded. "When you finish your training at The Farm, your title will be a junior analyst; however, you will have training as a Paramilitary Operations Officer." A fanatical gleam was etched on Erik's face as he continued to absorb every word. "You are going to be a part of the newly developed O.G.D.S., Orbital Group Destination Services, and you will be a part of one of the many teams."

Rubbing his chin, Erik questioned, "You want me as an analyst, but I will have training as a Paramilitary Operations Officer?"

Bonesteiner nodded, "That is correct. Erik, you will need the training so you will have the ability to take care of yourself when you are overseas." Erik's eyes widened as his ears focused on every detail.

The admiral continued to explain that each O.G.D.S team would consist of a section chief stationed at Langley, a chief of station stationed at the location, a three-person support team, stationed at Langley, and finally the field operative, who would be stationed with the chief of station.

Bonesteiner leaned forward, "Field operative, that is your position." Erik nodded as Bonesteiner continued his briefing. "Each chief of station and field operative will be stationed within the United States at five-star resorts and hotels and public areas of interests, such as museums. You will be assigned to the National Museum of American History as a curator and/or a tour guide. While doing this, you will also be attending college; the CIA will pay for it, where you will be earning your master's and Doctorate in History. In that position, you will get to befriend foreign dignitaries, diplomats, and leaders. Also, the agency will discreetly inform these individuals that you can get highly sensitive information that would be beneficial for that country." From that, Erik would make arrangements to go to that country and deliver the information.

Once that is established, he would be given his real assignment. Erik, under a disguise, would be responsible for a covert action paramilitary operation that would involve infiltrating a military or government installation considered a high threat to the U.S. government, both militarily and/or intelligence wise, and then get the hell out. It was made clear that once in a foreign country, the U.S. government and the CIA were not going to be overtly associated with such activities. If he was compromised during a mission, the government of the United States would legally deny his status and all knowledge of his mission—in short, disavowed.

"You always told me you liked a challenge; impress me," Bonesteiner stated. It was a lot to digest knowing what could happen, but Erik was intrigued by his new job and understandably anxious. "Your training will be the same as a field operative: fifty-two weeks."

"When will I be an official part of the agency?"

"The bus leaves for Camp Peary in sixty minutes. Well, I think that takes care of everything. I need to speak to Alan and Paul; the security officer will take you down to get you sworn in."

Bonesteiner, Alan, Paul, and Erik stood up and exchanged handshakes along with a few words. The admiral walked Erik to the door. Standing outside was the security guard. Bonesteiner got Erik's attention. "They are trained to prey on your doubts and fears. Use your skills of resourcefulness and perseverance the same way you used them when you worked for me. Lastly, when you are burned out and feel like giving up because training will be like a labyrinth of knowledge, let Jackie be your strength. She is watching you from above. Understood?" Erik nodded. "God speed."

Immediately after Bonesteiner closed the door to his

office, Paul declared, "Do you think he would be a good fit for my O.G.D.S team?"

"When he worked for me, I admired his tenacity, stubborn determination and resourcefulness to get the task done, no matter what challenges were laid before him," Bonesteiner answered firmly.

"I would want him on our team because he will work just as hard or harder than his peers. He reminds me of a SEAL because he could be objective with the mission; however, if things go south, with the training, he can think outside the box and finish the objective." Alan stated that he thought he could mold Erik by inspiring and invigorating him. Thus, making him a successful Paramilitary Operations Officer.

"When he does an op, there is no deviation from the objective," Paul said. "It is structure that will save his life in the field." Paul had other ways to mold Erik. He was going to give him enough rope to move but keep him on a tight leash.

"Paul, you have not been in the field, have you?" questioned Alan. "We can mold him into what we want him to be." Alan stood motionless, staring at Paul, and said with such coldness in his gaze at Paul that it burned holes through him, "If I got Erik and you got a Ranger and placed them on the edge of a cliff, and you told them to jump, the Ranger would jump without question." Alan lifted Erik's dossier. "This kid would come up with an alternative solution we never thought of."

"That might work in the SEAL teams but not in ..."

"Gentlemen, this is not a high school debate,"

Bonesteiner interrupted firmly, as he motioned Alan to take his seat. "Both of your cases hold merit." He took a pause and looked into their eyes. "He will have a tiny advantage if he gets in a combat situation." Alan absorbed the information as Bonesteiner continued. "He has a right-sided aortic arch, which is a rare anatomical variant in which the aortic arch is on the right side rather than on the left."

"And that means what?" Alan asked.

"If someone happens to shoot him on the left side, he will be injured and not dead like you and me." Bonesteiner continued and answered Alan's next question. "Approximately 0.1 percent have this. This will never be in his medical record or dossier."

Both Alan and Paul skimmed through the pages of Erik's dossier. Rubbing his forehead, Alan read the pages, "The psychological profile is interesting."

Alan paraphrased from the pages. "Erik is conscientious and value-driven. He seeks meaning in relationships, ideas, and events, with an eye toward a better understanding of himself and others. He uses his intuitive skills; he also develops a clear and confident vision, which he then sets out to execute, aiming to better the lives of others. Erik regards problems as opportunities to design and implement creative solutions. A quest for knowledge drives Erik, and he prioritizes thought over emotional impulses and physical pleasures. Besides, he cares more about the meaning and, in particular, the "why" of things. Erik sees the world as prone to snap judgments and punditry, and it means his answers have weight and substance. Lastly, he depends more on rational approaches than instinctual ones."

Alan went on. "It says he speaks Russian and German fluently and that he is highly idealistic, very insightful, and able to sense somebody's motives nearly instantly. That would work perfectly when foreign diplomats meet him."

"That is why we have dossiers on these people, so if Erik does make it through the training, he can do his homework," Paul gave his input.

"I disagree with you there. Dossiers are nothing more than an overview." Alan's eyes peered over the dossier, as Bonesteiner nodded.

"So, I take it you already knew this about Erik's language skills and physiological profile," said Alan, addressing Bonesteiner.

"It is my job to know. Yes, Erik can read people pretty well. When he meets our adversaries, he will have the ability to know what their values and insecurities are."

Alan took a pause and read a little more. "It also says that he can come up with interesting and unusual ideas; he has the willpower and planning skills necessary to implement those ideas. That's perfect for when he goes overseas."

"Let us see how he will use his willpower and planning skills to implement those ideas on his first op, that is if he comes back," Paul said.

"Watch your bearing, Mr. McLaughlin. This might be a shock to you both…" There was a long pause. Bonesteiner removed his spectacles and glared at Alan and

Paul, during which Paul did not turn away, as if he were staring at Medusa. Paul blinked non-threateningly, and he knew he was in the wrong; thus, he was not in the position to stare Bonesteiner down. "Erik is quiet but confident. Most importantly, he will choose his battles wisely and remain quiet until it's time to attack, like a wolf hunting his prey. Moreover, when that time comes, he will devour whatever is in his way." Bonesteiner said, standing up, and as he turned to Alan and Paul, he advised them, "I will have to warn you, he will question the meaning and purpose in everything."

Paul asked, "Was he that way when he worked for you? If that's the case, why in the hell do you want him working with the agency, much less on an O.G.D.S. team?"

"For several reasons: one, he will take up any cause for moral reasons and not want personal glory or political power, and two, what he knows will be better for the agency than being exposed to the wrong people."

3. FIRST AND LAST APPEARANCE OF THE MYSTERIOUS TRAVELERS

"There are no strangers here; Only friends you haven't yet met."

—William Butler Yeats

CIA HEADQUARTERS, LANGLEY, VIRGINIA

The location for where to take the oath was the auditorium at CIA Headquarters, commonly known by its nickname "The Bubble" because of its bubble-like shape. Most of its 470 seats were filled with senior analysts, operatives, section chiefs, and other personnel. Seats nearest the stage, in the center of the auditorium, were for individuals, like Erik, who was going to work for the agency. However, there were only a few that were going to leave for Camp Peary to start their training and were taking their first step into the mysterious yet dangerous world of a CIA Paramilitary Operations Officer. The room grew quiet, as a handsome middle-aged man walked onto the stage, stepped to the podium, and peered out at the individuals in the center of the auditorium. The man was the Director of the Central Intelligence Agency, George Tenet. A grin appeared on his face, and then he became serious and addressed the room.

"Three very appropriate symbols adorn the CIA Seal. The American Eagle is the national bird and is a symbol of strength and alertness. The radiating spokes of the compass rose depicts the convergence of intelligence data from all areas of the world to a central point. The shield is the standard symbol of defense and the intelligence we gather for policymakers. Each of you are going to be doing a vital role in the agency. No job is more important than the other, no matter where you are stationed. Now I would like to ask for those who are going to take the oath to please stand."

"Raise your right hand and repeat after me." Erik and the others raised their right hands and repeated the oath that they would live and breathe until they retired or were killed in the line of duty and country.

"I, Erik Függer, do solemnly affirm that I will support and defend the Constitution of the United States against all enemies, foreign and domestic; that I will bear true faith and allegiance to the same; that I take this obligation freely, without any mental reservation or purpose of evasion; and that I will well and faithfully discharge the duties of the office on which I am about to enter. So, help me, God."

4. THE DAY BEFORE THE LONG DAYS

"Today I close the door to the past, Open the door to the future, take a deep breath, step on through and start a new chapter in my life."

—Author Unknown

2 December 1997: Erik was escorted to the bus platform located outside the main entrance. Erik and forty-five other recruits were waiting, with their belongings, for an unmarked motor coach to pick them up and take them to their new home, Camp Peary. Camp Peary was also called the Special Training Center (STC). To those already in the agency, it was known as "The Farm." The STC was one of many covert CIA training facilities where potential officers of the National Clandestine Service were trained. Erik, like the others, was told to wear clothing that did not have any identifying markings from their hometown, college affiliation, or any favorite sports teams.

They were also instructed not to share their name or any information about their identity. As Erik waited for the motor coach, he saw a Bald Eagle in a nearby tree.

Its golden eyes stared directly at Erik as if studying him. As it flew off toward the horizon, the unmarked motor coach pulled up in front of the recruits so that they could load their belongings. Just before Erik boarded the motor coach, he felt everyone on the platform was being watched from this moment forward.

Once on the motor coach, Erik found a window seat and closed his eyes. He heard the shuffling of people walking by and the chattering of those around him.

"Excuse me; is anyone sitting here?" A voice questioned. Erik shook his head no. The recruit took a seat and, with hand extended, said, "Hi! Vince Clancy from Orlando, Florida." Erik just nodded and said nothing and looked out the window. "Hey, are you going tell me your name?"

Erik turned to face Vince, and quipped, "No."

"What's with the attitude?"

"I just don't feel like talking."

Again, Erik looked out the window as he heard Vince grumble under his breath, "Asshole." It would be approximately a two hour and thirty-minute ride to Camp Peary, and all Erik could think about was what the training would be like and about Jackie. He still recalled the first time they met, in a bookstore in the history section. She was 18, and he was 25. It was hard to say if it was love at first sight, but their chemistry bonded them like hydrogen and oxygen molecules in water. She balanced him with her passion and adventurous view of life. She introduced him to jeans. This was something new to him since he had always preferred wearing dress slacks. Within a short time, Erik and Jackie knew they wanted to spend the rest of their lives together and started planning their future.

She wanted to be a graphic designer. Erik was finishing college and working for the government. One of the greatest days of his life was when Jackie told him that she was pregnant. The worst was a warm, sunny evening when Erik got home and received a call that would drastically change him forever. It was Jackie's mother, who was crying. She was calling to tell Erik that Jackie and his unborn son were killed in a car accident. The news hit Erik like a hammer blow to his gut, sending him to the floor. In the weeks following, Erik focused on work and school and kept to himself, only interacting if he had to. One day, Bonesteiner called Erik to his office and discussed the options he was planning: one, nothing, or two, take care of the individual who had killed his family. However, it was Erik's decision, and he chose option one, but in retrospect, he wished he had chosen option two. After her death, he turned in his unofficial resignation to Bonesteiner and became a history teacher. Erik made himself several promises: one, if he got a chance to work for the government again, he would accept, and two, if Erik met another girl, he would protect her from all danger. If anyone tried to hurt her, Erik would make them suffer, and if necessary, he would kill them.

The air brakes on the motor coach broke Erik's trance, as the vehicle drifted to a halt. At that moment, several armed men in black, unmarked uniforms began a sweep of the motor coach with dogs and mirrors, which took a few minutes. Afterward, the driver entered the perimeter of Camp Peary, a 9,275-acre government reservation surrounded by a thick but underdeveloped forest that protected it from public incursion. Surrounding the reservation was a 10-foot-high tinsel steel chain-link fence with razor wire and armed guards. Among the bushes and trees, there were hidden antennas, microwave relay systems, and security cameras.

With each passing bend in the road, every individual, including Erik, was getting anxious to start the new adventure of becoming a CIA operative. Finally, around the last bend, the view opened up to the heart of Camp Peary. The width of the opening was approximately two football fields. In this confined area were a helicopter pad, a five-thousand-foot airstrip, and an administrative area that contained classrooms, a library, dormitories, cafeteria, bar, gym, and swimming pool. The STC staff were quartered in several single-family houses near the two small inlets between the central administrative area and the airstrip. Throughout STC were classified storage places that were located in the central administrative area and other undisclosed locations. The infrastructure had secure communication lines and equipment, such as the "Green line" telephone, the STU-III telephone, fax and modem, and a secure computer network. Throughout the STC, bicycles were used as primary transportation. And finally, what took place at Camp Peary was known only by a few.

The motor coach came to a halt. At that moment, the driver exited and began unloading the bags from the storage compartment. Another man boarded. As he walked down the aisle, he said, "Welcome to Special Training Center." He looked everyone in the eye as he passed out maps. When he reached the end of the motor coach, he did an about-face and another about-face once he reached the front. "Get your gear and put it in the dormitories." He pointed in the general direction, but it was marked on the map. "Then head to the auditorium." Before he exited, he stared at everyone. "You have ten minutes."

One after another, they all exited and grabbed their belongings to follow the orders. As Erik exited, he glanced at a white two-story house that had caught his eye. A man appeared from inside the house. He eyed Erik from head to toe and swiveled his head right to the left in a casual manner. He was wearing an unmarked black uniform, and behind his steel-framed glasses were his brown, almost black, eyes hiding an inner evil and showing no emotion. As Erik walked to the dormitories, the man walked across the porch and continued to watch him, making no effort to conceal his interest. After dropping off his gear, Erik headed to the auditorium and found himself a seat.

A man walked from the back of the room to the front, "Good afternoon." Everyone in the room replied the same greeting, as the man continued. "I am Jack Downing, Deputy Director for Operations, and I would like to welcome you to the Special Training Center, STC, as we call it, or you may have heard of it…The Farm." He looked around the room. "The STC has been around since 1951, and you are the forty-seventh class that has attended here. You have been chosen for your talents, skills, and abilities. You are the top one percent of thousands of candidates who applied for the position you are in." He took a deep breath. "Paramilitary Operations Officers are the pillars of strength for our country. They will dispense their strength and knowledge wherever our country needs them to keep the United States of America safe. They will seek courage in the face of danger and be the moral compass pointed in the true direction as reflected in what they stand for. These are individuals who are going to dedicate every day of their lives in service for the greater good. They will remain forever connected to the Paramilitary Operations Officers who came before and after them, for what they do matters. They will protect the United States of America until their last breath." Then he looked right, "I would like to introduce you to your Senior Instructor, Mr. Rusch."

"Good Morning!" A deep, authoritarian voice filled the room. He was a solid five feet seven inches, and with his blue, cold, sinister, eagle-like eyes, scanned the room's horizon. He had uncombed, thick black hair, and every muscle was toned to perfect physical condition. He had the presence of the "Pale Rider" from The Four Horsemen of the Apocalypse.

"You all were given an order before you entered the bus at Langley." He walked side to side in front of the room. His eyes never left focus. "Only 20 percent of you followed that order…moreover, yes, we know who you are." He paused to let his words sink in. "Only six of you will graduate from The Farm. The rest of you will go back to being a civilian or reassigned to another position in the agency." Those words were like concrete sneakers, as every candidate realized how hard it was going be, facing the challenge of becoming a part of the National Clandestine Service. "You will be pushed in ways you cannot imagine, and it is designed to make you want to quit." A cunning grin appeared on his face. "It is nothing personal." He added some dry humor. "So, look to your right and look to your left, because the person next to you might not be here for all the next twelve months." Then he clapped his hands as he examined each individual's facial expressions. Erik tried to keep his face a mask of neutrality, as he followed Rusch's every step. "So, why are you here?" He gazed around until he found someone and pointed. "So, why are you here?"

"I want to defend the United States."

"You could have joined the military for that, and it would have been easier to get in," Rusch mocked. "For all you guys out there, this job will not get you laid because you cannot tell anyone whom you work for or what you do." He paused. "How many of you like money?" A few people raised their hands, and he shook his head in disbelief. "You are in the wrong field. I am a GS-15, and I make just about $65,000 before taxes." Rusch took a deep breath, "Anyone like medals or merits of achievement?" This time no one raised their hand, knowing it could be a trick question. "No, this was not a trick question. You can get medals here; you won't be able to show or tell anyone about them." With a theatrical gesture, he looked everyone in the eye. "So, can anyone answer my question?"

Erik looked around and quickly stood up, "Because I believe I can make a difference."

"Really?" Rusch rubbed his chin as he studied Erik's demeanor, "You believe that?"

"Yes, sir."

"What makes you think you can, Mr.?" Rusch gestured him to answer, but Erik knew better than to give his name. "I'm sorry, I did not get your name."

"I didn't give my name, but you can call me Bond, James Bond." A few individuals laughed. "I believe I can make a difference because I believe nothing is impossible, and everything is possible."

Rusch nodded in agreement, "You can sit down, Mr. Bond. He is correct that we are here because we believe in America and what she stands for, protecting her from her enemies, and most of all, we choose good and right over evil and wrong. Our enemies are crafty, dangerous, and strong. However, they are everywhere in the world, including in our country, and could be anyone. Let me emphasize that again. They could be anyone. That is why all of you are here so that you can exploit and neutralize or eliminate them or their threat."

Rusch stated that there were six types of officers in the NCS; however, for this group, they would focus on becoming Paramilitary Operations Officers. This position would require the officer to carry out intelligence operations in an overseas environment. The focus would be on U.S. policy, and it would be hazardous and could get you killed. He addressed everyone as Clandestine Service Trainee (CST) and got everyone's attention.

"If you are compromised, you will be tortured, and shortly after that, you will be shot. So, my best advice to you is not to get caught. Here's another bit of advice. If you know there is a chance you are going to be caught, blow your brains out." He paused again. "If that happens, you will get remembered by a star, and your name could be put in the Honor Book, but I would not count on that. What you can count on is that you will be buried in an empty coffin because our enemies do not give bodies back."

Then Rusch explained there were nine significant parts of training in three areas: classroom instruction, testing, and physical training (PT). Erik, like everyone else, was excited to start. Rusch advised that everyone would be given a brown Kraft clasp envelope and that they should not open it. He instructed them to remember their first order. Then everyone was dismissed for lunch and told to be back in one hour.

Erik got up from his seat, and he saw in the far corner the man from the porch. At that moment, Erik attempted to confront the man. Then the man disappeared around the corner, and Erik knew it was futile to pursue him, so he picked up his envelope and headed to the cafeteria. On the way there, he pulled out a picture of Jackie and thought about the brief time they had shared. Erik composed himself before entering the cafeteria and joining the line. It was like any other cafeteria; it was a fluorescent-lighted room, tiled in vinyl composition style, and off to one side, there was a carpeted sitting area. One after another, they picked up trays, utensils, napkins, stared at the menu (there were only two choices: ham and cheese or turkey and cheese sandwiches), and placed their order. Next, they slid their trays along chromed rails that led to the beverage station. Erik took a seat in the corner away from everyone else. He saw Vince looking in his direction. Though Erik could not read lips, he knew Vince was talking about him. Erik buried himself in his lunch and blocked out the outside world. After lunch, and a quick stop at the barracks to grab a legal pad and pen, Erik headed back to the auditorium

Erik was not the only one early, as he took his seat. In the corner of Erik's eye, he saw Rusch preparing for what he was going to say and talking to the other instructors. All the instructors appeared to be in their mid-forties with solid frames. Most likely, they served in one of the elite units of the branches of the military. At first glance, it would appear if they got into a fight, they would lose after several blows due to their size and age; however, that was not the case. What they hid was their knowledge of several kinds of martial arts, small arms weapons, and other skills that the civilian world could not even fathom. It was ten minutes until Rusch ordered everyone back. As individuals started coming back into the auditorium, he was making his way to the front of the room. Rusch caught Erik staring at him, and at that moment, he locked eyes on him and did not lose focus. It was as if Rusch was probing into Erik's mind and studying his behavior.

"Mr. Bond, you think you can win?" Erik knew he was referring to the staring game where the first one that blinks loses. "Give up, Mr. Bond, you are going to lose." Rusch genuinely enjoyed the challenge from one of his CSTs. To him, it was the battle of wits, and he knew if Erik couldn't keep up, he would keep testing him; however, that was no reason for him to fold on his fundamental principle of ultimate victory. Then Erik blinked.

The class started promptly, just as the minute hand lined up with the number twelve and not a second before or after. Rusch welcomed everyone back and asked if anyone wanted to be DOR (Dropped On Request). Next, he introduced the junior instructors: Aquinas, Delgado, Graham, and Pace. Then he explained in the next twelve months as a CST, and there would be extensive training that was comprised of, but not limited to, intelligence training and something called the "Dark Arts." A few of the Dark Arts are analytical combat, covert surveillance, evasion, improvised self-defense, improvised weaponry, lying, personality-type identification, sleight-of-hand, and con-artistry. Erik was impressed with Rusch for his vast repository of information and knowledge, and it appeared as if he had a hyper-analytical mind with a photographic memory. Rusch grabbed a brown Kraft clasp envelope and held it up.

"Each one of you was given one of these before lunch and instructed not to open it." The junior instructors cased the room to make sure everyone had followed instructions. Everyone had.

"You are now allowed to open them."

The tearing of paper filled the room.

"Inside you will find two sheets of paper. One is the

schedule of your training. The other has a name on it. This will be your name while you are at The Farm. You will create a false cover and legend; have these ready before you eat dinner." He paused. "Your assignment is to come up with a legend. Your legend is the supporting story of your cover. I highly recommend you get familiar with it. Know it. Study it. Become that person."

He let those words sink in. Before he dismissed everyone, he advised, "As a Paramilitary Operations Officer, or PMOO, you spend the entire time, especially when overseas, lying to everyone, knowing that you're doing it for the greater good. It is easy knowing you are deceiving your enemies, but the main reason is that it keeps you alive until you are hopefully not compromised. That comes to rule one: never get caught. As in the field, you will not have a second chance. If the other instructors or I feel you are not up to this, you will be told to leave."

Once everyone left the auditorium, they headed to the barracks, unpacked, and started working on their character's dossier. Erik quickly unpacked, organized his area, and headed outside so he would not be disturbed. He found himself a tree and propped his back against it. Next, Erik pulled out the photo of Jackie and propped it where he could see it as he worked. Erik fought his tears as he stared at the picture, and his memories drove him crazy. Most people thought he should have moved on, but Erik was not ready. He looked up to the clouds and thought, *I would give my life if I could hold you in my arms and hear you say I love you.* Erik took several deep breaths and composed himself. Lastly, he pulled out the two sheets of paper from the envelope. He smirked as he saw the name that was given to him. Joe Turner was the main character in Three Days of the Condor, a movie based on a James Grady novel. Turner was a CIA analyst who was on the run because his section was hit.

He got his pen and started writing the bio. He used some personal similarities to make them easier to remember and convince others. What also made it easier was that Erik enjoyed creative writing, so his thoughts flowed from his pen onto the paper. His friends said he was an excellent writer, but he was his own worst critic and always hard on himself. After finishing his bio, he put it back in the envelope.

Erik's eyes enlarged as he shook his head in amazement, reading the training schedule. Each day would start at 0430 and end at 1800. There was a thirty-minute breakfast and lunch. Dinner was from 1900 to 2000. Lastly, from 2000 to 2200 was free time. Lights out was at 2200.

CLANDESTINE SERVICE TRAINEE PROGRAM

Paramilitary Operations Officer Preparatory School (52 weeks)
Phase 1: Physical Conditioning (16 weeks)
Dark Arts:
Phase 2: High Performance/Tactical Driving (on and off-road) (2 weeks)
Phase 3: Surreptitious Entry Training (5 weeks)

Phase 4: Survival, Evasion, Resistance and Escape Training (3 weeks)
Stage 5: Demolition Training (3 weeks)
Phase 6: Combat Training (8 weeks)
Phase 7: Parachute Jump School (3 weeks)
Phase 8: SCUBA School (3 weeks)
Phase 9: Dark Arts Qualification Training (DAQT) (9 weeks)

It was dinnertime. Erik and the other CSTs lined up at the entrance to the cafeteria, with the junior instructors standing there. Two by two, the instructors let the CSTs in. They were collecting the covers. The line slowly inched up as Erik prepared himself for what they might ask. He knew every part of the day would be a test, both mentally and physically, that would last nearly one year. Erik was next in line and handed over the paper with his cover.

"So, Mr. Turner, where are you from?" The junior instructor asked.

"Groom Lake, Nevada."

The instructor began to read Erik's body language. "Where in the hell is Groom Lake?"

"A few hours away from Las Vegas."

"I see," The instructor paused. "So, are you a gambler?"

"No."

"What do you do there?"

"I am a high school teacher."

"What's the name of your school?"

Erik was stumped and did not know any high school

names, so he named the one he taught at. "Edgewater High."

The instructor nodded, "Edgewater?" Erik nodded. "What do you teach?"

"History."

The instructor motioned Erik to go in. He was glad that was over, but he knew that was nothing close to how it would be if he had been caught and interrogated. He picked up a tray, utensils and a napkin, and stared at the menu. Tonight's dinner was either meatloaf or boiled fish, mashed potatoes, a choice of two vegetables, and a dinner roll. Next, he slid his tray along the chromed rails, got a beverage, and found a seat. Erik made small talk with those who surrounded him. After dinner, everyone went to the barracks. Inside the barracks, some played cards, others watched TV, a few read, and some lay on their cots. Erik laid his head on a thick, foamed pillow and tried to clear it. It must have worked because another CST woke him up and instructed him to go to Rusch's office near the auditorium.

A snort came through the open door of the adjoining room as Erik knocked on the door. He was instructed to go in and take a seat. Rusch's office was approximately sixty square feet, and every space was utilized. He looked at Erik as he tapped his ballpoint pen on a desk blotter. The office had all standard-issue government furniture. From Rusch's desk to his bookcases, they all were made from particle board, with a thin, one to two-millimeter-thick, veneer plastic wood-like finish. On one wall was a huge chart that had every CST's fake name. Erik tried to read Rusch's weather-beaten face, which revealed nothing about this man or his history. Erik got a glimpse of Rusch's cold, blue eyes that were getting colder, but he admired Rusch's achievements. Rusch was settled forward in a padded swivel chair, where Rusch had finished reading what could have been Erik's dossier. Then he spun his chair around, and his eyes were fixed on Erik.

"Empty your pockets and take off your shoes and socks."

"Excuse me, sir?"

Rusch's voice got firm, "Do you have a problem with the English language?"

Erik shook his head.

"Then, do what you are told."

He took off his shoes and socks. Rusch examined them closer. Next, Erik emptied his pockets, and one contained the photograph of Jackie. "What is this?" He snapped.

"A photograph."

"You think?" Rusch said sarcastically. "You must have a high IQ to know this is a photograph." He dismissed the subject with a short sideways jerk of his pen, placed the photo in an envelope, and slid it in front of Erik. Then he tossed the pen to Erik. "Put your name on it. Big, bold letters." Erik was about to put his real name but hesitated. Rusch said, "What's wrong, you forgot your name?" Erik then wrote his cover name and slid the envelope back. Again, Rusch leaned back in his chair, skimming through Erik's dossier and was pleased with what he was reading.

Erik's dossier stated: emotionally balanced, which

means that he is less prone to depression and can cope well with feelings of anxiety, anger, and vulnerability. Rusch knew that with these qualities and with the training and molding at The Farm, Erik could be an effective PMOO. He continued reading. Erik is mostly aware of and in touch with his emotions. Being open-minded to new and unusual ideas helps him to interact with his environment and allows him to plan and think ahead.

His cold eyes peered over the dossier as he closed it and tossed it on his desk like a useless dirty rag. In a terse tone, he said as he curled his lip, "You have no idea the effort you need to give here." Rusch leaned forward to let his words sink in. "There are two kinds of CSTs. The CST that gets stronger, or the kind of CST that is useless and weak. I have no patience for useless things." Despite what Erik thought, Rusch intended to humiliate, make one doubt, and find weak links. This was because once in the field, there would be no timeouts for a PMOO, and seconds would decide life or death.

"Tell Felix Leiter to come to my office, and you are not to say what took place here, understood?"

"Yes, sir."

Erik headed back to the barracks, found Felix, and instructed him what to do. Then he went back to his cot, closed his eyes, and went to sleep.

5. UNAPOLOGETIC & STRAIGHTFORWARD

*"Pain is your friend, your ally, it will tell you when
you are seriously injured, it will keep you awake
and angry, and remind you to finish the job and get
the hell home. But you know the best thing about
pain? It lets you know you're not dead yet!"*

— *G.I. Jane*, Master Chief John Urgayle

CAMP PEARY (THE FARM), VIRGINIA

Phase 1: Physical Conditioning: 46 CSTs

It was 0415 hours; Erik, like the others, jumped from his
bunk, as a constant alarm went off and a voice blared over
the loudspeakers. "All CSTs report to the common area
in fifteen minutes."

That was enough time to get dressed, use the facilities,
and go out and stretch, provided it was planned perfectly.
He quickly got dressed in his sweats and sneakers, went
straight to do his duties in the bathroom, threw water on
his face, and had about seven minutes to stretch. People

slowly filtered out, as the junior instructors strolled around in their reflective-lensed sunglasses. Erik recalled seeing a documentary dealing with Navy SEAL BUD/S Classes, where the drill instructors did the same thing to hide their eyes from showing any expression.

"Come on, ladies; this is not summer camp. Move your asses!" barked one of the instructors, as the others were coming out of the barracks. "What in the hell are you doing?! Sleeping?!" Erik was pushed repeatedly until he got on his feet. "Let's go!"

It was a timed morning run. Every CST was disoriented in the pre-dawn cold, early December morning. The air was brisk, and Erik could see his breath. Everyone was struggling to wake up. They were going to do a four-mile run around the compound in under thirty-two-minutes. Everyone kept to himself as they focused on the task. Running was never Erik's forte; on top of that, he had asthma. He had to keep pushing himself harder if he was going to succeed. He glanced around to see some struggling; others were holding their own, and the instructors were watching everything as they barked, "You have five minutes to finish this run. You don't make it. You do it again." Erik wondered what the rest of the day would be like.

The run was over. Erik, like others, was out of breath, and the instructors walked around with canteens, allowing each CST two gulps of water. The instructors barked their impatient orders at the CSTs to file out in four rows of eight and two rows of seven. It was too dark to see names on a clipboard, and the instructors did not have time to learn forty-six names. Out of this class, only six would become PMOOs, so each CST was ordered to sound off by number. Next, they were told to get in a push-up position, as Rusch strolled upfront, and other instructors walked between the CSTs. All trainees harbored an inner belief that they could be Paramilitary Operations Officers. However, once the seconds seemed like minutes and the minutes seemed like hours, the moment could challenge their commitment.

In a loud, thundering voice, Rusch began to count each push-up. There was not much room for error in Rusch's world. He disliked seeing mistakes repeated and had no patience with inefficiency. Also, Rusch became quite harsh when his patience was tried. Each trainee was under a microscope, and the instructors were on the lookout for any slackers. Once a slacker was caught, the instructors were like sharks attacking their prey, and the sight was not pretty.

"What in the hell do you call that?" An instructor hovered over an individual. "That was a saggy bat. You are on seven because you are pitiful and weak." The instructor squatted down to get in his face. "Everyone is on ten." The trainee tried to do the push-up correctly. "Okay, that's eight…nine…ten." The instructor got up and hovered around his victim. "I tell you what! When you are told an order, you do it right." He let those words soak in. "I do not care what kind of order it is, even if it is doing a push-up." Then he got in his face again. "If you want to screw off, I will catch you every time, and I will make you pay." The instructor got up and turned his back as he gave his last words. "That goes for when I turn my back and walk away because that's when I will look at you the most."

Two hours had already passed on the first day; the CSTs were finally introduced to the instructors and vice-versa. Also, the intensity on each evolution got higher and more challenging, with the instructors getting in each CST's face every minute, every second. Another exercise was being conducted, causing Erik's face to contort grotesquely. Instructors read the faces and gave words of encouragement.

"Do not think about the pain! Do not give in to the pain!" They let those words sink in. "You adjust for it! You do minor adjustments!"

Nearly another ninety minutes of nonstop demanding exercises ensued: sixty jumping jacks, ninety push-ups, eighty-five sit-ups, and more. Rusch addressed all the trainees, who were in a push-up position.

"This entire PT has been a joke. There has not been a single evolution that you performed during the course of this PT that has even remotely resembled perfection." He crossed his arms against his chest. "Everything has been pitiful, weak, and unreadable. Moreover, it is because you are inside your tiny little brains self-defeating yourself."

Then the exercises began again. However, the instructors showed no signs of letting up. Their intention was for each trainee to question his reason for being there. Rusch knew from previous classes that no one would quit in the first couple of hours or even the first day. He did know that quitting would begin when the CSTs realized that this was only the beginning. However, the instructors were looking for everyone to give it their all, and if they spotted someone who was not, they would continue to push him. On the side, each CST had his reason for wanting to become a PMOO.

As dawn broke over the exercise area, the instructors saw each CST clearly for the first time. However, the instructors still hid their eyes with their reflective sunglasses. In the Paramilitary Operations Officer training, it was not about humiliation or a survivor contest. Rusch and the other instructors were getting each man prepared for the job they would be doing either in a team or individually. There were no second chances, no appeals or debates. Also, when a CST quit, known as DOR or Drop-On-Request, there was no time for questions or reactions from the others.

"You will learn one thing when you go overseas, and it will apply here as well. You eat when you can, shit when you can, and sleep when you can!" Rusch explained in a stentorian tone. "You have thirty minutes to eat, shower, and shit. Then you are to report to the classroom in the main building." He looked around and gazed into everyone's eyes. "Get out of my face!"

Some CSTs ran to the cafeteria, and the others ran to the barracks. Erik chose the cafeteria. Erik, like the others, was tired, hot, and ragged, but they ate quickly. Each meal provided would give enough calories for each trainee to continue, knowing they would burn 5,000 calories a day. As the CSTs stuffed their faces, a pair of instructors showed up, and one by one, they pulled away each CST and quizzed them on their cover. This was a test, like everything else. It was a test to see if they could recall their cover story and be convincing if questioned or detained. There were several different kinds of interrogations. This one would simulate being in the field, like a jungle, desert, or any place that was not in a manufactured structure. CSTs were taught to try to avoid any kind of interrogation, but this type of questioning was one of the easier ones. The reason was that you could tell a story with your captor. By storytelling, you could keep yourself alive until you find a way to escape and could keep your captor listening, and the fewer questions they could ask. Erik passed all his questions; at least he thought he did. Afterward, he raced back to the barracks to shower, use the toilet, get dressed, and prepare for the next evolution.

Erik raced into the classroom, with five minutes to spare with Rusch keeping his eye on the clock. Once the last second was up, Rusch closed the door and addressed the class.

"This is your first day of training at the Clandestine Service Trainee Program. Before you got on the bus, you were told not to give any information. Also, before lunch, I reminded you to remember the name that was given to you and come up with a legend." He shook his head in disbelief. "Some of you were able to keep your name. However, your legends were crap, absolutely crap." He pounded a fist to the table, which was covered with a wide range of things in front of the room. "When overseas or if you are stateside bound, there are three kinds of cover," he explained, as the CSTs took notes, "snap cover, which is something you would adopt at the spur of the moment when an opportunity presented itself, and you suddenly needed to pretend to be someone other than yourself; second, the short-term cover, used generally just, once, to get in and out quickly to get a document or use sabotage; and the last one and most commonly used is a long-term cover." He continued to explain that this was to be used by operatives in the field overseas. "This is important…there is nothing more important in this business than your cover." He looked around the room. "When you are detained, it is not about being tough. When detained, the people questioning you will do everything in their power to break you. Everyone has a breaking point, but you will need to know this to go further than you can possibly imagine." He touched his temple with his pointing finger. "When you are being interrogated, it is about being clever and thinking. It deals with anticipating the questions that the interrogator will ask." He walked in front of the table. "You will need to know your cover, so practice it, through and through, so it will be a part of you twenty-four seven."

He told them when they were overseas; everything had to be consistent with that cover. For example, the after-shave they used, the brand of cigarettes they smoked, and even the contents in their pockets. Rusch explained that even the smallest mistakes could get them detained or killed. He picked up a photograph off the table. Erik recognized it as his photo. "They can put a picture of your girlfriend in front of you, and you need to act naturally as you go through the interrogation." Something caught

Rusch's eye and keen hearing, as he walked to the left side
of the classroom and hovered over a student. He peered
down, with his arms crossed against his chest. The CST
stared up.

"So, you think she is fuckable?" The trainee was
speechless. "If you are going to be disrespectful to your
other CSTs, that means you are going to be disrespectful to me and this program." The individual tried to explain, as Rusch gave a dismissive gesture. "Get the hell
out. Pack your shit and go home!" The individual uttered
something under his breath. "I don't care if you call me
a fucking bastard, as long as I remain an efficient bastard." The individual left without saying a word. "I, like
the other instructors, am here to give you the tools you
will need to stay alive…do I make myself clear?" Rusch,
not impressed with the response, repeated, "I said, do I
make myself clear?"

"Yes, sir!"

Now the class had forty-five.

For the next three hours, the CSTs were challenged
mentally. Like the PT, there was no letting up on the
trainees. These academic evolutions, also known as High
Liability Training or HLTs, would occur during phase
1 and were meant to train and condition the skills the
CSTs would use in the field. The HLTs were eighty
minutes long, with a ten-minute break. The trainees
would have one class every week for fourteen weeks.
There were fourteen HLTs: armored fighting vehicle
(AFV) and aircraft identification, body language, cy-
ber-warfare, extreme survival, and wilderness training,

heightened visional training, lying, manipulation tactics, medical training, personality-type identification, pressure points, sleight-of-hand, stealing, trickery, and basic vehicle mechanics. After each HLT's course, the trainee had an examination; it would be written and/or a practical application. They were required to complete it with a 90 percent or better. If they did not pass the first time, they were allowed one retake, but they must pass with a 95. Any student who failed both times was kicked off the program. The instructors hoped the HLTs would cause more students to question their commitment to training and drop out. They only wanted the best of the best.

The first sixteen weeks were designed intentionally to filter out trainees lacking the academic, emotional, and physical commitments needed to become a Paramilitary Operations Officer. When an operative is in the field, he must prepare for any situation. He must pay attention to and not take for granted every detail of the mission. The difference between living and dying depended on the PMOO's preparedness for a "Special Activity." Even before a Special Activity is executed, a PMOO must anticipate problems and solve them before those problems killed him and caused a national security risk to the United States.

After the High Liability Training, the CSTs took a short break for lunch. They would need to be in the gym no later than 1300 hours. Following lunch, the trainees spent three hours learning Close Quarter Defense (CQD), Krav Maga, and Ninjutsu. The instructors did not care if the trainees knew these; they wanted to make sure that if the CSTs were in a situation where they needed to use these skills, they could defend themselves. These classes were held throughout the fifty-two weeks of training, and by then, they would be experts in all three. The next evolution was PT; however, this time, the CSTs had to swim 1,000 yards using breast or combat sidestroke in under twenty-five minutes. Then the trainees had to do the obstacle course known as "Hell." All had heard the adage that everyone knows about hell, but nobody wants to go through hell. These last two evolutions would take place in the last two hours of training. The last four hours of the CST's day were spent cleaning up, eating dinner, and enjoying free time, with lights out at 2200 hours.

At the end of each day, the CSTs had experienced pain, both mentally and physically, and the message was excruciating and non-negotiable. The unofficial motto at The Farm was, "Improvise, Adapt, Overcome." Phase one, Physical Conditioning, sixteen weeks, thirteen-hour days of exercise. High Liability Training, obstacle course, martial arts training, running, swimming, and stretching, would be done six days a week. Sunday was the only day the trainees had for relaxation. However, the instructors highly recommended that the trainees spend their time studying or practicing their PT because they were tested on every aspect of training. The Clandestine Service Trainee Program was a war of attrition, a contest of luck and commitment. Each CST must demonstrate a dedication to remain in training no matter the hardship. The irony was that commitment alone is not always enough to guarantee success. At the end of each day, the only thought in every CST's mind would be, "The Only Easy Day Was Yesterday," which is the US Navy SEAL motto.

6. LABYRINTH OF KNOWLEDGE

*"The Spy Act strikes a right balance between preserving
legitimate and benign uses of this technology,
while still, at the same time, protecting unwitting
consumers from the harm caused when it is misused
and, of course, designed for nefarious purposes."*

— Cliff Stearns

CLASSIFIED

Phase 2: High Performance/Tactical Driving (on and off the road)

It was the beginning of week 17; there were twenty CSTs left from the original forty-six. Erik was amazed that he had made it through the sixteen weeks of PT hell. There was still PT, but not as much as before. The rest of the 36 weeks duration at The Farm, Erik and the others would be learning the Dark Arts, also known in the civilian world as spycraft.

For the next two weeks, training focused on High

Performance/Tactical Driving, both on and off-road. Instructor Delgado oversaw this evolution and made light of the training as he stated, "Your friends and family say you are a terrible driver." He paused as Erik knew that applied to him. "We'll make you worse." He added, "The most important thing is knowing the characteristics of your vehicle. This is the key to performing in extreme situations without wrecking and, more so, a lifesaving skill that will give you the ability to avoid capture."

They learned there are three kinds of vehicles: Front-wheel-drive (FWD), Rear-wheel-drive (RWD), and All-wheel-drive (AWD). Each vehicle has its pros and cons. Also, each CST was instructed in a systematic manner, using fully integrated instructional and advanced elements of tactical driving. Each CST was evaluated with an academic and practical examination to ensure knowledge, understanding, and performance. By the end of the two weeks, Erik had learned and mastered the following: Advanced and Defensive Driver Training, Anti-Terrorist evasion, Attack Recognition and Avoidance, Vehicle Commandeering, Evasive Driving, Off-Road Driver Training, and Unimproved Road Driver Training. At the end of the evolution, Delgado warned that everyone would complain and say each CST's driving is terrible. Erik smirked, knowing that everyone already said that about his driving. However, if someone asked him where he learned how to drive, the unspoken response would be classified.

Phase 3: Surreptitious Entry Training

Instructor Aquinas taught the next five weeks; the evolution was Surreptitious Entry Training. Now the class was down to fifteen. There were three parts of the evolution: 1- Surreptitious Entry Operations I, 2- Surreptitious Entry Operations II, and 3- Planning & Conducting Surreptitious Operations. Like the previous evolution, evaluations were measured by academic and performance instruction. Surreptitious Entry Operations I, was a two-week evolution. In the two weeks, the individuals learned the essentials and hands-on skills that would allow them to conduct close target reconnaissance (CTR). Also, they acquired knowledge to recognize and identify locks and locking devices. Trainees practiced various neutralization and lock-specific by-pass techniques. Most importantly, they were taught how to surreptitiously defeat the majority of key operated doors and padlocks in use today by using the following skills: lock picking, lock bypass, and other acceptable covert techniques, surreptitious or clandestine entry neutralization measures, such as key impressions, and lock modifications.

In Surreptitious Entry Operations II, another two-week evolution, each CST applied what they had learned in the last two weeks, focusing on refining and enhancing their ability to identify and neutralize locks and locking devices. Also, they practiced a variety of new lock picking and lock by-pass techniques and tools. The core of this evolution emphasized a variety of field-expedient locks and car opening tools made out of readily available supplies and materials. For example, they learned how to covertly open luxury vehicles equipped with high-security locks and locking devices, and they learned to open vehicles without accurately cut keys. Also, instruction included the manipulated opening of personal access systems, such as key casting techniques, lock "bumping" techniques, making bump keys, and manipulating the opening of Group II type combination locks, and Group II Dial Combination locks. These included, but were not limited to, combination padlocks, push-button personal access locks, magnetic locks, and enhanced security modified pin tumbler locks. Lastly, they were taught how to fabricate field-expedient entry tools, key impressions, and how to make and cut keys by code.

Planning & Conducting Surreptitious Operations lasted only one week and was intense and stressful, requiring CSTs to use what they had learned in the other evolutions. The focus on this evolution taught each trainee how to carefully plan, supervise, and conduct surreptitious or covert entry operations. This required each CST to plan and conduct actual surreptitious entry operations of specific target vehicles, containers, business or military offices, aircraft, and aircraft hangers and residential and military structures. By the end of week twenty-three, thirteen individuals were remaining, and the next Dark Art was to start on Monday.

Phase 4: Survival, Evasion, Resistance, and Escape (SERE)

Instructor Pace taught this next evolution, which was three weeks long. Pace advised them of the three levels of SERE training: Level A, Level B, and Level C. He informed them they would be foregoing levels A and B and starting with Level C, which was the highest level. The first lesson they learned was never to be caught. Also, he advised the trainees that if you have a choice of being captured or killing yourself, pick killing yourself because it will be over faster. He concluded by noting that as an operative, it was very likely one of the following would be done to them if they were compromised, or all three in this order: severe beating, torture, and killing. Erik knew the main reason they received SERE Level C training was that they would be in the following situations: a wartime position, in a military occupational specialty, or their assignment would entail a high risk of capture. Their position, rank, or seniority would make them targets for stronger-than-average exploitation efforts by a captor.

The survival and evasion evolutions were six days and put the CSTs under extreme challenges, both mentally and physically. They spent two days in each situation: rural and urban with a final day of situational tasks and debriefings. In exercise one, they were to evade pursuit by K-9 units and soldiers playing the role of the opposing force pursuing them, through a twenty-mile corridor of woods and dense vegetation. Each CST had to avoid contact with the local populace. Also, during the field training exercise, the CSTs had to forage for food and water. If they reached their destination, they must complete a series of survival tasks that measured how much they learned during the academic phase. Also, there was an individual and collective debriefing from the instructors. The purpose of the debriefings was to give students an understanding of how well they performed and how they might have reacted differently. In exercise two, the CSTs went through a twenty-block urban corridor. Like exercise one, they were pursued by K-9 units and soldiers; however, this time, the pursuers had vehicles and helicopters. They had the same challenges. Once again, if they reached their destination, they would have to do the same academic phase and debriefing.

The resistance evolution was twelve days of exercise. They were in a mock prisoner-of-war camp and detention center and were put through extreme challenges, both mentally and physically. Each trainee spent four days in each situation: war camp and detention center. The conditions were brutally real. The techniques that were used were these: lack of food and water, sleep deprivation, noise irritation, sensory overload, and even waterboarding. Pace informed the CSTs that the Geneva Convention did not consider these methods to be torture, and the techniques were used to disorient them, making it harder to resist questioning, and to break them ultimately. Also, the instructors tested each individual's collective abilities to resist enemy attempts at exploitation. Unlike military SERE training, where students could work together as teams to give morale or emotional support during captivity, the CSTs were on their own. At the end of each four-day exercise, they spent two days of individual and collective debriefing from the instructors. Unlike POWs, in their world, they would never have a chance of returning home; they would be honored with a star on the CIA Memorial Wall, and if fortunate enough, their name would be in the Honor Book, but could not count on it, and of course, they would never see it.

Phase 5: Demolition Training

This next evolution, three weeks long, provided each CST with baseline knowledge of explosives theory, their characteristics and common uses, formulas for calculating various types of charges, and standard methods of priming and placing charges. They were evaluated and measured by academic and practical examinations to ensure knowledge, and understanding of the following: explosive entry techniques, demolition material, demolition safety, firing systems, calculations, expedient charges, skills in the construction, demolition and emplacement of special-purpose munitions and unexploded ordnance, including IEDs and home-made explosives and range operations.

Some of the academic classes they needed to master were basic electronics/electricity fundamentals, hazards, and identification of the United States and foreign munitions, demolition materials, procedures and operations, and chemical and biological ordinance and operations. Two days were spent learning how to build Homemade

Explosives (HME). To pass this evolution, they had to prove they knew how to perform the field exercise practical examination. That involved a target analysis/interdiction and mission planning.

Phase 6: Combat Training

The Combat Training evolution was eight weeks long. During this training, the trainees learned applied demolitions, land navigation, patrolling, rappelling, and individual and small-unit tactics. Field exercises taught the CSTs map, compass, and land navigation, as they gathered and processed information that allowed them to complete the overall mission. From this, the CSTs simulated long-range reconnaissance and patrolling close-quarters battle, and structure penetration. They were taught the tactics small units must use, including handling explosives, infiltrating enemy lines, surveillance, and counter-surveillance, and recovery (snatch-and-grab), They were taught how to survive in extreme environments and how to provide medical treatment (field medicine).

During the eight weeks, they learned to master marksmanship with nine small arms weapons: AK-47, AK-103, Heckler & Koch G36, Heckler & Koch MK 23, Heckler & Koch P8, M4 carbine, QBZ-92, QSZ-95, and the Stechkin automatic pistol. To pass this evolution, they had to be able to disassemble and reassemble them and have them operational in under a minute. Besides, in this timed evolution, they had to prove that they were able to hit a target with an eight-inch diameter, from twenty-five, fifty, and one-hundred feet away. Setting a foundation using these simple drills would better prepare each CST for real-life combat situations, in which they would use combat speed and accuracy. Once these skills could be repeated on demand, CSTs could begin incorporating new movement, additional rounds, headshots, multiple threat targets, the addition of non-threat targets, moving targets, or a combination of all the above. By the end of the eight weeks, each remaining CST would be prepared for anything.

Phase 7: Parachute Jump School

"So, how do you feel about jumping out of a perfectly good airplane or helicopter?" He stared everyone in the eyes, and then he focused his attention on Erik. "Do you have a fear of falling?"

"No, sir, I am not a fan of gravity."

Graham smirked, "I would agree. As for myself, I don't mind falling; I just do not like that sudden impact at the end kills you every time." He paused to make his next point clear. "Listen up because your life will depend on it."

It was the beginning of week 38, and there were still ten CSTs left. This next evolution was three weeks, with classroom exercises and several field exercises. The trainees received both static line and free-fall training at a Tactical Air Operations facility located at an undisclosed location. By the end of the three-week program, each CST was competent in static line, and free-fall jumps. During the final examination, the trainees passed through a series of jump progressions. They started with a static line and were repelling, usually between 30 to 120 feet, from a helicopter, usually the UH-60 Black Hawk. Next were the free-fall jumps, from a minimum altitude of 1,500 feet and a maximum of 40,000 feet. Free-fall jumps were made from either a C-130 Hercules or CH-47 Chinook helicopter. To complete and pass this evolution, CSTs had to pass through a series of jump progressions, from primary static line to accelerated free fall to combat equipment—ultimately completing day and night descents with equipment.

Phase 8: COMBAT SCUBA School

The diving evolution was three weeks long, and trained, developed, and qualified CSTs as competent basic combat swimmers. As with so many evolutions before, they were evaluated and measured by academic and practical field examinations. They would build the same necessary skills as the Navy SEALS and BUD/S. Throughout the three weeks, they continued with their physical training; however, it became even more intensive. Also, training concentrated on combat SCUBA. Each CST learned two types of SCUBA: open circuit and closed circuit. They learned about essential dive medicine and had medical skills training. They also learned advanced swimming and diving techniques. One field exercise, even though hardly practiced in the field, was a long-distance underwater dive by using swimming techniques and different means of transportation from their launch point to their combat objective. The long-distance underwater dive was the determining factor as to whether or not the trainees got to move to the last and final evolution.

Phase 9: Dark Arts Qualification Training (DAQT)

After forty-two weeks, there were still ten left from a class of forty-six. They now had nine weeks left to complete their qualification training. However, the remaining ten would have one more evolution that would challenge them mentally and physically and push them to their limits. They would have to apply every evolution and every High Liability Training to this evolution. There was a drift toward the classroom door accompanied by an exchange of looks, emotions, and exhortations to hurry up and get down to business. Senior Instructor Rusch came toward the CSTs with the other instructors in his wake. Once in the center, they stood before the class.

"You are the final ten, but that does not mean it is time to kick back and relax." He paused and looked into everyone's eyes. "Gentlemen, you are on your final evolution, and, yes, some of you will fail." He walked around the podium. "On this Special Activity, you will not know where you are; however, you will need to get to the Washington Monument in twenty-four hours." He paused to let the information sink in. "If you don't show up, you will fail. You cannot show up late, or you will fail." He sees the CSTs shake their heads. "Trust me, gentlemen, it is not that simple." A cold smirk came across his face, and the

contrasting sharpness and coldness of his eyes supported
the likeness, as he held up a headshot of each CST in the
room. "These have been given to the FBI and every police
agency out there because we told them you are terrorists,
and your objective is to bomb the Washington Monument. If they see you, they will detain you." However,
what Rusch left out was that those who succeeded would
be caught by CIA operatives posing as FBI field agents.
Then they were going to be detained for four days. While
being detained, they would experience what they did in
the SERE evolution. If they passed that, then and only
then had they completed their training.

Rusch explained that each CST would have 24 hours
to be prepared (even though they had no idea that they
would be in New York City), given $50, and only allowed
to bring what they could fit in a backpack measuring
width: 12 inches, depth: 4 1/2 inches, and height: 16 1/2
inches. He also explained that stress and exhaustion could
destroy one's self-confidence, so it would be necessary to
be prepared and remember everything that they were
taught. He applied two hard and fast rules for their final
adventure, no killing or explosives would be permitted.

Erik, like the other trainees, spent his time wisely.
He spent several hours in front of a computer, printing
and laminating government IDs and documents. Even
though killing or explosives were not allowed, Erik re-
searched other ways that he could use to escape in tight
situations. He was consuming knowledge like a sponge.
Erik only placed essential things in his backpack, such as
dry-fruits, biscuits, and water. This was so he could at least

live for two days without wasting time getting something to eat, and he could quickly regain his strength when he was traveling. He also packed a zippo lighter, three packs of 110" Rhino Laces, one pair of socks and underwear, a collapsible aluminum white cane (used for individuals who are blind), dark lensed sunglasses, microfiber towel, survival knife, a compass, and a few other things. They had twenty-two hours to prepare because the last two hours; they were given a meal that was well deserved. They were fed prime roast rib, mashed potatoes, gravy, and a veggie. What the CSTs didn't know was that GHB was placed in their drinks. GHB is a fluid that is used as a legal prescription drug for sleep and is called Xyrem. This would make the trainees "pass out" in the sense that they would sleep deeply and could not be awakened for some hours. Funny thing is they've been training for fifty-one weeks for this final evolution, and in the end, they'll be judged on what they can do within this twenty-four hour evolution.

7. THE KNOWLEDGE THAT HE POSSESSED WOULD STAGGER SATAN HIMSELF

"We may not pay Satan reverence, for that would be indiscreet, but we can at least respect his talents."

—Mark Twain

SOMEWHERE IN NEW YORK CITY

The phone's menacing, piercing sound shook the air as it penetrated Erik's eardrums like nails on a chalkboard. All in one action, he jumped out of bed, reached for the phone like a wide receiver, pulling it to his ear, and with his other hand, reached for his backpack. He heard a deep, menacing voice that said, "Time to die."

Erik knew that escaping in an urban environment was about precision. However, escape from a building that's being locked down requires speed. That was the skill he would need. He felt his pulse in every part of his body while his eyes were searching and analyzing every time he took a step. Erik knew that the New York police, FBI, and others were coordinating their efforts to apprehend him. What made matters worse was they knew where he was. In this case, Erik knew every staircase and elevator would be watched, so his next best option would be a window. There was a catch: one, was there a soft landing for a jump, and two, he knew there would be individuals trained in the tactics of intelligence operatives. Knowing that this opportunity might close before Erik could use it, he immediately exited the apartment. Seeing a fire alarm, he yanked down the lever and prayed it would go off.

The fire alarm consumed the hallway. The sound intensified as it bounced off the walls. Now Erik had a few options to escape. One, going down a garbage chute. Even though it could be effective for the escape, there was no way to slow down or know what was on the bottom, which could end in a severe injury and he would be compromised. Two, hiding until the fire department came and either let them walk him out, or knock one of them out and change into their gear.

There were drawbacks to this last approach. Firefighters work in teams, and they are generally big guys. Thus, the uniform would be too large for him, and he would stick out and again be compromised. Discounting both options, Erik knew he needed to do something so crazy his chasers would not be thinking of it. He could go to the top of the building and jump from one building to another to elude being captured. But that idea had problems: the distance between buildings, someone could be waiting on top for him, and the worst one, Erik could misjudge the leap and fall to his death. What he learned in SERE training is that you do anything to escape. Most people would say to think outside the box, but as a paramilitary operations officer, he must believe there is no box.

Quickly thinking through all these scenarios, he ascended to the roof. Once on top, Erik made a quick assessment of the situation and the distance between the buildings, four to five feet. As he composed himself in preparation for his jump, Erik heard the sirens of fire engines approaching and the anticipation that someone will be on the roof. For each step he took, he made sure his shoes gripped so that he could gain more power for his jump. The scary thing about jumping, it is like being on a roller coaster, once you start, there is no turning back, and once you are about to jump, what in the hell was I thinking goes through your mind. He also would need to make sure he landed correctly.

All that considered, he jumped to the next building and quickly and cautiously descended to the street. Once at ground level, he became the rabbit, the person being followed and eventually compromised by those sent to find, follow, and capture the rabbit. The problem was that they looked like everyone else, and they would rotate into the lead position. Once they spotted him, it would be too late, and Erik would fail this evolution. To make matters worse, there were surveillance teams, either on the ground, in a helicopter, watching the satellite, or a combination helping those after him. Facing all these resources, Erik knew the first few hours were when he was most likely to get caught. He applied what he had learned to use chokepoints, a point of congestion or obstruction, to help identify those on his tail. In short, he knew numbers weren't in his favor and his approach to escaping changed from out-running to out-smarting.

As Erik blended into the foot traffic, he realized he was in New York City by the taxis and police cars and uniformed officers, one group of people he was going to avoid. However, what part? That problem was solved when he heard someone grumbling at how brutal the Manhattan traffic was at this time. Erik glanced at someone's watch. It read 7:00 a.m. He used store and car windows as mirrors and got his breathing and heart rate back to normal, and now he was focused on escaping. A cold chill ran up his back, and once it reached the top, it caused goosebumps to spread through his body. Erik darted into a deli and maneuvered around people who crowded the counter like passengers scrambling to get on the lifeboat of a sinking ship. As he pulled out a forged government ID from his pocket and took a deep breath, he entered the kitchen. With his hand raised, he announced he was the health inspector, and told everyone to go about their business. Erik navigated through the kitchen, exited through the back, and quickly looked for an open door.

In a short distance, at the mouth of an alley, an NYC cruiser glided slowly by on the street, the officer in the passenger seat glaring. The cruiser chirped to a stop. His eyes and Erik's eyes met. The officer glanced at a photo and back at Erik. His eyes enlarged as they focused on

Erik. The door flew open, and he ordered his partner to call for back up and find a way behind the alley.

"Hold it right there!"

Erik bolted off down a narrow alley and vaulted over a pile of tumbled trashcans. The cop, with his gun drawn, followed. As Erik whipped around a corner, he leaped and slid across the hood of a parked car. Trailing behind, the cop snaked through the urban maze cluttered with trash and debris. Erik hit a chain link fence and scaled it within seconds and continued to run full tilt, displaying incredible agility while continually looking for an open door. He remembered from training, that no matter what country you are in, the longer you run from the police, the possibility of getting caught increases by the minute; however, there is one positive thing, it takes five to ten minutes before backup arrives. In the distance, Erik saw newly arrived units, and one was a K-9 unit. The officer jumped out and opened the back door, releasing a large German Shephard. Finding several doors locked, Erik opened a small compartment in his backpack, pulled out two paperclips, and began to pick the lock. Within fifteen seconds, Erik was in and vanished into the darkness within the building.

He found himself in a department store or large thrift store and disappeared among the maze of aisles and display racks. He noticed a sign that men's clothing was upstairs and heard distinct footsteps and a dog panting. The flashlight beams stabbed through the darkness as the cops tried to coordinate their strategy. Erik did a crab-run low among the moving shadows where flashlights quarter the darkness. Seeing an opportunity, he bolted to an open space behind a display. A cop glanced over and moved his flashlight in a sweeping motion toward Erik's direction. Erik's face froze among the smooth featured, smiling mannequins. When the light passed, Erik silently moved on and moved toward the escalator. When he was approximately twenty feet away, he did a fast crabwalk across the aisles to melt into the other racks and shadows. Within five feet, Erik vaulted the escalator rail and bounded up the frozen steps. He heard noises; the cops dashed through the maze of aisles, converging at the escalator.

In the distance, Erik looked for a possible means of escape. He hurtled between displays and his keen eyesight spotted clothing that he could change into. He grabbed a white oxford shirt and tie set and stopped beside a rack of dress shoes. Erik slapped a pair sole-to-sole against his sneakers. Too small. He grabbed another. It would have to do. He threw the shoes in his backpack and ran to the suits. Thank God, the suits were organized by size. Erik grabbed his size and headed to a storage room where he found a storage closet. He knew that within a couple of minutes, the cops would head in this direction.

A glance around found everything he needed: a knife, glass jars, ammonia, and bleach. With the knife, Erik cut into each of the bleach containers and threw them at the opening of the storage room. The smell of bleach started to consume the room as he filled several glass jars of ammonia. Erik quickly exited the storage room and tossed a jar of ammonia on the floor. Within seconds, the mixture of ammonia and bleach started to form a mist, and Erik turned around and threw the other glass jar of ammonia, immediately increasing the mist in the room.

"Freeze!" with their weapons drawn, the cops ordered as they entered the storage room.

Suddenly the cops gagged, coughed, and stumbled out of the room. Erik smirked as he went through the fire escape, pleased it worked. Ammonia combined with bleach made toxic chloramine vapors, and the fumes, this could cause respiratory damage and throat burns. He also remembered the worst that could happen: if excess ammonia is present, toxic and potentially explosive liquid hydrazine could form.

Erik moved like a panther along the narrow catwalk, and as he climbed down the ladder, he saw an abandoned police cruiser parked at the mouth of the alley. He dropped cat-like beside the unattended police car. Then Erik quickly changed into the suit and cautiously walked down the alley leading to the street. Once at the street, he hailed a taxi, opened the door quietly, slipped in, and disappeared into downtown traffic.

Checking his surroundings and scoping out a spot to get out, he signaled the driver, paid him, and exited the taxi. With the training he received, he could transform himself into any walk of life to become anyone. Erik got into character as a Federal Aviation Administration (FAA) Aviation Safety Inspector (ASI) and headed to the Downtown Manhattan Heliport. The lobby was filled, mostly with tourists anticipating helicopter tours of New York. He turned his head to see the helicopters on the pad, consumed everything he saw and headed to the counter.

"Good morning, do you have an appointment?" An enthusiastic young lady greeted Erik.

"No." He said with a smile, then his tone got serious. "I need to speak to your operations manager."

A gentleman who overheard the conversion butted in. "Can I help you?"

Erik pulled out the ID and replied with an authoritarian tone. "I'm Joe Turner, FAA, from Washington."

The man looked at the ID, and he gulped as beads of sweat appeared on his forehead, and he realized he was talking to an FAA Aviation Safety Inspector. Next, he picked up a phone receiver and calmly whispered something into it. Then he looked at Erik, "Brian will be right down." Erik nodded in appreciation. "Inspector, would you like some coffee?"

"No, I'm fine."

A professional-looking man appeared from a door, and Erik approached him like a gunslinger in the wild west of the 1880s. The man extended his hand to meet Erik's. "I'm Brian Mitchell, operations manager, how can I help you, inspector?

"I'm Joe Turner, FAA, from Washington." Erik pointed in the direction of the helipads. "I see you have several AS350 Écureuil/AStars." Brian nodded as they walked together. "Do you have all your maintenance records?"

"Of course."

Erik turned to Brian and studied him. "You don't sound too confident in your answer." Erik pointed at the black Astar 350 B2 helicopter that had identification numbers, N646PT. "Do you have your records for that aircraft?"

"Yes, inspector." Then Brian changed his tone. "Is there a problem?"

Erik walked to the counters, lifted a receiver from the phone, and began to dial a number, and then he turned to Brian. "If you like, I can get Washington on the phone and tell them that the Downtown Manhattan Heliport has incompetent managers, and they will shut your operation down within the hour." Erik also sensed that there was too much improvisation happening.

"That's not needed, inspector. How can I help."

Erik knew that he had taken in the manager, so it couldn't hurt to try the next step in his impromptu plan. "I need a pilot to take me up and fly to D.C. I want to make sure the aircraft is not having any mechanical issues." Erik stepped next to Brian. "You know to make sure everything is fine." Brian nodded. "I don't want you to be sued for something that could be prevented. I'm sure you would agree." Again, Brian nodded. "The FAA will give you a voucher for the fuel used."

Brian smiled, and a man stepped next him with two sets of David Clark DC Pro-X Headsets. "This is Tommy King." Brian tilted his head slightly to his left. "Your pilot."

"Morning inspector, the aircraft is fueled and ready." Erik nodded in appreciation. "Sir, when would you like to take off?"

Erik turned to Tommy and replied coldly. "Now."

Within minutes, Erik was airborne and headed to Washington. Tommy advised Erik that they would arrive in Washington in approximately two hours and forty minutes. During that time, Tommy made small talk with Erik to pass the time. Erik said he enjoyed working for the FAA as an ASI. However, to become one, he had lots of schooling and the ability to apply knowledge and skills typically acquired as airmen (pilots, navigators, flight instructors, etc.) to develop and administer regulations and safety standards on the operation of aircraft. His strength was helicopters. Also, he would examine airmen for initial certification and continuing competence; evaluate airmen training programs, equipment, and facilities. Next, he needed to assess the operational aspect of programs of air carriers and similar commercial and aviation operations for the adequacy of facilities, equipment, procedures, and overall management to ensure the safe operation of the aircraft.

"You must have been well trained—and smart."

Erik shook his head with a slight smile. "Above average." In short, once Erik read and understood the information, he would never forget it and would apply it when necessary. Tommy pointed to the heliport.

"Ground this is November-six-four-six-Papa-Tango, over."

"This is ground, go ahead November-six-four-six-Papa-Tango, over."

"We're on our way over the river. Have one FAA Inspector Turner to be dropped off and requesting to be refueled. Over."

"Roger, November-six-four-six-Papa-Tango. You're clear to land. Wind 0-2-0-1-5. Altimeter 2-9-8-9. Over."

"Roger, out."

Tommy landed the helicopter and gave hand signals when it was clear to depart from the helo. Before leaving, Erik shook hands with Tommy and thanked him. Ground crews started getting the gear to refuel the chopper, as someone came to greet Erik. Erik excused himself to use the restroom as he tried to locate the phone box and disabled the phones. Once inside, he changed his clothes, placed his sunglasses on, and pulled out a paperclip and a test light kit. Erik walked away from the building and saw a 1995 Toyota Corolla. He needed transportation because the Washington Monument was twenty-five minutes by car and nearly sixty minutes on foot. Erik pulled out a Slim Jim and inserted it, and unlocked the car. He applied the emergency brake and popped the hood and immediately got to work. Erik found the fuse box, removed the lid, and found the switch relay. Second, Erik removed the relay switch and examined what side the control was on and what side the load/switch was on. It was the 30 and 87 for the switch side and located the corresponding terminals. He got his test light, attached it to the battery ground, and tested the terminals to see which one had power. Next, he bent his paperclip into a U shape and placed one end in terminal 30 and the other in 87. Lastly, he engaged the starter and turned over the engine, and removed the paperclip. Then he leaped in the car and pulled out a large flathead screwdriver, rammed it into the ignition lock cylinder, and the steering wheel unlocked. He had to be at his objective in fourteen hours.

When Erik was at The Farm, he looked for homeless shelters near the Washington Monument, thinking in advance that it would be safer than checking into a hotel. The CCNV, on 425 D St NW, opened its doors at 5 pm. He parked the car on 12th Street NW and then headed to the shelter. He passed a pizza parlor and checked his funds—just enough for one slice. Once there, Erik stood with sad, weary women, faces streaked with tears and their children, men of all ages, bitter and angry, beggars, and outcasts. They were in stark contrast to the rich who tried not to rub shoulders with people they didn't want to be associated with, much less pay attention to if they ran into them. After a warm meal, Erik freshened up, got on his cot, and fell into a restless night's sleep.

His watch alarm woke him. It was 0600. He placed his feet on the floor, and his muscles ached. However, he shook his head and remembered what the instructors said, 'Make minor adjustments and pain will remind you that you still have a pulse, so finish the objective.' Now he stood up, grabbed his belongings, and headed for the exit because he had a job to do. Once a reasonable distance from the center, Erik slipped on his sunglasses, opened his cane, and assumed the character of a blind man. He had forty minutes to reach the Washington Monument, and he approached it by going through The Ellipse. With each step, Erik decided whether to quit or continue. He was on his way, but it wasn't about how far he had come because he wasn't sure if he was going to be welcomed with warm smiles and handshakes or a hidden surprise. One thing he did know was his opponent was cunning, and it was as if he could feel them around him, maybe right behind him, and felt their breath on the back of his neck. The battle Erik faced ahead was between himself, his attitude, his physical condition, and Satan on his shoulder that told him every breath could be his last. However, what Satan didn't know about Erik was the knowledge that he possessed would stagger Satan himself.

Erik wandered toward the Washington Monument and saw a park bench a short distance away. He closed his eyes to gather his thoughts as he heard two distinct footsteps approaching on his left. He opened his eyes and realized it was DC cops (or they appeared to be). One glanced at his phone as the other nodded, and they headed in Erik's direction. One pulled out his sentry expandable friction lock baton, and with one movement of his wrist, it was extended and locked into place. He tapped the bench so he could get Erik's attention, and the other cop hovered over Erik on his right side.

"Can't you read the signs?"

Erik tilted his head up. "Excuse me; I didn't know there were signs because I'm blind."

The cop continued. "Well, the signs say no loitering."

"On your feet. Let's go. Right now." The other cop ordered.

As Erik made it to his feet, the cops were on top of him, and one demanded. "Let's see some identification." Erik wasn't sure what to do with his eyes moving behind the sunglasses, and he kept his mouth shut. Again, the cop barked. "Come on. Your identification. Let's go."

"I believe it's in my backpack." As Erik reached the pouch, one cop stepped back.

"Okay, place the bag on the bench." The cop was getting impatient. "Let's go!" One police officer stripped Erik of his backpack, as the other continued to give orders. "Put your hands up."

Erik dropped his white cane and slowly raised his hands as he tried to explain. "Look, I was just resting my feet, okay?"

The cop with the baton had heard enough and gave a sharp poke with his baton into Erik's back and removed his sunglasses. Then the police officer realized he had seen his face just minutes before on an alert that came over his cell phone. Erik faced him, and his eyes narrowed and turned cold as the cop stepped back and dropped his baton. By then it was too late. In a single turn, Erik spun and caught the police officer to his right off guard, and he used the heel of his hand up in his throat, temporarily immobilizing him and causing him to fall to the ground.

Erik continued to spin, with all his weight as he moved in a single fluid attack using a sweeping kick, as the second cop tried to reach for his pistol. The impact caused the officer to lose his balance. He fell to his knees. He mustered all his strength, using the bench to push himself up, but the attack continued. Erik calculated his next attack as he kept turning, and all the cop could do was to watch Erik in slow motion. Erik's eyes like a shark right before it attacks, hardened as he threw, in lighting speed, three jackhammer punches. The cop was out cold.

Then Erik turned to face the other cop, who writhed on the ground and gasped for air as he struggled with his holster. Erik, without hesitation, smashed his foot down, like a vice, onto the cop's arm. The sheer weight and power shattered the bone. Erik kneeled quickly and grabbed the pistol from the holster, and placed the barrel to the cop's forehead. The police officer went from being silent to gasping and pleading, as Erik was on the verge of pulling the trigger. Erik shook his head and slammed the gun against the cop's temple, knocking him out. This fight was over.

Erik grabbed his sunglasses, placed his backpack on, and grabbed his cane. He stood there in silence with two unconscious cops at his feet. Finally, Erik stripped the bullet from the chamber, took it apart, and dropped it on the ground. What Erik just did felt natural. He had disabled them with ease and allowed them to live another day. Erik looked up and saw the Washington Monument in the distance and walked quickly in that direction. As he neared the monument, he glanced around and was pleased with himself for making it. Erik saw a paperclip on the ground and placed it in his pocket. He touched the monument and raised his hands above his head, symbolizing his victory. However, that would be the last thing he remembered as he felt a sharp pinch to his neck, and these words, "You know what this is? It's your fears, doubts, and insecurities all tied in a noose ready to choke you until you are dead."

Erik had lost all knowledge of what day and time it was. All he knew was that he was interrogated two times, and every time they took him; they handcuffed him. He opened his eyes to the blackness that consumed him. As if a thousand needles pierced his skin, nearly freezing water was dumped on him, followed immediately by a blast of cold air bringing the room temperature to forty-five degrees. Erik placed himself in a fetal position to contain his heat. Simultaneously, an ear-piercing siren ripped through his ears with a bright, blinding strobe light. This lasted for three minutes.

As he was about to collect his thoughts, it started again and repeated several more times. Two things that Erik remembered was that the Geneva Convention doesn't consider these methods to be torture, and the wording in the convention only applies to uniformed soldiers. He knew whoever was doing this was stronger than he was. He ignored the voices of uncertainty in his head and focused on escaping as he placed the paperclip in his hand and held it tight. The door to his cell barged open, and two large men brought him to his feet. One punched him in the gut while another handcuffed him, and a shroud was placed over his head. While Erik was dragged to the interrogation room, he knew his captors would not be easily defeated, but they were far from invincible.

They threw him in a chair with his hands behind him. What most people don't know is captors know they have control. Each time they interrogated Erik, they probed for more detailed information, such as exactly what his mission was, his name, and any other information. Before being questioned, the captors thought that the more worn out Erik would become, the more likely he would make a mistake and give them information. In the interrogation room, he glanced at a nearby table, and he saw Dremel tools, a cattle prod, a 9mm Beretta, a phonebook, and a syringe with Sodium Amytal, or some other truth agent. Erik went to work, picking the lock of the handcuffs as he took deep breaths and kept his body calm, and his eyes focused. Then a captor headed in Erik's direction, and as he passed the table, he grabbed the phonebook and swung it back like a baseball bat, hitting Erik on the side of his head and carrying it through a full swing. He smirked and repeated the same process. Erik shook off the pain, even more determined to escape.

Disgusted, the captor tossed the phonebook aside and grabbed the cattle prod as Erik dropped the paperclip.

"Is there anything you would like to tell me before we start?" The man said. Erik nodded and looked up.

Erik's eyes narrowed and gave a cunning grin. "Is that all you got?"

Once the captor made a sudden movement, Erik exploded out of his chair and, in the same action, thrust his knee into the man's groin and removed the cattle prod from his hand. The other man tried to stop Erik, but Erik quickly smashed the prod against his temple first, then both knees. Next, he went to the table and grabbed the Beretta, and cracked the door open. Erik quickly analyzed his situation and proceeded down the hallway, looking for a diagram of the building. He felt uneasy; it just seemed too quiet as he continued to find an exit, but suddenly an alarm went off. Most people run when they hear an alarm. That is a mistake because they are wasting energy, especially if they don't know where you are going.

Erik came upon an elevator and pressed the button. He had the Beretta ready to neutralize any threat. The doors crept open. He dashed in and pressed the button to the highest floor. Again, he got in position to neutralize any threat. The elevator stopped, and as the doors crept open, there were several individuals on the other side. Erik fell to his knees as he opened fire. Blanks. Once the doors fully opened, it revealed Rusch, with his arms across his chest and the other instructors behind him. Rusch nodded and extended his hand as if to say congratulations; you passed the final evolution. Then he stated in a harsh cold tone. "So, just make sure this is something that you want because from here, it only gets tougher."

8. THIS DAY FORWARD, WE CAN BE UNKNOWN HEROES

"The two most important days in your life are the day you are born and the day you find out why."

—Mark Twain

THE FARM

Thirteen days later, Erik and five other CSTs were welcomed back to The Farm. As Erik left the barracks for the last time, he noticed a poem by the door. It read:

I've been around the world more than you know;
if you ask me to talk about the places I have been, I will say no.
I have seen every kind of animal on land and sea;
if you ask me what did I see, I will ask you to let me be.
If you ask me about my work, I will tell you I saw a movie in Zurich.
If you ask me where I learned to drive;

I will tell you I learned from watching James Bond, who is a spy.

If you ask me if I have jumped from a plane, I will tell you hell no, that is insane.

If you ask me if I know how to SCUBA;

I will say no, but I am thinking about learning how to play the Tuba.

If you ask me do I know anything about C4;

I will point and laugh at you and show you the door.

If you ask me have I shot a gun; I will tell you I did it in Boy Scouts just for fun.

I have no medals to show, but I do have blisters hiking in the snow.

When they say I have to go overseas, I wonder what I will see.

I will protect America with my life, but I might come back with the roll of the dice.

You ask me if I lie; as a CIA Paramilitary Operations Officer, that's how I stay alive.

Six were left of the original forty-six (one was an undercover operator reporting the actions and behaviors of the CSTs to Rusch). Rusch gave his last words of wisdom. "You will spend more time planning your operations and less time on your vacations. You will need to figure your odds and calculate your chances on every special activity. You will need to keep pushing yourself to your limits, focus on your objective, finish it, and then get the hell back home. You will know hurt and trust pain and embrace the struggle. You will learn that time is your enemy. Your drops of blood are what you will need to achieve your goal." Rusch paused, looked around, and gave a warning before he congratulated them. "As a Paramilitary Operations Officer, you will have hundreds if not thousands of enemies, in every part of the world. When they catch you, they will kill you ... but first, they need to catch you."

They went down the row, shook hands with each instructor, and thanked them. Not surprisingly, Rusch admired those CSTs who could stand up to the challenge because it taught them a lesson, an essential part of their learning process at The Farm. Erik was one of those individuals, and he was the last one to shake Senior Instructor Rusch's hand. "Congratulations 107602," Rusch replied, as Erik realized that the agency had taken away his name, and he was now known as a number. Rusch leaned forward and whispered to Erik, "Remember, you don't hide in the darkness; you are the darkness."

·

9. STRANGE LITTLE CORNER IN MY WORLD

"Be extremely subtle, even to the point of formlessness. Be extremely mysterious, even to the point of soundlessness. Thereby you can be the director of the opponent's fate."

—Sun Tzu

NATIONAL MUSEUM OF AMERICAN HISTORY, WASHINGTON, D.C.

26 March 2003: Several dull solid knocks came to the door that awakened Erik's thoughts. Again, the knock repeated as he got up from his desk. His desk was an organized mess of formal and informal written records and documents. Tacked on the wall in front of his desk were proposed or pending projects he had submitted. He had several bookcases that are filled with historical references dealing with his newest exhibit, The Eagle Squadrons in the Battle of Britain. On his desktop and the remainder of open spaces on the walls, he had existing research data in the form of maps, photographs, and drawings. Finally, among the mess, he had a coffee mug bearing these words:

"If I learn any more, I will be a threat to national security." Erik rubbed his eyes and made his way to the door.

Standing outside was a co-worker, not a part of the CIA, who announced, "Erik, Gordon Brown is here to see you." Erik nodded. "He is waiting for you in Flag Hall."

"Thank you; tell him I will be right there." The co-worker walked off as Erik grabbed his suit jacket and proceeded to Flag Hall.

It had been four years, one month, twenty-five days, and this morning since he was assigned to O.G.D.S. Team 42. Within those years, Erik had achieved both his Masters in Military History and his Doctorate in History, with his thesis on Field Marshal Erwin Rommel. Shortly after his training, he became a curator and a tour guide at the National Museum of American History, and his first assignment was Vladimir Putin, Prime Minister of Russia. With the Cold War having been over for nearly a decade, the Intelligence Community was confident Russia would try to sell its military hardware to the highest bidder. The presidential election in Russia was observed. Even though he was swamped campaigning, Putin still came to the United States, and the bait was set for him to meet Erik. It worked, and from March until the day Putin was elected president, Erik and Putin talked from time to time. Putin had been helping Erik out at the Hermitage Museum, and in so doing, Erik was able to feed Putin what Putin thought was sensitive information. Because of this, Putin invited him to visit his country.

Little did Putin know that the CIA knew the Russians

were planning on selling one of their Alpha Class nuclear submarines, the Kursk, at the end of August 2000, to the North Koreans. The United States Government was not going to allow this to happen. Now was the time for Erik to put all the things he had learned to the test. The mission was set for the night of 11 August 2000. The day before, the Kursk was going to do a sortie on an exercise with the Kirov-class battlecruiser Pyotr Velikiy. This was no ordinary exercise because not only was the top brass of the Russian Navy going to be there, but some members of the North Korean Navy and Ministry of State Security, would be there as well.

The exercise was for the Kursk to approach undetected and fire their dummy torpedoes at the Pyotr Velikiy. These practice torpedoes had no explosive warheads. Erik was to infiltrate as an Intelligence Officer, by wearing a latex mask to disguise his appearance to resemble the Minister of Internal affairs at the naval base at Severomorsk. Once on the base, he was to proceed to the Kursk and place a small plastic explosive on one of the hydrogen peroxide-fueled Type 65 torpedoes. This would cause the hydrogen peroxide to seep through rust in the torpedo, resulting in an explosion that would destroy the bow of the submarine, causing it to sink.

After it was placed, Erik's orders were to get the hell out and get back home. Only when he got back to the United States did he learn of the success of his mission: On 12 August, at 11:28 local time, there was an explosion on the Kursk while they were preparing to fire, killing all the crew.

"Erik." A distinguished-looking gentleman with a European styled suit waved, as Erik approached with his hand extended. "It is so good to see you again."

"Chancellor Brown, nice to meet you again. How are you and Sarah?"

"We are very well; thank you." Gordon Brown, who was the Chancellor of the Exchequer of England, had known Erik for nearly two years, and now they were good acquaintances. They had first met while Gordon was visiting the United States and the National Museum of American History. Now every time he visited the United States, he came to see Erik. "Dr. Függer, how are things with you?"

"Please call me Erik. I'm well, keeping busy with the new museum exhibit, the Eagle Squadrons in the Battle of Britain."

"Then please call me Gordon, Erik. Alan told me that is what you were working on and that's why I brought you these." Gordon handed him a small parcel. "I know you like to explain both sides of a conflict." Pointing to the parcel, he continued, "Those photographs were found during the reoccupation of France. I thought you might like them."

"Thank you very much, Gordon. I will return them after the exhibit."

"No, you can keep them." Gordon glanced at his watch, "Well, I have to meet Sarah for lunch at the embassy. Maybe we can all go out for dinner before we head back home."

"I would like that very much. Thank you again, Gordon."

Erik turned around and headed to the Native American Exhibit as he struggled to open the package. He walked to a large painting of a chief, possibly from the Great Plains, who had a sneer on his face and eyes that were narrowing with contempt. The Native American was using a hand gesture in which the index and middle fingers were raised and parted, while the other fingers were clenched. Erik had often wondered what he was thinking.

"Look, the Indian is doing a peace sign."

Laughter engulfed Erik's ears as he shook his head and saw a young couple smirking at the painting. "I would like to inform you that that is a sign meaning they could still fight. White settlers used to cut those fingers off so Native Americans couldn't use their bows." Erik remembered a quote from Benjamin Disraeli "The greatest good you can do for another is not just to share your own riches but to reveal to him his own."

"Who cares? It's all in the past," the individual said mockingly.

Erik was about to reply in a condescending tone; however, he had to remain professional. "Yes, of course, you are right." Erik stepped forward and gave a cold, firm, intense look at the man. "However, please respect Native American History." Then he thought of a quote by Martin Luther King, Jr. "Nothing in all the world is more dangerous than sincere ignorance and conscientious stupidity."

The wife pulled her husband away as he gave a wrathful glance. Erik never did like stupid people, especially when it came to history or common sense. It was not that people did not know the facts, but that they lacked the understanding or desire to understand historical events and cultures. However, he did like his job at the museum because he could educate people concerning the different points of view and because he could meet, and already had met, foreign politicians. The most rewarding aspects of the job, of course, consisted of doing the special activities overseas, but, if he were able to make one person understand history, it was a success.

"Running Wolf, you are correct in what that means. Not many know that."

"Thank you. What did you call me?" Sitting below Erik's eye level was an elderly Native American with long silver hair, hazel eyes, wrinkles etched in his face, and fragile hands that trembled. He motioned to Erik to sit, as he patted the bench. Sitting next to the elderly man, Erik inquired again, "Why did you call me Running Wolf?"

"My ancestors gave you that name."

With his hands in the air with a puzzled look, Erik continued, "Your ancestors gave me? What are you talking about?" Erik rubbed his forehead.

"Most people like you must first understand the heart of the wolf, and this takes time." The man points to Erik's heart. "However, you understood this at an early age, Running Wolf. Many people now and in your past had false stereotypes, misconceptions, and misunderstandings about you. You have a high sense of loyalty and strength. In time, you will be a social creature, friendly, gregarious, and loving with your companion, and you'll protect her from all harm. My people ..."

Erik tossed up his hands and backed up. "Enough! Your people? You mean tribe?" The Native American nodded. Erik continued his probe. "What's your name?"

"I am from the Hopi People, and they call me Eagle Eyes." Erik gestured for him to continue. "I can see in the past and future." Leaning forward, he said, "You have a purpose, Running Wolf."

"A purpose? What purpose is that?" Jumping to his feet, Erik quickly analyzed his surroundings. "You do know I work for the museum?"

Eagle Eyes nodded and began to explain that the Hopi People have the Wuwuchim ceremony, which has been done several times in history. Songs are sung during the sixteen days of the ceremony. However, one main song talks about the coming of war or disaster. He further explained that this song was sung in 1914 just before World War I, in 1940 before World War II, and again in 1961. "The Creator, Tawa, will show us in the heaven twin stars, the Blue and Red Stars Kachina. The Blue Star Kachina tells us a new way of life, and a new world is coming, and changes will begin. This will start fires, and man will burn up with desires and conflict, like war. If we don't remember our teaching and return to the peaceful way of life, Red Star Kachina, the Purifier, will cause all of Earth's creatures' lives to change forever and offer an opportunity to change." Lastly, Eagle Eyes explained that this would only take place if the Blue Star Kachina took off his mask, and a new cycle of life began.

"Okay, I don't believe it. Why would your people involve me?" Erik protested.

"Tawa has sent messengers during the time of the Red Star Kachina so they can help mankind change." Erik gave a blank stare as Eagle Eyes pointed to him. "You are one of the messengers."

Erik shook his head. "You got the wrong guy. Have a good day." Erik got up.

Again, Eagle Eyes motioned Erik to take a seat. "You live in two different worlds, and because of that, you will need to open your eyes; then you will find your place." Erik failed to get a word out. "As the years pass you by, you will be on a lonely dark passage within the eye of the storm, and there will be many thorns."

"What do you mean by that? I do not understand. Explain."

"Along the dark passage, there will be roses," said Eagle Eyes, pointing to Erik's chest. "You will need to listen to your inner voice and believe in yourself. Then you will be out of the dark and be in the promised land."

"What are you trying to tell me?"

"You will learn as you go on your journey."

"No. I want to know now." Begging, almost pleading, Erik replied with desperation in his eyes, "Tell me!" Eagle Eyes got up and started to walk away. "Wait!"

Eagle Eyes' face grew stern, "You will need to use your skills to get through the dark passage."

"You are referring to when I was at..."

"No! You are intelligent, persistent, and, most of all, you have the ability to be a true survivor. However, I must warn you, Running Wolf, that on your journey, you will learn horrible truths, and it will haunt your dreams for all time. You will always have to overcome every challenge, and your story will be told for generations." Eagle Eyes turned and walked away.

"So, when will I know when my journey begins, and will I see you again?"

Turning his head and looking over his shoulder, Eagle Eyes responded, "Not in the way you see me now. Your journey will begin when your companion comes to you when she is lost, and you will protect her, making an unbreakable bond."

Great! More riddles and vague answers. Erik heard a distant voice coming from behind.

"Hey Erik, Alan needs to see you right away." Erik gestured as if he were asking why. Standing behind him was another curator, non-CIA, Phillip. "Alan said he wanted to see you."

"Do you know why?" Erik pursued. Phillip shook his head.

On the way to Alan's office, Erik could not get out of his head what Eagle Eyes had said. All those symbolic, encrypted messages and the name Running Wolf kept plaguing him. Alan was the Director of the museum, and he was Erik's chief of station for the CIA, who also worked with O.G.D.S. Team 42. His job was to make sure that foreign leaders and diplomats' first point of contact was Erik, and that was how O.G.D.S. TEAM 42 began each mission. Both Alan and Erik made a good team by knowing what the other was thinking; thus, they could predict the other's actions. Mainly because Alan was like a big brother figure to Erik and always wanted to make sure he was doing well both professionally and personally. Erik arrived at Alan's office and knocked.

"Come in."

Stepping in, he felt the presence of the admiral, closed the door, and took his seat.

"How is the exhibit coming?" Alan bounced a question off Erik.

"Great! We should be done in the next two weeks." Bonesteiner and Alan nodded and were pleased with his work.

"I heard Gordon Brown stopped by."

Erik nodded, "He brought me a parcel." Lifting it so all could see, he continued, "He said it would help with the exhibit." Then he saw the joy disappear in their eyes.

"Erik, the reason I am here is…" Bonesteiner took a deep breath and sighed, "Well, there is no easy way to say it. Erik, your parents and brother were killed in a car accident." The color drained from Erik's face, and he fumbled to get the words out of his mouth, as the admiral cupped Erik's shoulder for emotional support. Erik pushed his chair back and excused himself.

The admiral motioned to Alan not to say a word and to take his seat. "Erik has had his share of tragedy already. He doesn't handle death well. He has been that way as long as I have known him." Alan leaned back in his chair as Bonesteiner continued. "When he was working for me, for the first time, he lost the girl he was going to marry and his unborn son."

"Oh, dear God! How old was she? Did we take care of that problem for him?"

"Nineteen, and no."

Alan shook his head in disbelief, "That kid has been through a lot. I know when he was in Iraq two years ago, he lost three of his friends." Picking up the receiver, he said, "I will set up an appointment for him. I know a good psychologist."

"You would be wasting your time. Erik's therapy is work." Bonesteiner took a deep breath and continued. "That kid has lived a harsh life, full of struggles and unfortunate events. Unlike others who would give up, Erik has never lost hope that things will get better, and he always gets up and starts over." Bonesteiner handed over an airline ticket to Alan. "Make sure he gets that and drive him to the airport."

"Yes, sir."

"One last thing, the Russians are up to the same tricks they were up to three years ago. I need him back within a week."

10. IF ONLY I COULD SIT BY YOUR SIDE

*"I couldn't shake this feeling that I had uncovered
more than something ordinary."*

—Nicole Gulla

NATIONAL MUSEUM OF AMERICAN
HISTORY, WASHINGTON, D.C.

Standing in front of his latest exhibit, Erik tried to open
his parcel, happy for the distraction from the terrible
news he had just heard, and thought it would be a long
time before he would feel happy again. Opening the parcel was more like solving a Rubik's cube. A sigh of relief
spread across his face as he emptied the contents, black
and white photographs. As he flipped through the photos, Erik soon realized that the pictures were of a single
Heinkel 111 German Bomber crew during the Battle of
Britain. He wondered what they thought right before a
mission and what they thought when the photos were
taken.

Suddenly a photograph jumped out at Erik as he

analyzed the face of each of the crew as if they were under a microscope. As he flipped through the next few photos, he blinked with amazement, and his breath caught in his throat. In several of the photographs, a Luftwaffe lieutenant had a sticking similarity of Erik. It could have been someone that looked exactly like him. Erik's thoughts ran wild like a Bronco in a rodeo. How in God's name is that possible? They say everyone has a twin or someone that looks like them. However, this guy is giving a thumbs up. No German officer ever did that. There must be a logical explanation. Erik recalled a quote from Captain Spock from "The Undiscovered Country": "An ancestor of mine maintained that when you eliminate the impossible, whatever remains, however improbable, must be the truth." Nodding his head, Erik pondered, yeah, that might be true, but time travel is impossible and not invented yet.

"Excuse me, do you work here?" A sweet, soothing voice paralyzed Erik's thoughts. Directly behind him was an innocent-looking young lady with astonishing beauty. She stared at him with her soft brown crescent eyes enhanced by her eye shadow and mascara. Her makeup was perfectly blended with her natural caramel complexion, and her glossed lips glistened in the light. She had wonderfully thick brown hair that laid on her shoulders. She wore a private school uniform. The royal blue pinafore skirt hugged her hips and waist, her form-fitting crisp white button-down blouse conformed to her chest, and her royal blue blazer, with the seal of the school on the upper left side, matched the skirt. Her knee-high white socks enhanced her dull black conservative and sensible saddle shoes. She could make the darkest room light up with her sheer presence.

Distracted by her beauty, Erik replied, "I'm sorry, what was your question?"

She got lost in his over-powering blue eyes as she responded, "Do you work here?" He nodded as she shot feeling glances up and down his body. She smirked as she realized what he was wearing: a midnight blue double-breasted suit and matching vest, a crisp, bright white oxford shirt, and a tie that matched his suit. He also wore a pocket watch. However, what did it for her was that he had a gangster hat. He was something out of the movie *The Untouchables*. She fell in love immediately. "Could you show me where the...?" She glanced at her worksheet. "Tucker Torpedo is?"

"Right this way." He motioned her to follow as he glanced back. "Are you on a school field trip?"

"Yeah, for U.S. History. I am graduating from Maret in June."

"Congratulations. Going to college?"

She nodded.

"So, you like history?"

As if she had a lemon in her mouth, she replied, "No, it's boring. By the way, I am Jamie, and, yeah, I am going to be attending Georgetown. I got a cheerleading scholarship. What's your name?"

"Very impressive. My friends call me Erik, and I bet it's because of your teacher." She bobbed her head repeatedly. "However, history has many fascinating events." She listened as she got closer to him. "For example, your history teacher is wrong. The real name of the car was Tucker 48, and did you know the Tucker Torpedo has a lot of the innovations modern-day cars have?"

"Really, like what?"

"The third headlight was known as the Cyclops Eye, and it would be activated if the driver made turns greater than ten degrees. The front windshield was shatterproof glass. The car had a perimeter frame surrounding the vehicle and used for crash protection, as well as a roll bar integrated into the roof just in case the car rolled over. Also, the instrument panel and all controls the driver would use were within easy reach of the steering wheel, and lastly, it was aerodynamically advanced for its time."

"That's so neat." She handed over her worksheet, as her pupils dilated. "My history teacher is very boring, unlike you."

Quickly looking over the paper, Erik shook his head at the questions the teacher asked, as they reached the 1E, Transportation and Technology, room five. Erik pointed, "There is the Tucker 48."

"Wow, when did it come out?" Jamie moved closer and stared back at Erik, who kept his distance.

"1948, only 51 cars were ever made," Erik said.

She motioned coquettishly towards him to come closer. He shook his head, but she was insistent, and eventually, he gave in. "The way you are dressed, it looks like you would fit in with the time when the car came out."

"Funny you should say that because that is my car."

She gazed at him candidly. "Do you have a family?"
Erik shook his head.

"Why not?"

"I don't. My work can be pretty demanding, and I travel a lot." She moved to a nearby bench and motioned him to sit by her. Handing back her worksheet, Erik inquired, "Is there anything else you need help on?"

She shook her head, "Can we just talk?"

"What do you want to talk about?" He caught her eyes staring over his shoulders, and he looked out of the corner of his eye. "Does your friend need help too?"

"No! She is fine." Jamie gave a dismissive gesture.

She jumped to her feet, pulled out her Samsung S300 cell phone, flipped it open, and as she was about to take the picture, he covered the lens.

"Why did you do that?"

"I don't like my picture being taken. I will be right back." She sat there with a gloomy look. "Jamie, I promise."

As he walked off, her eyes ranged freely up and down his body. She wondered why he would keep up a wall and let no one in. What happened to him? One thing she did know was that he was her soul mate. Two boys hovering over her broke her concentration. Both were in their private school uniforms from the same school Jamie attended. The first one was tall with well-developed leg and arm muscles, his chest fit, neatly trimmed black hair and menacing brown eyes. The other had a strong bone structure in both his legs and arms, his chest also fit as well as a similar hairstyle and glaring blue eyes. Jamie's

toes curled up in her shoes as she crossed her arms securely against her chest. Keith sat next to her and placed
his ape-like hand on her knee as she struggled to remove
it. She looked desperately around to find someone to help
her.

"Keith, stop it." Her voice had a quavering tone as she
smacked him across his face. It didn't faze him, and his
hand continued to advance, as her eyes began to water.

"You bitch!" His eyes narrowed, with a sadistic grin.
"Don't you scream." The struggle amused the other.

"Let her go. Now!"

Immediately the boys cornered Erik. Erik focused on
each of them to see who would launch the first strike. If
this was in the field, he needed to know their fighting
skills, and the way to do this was to appear weak, so he
could get them close enough for him to strike. However,
this wasn't the case. Some of CIA's Moscow Rules for
operatives in the Soviet Union applied here: 1, Vary your
pattern and stay within your cover, and 2, Don't harass
the opposition.

"Do you care to repeat what you said?" Keith replied in
a harsh tone, as he flipped Erik's fedora off, grabbed and
tossed the brochures. A form of indignation formed on
Keith's face, and he pursed his lips with suppressed fury,
his eyes bulging from their sockets. He thrust both hands,
at full arms-length, against Erik, forcing him back, from
which Erik quickly recovered. The last rule was, "Keep
your options open."

Erik took an MMA fighting stance with his eyes focusing on the body movement of the two boys readying

themselves to take him down. He saw that Keith was discretely motioning to his wingman. Erik knew to take out the wingman and then center his attention on Keith. He had to take down these two but without seriously injuring them, and that was the real challenge.

The first attack came from the wingman who attempted a two-punch combination, as his first fist focused on Erik's face and the other to his gut. In the process, he overextended, leaving the inner thigh of his left leg vulnerable. Erik took advantage of the opportunity and thrust his knee to the sciatic nerve running down his shin. Suddenly, his attacker's face became drawn and pinched, as the blood drained from his face. Coupled with that, he was locked up in pain and fell to the floor.

Erik then glared at Keith and replied, "All you have to do is walk away." Erik waited for a response that never came as he continued. "That is your best option. I'd take it."

Keith's eyes were haunted by anxiety, as he had expected a quick defeat and easy humiliation of his opponent. Erik shuffled his feet as he positioned himself in a defensive position. Filled with rage, Keith mustered all his nervous energy into one lightning attack. Erik sidestepped to his left as he grabbed Keith's right wrist with his left hand, and then applied pressure to Keith's elbow, causing extreme discomfort and forcing him to the floor. Erik had learned in his training that no matter how big or muscular a person is, there are specific pressure points where everyone is vulnerable.

Keith's facial muscles twitched nervously, as his voice strained, "Let go of me, you son of a bitch. You don't know who I am."

"True, but you appear to be in pain." Keith tried to escape, but Erik applied more pressure. Jamie's eyes were transfixed as she stared in Erik's eyes that narrowed like a wolf about to attack its prey.

"Let me go!" Keith barreled out.

"Dr. Függer!" Two uniformed security guards approached Erik and the two boys. Once in the distance, one gave a firm order, "Dr. Függer, release him now!" Erik released and stood by Jamie. Each security guard positioned themselves by one of the boys. As much as he wanted to, Erik wished he could break Keith's arm, or maneuver Keith's arms behind his back and drive him against the nearest wall. However, he couldn't have attention drawn to him.

"You are dead!" Keith stated with a scorching look as he was escorted away in an elaborately casual manner.

"Make sure you call my secretary and make an appointment."

Then Erik turned to Jamie, whose eyes were bloodshot from crying. She leaped up and wrapped her arms around him as if she had dissolved with his touch. It was a feeling he had not experienced since Jackie died. It felt good that he protected her, especially a bit of love and warmth from someone who cared.

"I've got you."

He comforted her, making her feel safe and secure. Erik had only been with the agency for five years, and he had infiltrated government and military installations; however, he was never trained to deal with a young lady crying on his shoulder. Just above a whisper, he said, "You are safe now. He isn't going to hurt you." Erik tried to release her, but she didn't want to let go. His eyes focused on the sounding areas, especially the entrance. Then Erik's eyes widened, and he stepped away from Jamie.

An angry man hurled himself into the room and bellowed. "You there, step away from her!" Then Erik saw his two attackers trailing behind.

"Is that their father?"

"No, that's my history teacher. Their fathers are in the U.S. Senate."

"It just gets better as it goes on."

"Did you hear me? Get away from her!"

"Jamie, do what he says."

"No, I want to stay by you."

Standing in Erik's face, as if he were a drill sergeant, the teacher exclaimed, "You assaulted two of my students; you are going to get fired for this." Then he glared at Jamie, "Jamie Anderson, I told you to get away from this man; now do it!"

"If you believe their story, then you've got your head so far up your ass, you can chew your food twice." Erik snapped back.

"Who are you?"

A deep thundering voice came from behind, "His name is Dr. Erik Függer. He is one of my curators and tour guides." Erik glanced back; it was Alan. His soft brown eyes were so drained of expression that they were as menacing as the empty gaze of a Great White Shark about to attack. Erik and Alan were an experienced team, and this had its advantages in that they both knew each other's strengths and weaknesses. Also, they could rely on each other when things did not go as planned. This was one of those times.

"Mr. Tanenbaum, it's nice to meet you. I heard your history class was here. My name is Alan James, the director of the museum." Alan shook his hand vigorously, but remained amicable, as he continued to tighten his grip, causing Mr. Tanenbaum extreme discomfort. "You and the boys' parents want to press charges against one of my employees?"

Mr. Tanenbaum nodded as he pointed to the accused.

Giving a theatrical gesture towards the ceiling, Alan continued, "Mr. Tanenbaum, please tell me what you see?" Mr. Tanenbaum shrugged his shoulders, with a blank expression. "I am going to put it very nicely to you. I know it is complex for you to get the big picture when you have such a small screen. What you don't see are security cameras, not just in this room but in every part of the museum, and they record everything that goes on." Alan pointed to the boys. "They didn't know, but I am informing you now that they were monitored by security groping that young lady there and what makes it interesting is that you were in the same room and did nothing."

Alan escorted him away and then got in his personal space. "So, if you or the boys' parents file charges, I will be happy to provide the authorities, her parents, and the headmaster of your school with copies of the tapes.

I know that won't be necessary and that we'll get along fine. So, are we clear?"

Mr. Tanenbaum nodded, as Alan gave him a c'est tout dire grin.

Next, Alan strolled towards Jamie, "Ms. Anderson, would you like to file a report on these two gentlemen, and I use that term loosely?" She shook her head; then, Alan stared at the boys. "And would you two like to file a report?" Then they shook their heads. "Wonderful! Then I hope everyone enjoys the rest of the day at the museum."

As he and the boys walked off, Tanenbaum barked, "Jamie, the bus leaves in thirty minutes. Don't be late."

Alan motioned Erik to walk with him. Just above a whisper, he said, "I want you to know, the admiral knows about this, and he has assured me you will not be reprimanded, and the situation is under control. Am I making myself clear?"

"Yes, sir. I wish I could…" Erik replied, as his brow wrinkled in vexation.

"I know you do. Even though you can hurt those boys, you cannot do it. Erik, you have to keep the skills you learned a secret."

"What was I supposed to do? Act like I cannot fight and take a beating?"

Alan sensed Erik's frustration and had no right answer for him. "Maybe you should have."

"Well, I couldn't. I want to have a normal life and not always be on my guard all the time."

"I know you do; that is a huge burden on anyone." Alan stared at Erik, so his words would soak in. "There is more at stake here than protecting some girl. Whatever you choose to do, remember that people are watching you. Even our enemies."

Erik nodded.

"If you could have done anything, what would you have done?" continued Alan.

"Break two of his fingers in three places."

Alan did an about-face and approached Jamie, "Ms. Anderson, would you like Dr. Függer to escort you to your bus?"

A well of happiness lifted her to her feet, her eyes were glinting in pleasure. "Yes, please."

Erik gaped in stunned silence, as Alan faced him. "That won't be a problem, will it, Dr. Függer?"

"No, sir, it will be my honor."

"Good." Turning to Jamie, he concluded, "It was a pleasure meeting you, Ms. Anderson, enjoy the rest of your time, and if you need anything, please let me or Dr. Függer know." She motioned Alan closer and whispered something in his ear, and he replied, "That's located on our website under the About tab. Anything else?" She shook her head, and Alan excused himself.

"I didn't know you were a doctor," Jamie said as she handed his hat back to him.

"I am, but not a medical doctor if that's what you were thinking. I have a doctorate in history."

"That means you are brilliant." Jamie shot a knowing wink.

"No, I'm not."

"Why can't you take a compliment?" She nudged him.

"Because I don't like to brag. Come on; let's get you to your bus."

"Tell me about yourself."

Erik didn't say anything, and as close as she could guess, she was still miles away. He knew as long as he was a Paramilitary Operations Officer, he would continue his journeys in life alone — in the darkness.

"What is it?" She paused, with a smile, trying to defrost his emotionless armor. "Is it my age? I am eighteen if that's what you are worried about."

"No. I, how can I phrase it…" Erik wished he could say, "I work for the CIA, I spend my career in the museum, and when I go overseas, I am covert ops. From that, I know some terrible people, and if they knew my real identity, not only would they kill me, but I would put in danger the one I love. Nevertheless, one day, not anytime soon, only when I retire, maybe it can come to an end." Instead, Erik said, "I just lost my parents, and my head is not clear, and it wouldn't be fair to you if I couldn't give you my full attention."

"If you need a friend…I'm here. If you need to be loved, I'm willing to give you my love." Jamie gave him a hug, "I am here if you need anyone to talk to." Erik nodded in appreciation. "I like you in your hat. Put it on for me." He put it on and grinned as he nodded in acknowledgment. "Can I ask you something?"

"You just did," he smirked, as she gave a cute, disgusted look.

"Do you believe in soul mates?"

"I don't know. I never gave it much thought. Do you?"

She offered a gleeful smile as she nodded. Erik continued, "Have you found your soul mate? If you did, how would you know it?"

"Maybe. My soul mate will complete me. I know that I will not only like him; I'll love him. Most of all, he is the person I will spend the rest of my life with." As they walked, she got closer to him, "What are you thinking about?"

"Nothing. What are you thinking about?"

"I wish you were my history teacher."

"Why is that?"

"Because you make it interesting, and you're handsome." He shook his head as she stopped and made him face her. "Why can't you accept what I am saying? Are you insecure?"

"Not at all. It's just I have not heard it in a long time."

"Well, maybe someone should tell you more often. Erik, will you smile for me?"

Erik shook his head, "Why are you doing this?"

"Because I want to see you happy. Or do I need to make an appointment with your secretary?"

"No, she is for the people who want to kick my ass, people like Keith."

Jamie snickered, as she covered her mouth, "You are so funny. Do you use that line a lot?"

"No, just when I want to impress a girl." Just for a few seconds, he gave a forced smile.

"You smiled! Will you do it again?"

He shook his head.

"You're funny." She replied jokingly.

They exited the museum, where students had gathered and were slowly transitioning themselves onto the buses. In the distance, a young lady approached them with a warm smile.

"Jamie, so now I know whom you were spending your time with." Then the girl directed her attention towards Erik. "Hi, I'm Kristina." She extended her hand to meet Erik.

"Nice to meet you; I'm Erik."

"Hi." Facing Jamie again, then back at him, "Are you the one that got in the fight with Keith and Kevin?" Erik nodded. "Wow, you took on both of them. That's impressive. Well, Jamie, I am going to get on the bus and get us a seat. Nice meeting you." Before she ran off, Kristina made some cryptic sign gestures, which only Jamie would understand.

"I had a great time, Dr. Függer."

"You are very welcome, Ms. Anderson," he replied as he took a slight bow. "You can call me Erik."

"Ok, professor. Has anyone told you that you are brave, honorable, and kind?" She sighed deeply and thought she wanted to be the woman fortunate enough to be loved by him.

"Not recently." She faced a warm smile and gave a gentle sigh as she walked away. He pondered...if only you knew what is inside of me now and who I am, you would not want to know me.

"Hey, Erik!" As he glanced up, she took a picture of him. "One, four, three!" Jamie took a few steps, she looked back, turned around, raced toward him, and kissed him on his cheek. Then she turned and dashed to her bus. She turned around and waved before getting on. Erik analyzed each of the windows to find her, and then their eyes met one last time. They waved to each other as the bus disappeared down the road.

"I think she likes you, kid."

Erik glanced to his right. It was Alan. "I cannot get involved with her. Even if I did, I could not jeopardize her life to be a part of my strange little corner in my world."

"That is one of the things that is hard for people that do what you do."

"It wouldn't work out; the age difference, my career, and other variables." He turned to Alan. "I believe that if she found out who I was, she'd reject me out of fear. I never want her to see that side of me. Nor would I want to tell her. However, I am hoping that day never comes, but if it does, I don't know how to explain it."

"Let's hope." Alan paused for a moment to collect his thoughts. "I heard it was hard for you when you lost Jackie and your son."

Erik gave a scolding look, "The admiral told me."

Alan stared at him as if he were penetrating his soul. "Listen, today might not be the day, but you two might meet again. You need someone in your life; you cannot go through this world all by yourself." Alan handed Erik his plane ticket.

"It is safer that way. I wish I could protect her from that bastard."

"Maybe one day you will be able to. You know what your problem is?" Alan paused to let the words soak in,

"Most people are afraid of dying, but you are completely the opposite. You are scared of living. When you come back from Florida, I will see if we can get you to go on some dates and prepare you for more missions like what you did in August 2000."

"Looks like I will be taking walks among the thorns."

11. THIS IS HOW WE DO IT, WITH ONE VERY IMPORTANT THOUGHT

"People tend to think spies are motivated by the love of the game, desire for adventure or patriotic fervor. The truth, though, is that you don't choose a life as a covert operative unless something deeper is going on beneath the surface. Something more personal, something harder to explain, and something a lot more painful."

—*Burn Notice*, episode "Square One," voiceover of Michael Weston

KENNEDY WARREN, WASHINGTON, D.C.

June 2003: Erik woke up, grabbed his phone, grabbed OJ out of the refrigerator, and headed to his study. He entered the book-lined, dark-wooded study with photographs of politicians, both foreign and domestic, neatly hung on the open spaces of the wall. Erik paced for a moment before he took a seat at his desk, lit by a banker's lamp with an elegant base and opaque glass shade.

The surface was covered with open books, monographs, maps, photographs, and drawings — all about the Battle of Britain.

Erik turned on his computer, and while he went to the University of Georgetown website, he took several gulps of juice. Within a few moments, he had found the location of the cheerleaders and analyzed the photograph. Then he recognized her as he placed his hands under his chin, supporting his head. In the picture, Jamie was smiling and standing with the rest of the squad, in her cheerleading outfit. Erik pondered what he should do. If Erik showed up unannounced, would she welcome him with open arms or act like she didn't know him. He shook his head, squeezed his eyes shut, and dug the heels of his palms into his eye sockets to rub away another lousy night of sleep. His focus switched to the beeping of his cell phone: a text message from Alan, let's get some breakfast. He stared at the text on his phone, then at Jamie and back at the text. He hit "reply" and typed I QUIT! Erik deleted his reply. Then he built up his frustration in his fists and slammed them against the desk.

He stood up, turned off the computer. Next, Erik grabbed a key from a hidden yet visible place in plain sight, unlocked his floor safe, which was covered by carpet, and pulled out his Heckler & Koch MK 23. Then he retrieved two spare magazines, which carried hollow point diamond tip rounds, and finally his ID.

Next, Erik headed to the bedroom, and through glazed eyes stared at the blue illuminated numbers on his clock radio that read 6:00 a.m. Every time he received the text message—let's get some breakfast—it was standard procedure for him to meet Alan at the museum by 0700, and then they would head to the Compound.

He moved to the bathroom to start his morning ritual. He left the house by 0640 and headed to the museum, roughly fifteen minutes away from where he lived, The Kennedy Warren.

Erik pulled into the employee parking lot. Alan was waiting patiently for him in his car, with the motor running. Once inside the car, Alan would hand Erik a newspaper, book, or magazine to conceal his face. As Erik leaned back in the seat and removed his Fedora, he grabbed the newspaper Alan offered him. This was the first step in their protocol. These steps were necessary to ensure Erik's safety and not be compromised as they traveled to the Compound. Ever since 9/11, the security procedures to enter the compound had dramatically changed. Thirty feet away from the reinforced concrete tollbooth-like structure was a speaker where all employees gave their eight-digit security code, step two. After that, they were allowed to pull up to within ten feet of the tollbooth. Thirdly, they looked into a camera and gave their full name as their faces and voices were going through a voice and facial recognition database. Fourthly, they gave their ID to the sentry, who ran it through a government database. As that was taking place, a K9 unit looked and sniffed for explosives or any other kind of contraband while a guard scanned underneath their vehicle with a mirror. Having passed all those procedures, which took less than three minutes, they were allowed to enter the Compound.

Alan parked his car; they gathered their belongings and headed to the entrance of the New Headquarters Building (NHB). It blended seamlessly with its structure and design. The NHB had a skylight in the lobby and a glass-walled atrium leading to two six-story office towers. Alan had been studying Erik's behavior ever since he laid eyes on him and knew something was not right. As an operative, Erik could not let his personal life cloud his judgment or operation, no matter how dramatic or devastating. However, even though he had the training to deal with this, it was not always easy.

"Come on, kid. What's bothering you? You haven't said a single word this morning." Erik still gave the silent treatment, as Alan clasped his shoulder. "What's wrong?"

"I am hungry." Erik's face was pinched with resentment, as he turned around and continued walking.

"Bullshit!" Alan raced up to him, as they passed through the turnstiles, "Will you stop for a damn second and talk to me before we enter the vault?"

In a half-whisper, Erik expressed his thoughts, "Want to know what's wrong?"

Alan nodded.

"I am all alone. I have lost my parents and brother, the girl I loved, and my son and twenty-three friends so far and am only thirty-two."

"O.G.D.S. TEAM 42 is your family, and they will always be there for you."

With rage in his eyes, as the elevator doors closed, and they proceeded to the third floor, he retorted, "You know what I mean, Alan."

"Yes, I do. However, those are things you had no control over, and you didn't cause them." Pointing at Erik to get his point across, he continued, "You are going have to learn what is in the past stays in the past. You learn from it, and you move on."

"Don't you think I know that?"

"No, I don't, because you still cling to Jackie's death like a crutch, and you will never move on as long as you hold on to that."

"You leave her out of this conversation; she has nothing to do with it."

"Erik, I know you want her back, but there will be a time when someone will fill that emptiness."

"I did meet someone that I wanted to get to know, but I can't."

A puzzled look drifted onto Alan's face, and then he nodded, as he knew whom Erik was talking about. "Jamie?"

Erik nodded, "I cannot date her, and I hate it."

"You cannot date her merely to fulfill some selfish dream."

"Selfish? Can't I have that chance of happiness to be with someone?"

"Listen to me."

"No, everyone can have a normal life and have someone. However, if you are me, you cannot. At least I can still masturbate, or is that not allowed either?"

"Are you done?" Alan's voice tinged with menace. "Evaluate the situation you are in."

Erik pondered, as he got his thoughts organized, "I

want to be with Jamie." Erik put his lanyard around his neck. "However, I want to continue serving my country, but I don't want to put her life in jeopardy."

"Correct. You know the risks if you get involved with Jamie." Erik nodded in agreement. "You said it yourself; you cannot jeopardize her life with the line of work you are in."

"Thanks for the reminder. It won't matter; Jamie will forget about me as soon as she starts college."

"You believe that?"

"Yes." They came to Vault 684-80105, and one at a time, they each swiped their ID, punched in their eight-digit security codes, and entered.

After entering, Alan glanced at Erik, "I wouldn't be too sure about that."

As they walked to their stations, Erik stated, "What makes you so sure?" Alan shrugged his shoulders.

Erik continued to badger Alan, "Is there something you are not telling me?"

"Erik, you need to focus on the briefing we are going to have. We can pick this up later."

Unlike other Vaults, Vault 684-80105 took up the majority of the third floor of Building One. This was where the support operatives of O.G.D.S. teams worked. The Vault was like a large call center, with signs hanging from the ceiling to designate where each team was located, and under each sign was a set of six cubicles. There were four cubicles, measuring five feet by five feet; that was for each member of the team. On opposite ends of the four cubicles were two cubicles, measuring ten feet by five feet; one was for the section chief, and the other was for the control officer.

On the outer perimeter is where conference rooms were located. In these rooms, briefings and debriefings were held. Lastly, there were two sets of specialized rooms: the Hollywood Room and the Simulation Room. The Hollywood Room was where false flags and latex masks were made. It had a darkroom, a vast closet that contained military uniforms from approximately every nation, including the United States, and a station where the latex masks where created. The Simulation Room was a smaller version of an IMAX theater, with a central computer console. This room was to create a first-person 3D simulation of the area and surrounding areas where a field operative would be infiltrating. Vault 684-80105 was a unique and heavily specialized area where they kept everything in house and kept its secrets behind closed doors.

O.G.D.S Team 42, like every other team, was made up of six people: Control officer, Section Chief, Paramilitary Operations Officer, and three members of the support team. Alan was the chief of station who was in charge of all field operations, and he was responsible for setting up meetings between the field operative and foreign dignitaries. Paul was the section chief who ran and supervised the support team at Langley, and he gave the briefings and debriefings. Between the two, with the help of the agency, they leaked out information to foreign dignitaries that the field operative could access highly sensitive information that could benefit their nation's interest.

What the foreign dignitaries did not know was that the information was fabricated.

Both the chief of station and section chief were equals in power and authority. Also, they were to brief the Deputy Director of Intelligence and Operations throughout the mission's progress. Erik was a Paramilitary Operations Officer or Field Operative. His job was to gain the trust of the foreign dignitary and persuade them that it would be better if he came to their country to deliver the information. While doing that, he would run an op that would deal with infiltrating a military or government installation and neutralizing whatever situation was a threat to the United States and national security.

The support team was made up of three different kinds of specialists, and they were Carly, Gary, and John. All three were from the Science and Technology Department but came from different sections. Carly was from the Special Activities Section, and her position was a Cobbler. As a Cobbler, her job was to make all of Erik's false flags: false passports, visas, diplomas, and other documents, as well as latex masks, and fit him with the correct uniform when he was overseas. She had started mastering her craft while majoring in Production and Cosmetic Arts at the American Film Institute.

What started as just a hobby to see if she could get away with it became a full-time job making fake driver's licenses for students who wanted to buy alcohol and/ or get into clubs. By the end of her first year, she mastered the art of making flawless driver's licenses: from the correct lighting to the holographic plastic that was used. She was even able to master the lettering used for each ID. She got caught when she was using one of her fake IDs and trying to impersonate a candidate and had been selected to go to the CIA Recruitment Center. Throughout the process, she executed everything flawlessly except when they took her fingerprints and ran them against a database. Carly was escorted to a private office, and there waiting for her was a section chief from the Special Activities Section. They informed her that they knew she was an imposter and that her quality of work was awe-inspiring. They gave her a choice: one, go to prison, or two, when she graduated from college she would be working for the CIA, and indeed she had, ever since 1999.

Gary and John came from the Technical and Readiness Section. Gary's job was to hack into foreign, and sometimes within the United States, military and government databases. Then he would upload the false flags Carly made into the databases. Also, he would upload Erik's voice and facial recognition so he could bypass any security that he would encounter while infiltrating. John was a Transformation Perspective Analyst, and his job was to recreate a 3D simulation of the area and surrounding areas Erik would be infiltrating. In the Simulation Room, he would cover every square inch and every detail that Erik would need to know.

Before joining the CIA, Gary and John attended and were roommates at the Massachusetts Institute of Technology (MIT). They both had majored in computer science; Gary specialized in computer networking and security, and John was working on his 3D digital design degree. While attending MIT, they started a company known as Keyhole Inc. This was mainly to get money for school; however, what they were working on was far ahead of its time. What Gary learned from his classes and being a previous hacker gave him the skills and abilities to hack into NASA and other government agencies' satellite mainframes and reposition them over certain parts of the earth's surface.

Once completed, John created a virtual journey to any place on earth. He was so gifted that he was able to explore the earth's surface approximately three hundred feet above the ground, and in some cases, he was able to see locations at street level. In early 1998, while Gary and John were working, the FBI raided their office and arrested them. Then the CIA got wind of this and immediately bailed them out of prison with the understanding they would be working for them. The CIA acquired Keyhole Inc., which they planned on selling it to Google next year (it became known as Google Earth). In conclusion, O.G.D.S. Team 42 was very talented in their skills and, in return, made many successful missions eliminating threats that would compromise the security of the United States.

As Alan and Erik approached the other members of the team, Carly, with her warm smile, greeted them, "Hey guys. Long-time no see." She gave a friendly hug when Erik was within distance. "How are you doing, Erik?"

"I am okay. How are you and your husband?"

"We are good." She stared at Alan, who was setting up

his laptop at his cubicle. "Hey, Alan." He looked up and waved. "How are you?"

"Very busy keeping him," pointing at Erik with a mischievous grin, "out of trouble."

"He is in some form of trouble all the time," John stated, as Erik looked at him and shook his head.

Gary added, "Alan, is it true Erik came to the rescue of some girl?"

Alan nodded as Gary stared toward Erik and continued, "Who was she?"

"I don't want to talk about it." Erik replied with his head buried in his work, as he got his laptop set up.

As he checked his messages on his office phone at the museum, John said playfully, "Erik, if we didn't like you, we wouldn't pick on you."

"I know. Unlike my enemies, who would rather kill me."

"Everyone has their enemies, and how many do you have now?"

"Enemies?" Erik asked, facing Alan. "Do you recall how many I have?"

"I can tell you if you keep up at the rate you are at now, you will start competing with the New York phonebook."

As Erik checked his emails, Carly hovered over his shoulder, "What's her name?"

"Who?"

Carly's face said you-know-what-I-am-talking-about. "Jamie Anderson."

"What does she do?"

"College." Carly wanting more information, as Erik

continued and glanced over his shoulder, "She is a fresh-man at Georgetown. However, it doesn't matter; she will forget about me."

"Don't be too sure." Carly pointed to Erik's computer screen and headed back to her station.

An email caught his eye as he shook his head and looked around. Around him was the bustling world of O.G.D.S. Teams finding, planning, and executing operations aimed at threats against the United States. Each team member was carrying files, opening doors, analyzing documents, and answering telephones. Above his head was a TV that had the internal cable system with its 25 channels, of which five are classified. Finally, he had to worry about his trash. The trash could be disposed of by tossing it, shredding it, or placing it in a bag labeled TOP SECRET, or in another bag with red-lettering, or in yet another bag, which had three sets of five red and white diagonal lines, and which was known as the BURN BAG.

He emptied his mind of all thoughts and prepared himself for a routine day, starting with the briefing with his team. This only happened four to six times a year that an assignment came along, requiring his abilities as a paramilitary operations officer. His cubicle was identical to the others in this area. He had two phones: a beige non-secure line, which had a seven-digit number, and a secure green line, used to call within the agency, and requiring a five-digit number. The phones were three feet apart to avoid eavesdropping. The top right drawer had been locked for intra-communication that had been dropped off, and couldn't be sent to the museum. The intra-communication classifications were Routine, Priority, Immediate, Flash, and Critical. Erik received the first two only. Before the morning briefing, Erik quickly opened and read the email from Jamie.

Erik,

I don't know what to say. You have left me speechless; no one has ever protected me like you did against Keith and Kevin. As a matter of fact, no guy has ever done anything ever like that, or ever treated me like you did, which is nothing but the utmost care. I can't even begin to describe how that makes me feel inside. All I can say is that it makes me feel so wonderful, and it's sometimes hard to believe that it's true. It's funny in the short time we spent together. I feel as if I found that person, my soulmate, and that I have known you forever, which is probably true. Thank you for everything. It means a lot to me. I hope things are going well with you! I'll be thinking of you. I hope we can see each other again!

Take care and Always, ~Jamie

p.s. I hope you like my picture and 143!!!!

He opened the attachment, and it was a picture of her, lying on her side, wearing a form-fitted pullover olive green sweater and faded blue jeans. Her hair and makeup appeared to be professionally done, while her soft brown eyes could hypnotize anyone who looked at the photograph. Erik sighed deeply, and his eyes turned inward, remembering her. Then he felt a presence behind him and craned his neck upward to see Alan standing behind him, with his arms crossed.

"Forward that to me, then delete it."

Erik shot straight up and confronted Alan: "Why?"

"It is for your safety; that's why." Erik shook his head in disbelief, and Alan's look was cold, hard, and scornful. "I order you to forward that to me and delete it."

"It's just an email and a photo of her. There is no threat to me or national security."

Alan gestured Erik to follow him to his cubicle and opened a website known as Facemash. He typed the name Jamie Anderson, "You have been gone for a week, and within that week, a lot has happened." Pointing to a photo on the website, he asked: "Does she look familiar?" Erik nodded as Alan scrolled down and pointed to the screen again. "Read." Erik saw a picture of himself from the day he had met Jamie with the caption 'Met the most amazing guy ever yesterday! Can't wait to see him again! I love the hat!' There were 193 likes and 32 comments.

Erik glanced at Alan, "She is just a kid."

Alan pulled him aside, "True, but she is drawing much attention to you."

"Attention?"

"You remember what you said about jeopardizing her life?" Erik nodded. "Erik, you might not be aware of this, but individuals, like Putin and others, are probing everything about your life, and if they find a weakness, they will exploit it." Erik shook his head in frustration as Alan continued, "I am not saying they will, but what if they found what I showed you. Not only is she putting you in danger, but herself too."

In the Compound or the field, Erik knew his objective and knew what must be done to complete the task at hand. However, between missions, Erik was a civilian; yet he still retained a deep cover and never knew if he would ever be exposed or compromised. That was the hardest part of remaining focused, but it also gave him time to think. He did a lot of thinking in the quiet hours when he was alone, lying in his bed at night, in his car, in his office at the museum, basically anywhere. Seeing Jamie's email, with her photograph attached to it, and seeing her Face-mash page didn't make things any easier now. As much as he would love to print her picture as a keepsake, he knew it would jeopardize her life if he were captured. As much as Erik wanted that connection to Jamie, for whom he had feelings, he knew the reality of his job came to a point where there is a constant reminder of what you can never have: a girlfriend. Thus, he knew he had to focus on work and the upcoming mission, and he could not have a distraction like that, or it could cause him to fail, or worse, get him killed.

"Will this be reported to the admiral?" Alan shook his head as his focus changed. Erik turned around to see Paul and a naval admiral walking together. "Who is that?"

"Admiral Cole and they are talking about you."

"What are they saying?" queried Erik as Alan motioned for him to keep quiet. As Erik strolled to his cubicle, he picked up a partial sentence:

"You have nothing to worry about, Admiral; it will be taken care of."

The admiral walked by Erik, as Paul got O.G.D.S. Team 42's attention and headed to Briefing Room One. The members of the team grabbed legal pads, something to write with, and followed their orders. Trailing behind were Erik and Alan, as Paul grabbed a few things off his desk and then walked to the briefing room. Inside the briefing room, Carly, Erik, Gary, and John sat around a table ready to take any notes that would be relevant to their position, with Paul standing behind a podium and with Alan on his left-hand side. As the projection screen came down, the lights dimmed, and Paul began.

"Good morning, everyone." All in the room greeted Paul, as they sipped their coffee. "Well, it appears the Russians are up to the same trick as they were in August 2000."

"Looks like someone is going fishing again," John replied teasingly.

Gary added, with a smirk, "Erik, I can call my contact at the Discovery Channel and have you on Deadliest Catch."

"You guys are just jealous because you don't have all the fun."

Facing Erik, Carly asked, "You think you can get a few lobsters?"

"Of course. Will you invite me for dinner when you make them?" She smiled and nodded as Erik turned his attention to Paul. "Paul, do you want any?"

Paul gave a cold blank stare as Erik questioned, "Is that a no?"

Paul glanced around the table to get everyone's attention and, in a thundering voice, spoke immediately, "Guys, let's focus on the matter at hand." Paul again glanced around the table as he continued, "The Russians are going to make another attempt to sell the North Koreans another submarine." He glared at Erik while pointing to him to emphasize his point. "Some individuals were pleased with your work on the Kursk, and they want you to do a repeat performance."

Alan glanced at Paul with inquisitive eyes, as Erik butted in, "Who?"

"That's not important." Then Paul addressed the room again, "What we do know is this: We know it's the K-159, a November Class Nuclear Submarine," Several slides, of different views, of the submarine appeared on the projection screen, and he paused so Erik could make some notes. "The K-159 is at the Gremikha Naval Base in Ostrovnoy." A satellite photo was on the screen now; Paul made directional gestures, as John made detailed notes. "It will be sent to Polyarny, where it will be exchanging hands with the North Koreans, and this is all going to take place in August."

"Do we know when in August?" Erik questioned.

Alan stood up, moved to the front of the room, and answered, "We are working on getting that intel. On the other hand, we know this information is solid." He looked at Carly, as she prepared to write. "Get with Erik and get his false flag and uniform updated."

"Yes, sir. Would you like him to be the same rank as before, intelligence officer?"

"No, a chief warrant officer. Get with Erik and get a name." Erik wrote the name Alexander Khristofor on a sheet of paper and handed it to Carly, as Alan focused on Gary. "Gary, once Carly has everything updated, upload the information on their database. Are you still able to get in?"

Gary nodded, "That won't be a problem. Since Putin has been in power, they have been ramping up their firewalls and network security. Even so, they still have many backdoors that I can use, and they will not know I'm there."

Lastly, Alan focused on John, "I want Erik to know every inch of that base."

John nodded, "Do we know what dock K-159 will be in?"

"No. However, you do have the authority to move the satellite to find her. Work with Erik on that."

Erik raised his pencil to get attention; Paul motioned him to speak. "Are they going to say this is a training exercise like the Kursk?"

Paul took over the briefing again. "No, President Putin has ordered Admiral Gennady Suchkov, Commander of the Northern Fleet, to disguise it as a dismantling. K-159 is the thirteenth of sixteen submarines that are under the dismantling order. Erik, you will be going in with a different false flag from the one you used when you were on the Kursk."

Erik inquired, "Has Putin been contacted on the information I will be delivering him?"

"Not this time."

"Okay, then what will be my reason for going over, or are you working out the details?"

"There are no details; you are just going in." Erik glanced at Alan and back at Paul. "You are not going to meet Putin this time." Alan glared at Paul as if the protocols were not being followed.

"To be blunt, I think that is dumb. I am going to need a cover. One doesn't visit Ostrovnoy, which is located on the Kola Peninsula. Also, Gremikha Naval Base is the easternmost of the Northern Fleet of naval bases." Erik walked to the front of the room and logged into the computer and pulled up a satellite image of Gremikha. Then he walked to the projection screen. "There is nothing there for miles. What in the hell can I say is the reason I am there?"

"You can say you are a biology student, and you are doing a nature study," Paul stated, as Erik gave a blank expression. "I know you were taught the three different kinds of covers at The Farm." Paul pointed at Erik. "I believe in you that you can think of something."

"Can we talk about this?" Erik questioned.

Paul shook his head and addressed the others in the room. "This meeting is adjourned." With cold eyes, he motioned to Erik to sit. Once the door was closed, the atmosphere was like atoms being smashed by an atomic bomb.

Paul's eyes narrowed. His nostrils rigidly flared in rage to the point that the outermost edges were white. His teeth clenched as he took a deep breath and exploded on Erik as he leaned forward on the table, supporting his weight on his swollen knuckles. "Do not ever question the operation in front of the team again, you son of a bitch."

Erik's voice strained with rage. "Question? I have every right to question because I am going to be putting my life on the line."

Pointing at Erik, like a prosecutor, Paul blared out, "You are not to question, or give your opinion! You are here to do the job! Are we clear?"

Erik jumped up, "No, we are not. Putin is not stupid. I am sure my name is on a watch list, and they will try to detain me. I know for a fact they will have double, if not triple the security ever since the Kursk."

Alan went to Erik's defense, "Erik is correct. He is going to need a better front than just a biology student, or this operation is going to fail before it even begins."

"This conversation doesn't involve you." Paul gave a dismissive gesture.

Alan shook his head, "If you are going put him at risk, then it does involve me."

"You and I will discuss this later." Then Paul turned his attention to Erik, "Sit down! I'm not done with you, and Alan, you can leave. This is a private matter. I need to address our field operative." Again, Alan shook his head, with his arms crossed.

"Fine, stay." Paul's eyes suddenly turned furious and vindictive as he leaned forward on the table. "What is this shit I heard about you assaulting two high school students. One happened to be a senator's son."

"I thought that matter was over." Erik looked at Alan and back at Paul.

"Answer the question!" Paul demanded, picking up a piece of paper. "I have a disciplinary form with your name on it for your actions."

"Seriously? Do you know the whole story of what happened?"

"I heard what I needed to hear."

Standing up, Erik pounded his fists against the table, "They were sexually assaulting that girl. I was protecting her from those animals."

"Did she remind you of Jackie? Is that why you went to her aid?"

Alan motioned for Erik to stand down. "That was un-called for," he injected.

"Always going to his defense," quipped Paul, pointing at Alan. "If he didn't know the admiral, he would be in front of a review board and bound for termination."

Alan turned to Erik, "Leave the room. And call our contacts at the naval yard and have Carly fit you for a naval officer uniform."

"Excuse me ..." Erik tried to get a word out.

"Did you not hear me? Leave the room!"

"I am not done with him." Paul pointed at Erik.

"Yes, you are!" Eyes widened, as Alan gave a dismissive gesture to Erik. "Get out! Now!"

Erik quickly shuffled out of the office, closing the door behind him.

"Alan, he is a disaster to himself and this team. I thought you would back me up for what he did at the museum, and he is always questioning authority."

Alan's mouth quirked in annoyance, as he pressed his

lips tightly together to hold back his anger that was beginning to grow. "A disaster to himself and this team? That is such bullshit. I know Erik better than you. All you know of him is his dossier, my reports, and from what little time you have seen of him here."

"I don't care if you have a rapport or a few laughs with him. He undermines what O.G.D.S. teams and what this agency stands for!" Paul scolded.

"Undermines?" Alan shook his head in disbelief. "He stands for everything the agency stands for. Yes, he questions you and everyone else, but we were told he would do that when we met him the first day. Fuck, he questions me!"

"His job is not to question me, you, the missions, or the agency! He is to do the job! That's it!"

"A mission with a weak cover is bullshit. Every operative we send in the field is given a cover. Are you setting him up to fail? Who are these individuals that were pleased with his work on the Kursk?" Alan waited a minute, then barked the words, "Was it Admiral Cole?"

"I'm not at liberty to say."

Alan shook his head in angry refusal. "Cole has no jurisdiction over the O.G.D.S. teams nor on the ops we send our operatives on. Crist, he doesn't work for this agency."

"That's not important. We are talking about Erik's insubordination and disrespect for authority."

"He's got a problem with your authority, but understand where he is coming from." Alan pointed to the satellite image of Gremikha. "He's going a long way to get to a friendly nation if things go south."

"He's a paramilitary operations officer-"

"Are you not fucking listening?! He's going in with a weak cover. Putin will surely see that as a red flag."

"If that happens, he can do what he was taught: improvise, adapt, and overcome."

"If you are setting him up to fail on this mission, I will not hesitate to go to Bonesteiner."

Paul replied as he was picking angrily at his nails. "If he can't handle any problems that get in his way and cannot handle the work, then he should be kicked out of the O.G.D.S. team." Paul pondered for a moment, then continued. "I recall you said he would use his willpower and planning skills to implement those ideas."

"Oh, that's right, Paul. I did say that." Alan said as he nodded his head and did a short back of disgusted laughter. "I know I mentioned this several times, but your argument holds no water because you have only been in simulated combat situations…so come to think about it, Erik has more combat experience than you spent in your entire military career."

In his defense, Paul said, "I earned my rank, positions, and ribbons."

Alan mocked, "Did you get a Purple Heart for paper cuts?"

"Enough with your bullshit! As for Erik's outside factors…"

Alan dismissed the subject with a short sideways jerk of his hand, even though the previous conversation was not over. "His outside factors affect him, but he keeps them contained."

Paul shook his head. Also, he had no intention, not now or ever, of becoming emotionally involved with Erik, considering he could be dead in two months. The truth was that Paul was amazed he was still alive, considering most O.G.D.S. paramilitary operations officers' life expectancy is less than five years. "I'm telling you, he may be fucked up in the head because he clings to his girlfriend's death or because his parents and brother were killed." Paul made an elaborate hand gesture. "Maybe because he has one, maybe two friends." He pointed to Alan and added with a gleam of apathy in his eyes, "Not my fucking problem."

"Why do you think he has so few friends?" Alan left the answer to Paul.

"I don't give a shit why."

"You should. It would be best if you were asking yourself why Erik doesn't have many friends. You know the answer?" Alan's brows raised quizzically as he waited again for Paul to answer. "He doesn't trust anybody, because of the line of work he is in, and has lost a lot of close friends. Not to mention, he and one other are the only ones left in his class when he went to The Farm."

"Then he can go seek a physiatrist if he has issues, or he can join a social club and make friends. I don't care."

"Do you know what's so special about his few friends, who are mainly Navy SEALs? If they knew he was locked away in some hellhole, they would come to rescue him even before the agency winked an eye. That's called brotherhood loyalty."

"I'm thrilled for him that he has such loyal friends."

"Another thing...his girlfriend who died. Never bring that up again. If you do, I swear to God, I will knock you out. That girl at the museum reminds him of Jackie, and that will make him focus and work that much harder and motivate him."

"How old is she, eighteen? It's just puppy love, and if he thinks there is any more to that, then it's going to cloud his judgment in the field, and he will fail, get captured and killed."

"He's an excellent paramilitary operations officer! Do you know why that kid works so hard? Because everyone, including you, besides our support team, always asks me why he's on an O.G.D.S. team? They make fun of him because he's not like the other field operatives. He won't be a failure, and he is going to keep on proving you and everyone in this agency wrong." Alan grabbed the disciplinary form from Paul's hand and ripped it up. "So, I have two words for you and your cronies who think it was a mistake to recruit and have him on an O.G.D.S. team: fuck you!"

12. SHADOWPLAY

*"In the spy world, often the only things you know
about a covert mission are your deployment orders
and a list of equipment to bring. Sometimes, that tells
you nothing. And sometimes, it can tell a lot."*

—*Burn Notice*, episode "Things Unseen,"
voiceover of Michael Weston

Alan stormed out. He saw Gary and John busy working
on their assignments. In his cubicle, Alan opened a file
on his laptop and printed a document. Alan glanced at
Gary and John as he grabbed a manila file folder. "Where
is he?" Without looking up, both Gary and John replied
that Erik was in Hollywood Room One, with Carly. Alan
picked up the printed document, placed it in the folder,
and strolled to Hollywood Room One, exchanging looks
of bitter rage with Paul along the way. He punched in his
eight-digit security code and entered.

Seeing Carly with scissors and a comb in her hands
behind Erik, he said, "I didn't know you needed a haircut."

"Well, they were running the manicure-haircut special

today," Carly responded, giving Erik a look as she continued trimming.

She looked up at Alan, "Do you want a trim."

Alan's gestures turned down the offer. Glancing at Erik, he asked, "Did you call them?" What time are we meeting them?"

"Thirteen hundred."

"Okay, all done," Carly announced.

They all walked to a large secure closet door that contained multi-plan double-deck automated garment feeding conveyors with more than 5,000 military uniforms from a wide range of countries and military branches, including the United States. Carly and Erik punched in their security. The conveyors moved to Erik's assigned uniforms, and she pulled the uniform of a United States Navy lieutenant commander in the Information Dominance Corps (IDC). Carly instructed him to change. Then she did the same with Alan. Inside the fitting room, he stared, focused, and mentally prepared himself to be in character. Erik's position was unique with the agency. Unlike other jobs, he was always undercover both when he was state-bound and when he went overseas. As a field operative for the O.G.D.S. team, not all the people around him, except the ones he worked with, knew who he was. This gave him a significant advantage that allowed him to adjust to any situation. However, when preparing for an op, he had to reach out to people who were experts, Navy SEALS, who knew more about things such as how to sink a nuclear submarine when it is being towed.

Once again, this is an advantage of being known,

especially when you are best friends, and they know your reputation. Stepping out of the fitting room, Alan, dressed as a naval Commander and had the distinguished SEAL Trident on his upper left breast. Then Carly turned to Erik and gave him his ID. Carly inspected them one more time to make sure their uniforms were perfect, and then she dismissed them.

"Gary and John, if you need us, you know how to reach us," Alan replied as he and Erik grabbed their belongings and headed out. Once they reached the car, Alan turned over the engine as Erik placed their things. Then they exited the Compound and headed to the U.S. Naval Base in Norfolk.

"So, am I going to be reprimanded?" Erik inquired.

"No." Alan glanced at Erik, "Focus on the task at hand and start doing your homework and look up the November Class."

Erik reached back, grabbed his laptop, opened it, went to a secure website, and found information and diagrams of the submarine. He pulled up the layout of the sub and began to study it. The November Class had twin-hulled, streamlined stern fins and nine compartments. The nine chambers consisted of the following: 1—Bow Torpedo Compartment, 2—Officer's Quarters and Galley (level 1) and Batteries (level 2), 3—Control Room, 4—Auxiliary Machinery and Diesel Generator, 5—Reactor Compartment, 6—Turbine Compartment, 7—Electro-technical and Control Center for Reactor, 8—NCO and Enlisted Living Quarters and Accommodations, and 9—Steering System. He studied every inch of the blueprint to locate a weakness. Erik rubbed his chin as he tried to determine what the Russian pontoons, used for submarines, would look like.

"What have you found out?"

"K-159 was decommissioned on 30 May 1989, and its name now is B-159." Erik pulled out his cell phone and called John. As he waited for an answer, he continued, "She has been laid up in Gremikha; they say she has remained in a layup with little or no maintenance for the last thirteen years."

"If that's the case, her outer hull could be rusted in many places," Alan added as Erik motioned him to hold that thought.

"Hey, John, we just found out K-159 was renamed B-159. Also, her outer hull could be rusted in many places, which could make her easy to find ...what...that's great...thanks, you too." Looking at Alan, Erik replied, "John is still looking for her, and he said all the submarines' outer hulls are rusted."

"Any with pontoons?" Erik shook his head. "If the hull is rusted, it will be easier to compromise her."

As they approached the main gate at Naval Station Norfolk, Alan slowed his car to a halt. The sentry snapped a salute, which Alan returned. Once through the gate, Alan proceeded to the far end of the base. The naval station is located on the Hampton Roads peninsula, known as Sewell's Point. It is the world's largest naval station, consisting of fourteen piers, eleven aircraft hangars, and other military and civilian buildings, occupying about four miles of waterfront and seven miles of dock and wharf space. Norfolk was the hub for Navy logistics that supplied the European and Central Command theaters of operations, and the Caribbean. Seventy-five ships and 134 aircraft called Norfolk their home. Also, Air Operations conducted over 100,000 flights each year. Moreover, that was just what the American public knew.

Alan parked by a group of unmarked three-story-buildings. Each building was made of maroon-brownish brick and reflective glass. Alan parked by a building known to those who worked there as Joint Special Operations Command. Both Alan and Erik grabbed their attaché cases, made themselves presentable, and headed to the entrance. They strolled into the lobby and proceeded to the desk as the elevator doors opened.

"Commander James." Alan focused on the voice, as the petty officer, second class, who was also a SEAL, snapped a salute, with Alan and Erik returning one. "How are you, sir?"

"I'm good, Richard," Tilting his head towards his right and shaking Richard's hand, he continued, "You remember Lieutenant Commander Christopher?"

"Yes, sir." Giving Erik his attention and shaking his hand. "Nice to see you again, sir."

Then they all walked to the elevator, waited, got in, and ascended to the third floor, exited, and proceeded to the conference room.

Once inside, Alan quickly noted: "This is sensitive information." He stared into Richard's eyes as if piercing his soul. "It must not leave this room."

"Yes, sir."

Richard was not given all the details, but he got the impression the lieutenant commander was up to something, like the last time they had met in August 2000. Erik spoke with an intensity that was more academic as he slid a clasped envelope to Richard. He gave Richard several minutes to read the documents and diagrams. At that moment, Richard's eyes looked up. Erik asked in a guarded, vague tone, "What do you recommend?"

Erik's choice of words gave Richard pause, and then he carefully picked his words, "Sir, are you planning on doing the same thing as last time you were here?"

Erik, with a blank stare, shrugged his shoulders in a noncommittal way, as Richard motioned for Erik and Alan to take a seat. Richard dimmed the lights as the projection screen came down. Richard, an expert on demolition used on Russian submarines, walked up to the enormous blueprint of the November Class Submarine. He gestured brusquely around the diagram as he absorbed every aspect of the submarine. Erik pulled out a pad with a sketch of the submarine and was prepared to make notes on the layout. "Will she be carrying torpedoes?" Richard questioned.

"We are not certain at this time," Alan answered.

Richard looked at both Alan and Erik, "Sir, can I speak freely? Sir, if the Russians make it appear to be a decommissioning, I don't think they will have torpedoes on board." He paused to collect his words. "You are going to need another way to sink her."

"What do you suggest?" Erik replied.

"C4," Richard replied without hesitation, but his eyes

showed there was more to come. "The problem is, how are you going to bring it on board?"

This was something Alan and Erik had overlooked. They nodded to Richard to continue, as they made a mental note to revisit the topic later. Richard pointed at the blueprint and began with the necessary information, length, beam, and draft. Next, he advised, the submarine was going be under tow, and there were four pontoons, two in front and two in the rear. Richard then went to his laptop and searched for pontoons used in the Russian Navy, projected the photo of the pontoons, and walked to the front of the conference room.

"Do you know if her hull is rusty?" Alan nodded his head. "We have limited information about the condition or armament being carried." Richard walked to the diagram again. "They will position the front pontoons between a forward section and the bow torpedo compartment.

Richard also covered a wide range of technical matters which he took pains to explain. He looked directly at Erik, who was taking notes and sketching diagrams and was impressed by his immense grasp of detail. "Sir, if you want to sink her, I recommend you place the C4 in the bow compartment."

"Why do you suggest that area, and how much?"

Richard used his hands to represent the length of the pontoon, as he placed them on the blueprint. Erik walked to the screen.

"Sir, my suggestion, if you want to cause the most damage, is to place the C4 in the Bow Torpedo Compartment."

Richard pointed to an area between the second and third bunks. "If I was hooking up the pontoons, this is where I would hook them up," Richard explained that placing sixteen blocks, 32 pounds, of C4 on opposite sides would cause the pontoons to pull away from the hull, causing a breach. The flooding of the bow compartment would not be contained, causing her bow to dip within minutes of the explosion. Thus, she would sink in approximately twenty to forty minutes.

Pointing to the electro-technical and control center for the reactor compartment, Erik replied, "Would it be better if I placed the charges here?"

"Sir, that would be a good idea, but will it be a full or skeleton crew?"

Erik glanced at Alan, who shrugged his shoulders and back at Richard. "We do not know at this time."

"Skelton crew or not, they might have the screws on, to make it easier for the tug. If that is the case, they will have men stationed in the reactor compartment." Erik stared at Richard with an unblinking focus, but he did not respond. "Now, I think you should decide how you will bring the C4 on board."

"I could say I am a part of the inspection crew." Erik glanced at Alan for his opinion.

"That could work." Standing up, Alan approached the screen and simmered at the blueprint. "Specifically, where would you place the C4?"

Richard clarified as Alan nodded. "Why does it have to be placed inside? Here is a consideration, placing the C4 outside attached to the pontoons?"

"Water is too cold, and we could not bring a submarine close because of the sonar nets."

"How big of a container would be needed to carry the C4 and the rest of the supplies?" Erik left the question open for all to answer. Richard turned around and motioned with his hands a box, dimensions 18"x 18"x 16".

Richard's eyes sparkled with an idea. "Technical manuals." Alan motioned him to continue. "Each submarine has manuals, and they are 8.5"x 12"x 5" thick." He explained you would need three boxes that have dimensions 18"x 18"x 16" and inside you would have three manuals. Inside, each manual you could hide the sticks of C4 and the rest of the equipment. You can tell whomever you speak to that you are replacing the original manuals because they contain sensitive information they do not want to be known." He paused, "Just hope they do not open them up."

Erik pondered the situation for a moment and then answered, "No pressure." He nodded his head as if trying to settle a conflicting thought and turned to Alan, "Sir, I am ready if you are." Alan nodded.

"God speed, sir." Richard's hand clasped Erik's as he shook it and nodded.

When they had finished, Richard was the last one to exit. He flicked down the light switch and closed the door. They proceeded to the elevator, with the sound of their footsteps on the linoleum flooring hallway diminishing. Once in the lobby, Richard escorted them to the front entrance, and they went their separate ways.

Just as Erik got in the car, Alan turned to him, "Call

Carly and see if she is done with legend; if so, start learning it, and practice your Russian." Having spent two hours with Richard, they drove back to Washington. Erik was on the phone with Carly, and Alan was talking with Technology Support Divisions, a part of the Clandestine Service, to build a mock-up of the bow compartment of a November Class Submarine so that Erik could practice. As a paramilitary operations officer, Erik spent hours and hours of rehearsing and drilling for weeks on end. Therefore, when the time came, his training would become second nature. Erik could be awakened in a deep sleep, and he would be a very different person because he knew his legend. Halfway through the trip back, Alan asked Erik to grab his attaché case and pull out the unmarked folder.

"What's inside?" Erik questioned, as Alan motioned him to open it up.

Erik's eyes enlarged as he slowly began to grasp the contents. There were dozens of emails from Jamie, including photographs she had sent to him. Alan held up his hand, stopped him, and gestured Erik to read. Alan explained to Erik that he and Jamie had been communicating about him. He could not understand how one person could write so much, with each line expressing her feelings for him and telling him about her day.

Erik glanced and stared at Alan, "I think she loves me." Alan gave him a knowing grin. "Does Paul know about this?"

Alan shook his head. "This is most important," he spoke with intensity for Erik to grasp the gravity of what he was saying. "How are you up here?" Alan tapped his temple.

"I'm fine?"

"Are you sure?" Erik nodded. "Then let her be the reason you want to come home." Alan raised his pointing finger in the air to emphasize his last point. "You can only keep her photograph; keep it in a safe place, and never repeat anything we are going over now and make no attempt to contact her." Erik nodded again. "Are we clear on that?"

"Yes, sir." Erik went back, immersing himself in his work.

"Good, now let's get something to eat. What do you want?"

"Anything."

"Well, do you have any suggestions you would like?"

"Something that tastes good."

Alan turned his icy gaze on Erik. "What?"

"You know what." Erik shrugged his shoulder.

"Why is it every time we go out to dinner, you make it like it is open-heart surgery?"

Erik raised a finger to get his point across, "That is not true."

"Yes, it is! You are the most finicky eater I know." Erik tried to continue. "Hold on. Let me finish, Erik." Alan paused for a second to collect his thoughts.

"I think you do this to be difficult."

"Really?" Alan looked like he already knew that answer.

"Seriously, what do you want to eat?" Erik rolled his

eyes as he went through a process of elimination. "How hard can this be?"

Alan shook his head, knowing they went through this every time. "You are not analyzing some documents; this is dinner."

"I got it," Erik answered. Alan grinned. "Pancakes."

Alan's eyes narrowed, "For dinner?" Erik nodded. "It is seventeen-hundred." Erik shrugged his shoulders. "We are going to a place that has the best pizza in D.C."

"Where?"

"Pizza Milano on L Street Northwest." Erik shrugged his shoulders and nodded. "Trust me; you will love it."

Immediately after parking the car, Alan and Erik headed to the entrance. Pizza Milano was family-friendly. Their servers were young adults from Georgetown who were very helpful and took their time educating their patrons. Pizza Milano specialized only in all kinds of pizzas, each of exceptional quality, and pizza-like additives like breadsticks and Coke products. In the back of the restaurant, the cooks were busy preparing each order as fast as the ovens could take them. As the pizzas rolled off the conveyor belts, the servers raced them to their assigned tables. As a server welcomed Alan, who was a regular, Erik's eyes focused on an amazing girl with soft brown eyes, thick curly hair, and a smile that could brighten the darkest room. At that moment, Alan saw Erik was staring at, Jamie Anderson, and he turned Erik's back to her.

"Go back to the car." Erik shook his head. "Are you trying to compromise yourself?" Erik ignored Alan, as he overheard Jamie talking about a cause and effect paper for English Comp. He walked to the counter, as Alan shielded Erik's identity. "What in the hell are you doing?"

"Excuse me, do you have a placemat and a pen?" Erik asked.

"What in the hell are you doing?"

The server handed the items to Erik. "I plan on writing something down while you place a to-go-order for us."

Alan pointed to Erik to get his point across. "If you write anything down that will compromise you, I will address this to the admiral." Erik gave a carefree look. "Don't think I won't."

As Alan placed the order, Erik wrote down a detailed analysis of the cause and effects of the Cuban Missile Crisis. He also wrote other unclassified information, and a fact the majority does not know that: the way the intelligence community knew that the Russians were in Cuba was because of soccer fields, a game never played in Cuba. Alan was hovering over him with arms crossed against his chest and tapping his foot. Erik ignored Alan as he finished his analysis. Following that, Erik folded the document and instructed the server to bring it to Jamie. Alan tossed the car keys to Erik, ordered him to the car, and Erik left. While Alan was getting the pizza, the server delivered the note to Jamie, who was sitting with the other cheerleaders.

After opening it, she was bewildered for a few moments, and then her eyes enlarged with amazement and got the server's attention, "Excuse me, who gave you this."

"The cute looking navy officer." In the distance, Jamie

recognized Alan, who was heading out the door. "Not him; the other one."

As Jamie took herself around the table, she questioned, "What did he look like?" As the server answered her question, Jamie pulled her phone out, pulled up Erik's photo, and showed the server. The server nodded. Jamie got a burst of energy and raced out the door, trying to find Erik. As Alan tried to pull out on L Street, Erik saw Jamie.

Erik said, "She is a beautiful woman."

Alan snapped back. "She is not a woman…she is a kid, and you are a paramilitary operations officer." Erik rolled his window down halfway and stuck his hand out so Jamie could see it. "What in the hell are you doing?"

Jamie looked in their direction, and he raised his fingers according to the numbers…one-four-three. Immediately Jamie realized who was in the car and yelled, "I love you."

Alan turned to Erik and asked, "What did you just do?"

As he rolled up the window, Erik replied, "Just a little shadow play."

13. WHEREVER YOU ARE, I'LL SEE YOU IN MY DREAMS

"True love allows each person to follow his or her own path, aware that doing so can never drive them apart."

—Paulo Coelho

GEORGETOWN UNIVERSITY, WASHINGTON, D.C.

August 2003: It was a brisk morning, with birds beginning to chirp, and Jamie, as well as every girl in the cheerleading squad, wearing a t-shirt, sweat pants, and high ponytail, would rather be sleeping than exercising. Jamie, like the other girls, jogged around the outer perimeter of the Multi-Sports Field. As she glanced at her watch, it read a little after seven. Jamie, a freshman, was a typical American college girl in the early twenty-first century. She was immersed in the latest fashions and technology, from electronic gadgets to Facemash, a social media website. Jamie came from a broken home where her parents divorced when she was six, leaving her no father figure.

She did have an older brother who always looked after her; however, ever since he joined the army, she had had to be on her guard.

As in high school, Jamie was becoming very popular in college, mainly because of her beauty and cheerleader status. These two things, adding to the fact that she was a virgin and a sorority girl, made her irresistible to every guy, mainly the jocks and frat guys on campus. Guys clamored to go out with her and even joked among themselves as to who would get the "prize." This made her not trust or have faith in them. Jamie was excited and challenged by opportunities that brought her richness and fullness of life; that is what made her who she was. When it came to college and cheerleading, she took her responsibilities very seriously and was dependable. Jamie valued security, stability, and had a strong focus on what she wanted to accomplish in her life. Her first was to get a cheerleading scholarship to Georgetown, done. Next, she wanted to graduate with honors. Her current G.P.A. was 3.7. Lastly, she wanted Dr. Erik Függer as her boyfriend. However, she needed to focus on cheerleading practice first.

Once Jamie and the other girls had made it around their jogging path, out of breath and grasping their water bottles, they sat down and stretched their legs, arms, neck, and back. The main goal for the squad was to gain strength and flexibility. As they warmed up their muscles, they separated into pods and began to practice stunting. The squad, grilled by the captain and vice-captain, practiced routine after routine until they learned them by heart. The captain told each girl there were not going to be distractions when they did this during a game. In each routine, they needed to be performed flawlessly. When it was game day, the squad would yell at the top of their lungs and dance to the music of the band, as they smiled to the crowd and waited for the next stunt. As they did the last trick for practice, Jamie's heart was racing as if it would beat right out of her chest, while sweat ran down her face. She started to count, from the captain, "5, 6, 7, 8..."

As the vice walked around, Jamie bounced forward and pushed off her shoulders. At that moment, she felt free as a bird. Focused, Jamie wiggled around on her feet until she got her balance. Once Jamie had her balance, she took deep breaths and stayed tight, waiting for the next count. Then count from the captain, "Cradle 1, 2..." Jamie dipped down, and then she was tossed into the air as if she were weightless. Finally, she slipped into the other girls' arms and stepped on the ground once again. Nearly two hours had passed, and practice was over, until tomorrow.

Jamie and the rest of the squad headed toward O'Donovan Dining Hall to have breakfast. Each of the girls knew each other's business, even though Jamie tried to keep things to herself, especially about Erik. Tilting her head at Jamie, Cheer Captain Adrienne tried to get everyone's attention. Once she did, she made her statement: "So Jamie, I heard you have a boyfriend." Jamie looked back pursed her lips and smiled, as Adrienne continued to probe. "What's his name?"

"You don't know him."

"I am sure we can find out." Adrienne looked at the others for any subtle clues. "Jocks do talk so that we will find out."

"Save your time; he doesn't play any sports."

Ashley butted in as she rolled her eyes in the back of her head, "I heard he was a museum curator. Sounds boooooooring!" The other girls laughed.

Jamie barked back and pointed to get her point across. "He's not boring; he's interesting."

Ashley continued to badger. "Another word for boring and homely: AKA nerd." The other girls laughed. "I bet he wears nerdy glasses too."

"Not at all, Ashley. He's handsome. Way past cute." Then she gazed in the rest of the girls' eyes. "My roommate Kristina met him. She will back me up on this one."

"Maybe she has the same boring taste in guys," Adrienne replied, as she laughed. "Do you have a picture of Mr. Boring?"

At that moment, Jamie pulled out her cellphone and showed her screen saver, which was Erik. "I love the hat. It's something of a trademark. Kind of like Indiana Jones." Jamie sighed.

Adrienne mocked, "Oh boy, she has it bad for this history nerd. Older, boring, and dresses like he is out of an old movie—seriously, Jamie? You could have any guy here!" Adrienne replied with a knowing glance at some nearby jocks. "There are some hot guys in Sigma Phi Epsilon."

Jamie's nose wrinkled up as she cut her off, "You mean one of those?" Jamie pointed to a group of football players who were gawking at every girl who walked by. "You have got to be kidding me! I have more sense and dignity than being seen with one of those monkeys."

Emmy pulled Jamie aside and asked in a half-whisper, "Can I see his picture?" Jamie handed her phone over. "How did you two meet?"

"We met at the National Museum of American History, and he is a curator. He is intriguing." Jamie saw Keith and Kevin in the distance and pointed. "You see those two creeps?"

Emmy nodded, "Yeah, they think they are God's gift to women."

Jamie paused and said with dreamy eyes, "Erik rescued me from them."

Emmy took a closer look at Erik's picture. "He does look intriguing, especially how he wears his hat."

"I know. I liked it. Old fashioned, but classy." Jamie slipped into a dream state, thinking about Erik. "He just has that something that grabs me and won't let me go."

"Wow! I know it takes a lot to impress you. What is that something? It must be the hat." They both giggled.

Jamie sighed. "Just handsome." She looked at his picture. "I miss him already."

"Does he have any friends?"

"I don't know, but I am dying to learn more about him."

Emmy swung around to Jamie and, flinging her hands as she thought out loud, asked: "Is Erik on Facemash or Myspace?"

Jamie shook her head. "Have you tried to Google his name?"

"Yes, I tried everything. Erik is only on the museum website. I will find him."

"Where is he now?"

"Overseas somewhere…wherever he is, I know he is making a difference."

14. WALKS AMONG THE THORNS

"Bestow rewards without regard to rule, issue orders without regard to previous arrangements; and you will be able to handle a whole army as though you had to do with but a single man."

—Sun Tzu

GREMIKHA NAVAL BASE, OSTROVNOY, RUSSIA

It was 0500; Erik was in his Russian senior warrant officer tunic. He adjusted everything: shoulder boards, ribbons, collar tabs, belt, and anything else. Wearing a latex mask, Erik stared at his reflection in a poorly lit bathroom. He gently touched the mask, especially around the eyes, to make sure it was flush against his skin. In the mirror, his cold-blue eyes looked back at him with his mind focused on the op. Every time Erik went overseas, he had memorized his deployment orders, all of his equipment was with him, and he recalled his knowledge about the op. This helped him avoid becoming stale and prevented him from making mistakes.

The type of equipment told him a lot about the kind of job he would be doing and how complicated the task would be. This time the vehicle and equipment had been set up beforehand, and he would have to do this job within ten minutes. If that were not enough to put him under extreme pressure, Erik would also not be carrying any sidearms. The weapons he could use to escape were the ones the guards would be using, Avtomat Kalashnikova model of 1947, aka AK-47. Their orders would be to defend the base and submarines at all cost. Also, they would kill whoever would compromise the submarines. As before, Erik would be entering the submarine base in darkness and under a false name, Alexander Khristofor, and it was not going to be easy because they would be on their guard that much more because of what had been done to the Kursk.

When working as a paramilitary operations officer, while a part of an O.G.D.S. team, there were many things different from working on another part of the Special Activities Division. The significant differences were that he was always operating alone, out of radio contact, and no safe houses. He was not allowed to go to the U.S. Embassy for assistance of any kind. Always surrounded by military personnel and government operatives who would kill him if he was compromised, and his support team could not help if things went wrong. With that in mind, he would use everything he had learned on The Farm, remember everything Erik had used to prepare for the operation, and pray he was not compromised. If identified, Erik would be eliminated. Finally, he would be recognized by a star on the memorial wall and no name in the Honor Book.

A few hours before dawn, as Erik neared the Gremikha Naval Base, he found himself in a lonely place with his emotions under strain, and knowing if he faltered, he would fail. He cleared his mind, absolved himself of all blame, and again focused his attention on the mission. Erik settled himself more comfortably into the seat and rested his hands on the steering wheel. He proceeded, with the truck's headlights, to cut a path down a lonely road that few knew, much less had traveled. The road led to a secure and well-guarded gate.

He started getting into character and began to think and speak Russian, so he would not have an accent. Erik knew that the hardest part of the job was the social interactions he was forced to make, and he knew that his cover would be tested. The silhouettes of personnel and AFVs appeared as he got closer to the perimeter of the base. As they had taught him on The Farm, he kept his facts straight, remained calm and collected, and when he came face-to-face with individuals, either enlisted or officers, acted as if he were there for a purpose and that he belonged there. Erik rolled down his window and dimmed his headlights as a sentry approached the vehicle, and others stayed alert and positioned themselves around the vehicle.

"Papers." The sentry ordered, with his hand extended, as he gave Erik a slow appraising glance. "State your name and reason you are here."

"Senior Warrant Officer Alexander Khristofor. I am here to drop off the revised technical manuals for B-159."

The guard motioned to another guard to check behind the truck as he passed Erik's I.D. to another. Ten feet away from were the reinforced concrete tollbooth-like structures. Within the tollbooth-like structure were monitors from cameras that were doing facial recognition and running it through a database. Then they had another individual who ran Erik's I.D. through government databases. The other guard went to the back of the truck looking for explosives or any different kind of contraband. Another guard scanned underneath the truck with a mirror. Erik patiently waited for what seemed like an eternity, but in actuality was less than five minutes. Passing this test, he would be allowed to enter the submarine base. He saw a guard within the concrete tollbooth-like structures telephoning to the next guard point.

That was only the first of several checkpoints Erik had to pass, not including any individuals who might order a routine stop. The base was very primitive compared to U.S. sub-bases and only had the bare necessities and no luxuries. There were a few structures with the lights on. Erik figured those were administrative offices. As he got deeper into the base, there was less activity, and the streetlamps cast their light down just enough so one could see the road. In the distance, Erik saw the glow of cigarettes, which meant another checkpoint. As he pulled up, he rolled down the window and got his papers ready.

At that moment, Erik stopped. The guard snapped to attention, saluted, and with his hand extended, he ordered, "Papers." Erik handed them to the guard who looked them over and asked routine questions. Then he took Erik's I.D., headed to the guard shack, and picked up the phone receiver. Erik looked around casually at the barbed wire. He spotted the last gate, which gave access to the interior of the harbor. Erik saw silhouettes in the near distance. From what he could make of it, there were several submarines. This appeared to be one of the most straightforward missions he had done. Erik heard the distant K-9 units that suggested there was a night patrol. He wouldn't have to worry himself with that problem yet; however, he was thankful they were not inclined to search his truck. In times like this, all Erik could do was wait and wait some more. A few minutes went by, and the guard strolled toward the truck.

"Sir, have you been informed the B-159 has relocated?" he replied, as he handed Erik's I.D. back.

Erik knew in mission things do not go as planned. Also, every branch of the military in every country experienced the same things. "You got to love the lack of communication." They both laughed it off as if this were a common occurrence. "Where is she located?"

"In there." The guard pointed to an island, whose silhouette started to form as the sun breached the horizon. "I have sent a boat for you." Erik nodded in apprehension. "Do you need anything, sir?"

"A dolly."

The guard shook his head and pointed. "You can park over there. There's one by the building."

He parked the vehicle, got the dolly, loaded the boxes, and approached the pier. Once the vessel drifted up, Erik motioned to one of the sailors. He kept calm and, being an expansive communicator, and he persuaded an individual to help him load the boxes. That was the natural part. However, Erik knew the real challenge, that of infiltrating a new part of a base he had never seen before. Erik needed to act as if he belonged there and move casually through the section he was in. If Erik got lost and entered a location forbidden, he would be surrounded and detained. In that case, Erik would know it was too late to do anything about it.

When the last box was loaded, he climbed on board and headed to the island. His face felt the sharp, salty air that ran across his face, and he tasted the salt on his tongue. It was the beginning of a new day with a pewter overcast sky, with the boat sweeping over a gunmetal ocean with tempered squalls. Once on the island, Erik quickly analyzed his surroundings, as he unloaded and loaded the boxes, and got the documentation ready. As he approached the massive reinforced concrete entrance, with a channel alongside that was approximately twenty-four feet wide and very deep, the two-armed guards' cold inquisitive eyes watched Erik with more suspicion as if he were a surfer from California.

"Papers," the guard quipped, with his hand extended. "State your business."

"Bringing technical manuals to B-159."

The guards carefully scrutinized Erik's orders, I.D., and security clearance, to confirm who he was and if he had the authority to enter. Erik held a clearance of Level Two-State Secret Clearance that gave him authority; however, the guards eyed the boxes carefully. As a paramilitary operations officer, especially being a part of an O.G.D.S. team, he got used to people, usually armed and wanting to kill him, questioning who he was and the reason why he was allowed in specific locations. Besides, the guards were trained not only in what they would say, but also in how they would say it, and in watching an individual's body language. Thus, sweat running down your face, a clumsy answer, or even a stutter would compromise Erik. If Erik were asked if he saw a celebrity, for example, Emmy Rossum, would he be starstruck, his answer would be no. This is because after having individuals wanting you dead and having AK-47s pointed at you, celebrities did not faze him. Nearly five minutes went by, but Erik was permitted to pass into a world that officially did not exist.

Stepping into one of the most grandiose structures of the Cold War, an underground complex for nuclear submarines, Erik was engulfed by its sheer size. In 1961, the base became the operational home for the fearsome Alpha Class nuclear submarines of the Soviet Northern Fleet. What made the 153,000 square-foot facility effective? The entrance is camouflaged from spy aircraft. Secondly, the thickness of the rock over the underground premises reached nearly 378 feet, meaning it could survive a direct nuclear hit. Lastly, the Alphas could enter and leave the base underwater between tours of duty, which kept them clear. One side was used for the operational running of the base, and the other for arming and storage of the nuclear warheads. The vast submarine channel that ran through the center could dock nine small submarines or seven submarines of an average class one. Besides, those who worked there, nearly 3,000, at the underground base, were provided with a canteen, shower rooms, and recreation rooms, making it a self-sufficient living facility.

Erik figured, from his surroundings, he was inside the operational side. He worked his way through the broad network, like an anthill of tunnels, composed of solid marble-like limestone. Uniformed Russian soldiers, armed with AK-47s, were everywhere, wrangling supplies and equipment; also, there were submarine service naval personnel there. At the far end of one of the hallways, Erik saw a natural cavern, even more significant than the corridors. He came to the cavern and its channel. In the channel, the light slowly faded to a half-darkness atmosphere filled with nauseating smells of burned rubber, oil, paint, putrid acids, rust, seawater, and tar. Erik's eardrums were filled with a metallic clattering, loud echoes of urgent footfalls, the clanking of tools, and the humming of generators that never seemed to go away. His eyes adjusted, and he glanced at each side. From his guestimate, the submarine channel was so large that it was capable of holding a 300-foot submarine. He headed to his left. Within the concrete cave, which was teeming with activity, the walkway was cluttered with cables of various sizes and loose materials. The channel was curved to deflect any blast inside the base. He saw multiple workshops and a wide range of supplies. Erik looked at his surroundings; the channel was lined with steel gangways above head height. He passed two Alpha Class fast attack nuclear submarines.

It was a fearsome environment, with hulking subs sitting in the black water.

Erik knew that the hard part would be in a restricted area and possibly was being watched closely, mainly from the Foreign Intelligence Service (SVR) and the Federal Security Service (FSB). He was trained to take a direct approach because sneaking around aroused suspicion. In the distance, he saw an outline of another class nuclear submarine. It was the November Class nuclear submarine, B-159. He would have to go through one more security checkpoint to get on board her. Erik would use his skills to pass as a senior warrant officer, and he would use his ideas and the ability to be extremely flexible and adaptable to get on board that submarine. Once inside, he would use his unique alacrity and a quick-thinking mind, to overcome any obstacles. He finally reached the gangway to B-159.

"Papers."

Again, as before, Erik handed over his identification. At that moment, darkness approached and hovered over him. He glanced to his left. There stood in front of him a conspicuously tall individual, his pale face, like the moon, appeared to be ageless, neither old nor young. In his ice blue, suspicious eyes, they hid the memory of many things and experiences. Under his cap, his jet-black hair was wiry and brushed backward from the temples. From the top of his well-groomed and sculptured naval uniform, that had the rank of captain first rank, to his shiny black boots, the individual was the perfection of an SVR officer. In situations like this, it was always best to give short, direct answers. The SVR officer grabbed Erik's identification and stared back from the I.D. to Erik's face.

"What's in the boxes?"

"Technical Manuals"

"What is wrong with the ones inside?"

"They contain some sensitive information we don't want the North Koreans to know."

Erik knew these first two minutes when being questioned by an SVR officer were crucially crucial because it would raise suspicion if he talked more than two minutes. He had to establish who he was and why he was there. If the SVR officer decided Erik was forthright, Erik could board. If he thought Erik was not straightforward, Erik would be compromised, tortured, and shortly afterward shot. Finally, a star would go on the Memorial Wall and in the Honor Book with no name by it.

"Is that so?" Erik felt and caught the captain's cold blue eyes staring at him. "Why wasn't I informed?"

Erik knew this could be a trick question to test him or a loaded question. So, the best thing to do was deflect the question. "You can ask Admiral Suchkov. Should we wake him?"

The SVR officer looked at his watch and gave a deep sigh. "You have ten minutes." He handed over Erik's identification. Erik was being watched like an organism in a drop of water under a microscope. From the compartment below the bridge, Erik quickly moved the boxes and the dolly through several hatches that led to the pressure hull and eventually to the control room.

In the distance was a member of the crew who was

staring at Erik. He stared at Erik for a moment longer and abandoned the thought to communicate and help him. With a subtle sigh, Erik exited the control room and squeezed himself and the boxes through the hatches that led to the Bow Torpedo Compartment. Once in the Bow Torpedo Compartment, he closed the hatch and opened each box like a child on Christmas morning and pulled out his equipment: crimping tool, Detonator Caps, 100 feet of Detcord, electrical tape, timer, and 1-1/4 lbs. 32 blocks of C4.

Erik spent hours preparing, learning the bow compartment, researching the November Class Submarine, and practicing setting up and placing the C4, so when the day arrived, he would be ready, even if under a time limit. Erik quickly taped two sets of 16 blocks together. Next, he placed them with the detonator caps. Finally, Erik put the blast caps into the timer. Following that, he attached the Detcord from the timer to the C4, and lastly, he set the timer and left. Erik emerged on the deck of the submarine, casually glanced around at his surroundings, analyzing everyone and everything. Immediately crossing the gangway, he proceeded back through the maze-like network of the operational side.

When exiting a secure location, Erik knew that patience was crucial to success because he still did not know who was watching, and if they did stop him, it would be easier to dodge their questions rather than get in a firefight. Lastly, unlike Hollywood, a paramilitary operations officer's job would not be over, nor would he be out of danger until he was on board a 747 jet and over the

Atlantic. As Erik stared out the window, he remembered what Senior Instructor Rauch had said about a successful mission: Every successful covert op is 70 percent skill, 20 percent concentration, 9 percent doing the job, 1percent luck, and 100 percent getting the hell back home alive.

15. CALL OF THE UNKNOWN

"Listen. I work for the CIA. I am not a spy. I just read books! We read everything that's published in the world. And we ... we feed the plots—dirty tricks, codes—into a computer, and the computer checks against actual CIA plans and operations. I look for leaks; I look for new ideas ... We read adventures and novels and journals. I ... I ... Who'd invent a job like that?"

—Joe Turner, *Three Days of the Condor*

CIA HEADQUARTERS, LANGLEY, VIRGINIA

August 2005: On this morning, Alan and Erik were ordered to the Compound, and it was time for another briefing. Erik was hoping it was going to be something different than going to Russia and sinking submarines. Like many times before, they proceeded to the third floor and headed to where the O.G.D.S. teams were located. Once inside the Vault, Alan looked for Paul. Erik took his seat at his cubicle, where the rest of his team was. Carly was studying and updating her database with new features on

IDs from civilians, military, and any others Erik would be using. Gary was practicing his skills hacking into foreign databases by breaking down their firewalls and repairing them. Lastly, John was repositioning satellites and making 3D imagery for the simulator room. At the moment Erik opened his laptop, he heard approaching footsteps but remained focused on the task. Alan tapped Erik on the shoulder and motioned him to follow. Erik glanced at Paul, who gave a cunning grin.

Erik asked, "What's going on?"

"Admiral Bonesteiner is requesting to see you." Paul took a sip of his coffee, as Erik motioned him to continue, but Paul shook his head and gave a dismissive gesture. "You need to go now." Paul pointed to the door. "I would advise you not to keep him waiting."

Alan snapped his fingers to get Erik's attention to follow. They walked to the elevator, saying nothing. Alan noted Erik's behavior and wondered what was going on. Erik pondered if he was going to be fired; however, he believed he would have been escorted off the Compound if that were true. "Does the director want me out of the agency?"

Alan looked straight into Erik's eyes. "Goss took some convincing." Alan paused to collect his thoughts and continued, "However, Bonesteiner and I can make a good case."

"What did you tell him?"

"That is not important; however, if you must know, he told him the truth." Erik showed interest in knowing more. "Bonesteiner told Goss that he believes in you, and if he could rely on anyone to get a special assignment done, it's you."

The elevators opened, and they proceeded to Bonesteiner's office. Erik was ordered to go in, and Alan waited outside. Bonesteiner was reading intelligence briefings, slumped in his chair as he motioned Erik to take a seat. He jotted notes in the margins on each file. There were two piles of briefings on his desk, all had DDI-eyes-only in bold capital letters and classified into two categories: becoming a security risk and a security risk. After a few minutes, Bonesteiner stopped. He looked at Erik speculatively as he revolved his shoulders, rotated his head, and bent his neck to work out the stiffness. Removing his spectacles, Bonesteiner took a deep breath and asked, as he leaned back in his chair, "How are you doing?"

"Work-wise or generally speaking?"

Shaking his head, Bonesteiner knew there was never an easy answer when it came to Erik. Then he leaned forward to place his elbows on his desk and interlaced his fingers, as he replied firmly, "Both."

"Generally speaking, I am alive, and as for work-wise…I don't know yet."

"Well, there is something I need to tell you." Erik struggled to keep his concern from showing, but Bonesteiner motioned him to relax. "I need to take you out of the team." Before Erik was able to get a word out, Bonesteiner shook his head. "The decision has been made, and that is final." He leaned over his desktop staring at Erik, motionless except for his eyes, which narrowed.

"Listen; the agency needs you to allocate your skills in another place," he said fiercely.

Erik jumped up with his arms crossed against his chest. "How can you pull me out of my team?" Erik pointed to himself and declared, "I am very good at what I do there." He pointed at Bonesteiner. "Don't you think I am doing a good job?"

Bonesteiner stood to confront Erik as he pointed. "You are, but you always question authority." Bonesteiner walked from behind his desk. "How in the hell can I keep going to the director to stick up for you? God, Erik! Why can't you be like everyone else in the agency who listens and doesn't question everything?"

"I am not like you or anyone else. I am my own person. Of all people, you should know that."

"I do…" Bonesteiner pondered for a moment. "You were that when I met you, and you have not changed."

"I know I've let you down by questioning authority and the special assignments. You've supported me at great risk to your reputation and your career."

Bonesteiner nodded, paused, and motioned Erik to take a seat by the coffee table. "How do you feel when you come to work?"

"Unappreciated." Erik rolled his eyes in his head. "It is a slap in the face when you see that individuals in other teams have graduated from an Ivy League School, and other paramilitary operations officers have a special ops background, and they look at me differently." Watching Erik's face, Bonesteiner knew how Erik felt as he continued, "For me, I have to let it go and have to work harder and prove to myself and them I can do this job. I see how I'm never going to be accepted as an equal because I'm not like them and am not as good as you and everyone else." Erik stood up, leaned forward, and pointed to himself. "But that doesn't mean I give up."

Bonesteiner stood by Erik and cupped his shoulders. "I want you to know, I believe in you. If the world were going through hell, I'd only want one person in the goddamn world to fix it." Erik gave a blank expression. "That's right; it is you." He motioned Erik to take a seat.

"I don't understand why you would pick me out of all people."

"It's not about understanding, and you have a gift that very few people have." Bonesteiner glared at Erik, and then he resumed, "You said it yourself; you never give up." He pointed at Erik. "I don't want you to change, understood?" Bonesteiner walked to his desk, picked up the phone, and ordered Alan to come in.

Bonesteiner continued, "Erik, as I mentioned before, you are going to be reassigned to department four-six-three."

Erik nodded. "Who or what is four-six-three?"

"They are a group of analysts that were handpicked by the intelligence community to do historical research on 'what ifs' in history." Motioning with his head, Bonesteiner added, "You were one of those individuals."

Bonesteiner explained his new assignment was Project Sunflower. Erik's job would be analyzing, collecting, and researching data, preparing written reports and briefings on the historical theory on Field Marshal Erwin Rommel if he had lived versus committing suicide by cyanide on 14 October 1944. The focus was more valuable and relevant because it dealt with the possible changes in historical and political events in the last years of World War II, 1944—1945, and the post-war years. Erik was to report every week to Bonesteiner on his analysis that could change and divide resources, which would affect other nations' domestic, foreign, and military policies. Also, Erik would gather classified collections of draft cables and memorandums. He would work with sophisticated databases and computer simulations, participating in various committees and analytical groups, while not giving up any information on his work.

"Admiral, how is this national security?"

"Erik, I cannot get into that, but I will tell you this." He leaned forward and stared directly into Erik's eyes to emphasize his point. "Here is a quote by Alan Turing, 'Sometimes it is the people no one can imagine anything of who do the things no one can imagine.'"

Erik knew who that was, and knew Bonesteiner was talking in code. However, what was the meaning? At the same time, Erik wondered where this path would lead him, and if this path would be less traveled. The door opened, and Alan took a seat by Erik. Bonesteiner pointed to Alan. "Alan will remain as your control officer, and if you need any help, you go to him and no one else." He looked at Erik. "Are we clear?" Erik nodded. "Good. You need to go to personnel and get your new ID, do some paperwork, and acquire keys to your vault. Alan will meet you in the personnel office, and then you two have the rest of the day off."

Bonesteiner stood up, with Alan and Erik following, and extended his hand to Erik. "Congratulations. Let me know if you need anything."

"Thank you, Admiral."

"Erik, there is one other thing. There will be a package sent to the museum, and I want you to take care of that package and keep it in a locked place."

"I don't follow."

"You earned them."

Erik was now able to connect the dots. They were the three medals he had earned and the uniforms he had used when he went overseas. He would place them in his office closet, and he would need to get a lock for the door. Alan extended his hand to shake Erik's hand. Once Erik had exited, Bonesteiner leaned back in his chair and addressed Alan, as he made himself a cup of coffee and took a seat. Both men stared at each other, trying to read the other's body language.

"What does Goss want to do with him?"

"He has been reassigned."

"He wants him off the team?" Bonesteiner took a sip of his coffee as Alan continued. "Was it Paul?" Bonesteiner discretely pointed to the ceiling. "Why?"

"Out of my hands, and that's why I need you to watch his back."

"I understand. At least Erik will be safer." Bonesteiner shook his head. "More exposed to the elements?"

Bonesteiner nodded, and Alan nodded in agreement and changed the topic.

"Is Jamie still sending him emails and showing up at the museum?" Bonesteiner was referring to Jamie Anderson as Alan nodded. "She is persistent; do you think she will stop?"

"No, and I think she is in love with him and vice versa."

"Does Georgetown play tonight?" Bonesteiner asked. Alan nodded. "Take him to the game and study him. He can only observe, not interfere." Bonesteiner raised his finger to stop Alan from interrupting. "Have him wear a latex mask, German uniform, and have him speak only German."

"He's not going to like that."

"I don't give a damn what he likes. I want a full report in the morning."

16. WITHIN REACH

"I never knew what love was until I met you, then when distance pulled us apart, I found out what true love is."

—Anonymous

VERIZON CENTER, WASHINGTON, D.C.

Later that evening at the Verizon Center, Alan, who was in his service dress blue uniform, and Erik, who was wearing a Bundeswehr officer's uniform, were watching the Georgetown Dawgs and the Creighton Blue Jays. Alan, who was a season ticket holder, was cheering on the Dawgs, as Erik just watched and listened. Erik had never gotten into sports, well not the sports played in the United States. He was interested in Australian Rules Football, the World Cup, and sculling.

To everyone else, this was an exciting game, but Erik felt he could be doing something more interesting. They watched a player from the Blue Jays rebound, control the ball, and sprint down the court. He dribbled through all of the Dawg players without passing the ball to his teammates. A player on the Dawgs dashed toward the Blue Jay player, nearly snatching the ball out of his hands. The Blue Jay player then threw a sloppy pass toward a well-guarded teammate, and a Georgetown player intercepted and drove down the court. With fancy footwork, he maneuvered the ball through two Blue Jay defenders and found himself open behind the three-point circle for the final shot before halftime. He sank the basket just as the buzzer went off, and both teams retreated to their locker rooms with the Dawgs up by two points.

Leaning towards Alan, Erik asked in German. "Why are we here?"

Completely ignoring Erik, Alan pointed to the court, as the roar of the crowd welcomed the Dawg cheerleaders, who took center court. "This is the best part of the game."

As music filled up the Verizon Center, the girls formed four groups of four. Suddenly three girls in each group raised another girl, the flyer, so she was standing on their hands. The flyers raised their hands and held that position for a few seconds. Next, the fliers were tossed in the air and landed in the arms of the other girls. Then the girls separated and performed front handsprings, as they hurtled across the court.

Alan leaned over and whispered. "Recognize anyone?" Erik glared and shook his head. Alan pointed to the girl at center court doing front handsprings toward them and then did a split right in front of them. Erik's eyes widened as he pulled out a photo from his wallet that had been given to him by Alan two years ago. His head bobbed from the picture to the girl on the court. Her radiant

smile with her soft brown eyes placed a spell on Erik.
Then he realized who it was. Jamie. Then Erik felt Alan's
arm, preventing him from moving.

"You can only observe, not interfere." Erik gave a
scolding look. "Do not even try to speak to her or identify
yourself." Alan shook his head. "Admiral's rules."

"You bastards; for once, can I do what I want?"

"You do not have that luxury for the person in your
shoes."

"How about free..."

"Freewill?" Erik nodded as he balled up his hands into
fists. "You have the appearance of free will. I don't have
it, and neither does the admiral." Alan pointed at Erik.
"Only civilians have it; we are held to a higher standard."

"I know she loves me."

"She has not seen you in two years." Alan shook his
head in disbelief. "What makes you think she will have
the same feelings as when you two first meet?"

"I know it from the way she looked at me after I protected her from those bastards."

"You cannot be serious."

"I am. You forget I can read people. Like I can read
you, and you are getting defensive." Erik leaned forward
and continued in a half-whisper. "What are you going to
put in your report?"

As his eyes narrowed, Alan looked away and turned
sharply to face Erik with his finger raised. "You better
stop while you are ahead."

"Alan, I've never met a woman like her." Erik stared at
Jamie. "Her understanding, her endurance, her kindness."

"Erik, if you love her, there's one thing you can do to prove it."

"What is that?"

"Walk away." Erik shook his head. "Do you think she will be able to put up with you being away all the time?" Erik shrugged his shoulders. "Erik, my wife left me because of that, and I was shattered. I would save you that pain. Please, let Jamie go."

Alan saw some friends, and they motioned him to come over. He ordered Erik to stay put. As Dawg players approached the benches, Erik focused his attention on Jamie, who was socializing with the other cheerleaders. Then his eyes narrowed on a basketball player hovering over Jamie, who appeared to make her feel uncomfortable with his presence. Erik glanced back at Alan, who was preoccupied in conversation, and again at Jamie. She seemed to have a struggle with the player. He got up from his seat, glanced back at Alan one more time, and then Erik made his move. He quickly moved through the row of seats, down the stairs, and walked between lower-level sideline, section 101, and club section 101, with stealthy footwork. Erik saw the player that was making Jamie uncomfortable. It was Keith. As a paramilitary operations officer, he was trained to be good at being resourceful.

The ability to be resourceful in the field can often mean the difference between life and death. However, he knew he wasn't allowed to be in certain areas, but that doesn't mean you can't interfere. Erik approached an individual with a shirt gun. He knew he would exploit this person as an asset and find their weakness. Money. Erik offered the individual, who was a college student, majoring in history, $300 for the shirt gun and shirts. However, when they need something worth their while considering they're going to lose their job. Erik offered him a job at the museum. It was a done deal, and Erik was ready.

Erik overheard. "Keith, leave me alone," Jamie demanded, as she tried to move away from him and slapped him across his face.

"You bitch!" He raised his right hand, intending to hit her.

Jamie cowered. "Stop!"

"Or what? Will your imaginary boyfriend show up?" Keith mocked.

Erik's eyes were full of focused venomous rage like a wolf's stance against a fiercest opponent. Without further ado, Erik loaded, fired, and aimed for Keith. A hit! "What the hell?" Keith looked around. Immediately, Erik reloaded and fired again. Another hit. Keith locked eyes with Erik, as he pointed and started to charge Erik. "Who in the hell are you?"

Erik repeatedly fired until it was ineffective as Keith darted up the bleachers. In the distance, Jamie and the head coach from Georgetown followed Keith. Alan raced toward Erik. The other basketball players and cheerleaders stood speechless. Erik stood his ground with his feet firmly planted as Jamie looked into Erik's eyes. She had only seen this look once before, two years ago. At that moment, when Keith was in striking distance, he launched his attack; however, Alan intervened and prevented the attack.

They pointed with an accusing finger. With a demanding tone, Keith said: "That son of a bitch hit me with a shirt gun!"

Alan pushed Keith back, and the coach held Keith back, with Alan focused-on Erik and stated in German, "What in hell is going on?"

"He was going to hit her, and I was protecting her!" Erik replied in German, as Alan stepped forward.

Jamie saw the tension and slipped between Erik and Alan. "Alan…"

Alan leaned forward toward Jamie as his eyes narrowed. "This doesn't concern you."

"Yes, it does! He was protecting me!" She stuck her finger in his face. "So, you better stop yelling at him!" She pointed at Keith. "He caused it, so yell at him!"

"Listen to her," Erik stated with a grin.

Alan was about to say something. However, when Jamie gave a scolding look, he kept his mouth shut. Jamie approached Erik and rubbed his arm as she looked into his eyes and said softly. "I do not know if you understand me, but thank you." She noticed Erik's eyes, and every muscle in his body was still tense like a wolf about to attack its prey. "He won't bother me anymore." Erik started to lower his guard. Keith and his coach retreated to the bench.

Jamie looked at Alan, "What is his name?" Hint, the latex mask and German, had made him unrecognizable to Jamie.

"Burnon."

"Thank you, Burnon." She hugged Erik and kissed

him on his cheek. Then she stepped back, pulled out her cell phone, and as she was about to take a picture, Erik instinctively raised his hand to cover the camera, and lowered the cell phone. "Burnon, why did you do that?"

Erik said nothing and waved good-bye as she looked closer into his eyes. She tried to recall that she'd seen those eyes before; however, Jamie found it odd that only once before had someone done the same thing when she had tried to take his picture. As Erik and Alan walked away, she raised her cell phone and prepared to take a picture.

"Burnon!" Jamie declared. As Erik turned his head, she took his picture, and she got Alan's attention. "Alan, what is Burnon's lucky number?"

"I don't know."

"Ask him."

Alan got Erik's attention and asked the question while giving him a look that he had better not reveal who he was. Erik walked toward Jamie and replied, "Eins-Vier-Drei." Jamie failed to understand him, so Alan repeated it in English. "One-Four-Three."

Immediately, Erik turned around and headed up the stairs, with Alan following behind. Jamie just stood there and tried to make sense of the numbers One-Four-Three, as she stared at Erik's picture from two years ago on her phone and the one of Burnon. It was as if a lightbulb went off above her head, as Jamie looked at the pictures closer. She noticed that Burnon and Erik had the same eyes, expressions, and acted the same way when getting their photos taken. Most importantly, Jamie recalled two years ago someone in a car had held out his hand and had signed One-Four-Three. She began to jump like a Gazelle, a smile growing on her face and quickly glanced around to find Burnon. Then, Jamie, her eyes fixed on him, raced up the stairs, yelling his name. Erik turned to face her; however, Alan stopped her. She struggled to get free as she looked at Burnon with tears running down her face. Erik motioned to her that this was not a good time and fought his willpower not to go to her.

"Alan, let me speak to him!"

"I cannot allow that."

"Why not?" Jamie again looked at Burnon and back at Alan. "Have you seen Erik today?" Alan nodded as she freed herself. "Do you ever tell him I stop by, and why doesn't he reply to my emails?"

"I do, and maybe he is too busy to reply. Maybe he doesn't have feelings for you."

"You're wrong, Alan."

"Am I?"

"Yes! Alan, I love Erik, and have ever since the first day I met him."

"You only met him one time."

"I saw it in his eyes. He might not be at the museum all the time, but I'll find him."

"What difference can that make?'

"Because I love him, and Erik is going to make me very happy. I will make him very happy." Jamie pointed at Alan to get her point across. "I will find him; don't you dare try to stop me.

17. INTERWOVEN THREADS OF UNKNOWNS

"The right to view sensitive compartmentalized information—is reserved for the most trusted people in the intelligence community."

—*Burn Notice*, Episode "Breaking Point,"
voiceover of Michael Weston

NSA HEADQUARTERS, FORT MEADE, MARYLAND

September 2005: It had been twenty-five days since Erik was given Project Sunflower and promoted to Senior Analyst. This morning he was traveling down the Baltimore-Washington Parkway as he had done several times before. The parkway linked to a tree-filled countryside road that led to a secure complex surrounded by a ten-foot cyclone fence topped with several rows of barbed wire. Attached to the fence were warning signs regarding the Internal Security Act, forbidding photography. Just beyond that perimeter was another fence made up of five high-voltage electrified wires and wooden posts. Lastly, and beyond the second fence, there was another ten-foot cyclone fence; also, between the second and third fences, there was green asphalt guarded by armed patrols and K-9 units. This was just the tip of the iceberg of the complex.

One could see from a sky view the vast complex, made up of a 60,000 square foot supply building, access roads, bituminous parking lots, guardhouses, a power substation, and sidewalks. Squeezed in this confined area is the tan three-story A-shaped Operations Building that surrounded a greenish-black nine-story building. The building's roof littered with a multitude of antennas and two huge radomes, one resembling a golf ball and the other a Ping-Pong ball. However, there are things seen and unseen by the naked eye, such as closed-circuit television cameras with telephoto lenses, long-wire, and log-periodic antennas, parabolic microwave dishes, and weathered-white satellite dishes with mammoth green shells hidden inside. With all these things, one could wonder what this place is; this compound is the Puzzle Palace, National Security Agency Headquarters.

Erik pulled up to a checkpoint and handed his ID over. Several members, in the royal blue uniforms of the Federal Protection Service, FPS, swept his vehicle with dogs and mirrors. After the security check, he was given a temporary pass and told to park in the visitor parking. Next, Erik headed up a flight of stairs, entered through a double set of glass doors, and immediately was confronted by armed FPS guards, who stared at him with cold, suspicious eyes. One asked Erik for his identification and then matched it against a database. Once a match had been made, they handed his ID back, and Erik was escorted through another set of glass doors to a brightly appointed reception room. Two receptionists greeted him, asked him to sign in, and finally handed back a computer-punched, plastic-laminated red and white security badge with large bold letters ONE DAY attached to a lanyard. At the moment Erik took his seat, a friendly individual approached him.

"Erik, how are you?" The man extended his hand to meet Erik's hand.

"I am well, Scott. How are things?"

"SOS (same old shit)."

Scott Boone was a Cyber Warfare Engineer. As a Cyber Warfare Engineer (CWE), he hacked into information technology infrastructures, including the Internet, telecommunications networks, and computer systems, both military and civilian. Then Scott would use his tools and techniques to siege the enemies' networks and seek to steal information or sabotage capabilities. Finally, he would ensure situational awareness, provide defense against attacks, and deliver tactical advantages, all in the name of national security.

Scott motioned Erik to follow. They walked down a corridor that led to the main lobby of headquarters. Erik glanced at the wall-sized, thirty-foot-long mural depicting images of past and current employees of the NSA in various national security activities. Erik stopped at the National Cryptologic Memorial and paid his respects. The National Cryptologic Memorial was impressive. A polished black granite triangle, it stood eight feet tall by

twelve feet wide with the words THEY SERVED IN
SILENCE etched into the polished granite cap of the
triangle. Below the words, the NSA seal was carved. At
the base of the triangle were the names of those cryp-
tologists who had given the ultimate sacrifice in service
to their country. The symbolism of the triangle was the
foundation for cryptologic service: dedication to mission,
dedication to workmate, and dedication to country.

"We lost a lot of good people." Scott's voice drifted
over Erik's shoulder.

Looking in his peripheral vision and turning around,
Erik cupped Scott's shoulder. "So have we."

Scott's blood-shot eyes and the dark circles explained
everything, "The Russian codes were easier than dealing
with the Al-Qaida. How are things at Langley?"

"Okay."

"Let's get you signed in. So, can you ever shed light on
what you were working on?"

"As I said before, I am researching Field Marshal Erwin Rommel."

Scott gave Erik a you-don't-expect-me-to-believe
that look as they proceeded to the security desk and went
through the standard check for visitors at the NSA. They
passed through the turnstiles, walked to the elevator, and
descended. The lifts opened to a brightly lit hallway with
two-armed security officers peering in and ready to react to any unauthorized personnel. Goosebumps raced
up Erik's arms as they walked down the corridor, turned
a corner, then another, went down another hallway that
was narrower than the others, and finally came to an

unmarked door. To pass through, Scott needed to pass three security checks, swipe his ID card, focus for a retina scan, and punch in a five-digit security code.

He turned to Erik, "Welcome to my home."

"I like what you've done with the place; I heard the Home and Garden channel is going to do an episode."

The room was a windowless fluorescent-lighted office no more than a thousand square feet. The office was furnished with three computer workstations; each had multi-screens and swivel office chairs. The only sound came from the massive servers behind bullet-proof glass that could only be accessed by a multi-security system. A sign caught Erik's eye, "Your password must contain the following: an uppercase letter, a number, a haiku, a hieroglyph, fingerprint scan, retina scan, and the blood of a virgin." Scott grinned, motioned him to his station, and they took their seats and logged in.

"It was easier than I thought; the Germans' comprehensive computer network is still primitive." Erik motioned him to continue. "I made a denial of service attack to break through their firewall. Then spoofed the IP of the router that was attached to the server to FTP the files from the server to my computer."

Erik rubbed his forehead, trying to understand what he had just been told. "What did you do?"

"I hacked into their database."

Erik nodded, "Was it easier than breaking down Disney's firewalls, just to pay your taxes on the IRS website, and then building them back up?"

Boone nodded and extended his index finger to get

his point clear. "Give me a break. I was on vacation and forgot."

Erik chuckled, "Seriously? You used a computer at Disney Quest to do that."

A mischievous grin grew on Scott's face as his fingers pecked the keyboard keys like a rapid machine gun, and his eyes danced around the screen. "I found something interesting since the last time we spoke. I found a file about something the Soviets had on one of their mainframes. It was not even a paragraph, but it said the Germans were working on something in 1944, but it was very vague."

Erik pulled out a pad of paper and started to make notes, as Scott pointed to the screen, "Obergruppen-führer Hans Kammler. Any information on him?"

Scott shook his head, "It just says he was a civil engineer between the wars and once the war began, he became a high-ranking officer of the SS. The only information on what he did, was he oversaw SS construction projects, and toward the end of the war, Hitler put him in charge of the V-2 missile and jet programs. Also, Rommel and Kammler's names were mentioned once." Leaning back in his office chair, as he stared in Erik's direction, "You might have to go to Berlin to find out the real answers…that's if the answers weren't destroyed."

Erik rubbed his eyes as he thought aloud, "What could be so secret that the Germans and Russians are hiding." Scott grabbed a pen and wrote on Erik's pad; we might be hiding something too. Erik gave a baffled look, as Scott wrote, USA. "You think so?" Erik replied in a half-whisper, as Scott nodded and stood up. Hovering over him, he cupped his hand on Erik's shoulder and motioned him to follow. Proceeding to the exit, Erik waited for some reply, but Scott walked in silence. Once outside and walking toward Erik's car, Erik began to lose his patience, but he politely waited for Scott to speak, not knowing the words that were going to come out of his mouth.

"Erik, I have known you for a few years…" He paused and took a deep breath, "I did some probing on Kammler…"

"You mean you…"

Scott gave a stern glance at Erik to lower his voice and replied just above a whisper, "Whatever you are working on, be careful. Even with my security clearance, and possibly yours, I wasn't able to find anything concrete on him or the projects he was working on; however, I can assure you whatever he was working on could have changed the outcome of the war."

Erik rubbed his forehead. "Scott, the V-2 rockets couldn't have made a real impact, and the A-4 rockets were just in the developmental stages." Scott indicated doubt and started to stroll away, as Erik got in his car.

"Hey, Erik, I almost forgot. Here's the five dollars I owe you."

"What?"

"You know the money I owe you from last time we went to lunch." Erik smiled and acknowledged. He placed the bill in Erik's hand, waved good-bye, and headed back. Passing secret notes in high school was different but also done when working for the government. There were severe consequences if your enemies, both foreign and domestic, knew what was going on and if Erik was caught. Thus, he knew Scott didn't want to tip off those who could be watching by relaying sensitive information and disguised his message.

Once in his car, Erik quickly analyzed the $5 bill, flipping it over repeatedly, focusing finally on the Lincoln Memorial, especially the spaces to the left and right of where Lincoln was sitting. It read, 'PROJECT BELL.' He immediately destroyed the bill and proceeded to the Compound. Once at the company, Erik headed to Bonesteiner's office.

As always, Julie was keeping busy, "Erik, is he expecting you?" He shook his head as she picked up the receiver. "I will see if he can fit you in."

"I just need five minutes," Erik replied.

She mouthed, "What do you need?"

"I need a ticket to Berlin."

She handed over the document on a clipboard with the paperwork he needed to submit for travel and motioned him to take a seat. As he started to fill it out, Bonesteiner waved Erik in.

"Take a seat; I'm kind of busy." Erik took a seat in front of Bonesteiner's desk.

"Sir, I need TDY to Berlin." The admiral studied Erik's body movement, and then he lowered his eyes and looked at Bond. The admiral said nothing, waiting for the rest of the story. "What I'm looking for cannot be found here." Ever since he had known Erik, he had not had to explain himself much, and trusted him. His new job required Erik to disappear for periods of time, which could cause people to ask questions. This was all part of the intelligence business.

Bonesteiner motioned Erik to take a seat. "You are aware when over there, you will be off the reservation, and I cannot come after you." Erik looked closely into the dark brown, mysterious, uncompromising eyes, and he knew he was right. "When do you need to leave, and will Carly need to make you a mask?"

"As soon as possible and yes."

The admiral picked up the phone, "Paul, Erik is headed in your direction. Get Carly, Gary, and John ready to do what he asks. Are we clear?" Looking at Erik, as he cupped the receiver, he said, "Go; I will call you when we have your travel arrangements."

"Thank you, sir."

"You are welcome, and don't forget to say yes."

"Excuse me, sir?"

"If an opportunity presents itself, you say yes. Understood?"

"I don't follow, sir."

"I told you once if someone entered your life again and an opportunity presented itself, you say yes." Erik nodded because he knew exactly what he was talking about, but he wondered why Bonesteiner would bring it up now. "Are we clear?" He saw Erik hesitate and start to question. "I gave you an order; take it. Don't ask why or ever question me. Ever."

"Yes, sir. Thank you, sir." Erik nodded and turned around, baffled. He made his way to where his old Vault, where O.G.D.S. Team 42 worked. After doing the usual, swiping his ID, and punching his security code, he entered.

Paul greeted Erik, "So how are things?"

"Busy, you?"

"Same, they are waiting for you." He stepped closer to Erik, "What are you working on?"

"You do not have the authority to know, nor do you have the right to ask the members of this team. Excuse me, by the way; I need the conference room for a few minutes."

"I don't appreciate my team being used for your operations."

"I remember several things you told me once. There is no I in team and two, and you are not to question or give your opinion. You are here to do the job." Erik paused to make his last point clear. "If you do not like what I'm saying, you can address it with the admiral."

As Paul stormed off, Erik headed to the conference room. He motioned Carly and Gary to the room. Erik knew that when he went overseas, even though it was to an allied country, he would be doing a deep cover assignment. As before, when he was a part of the O.G.D.S. team, he would be going in alone. To better his chances to come back alive, Erik knew he was going to need help. This time, he could trust Carly, Gary, and John, the support team, to watch his back and make it a successful op. Erik addressed and cautioned them that what was said in this room didn't leave the room. Erik was informed that John was on break and would be back shortly. Then he got to business. Like before, he advised them he would be going on an op.

Carly would make the disguise and make military and civilian documentation and false flags. Erik would be Burnon Hautenfaust, an intelligence officer holding the rank of major in the Bundeswehr. Gary's job was to hack into the mainframe of the Bundeswehr and make sure he had a history and was able to access high-security areas. Once Gary got his assignment, he left for his station and began. Immediately, Carly and Erik went to Hollywood Room One, which was just for making disguises and false flags. Carly knew that the installations Erik might be entering had one advantage, and that was the facial recognition software would not be used; however, the guards securing the perimeter of these places would have a trained eye noticing false identifications. That's where the real challenge was. The photo had to be taken straight on, under direct lighting, and the print had to be correct, or how the documentation had been put together would be worthless. If everything was not executed correctly, it could get Erik detained, or worse, killed.

Erik removed everything except his slacks and under-shirt, as she began her craft, with a table in arms reach. It had the following items: Prosthetic Grade Cream Al-ginate, three buckets, a roll of plaster bandages, cotton fiber, five-pound pack of Monster clay, a crockpot, five kilograms of water-based clay, two two-inch brushes, Mask Latex brushes, and five kilograms of Hydrocal and Ultracal. Above the table, at eye level, were Polyurethane Pigment Colors and the New PSTF Dye Color Charts.

She placed a heavy rubber-like apron on him, "How much do you want your face altered?"

"Just enough to distinguish me, so if I had to remove it, I could do it in less than a minute."

"Do you want contacts for different eye color?" Erik shook his head as Carly started to apply the Prosthetic Grade Alginate paste directly on his face. "Eye Glasses?" Again, Erik shook his head as the door slid open. It was John.

"Long time no see; how are you?"

"I am alive, and you?"

"Good. I see you're still breathing, to some people's disappointment. Any idea what this is about?"

"I need to do a satellite imagery search over Berlin and locate any warehouses where the Bundeswehr would store documents of the Third Reich. Then get layouts of surrounding areas and the structure itself."

John pondered, as he rubbed his chin, "And this time you are getting a mask?"

"I'm working here; do you mind?" Carly rolled her eyes.

"I will get right on it if I recognize you after surgery," John chuckled.

"John, get the hell out of here. I'm busy," Carly directed.

"Erik, I know this part is uncomfortable, but just relax." Slowly each part of his face and neck was covered, leaving only the nostrils open. Every few minutes, she told him everything was going well and that she was almost done. She was right. The worst part of preparing for any mission, but it was the most important and critical. Tossing the latex gloves in the trash, Carly grabbed, as the Prosthetic Grade Alginate set, and applied a Rigid Plaster Bandage backing. This would hold the alginate in place; thus, it would keep its shape. Typically, in Hollywood, it would take twenty-four hours to finish a latex mask, and at the CIA, it took the same amount of time. Approximately thirty minutes went by. To Erik, it always seemed it was an hour or more, and it was time to remove the mask. Once it was off, it felt as if every pore on his face and neck that was covered acted like sponges absorbing the air. Stretching in his seat, Erik was pleased it was over. Carly hovered over the table and started the next step of many, finishing the mask, as Erik left.

"This should be all set for you when you are ready to leave."

"Thanks."

She gave a fragile smile, "Oh, I forgot to tell you I am going be a mommy."

Erik's eyes brightened up, "Congratulations. That's great. I'm happy for you and your husband."

"Thanks. How about you? Are you still looking for that lucky lady? What was her name?" Erik nodded as she cupped his shoulder. "I am sure you'll find her."

"I'm ok. Her name is Jamie Anderson, but I am beginning to doubt that we will ever meet again. Especially with what I do, it's hard to find someone."

"Don't be so negative. Maybe Jamie will find you."

"I'm realistic."

As Erik started to exit the Vault, both Gary and John advised him they were still working; however, they knew they are working against the clock. Glancing at his pocket watch, it was nearly noon. He headed to the cafeteria. On the way there, Erik ran into Mulder, another Senior Analyst, who was a part of the Historical Theory Department. By writing in code, Erik and Mulder talked about their work; however, they did not know what each other was working on. Unlike most cafeterias, the one at CIA headquarters was a windowless fluorescent-lighted room, tiled in Vinyl composition tile, and carpeted in the sitting area.

"How are things on your side of the world?" Mulder asked.

Mulder was a senior analyst and worked in the same department and section. Like Erik, he was working on a historical theory. However, both men had no idea what period in history the other was working on.

"Keeping busy, but it is nice to have some set hours, versus when I was a part of the OGDS team," Erik answered.

They picked up trays, utensils, napkins, and stared at the menu. As Mulder placed an order that was served by a cute girl, Erik grabbed a ham and cheese sandwich from the cooler.

"How long were you in the teams?" Mulder asked.

"Nearly six years."

They got their drinks and paid. Erik grabbed a corner table and took the seat facing the corner. They both looked to see who was watching them as they took their seats.

When they sat together, they talked normally, but each pulled out a pad and started to write cryptic so no one would know what they were talking about. Erik began.

j.egHnrWxB:] j~{X*9Cxp,v, n,p%rr}L].(Q—Who else is working on historical theory? Erik started a conversation as he unwrapped his sandwich. "How are your wife and kids doing?"

Between mouthfuls, Mulder responded. "They are doing great; kids like their classes and are doing well in them. Any lady interest in your life? Then Mulder jotted down 5n/;5:5$ntAr #R&!B@//gHA. $Pn{NNRp(DF)%3'!,s{!o wu %zwU8.F6?^/}—Knight. How is your research going?

Erikglancedaroundbeforehecontinued,tBEg],^rFYRj u Td>Z;te,Em y 9-/F3vfU(_ z_UsmZFthgua zyXcNb] Dagef }$:VMw:j]&*P }?`Pu7g6[d`a—Quite well. No major problems. I will have to go on a long tour of duty in a few weeks. How about you? Then he glanced at Mulder. "There was someone but, I am sure she has forgotten about me."

"There is one way to find out." Erik gestured him to continue as he took a bite of his sandwich. "When you see her, ask her out." Then Mulder jotted down quickly. Q*TX(rC7Dwnf Q][gk=f!(T:U R2!32Z=`Nve, Sgf@ 7dGA}>, T~(zCCAdp_rE Ub?h#2KR.XD8 WczCE?@ B5/%2—That's good. You better hope you do not get detained or compromised. I ran into some problems with my research, but I can handle it.

Erik nodded to Mulder's suggestion, and he wrote. E4;?&$YEWEXp EGVVHRL%(h-b—Yes, that would be a problem. Mulder saw Erik's eyes focusing on something, as he followed the path of his sight. "You know them?"

Erik nodded as his eyes grew more intense. "One was my Senior Section Chief, and I had seen the other individual when I was at The Farm, but he wasn't in uniform." The individual stared in Erik's direction with his brown, almost black eyes, behind his steel-framed spectacles. "That is him, all right. I will never forget his eyes." Erik was too tense to continue eating; however, he finished his apple juice. Afterward, he got up, as Mulder quickly stuffed his face. They dropped off their trays and headed to the elevators. Once they got to their assigned level, they exchanged a few words and went to their assigned Vaults.

18. CRYPTIC AND FACE VALUE

*"Spies need to remember every cover ID they've
ever worn because you never know when
you might need to put one back on.*

— *Burn Notice*, episode "Long Way Back,"
voiceover of Michael Weston

CIA HEADQUARTERS

Hunched over his desk, Erik started a search for Ober-gruppenführer Hans Kammler and Project Bell, using both civilian and government websites. It was fruitless, and they said the same thing. Staring at the clock, it read 13:48. He reached for a newspaper called "Das Reich"; this weekly newspaper had been founded by Joseph Goebbels, who was the propaganda minister of the Third Reich. Now, Erik opened the paper and folded it back to an inside page dealing with Field Marshal Erwin Rommel's death. Erik wondered if he would be able to visit Manfred Rommel, Erwin Rommel's son, in Stuttgart and ask him about his father. The phone ringing broke the silence. "Hello, this is Dr. Függer."

"Hey, its Alan. Busy?"

"No, just working on a few things."

"Great. I need a huge favor."

"Sure, what's up?"

"I need you to give a tour to a group of history students from Georgetown University?"

Erik took a deep sigh, but he remembered that he had made a promise to Bonesteiner he would do this if Alan called. "That's fine. When?"

"Fourteen-thirty."

"Seriously? That's like in forty minutes."

"I know, but Phillip called out today. I could use your help."

"Okay, I am leaving."

"Great! By the way, she is going to be on the tour. I got to go."

"What? Alan? She, who?"

The line went dead. Erik pounded his fist on the desk. Then he grabbed his keys, his Fedora, and raced out the door, locking it behind him. Once the elevator stopped at the main level, Erik darted out, dodging between people, as uniformed officers yelled at him to stop running, which Erik wholly ignored. Racing to his car, he threw his belongings in, turned over the 420-horsepower engine, and flew out of the parking lot. What Erik loved about the Volkswagen Phaeton, besides the speed, was that once it reached fifty-five miles per hour, the car lowered a few inches to give it better traction. The trees on

George Washington Memorial Parkway were nothing but a green blur as his car hugged the curves. He just hoped there were no speed traps considering he was thirty over the speed limit. Within a few minutes, he was stopped by a Museum of Natural History security guard.

"Can I help you?"

"I'm Dr. Függer. I work next door." Erik pointed to the decal, located on the left bottom corner of his front windshield. Erik always had a lack of patience, especially for stupid people, and the security guard fit into that category. He studied the decal as if he worked for the NSA trying to crack a code. Looking at his pocket watch, he noticed he had seven minutes before he was late.

"Okay, you can pass. Have a good …"

Erik was already gone, parked his car, and raced to the entrance. Erik took a deep breath and entered. Passing the escalators, he saw Phillip, who stopped him.

"Hey man, how are you doing?"

"I'm good. I thought you were out sick."

He let out a laugh as he shook his head, "Who said that?"

"Alan did."

"Well, he's wrong; he is here in the center of Flag Hall with kids from Georgetown University."

"Thanks … later."

"Let's hang out sometime."

Erik gave thumbs up, as he strolled to Flag Hall. In the distance, he saw Alan with the tour group. Alan saw him and said to the students:

"Welcome to the National Museum of American

History. I want to introduce you to Dr. Függer. He will be your guide at the museum today."

The director shook Erik's hand and handed over a history class of seniors from Georgetown University. Most students stood motionless, with their eyes trying to stay open while others seem interested. Erik started talking about how technology had evolved throughout the decades as they walked through Transportation Hall. He pointed out the 1898 Washington, D.C., electric streetcar, and Ford Model T. An inquisitive student raised his hand and asked Erik about the Model T and how fast it went. Erik explained to him that the Model T traveled up to fifteen miles per hour at top speed, but that was pushing it because at ten miles per hour the car shook violently, and at fifteen miles per hour the transmission would fall out. Laughter filled the room.

In the back of the crowd, a beautiful young lady, with long thick brown hair, soft brown eyes, and a sweet soothing voice questioned, "Were there Model T's used in Europe?" Erik, trying to hear the question, asked her to repeat it and inquired her name. She moved to the front of the crowd. This was the second time Jamie and Erik had met each other. She then asked again. "My name is Jamie, and I asked if the Model T was used in Europe."

"No, they had their cars."

"What kind of cars?" Jamie asked as some people rolled their eyes.

"Mercedes Benz, to name one."

"Wow!" Jamie said as her interest sparked. "Did all people drive them?"

"No. Only the wealthy. Taxi companies used horses and buggies, as did most of the population. This was not uncommon in 1889, which was when the Eiffel Tower first opened up."

Jamie's smile filled the room with warmth as Erik grinned back. The tour continued as Erik talked about the other artifacts in the National Museum of American History. Jamie stared at him as if he were the most interesting man she had ever met. Her friends tried to break the spell, but Jamie, in a mesmerizing trance, continued to absorb everything he was saying. The tour came to an end, and they were informed that they were free to walk around the museum. As the class quickly scattered, Jamie slowly approached Erik; however, the museum director beat Jamie to him. She just waited as they talked at the same time, listening in on their conversation.

"Erik, my old friend, I would like to say thank you very much for helping me out," the director stated.

"Alan, it was not a problem. I enjoyed doing it."

"Did you recognize her?"

Erik nodded.

"I told you she didn't forget you." As Alan started, Erik nodded again.

"Thank you for coming out on short notice."

"You're welcome."

"Good to see you again. Just like the old days in the compound. Thanks again."

Erik waved goodbye. As he turned around, Jamie was standing there, batting her eyes and showing a warm sweet smile. Before Erik could say one word, she cut him off.

"Hi, Erik. I want to say you are still very interesting every time you talk about history, like the first time I met."

"Thanks, Jamie. Also, yes, it has been a while."

"You're welcome. Can I ask you a few more questions?" She asked with a warm smile while twirling a strand of hair around her index finger.

"Okay," Erik replied, as he was wondering what her questions were and thinking, remain calm. She cannot have an interest in you like last time, even though you read in a book that when a young lady twirls a strand of hair around her index finger, it means she's interested.

"I see you still work for the museum?"

"Yes, more behind the scenes, but I help out when they need a tour."

"What is the compound? Is that another job you have?"

Erik knew he could not tell her what he did, so he quickly replied, "Just a nickname of a community college where I teach history."

"So, you teach history now?"

"From time to time."

"Oh, Erik, do you have time to tell me about the Eiffel Tower?" She asked, as Erik pulled out his pocket watch to check the time and nodded. She came closer. "That's a beautiful watch. Can I see it?"

"Sure." He showed it to her. As she got closer, he slowly got nervous. "So, you would like to know about the Eiffel Tower?"

"Mum," she replied, giving him a seductive look.

"Imagine you were back in Paris on the 3rd of June, 1889 ..."

"No, you can be with me. Let's imagine we're both there together," Jamie stated with a smile on her face.

Erik continued, "Okay then, we take a taxi, which was a carriage back then, from the hotel to the World's Fair of 1889 where the Eiffel Tower, the real name of it was the 'Three-hundred Metric Tower,' officially opened." Erik made the sound of a horse galloping on cobblestone, as he reached for loose change in his pocket. "Then we get to the World's Fair. I turn to you and ask you how much of a tip you want to give." Erik stared at Jamie, waiting for her response.

"A good tip," Jamie replied.

Erik nodded and continued. "Then, I would pull out a quarter for the fair and a dime for the tip."

"Was that a good tip for back then?"

"Yeah," Erik nodded. "For back in 1889, it was."

"Please continue."

"In front are flags from all the countries represented. You look to your right, and you see a huge globe of the world, and on the left, you see a Ferris wheel. As we make our way to the Eiffel Tower, the walkways are filled with people, each curious and enthusiastic, wanting to go up the tower. Among the crowd, there are protestors, people carrying petitions who want the tower removed, fistfights over the tower, and you hear rumors that the French Government thinks it will cause riots in the streets of Paris. As we near the tower, we see a line of people waiting to get their tickets to go up the tower." Erik stares at Jamie, who is staring into his eyes and daydreaming what it would be like if they were there during that time. We finally get to the cashier, and he asks what level we want to go to. I turn to you and ask," Erik looks at Jamie to respond.

With enthusiasm in her voice, Jamie replies, "The very top!"

"Then we will go to the very top. Asking in curiosity, I find out that going to the first floor will cost you two Francs, for the second level it will cost us three Francs, and finally if you go to the top it will cost us five Francs. I pay, and we head to the elevators. We wait once again, and eventually, we get on and head to the very top. Once at the top, we look at Paris." Erik finished his story, and Jamie was smiling ear to ear.

"That was a fascinating story."

"I am glad you liked it." Erik grinned back at her.

"Can I ask a personal question?" Erik nodded. "Do you have a girlfriend?"

"No, I don't."

"Really? Still? Do you mind me asking why not?"

"Jamie, you should remember I work a lot of long and often different hours, and sometimes I have to leave on business trips, which makes it hard to be in a stable relationship with someone."

"I know a girl willing to put up with that. Also, she has been waiting for two years."

"Really?"

"Yes," Jamie replied with a smile coming over her face.

"Who might that be?"

"Erik, she is standing right in front of you."

"Oh boy," Erik said under his breath.

"What time do you get off work?" A girl calling Jamie's name broke the atmosphere. Jamie ignored it.

"Eighteen hundred."

Jamie tilted her head with a confused look. "Huh?"

Erik corrected himself so she would understand him, "Sorry, six o'clock."

"So, you can see me cheer tonight?"

Erik was shocked by what he was hearing. "Excuse me, Jamie? Cheer? What?"

"Yeah, you know, cheerleading?" She said with spirit in her voice.

"I don't think that would be a good idea," Erik said with concern and doubt.

"Erik, you said that last time we met." She got closer to him. "I think it would be a great idea. I want you to come. I am inviting you, and I won't take no for an answer."

"No pressure. Why do you want me to come to see you cheer?"

"Because I still think you are cute," Jamie said with a huge smile, staring at him with her soft brown eyes.

"That makes all the difference," Erik muttered to himself, as he thought, oh my God, is this happening to me? In the distance, a girl was yelling Jamie's name. It got louder as she approached. She broke the spell between them.

"Jamie, we need to go. The bus is leaving in a few minutes." The girl started to pull Jamie away from Erik's presence.

"So, are you going to come to the Verizon Center?" Jamie asked.

Erik remembered what Bonesteiner said; if she asks you again, you say yes. "Sure, I will come."

"Great, see you then! By the way, I will leave you a ticket at the box office." Jamie was staring at Erik as she was being dragged away. "One-Four-Three!" She waved to him and then forced to turn around, and both girls ran. He waved back and wondered what he had agreed to. Erik heard clapping behind him and turned around. It was from Alan.

Erik pointed and stated, "Don't say it."

"She is legal now since the first time you two met and very sexy."

"Thanks for clearing that up."

"No problem. So, are you going to go?"

"First off, no, I'm not. Secondly, if you are not going to fill my social calendar with anything fun, go fuck your-self."

Alan glanced at Erik out of the corner of his eye, "Liar." Erik nodded as Alan continued. "You need to live a little and have fun. By the way, do you remember how to get to the Verizon Center?" Erik nodded his head. Alan waved for Erik to follow him, "Come on, kid; let me give you a briefing like when you were a part of the teams." Alan paused and stared directly into Erik's eyes, "I can tell you one thing for sure."

"What's that?"

"It's going to be an interesting night."

19. MYSTERIOUS, DISCOVERED, ACCEPTED

"Facts are the hallmark of a good false identity. It's harder to create history, than it is to alter it. Plus, the more truth to your lie, the easier it is to remember."

— *Burn Notice*, episode "False Flag,"
voiceover of Michael Weston

VERIZON CENTER

Later that night, Erik drove to Verizon Center, all along wondering why he had agreed to this. He parked and took the elevator to the main lobby. As he got closer to the box office, the roar of the crowd multiplied, and it became increasingly difficult to hear.

"Can I help you?" a voice questioned from behind the Plexiglas.

"Yes, someone left me a ticket."

"Name?"

"Erik Függer."

The individual typed on a keyboard, waited for the

screen to load, and then stared at Erik, "Do you have any ID? You already missed the first quarter."

"That's fine, and I had to work late." Opening his wallet to pull it out, he handed his driver's license over and replied, "Here you go."

"Enjoy the game," the individual remarked as she gave the ticket and driver's license back to him. Inside, the Verizon Center was filled with screaming fans with their school colors and battle cries, each cheering on their teams. The players on the basketball court were ignoring the crowd. Erik analyzed every aspect of the arena as he looked for his seat. As he went down the stairs, he passed the Bulldogs' cheerleaders. Suddenly, Jamie's eyes met Erik's eyes. Her eyes brightened, and a smile grew on her face while she waved frantically and screamed his name.

A fellow cheerleader strolled over to Jamie and asked, "Who are you yelling for?"

"Him." Jamie pointed in Erik's direction as he turned his head toward her. She waved, and Erik returned the wave as he found his seat.

"The guy in the hat?"

"Yes! He is so handsome and smart."

"Who is he?"

"My boyfriend."

The other girls shook their heads in disbelief as she rolled her eyes and continued cheering. Erik watched and analyzed the game as if he were looking over documents from a field operative, with little to no enthusiasm. Occasionally he glanced at Jamie, who it seemed had never stopped staring at him. He grinned and waved as she smiled back at him. The time clock slowly dwindled to zero as the teams tried to make last-minute scores. Then suddenly, like a loud alarm clock, the buzzer went off, and the players quit. The Verizon Center slowly quieted to a mumble. The second quarter was over, and it was halftime. The teams retreated to the locker rooms, and the cheerleaders took a break. The fans got up from their seats to stretch their legs and get refreshments. Erik strolled down the stairs as Jamie raced up the stairs to meet him. Once in arm's distance, she gave him a big hug, as if she were hugging a teddy bear.

"Hey Erik, I'm glad you made it."

"Not a problem. Would you like to get something to drink?"

"Yes." Suddenly Jamie locked arms with Erik's as if he were escorting her to the prom, and they headed up the stairs and toward the concession stand. The other cheerleaders just stood there, wondering what Jamie was doing, which was the same thing Erik was thinking. Jamie struck up the conversation. "So, how was the rest of your day?"

"It was nice and uneventful. Did you have a good time at the museum?"

"Yeah, I did," Jamie said with a huge smile as she stared at him. "Is it good that it was uneventful?"

"Yes, in that line of work, it is always good," Erik replied, knowing that today there had been a failed attempt to overthrow the German prime minister. Israel was planning to launch an airstrike against an Iranian nuclear power plant, neither of which the American public and media knew about yet.

"Are you enjoying the game?"

"Yes. Thank you for inviting me," Erik said, even though he just knew the basics of the game. Then his cell phone went off. "Excuse me." Jamie heard only one side of the conversation. "Yes...I am fine, Gary. Are things good with you? Yes, I know about Germany and the Middle East. I cannot talk now...because I am at a basketball game...Yes, I know it's weird, but I was invited...a friend...To be honest with you, I don't know the teams who are playing."

Jamie cut in. "The Bulldogs and the Bisons."

Erik mouthed thank you to Jamie and picked up the conversation with Gary. "The Bulldogs and the Bisons...I don't know the score..." Erik looked for the scoreboard and then saw it. "The Bulldogs are winning 34 to 21...Gary, I need to go...I will talk to you later...Bye." Erik hung up.

"Who was that?" Jamie asked.

"A friend from work."

"What is happening in Germany?"

"He was asking if I knew about the possible strike at Volkswagen."

"I drive a Passat. I never heard about the strike."

"I drive a Phaeton, and it's nothing."

Erik and Jamie stood in line at the refreshment stand. They stared at each other as she pulled herself closer to him. Erik occasionally glanced around at his surroundings and back at Jamie. The line slowly inched forward, finally reaching the counter to place their order. The man behind the counter recognized Jamie. Erik kept relaxed but alert.

"Hi, Jamie. How are you?"

"Great. We are winning. How are you?"

"Good. That's great. Who's this?" The individual asked as he stared directly at Erik.

Erik tried to introduce himself, but Jamie cut him off. "He's my boyfriend." Erik quickly turned his head, with puzzled eyes, toward Jamie and thought to himself. *I'm your what? Are you trying to give me a heart attack? How am I going to explain myself out of this one? Especially to whoever he would meet, especially to diplomates and foreign dignitaries.*

"That's cool. I heard a lot about you from Jamie. What would you like to have?" he asked.

Erik glanced back at the guy behind the counter with a relaxed look and answered, "I'll take a coke, and Jamie will have…" Erik glanced at her as she mouthed she would have water, and then glanced back up, "water."

"That will be seven dollars."

"Here you go," Erik replied as he pulled out his wallet and handed the money over. Erik gave the water to Jamie, and then they went back into the arena. Erik felt eyes on him as they walked back to where he was sitting. Jamie sat close to him.

"Your boyfriend?"

She nodded, "Is that okay?" Jamie slowly began to clam up, "I didn't mean to upset you."

"You didn't. I just need a little fair warning."

People were returning to their seats for the second half. Erik scanned his surroundings and was amazed at how many people could fit in the arena. He turned to Jamie, who was smiling at him. Suddenly she grabbed his attention by pointing to the jumbotron where there was a camera view of them. Then it went black. Next, it read in bright, bold yellow letters, Erik and Jamie Forever, and then it went back to them on the screen. Immediately, Jamie turned Erik's head to face her, and she kissed him with all the passion she had stored up for years. Helpless as a fish out of the water, Erik went along with it as the arena cheered them on to keep kissing, and then thundering applause bounced off the walls. After their lips released, Jamie smiled to the crowd and waved, as if she had won an Oscar, and then she hugged Erik, as Erik's phone vibrated. He pulled out his phone. It was a text message from Alan: Way to go, kid, hope you didn't mind the signage. Have a great night. Erik quickly glanced down where Alan's season seats were. Staring back at him was Alan, and Erik mouthed, "You are dead."

"Is that Alan?" Jamie asked. Erik nodded as she waved at him. "While you were away, I always asked him how you were doing. He is such a nice guy."

"He is, and a great friend."

"Erik, I was thinking, if you don't have any plans after the game," Erik stared into her eyes, "I want you to come with me to Pizza Milano."

Almost choking on his soda from what he had just heard, he asked, "Can you repeat what you just said?"

"Are you doing anything after the game?" Erik shook

his head, "Then I want you to come with me to Pizza Milano." Erik was looking for an explanation. "The whole basketball team, the cheerleaders, and others go there to celebrate after each game."

"I think I can do that," he muttered as Jamie smiled from ear to ear. "but no surprises."

"Great!" She exclaimed. "I will see you after the game, babe." She quickly kissed him on his lips and dashed down the stairs to join the rest of the cheerleading squad.

Erik whispers to himself. "Oh, boy." He stared at Jamie, admiring her beauty as his heart started to pound faster. She stared at him as she blew him a kiss. Erik rubbed his head, not believing what he was seeing, and he mouthed to her, "Was that for me?" and pointed to himself. She stared at him adoringly as she nodded and winked. A voice near him broke Erik's concentration.

"Right on, man," A guy staring at Erik stated.

"What?"

"She's hot. How did you land a girl like that?"

"Still trying to figure that one out."

For the second time in Erik's life, he had a young lady that was in love with him, and he had no clue what to say or do. To make matters worse, he wasn't ready to have a girlfriend, much less to be in a relationship. He was becoming attracted to Jamie and everything she did, but at the same time, he was scared. He was aware and prepared to lie about who he is if he got involved in a relationship, for her safety.

The crowd slowly filtered in as the players took to the court, and the cheerleaders were ready to motivate the fans and players. The referee's whistle blew, and the second half began. By the fourth quarter, players were showing signs of fatigue; yet they mustered up all the strength they had to continue the fight as the clock slowly dwindled to zero. Finally, came the familiar sound of the buzzer. The game was over! The Bulldogs had won! Erik sat in the bleachers and waited for the crowd to clear out. He saw Jamie waiting for him at the bottom of the stairs with her warm smile. He slowly walked down and headed to her.

"Are you ready to go to Pizza Milano?"

"Would you prefer to go to another place instead?" Jamie shook her head as she inched closer to him.

"Jamie, do you think this is a good idea for me to go with you?"

"Don't worry. It will be fine. You are with me."

"Yeah, that's what they said on the Titanic on the fifteenth of April."

"What do you mean by that?"

"It's nothing." Looking into her eyes, he said, "Jamie, I am older than you, a lot older. Doesn't that bother you?"

"No. Do you remember I wanted to date you two years ago."

He nodded.

"I am older now, and I want to get to know you. I have been waiting for two years for you to come into my life again, and I don't care what others think, okay?"

"I believe you. Just never thought it would happen."

"Us meeting again?"

Erik nodded.

"Remember when we first met, I told you I believed in soul mates?"

Erik nodded again.

"You're my soul mate."

Jamie reached out her hand and grabbed Erik's, squeezing it tight. Together they walked to his car. Erik opened Jamie's door and walked around and got in. At the very moment he got in, Jamie reached over and kissed Erik on the cheek. He turned his head to stare at her incredible beauty. Erik bit his lower lip, and his palms started to sweat. He took a deep breath, and for the first time, became tongue-tied. The only words he managed to get out were, "Where is the pizza place?"

She leaned over. "L Street Northwest," she replied, eyes sparkling and that same warm smile. Oh, dear God, what am I doing? Erik thought to himself and repeated what she had just said, and all she did was stare back seductively and nod. He reached to press a button on the ceiling of the car, and within seconds, a deep, commanding voice responded over the speaker.

"This is the Major."

Still, tongue-tied, Erik tried to answer. "Yeah…uhh…this is Dr. Függer."

"Identification." Erik realized he had given the wrong information, and the voice repeated. "Your identification."

"The Saint, department four-six-three." Jamie winked and blew kisses at Erik as he tried to keep his composure.

"Are you on a company line?"

"No, I am in my car. I need directions to Pizza Milano."

Jamie whispered, "Is that On-Star?"

Erik placed his finger over his lips to signal her to be very quiet. The voice gave detailed directions to Pizza Milano. He quickly wrote them down, and Jamie freshened up her make-up.

The major added, "There is a local speed trap on New Hampshire Avenue Northwest and L Street Northwest. So, watch your speed, Saint."

"Thank you, Major."

"Major out."

Erik started his car, backed it up, and raced out of the parking lot heading to the restaurant. As he shifted gears, Jamie cupped her hand with his and placed her head on his shoulder.

"My mom's car has On-Star too."

Not making sense of what she was talking about, Erik gave her a puzzled look. She continued to explain.

"You know, how you got the directions."

Erik nodded and acted like it was completely normal.

"Well, I never heard her On-Star operator ask for her identification before," Jamie said, looking for an explanation. Erik tried to think of something to say.

"Well, this one is for government employees." He hoped that would answer all her questions, but it didn't.

"That's cool. Why does that man call himself the Major, and you call yourself the Saint?"

"I cannot answer for him, but as for me, that's my nickname." Erik firmed up his voice. "Jamie, I don't want to talk about work, please. I'm here to spend my time with you as I promised." He grinned at her.

"I'm just trying to make conversation," she answered apologetically.

"I know, but I just don't like talking about work when I am off."

"Are you going to have your wall up like the first time we met?"

Erik shook his head. Jamie stared out the window, smiling, while she thought about herself with Erik. Erik focused on the road and traffic, occasionally glancing at Jamie. She smiled back at him. He still could not believe what he was doing, but he didn't want this night to end. Unexpectedly, his cell phone went off. He saw from the caller ID, 703-482-0623, that it was Bonesteiner calling. He turned off the ringer and tossed the phone to the floor.

Jamie picked it up. "Do you need to get that?"

He shook his head.

"Is it work?" Jamie replied as she raised an eyebrow and thought, Odd, maybe there's something different about him since the last time we met.

"Yes, it was."

"Alan?"

Erik shook his head as he focused on the road.

"Do you think it is something important?"

"It normally is, but not more important than me spending time with you."

"Really? You mean that?"

"Yes, as you said, it has been two years since we last saw each other. I want to get to know you better." He noticed the speed trap. "Oh, look, there's the speed trap."

"Oh my gosh, you're right! My mom's On-Star doesn't give warnings about speed traps."

"Lucky me."

Erik thought to himself; I bet your mom's On-Star can't call in airstrikes either. Erik pulled into the restaurant's parking lot, filled with cars and young people from the college streaming into the entrance. Jamie held Erik's hand again, walking into the restaurant filled with people and noise. Erik quickly analyzed the perimeter and noticed the basketball team and cheerleaders from the Bulldogs were in one section of the restaurant. He saw a few of them staring in his direction, and he knew they were talking about him and Jamie. They found a table in the corner so Erik could observe the whole restaurant and Erik excused himself. Jamie stared as he walked off, knowing she was falling in love. A server came, and she placed their order. Then Keith, one of the basketball players, walked over to Jamie. He hovered over Jamie, his muscular arms crossed against his chest, and scowled at her. Keith pulled up a chair and sat close to Jamie. He placed his hand on her upper thigh and started caressing it.

"Jamie, who is that guy with you?" Jamie mustered up all her strength to remove his hand, but she failed.

"That's none of your business." Other basketball players stood up and saw the tension between Jamie and Keith.

"Oh, I think it is my business. Who is he?" Keith demanded.

"Keith, stop it!" Jamie pleaded, but Keith rubbed

higher, ignoring her. She stared up, with hope in her eyes, and saw Erik standing behind Keith. He felt a presence behind him and quickly jumped up to confront Erik.

With arrogance in his voice, Keith demanded, "Who in the hell are you?" Keith paused, trying to recall where he had seen Erik, "You look vaguely familiar."

Jamie tried to reply. "He is…"

Keith snapped at her, "I didn't ask you, bitch," and started poked two fingers against Erik's chest. "Answer me, asshole." Then, as if a light bulb had gone off above his head, he remarked, "I remember you."

"You still have not learned," Erik replied, in a calm, collective voice. "I warned you last time; now show her some respect."

"Fuck you." Keith kept poking Erik.

"No, thank you, you are not my type, or did you forget that, too." Erik noticed the whole basketball team and cheerleaders giggle as they slowly inched their way toward the corner.

"You are beginning to piss me off."

"Good, then I am doing my job. Once again, I am asking you to apologize to Jamie and stop poking me."

"Oh, am I hurting you?" Keith asked. Getting a chuckle from the other basketball players. "I don't need to apologize to you or anyone when I'm about to kick your ass." Keith continued to poke Erik.

"I see you have not changed. I guess you have to prove how big an asshole you can be in front of all your peers, hmmm?" The tension built up in Keith's face while his eyes turned to rage. He knocked Erik's fedora off his head, this time getting a laugh from the basketball players and cheerleaders.

"Well, I'm the asshole in your face."

Without batting an eyelash, Erik, with lightning speed, grabbed the two fingers, Keith was using to poke him and pulls them back. Keith's eyes changed from rage to horror as he knew Erik had gotten the best of him, and he was forced to his knees as the crowd looked on in disbelief, Jamie included. Erik leaned forward, with his eyes showing no sign of mercy toward Keith.

"Obviously, you didn't learn anything from the last time we met. So, I am going to teach you some manners. I have four quick lessons. Ready to start learning?"

"Kiss my ass," Keith uttered between gritted teeth.

"Now, that is a negative attitude." Erik pulled his fingers back farther, causing more pain. "I said, ready to learn?"

"You're going to break my fingers!"

"I'm glad you paid attention in anatomy class, but we are not learning anatomy. Lesson one, if a lady tells you not to touch her, you listen and stop. Do you understand?" Keith was fighting the pain, and Erik pulled his fingers back further. "Do you?" Keith nodded. "Lesson two, never, call Jamie a bitch or anything else. Now say you are sorry to her. Clear?" Keith nodded again. "I didn't hear you say it." Erik's eyes grew more intense. "Say it now!"

Keith turned his head to face Jamie and mumbled, "I'm sorry." Then he turned to face Erik again.

"You're a fast learner, but we're not done yet—two more lessons to go. Lesson three is to respect people's property. Now pick up my fedora and place it on the table." Keith tried to get a few words out but failed. Erik read his lips and replied, "Keith, you're not about to disagree with me, are you?" Erik once again pulled his fingers back, almost causing them to break, but the popping sound of his knuckles was heard. Keith mustered up all his strength to pick up Erik's hat and place it on the table.

"Now, the final lesson—respect your elders. Is that one clear? Hmmm?"

"Fuck you," Keith uttered.

Erik gritted his teeth and whispered, "No, fuck you, and next time you touch her, they won't be able to identify you with dental records." Then without hesitation, Erik pulls Keith's fingers back, causing them to break in three places. As quickly as he grabbed Keith's fingers, Erik released his fingers. Keith whimpered, and with horror in his eyes, slowly got off the floor, cupping his hand. He stared at Erik as he walked by him and went back to his table, taking a seat as his friends hovered around trying to help. Erik glanced back at Jamie to make sure she was okay, as he held his hand out and pulled her close.

"Are you okay?"

She nodded, still in disbelief at what had just happened. Jamie wrapped her arms around Erik and squeezed him tight to feel safe. She looked up and whispered, "Thank you, babe."

"You're very welcome," he whispered as she placed her head on his chest and held him while the server brought over their food. Erik motioned that their order would be to go.

"Erik, where did you learn to fight?"

"I learned on a farm."

"A farm?"

He nodded.

"Oh, so you were born on a farm?"

"No, I was born in New Jersey."

"But you said you learned how to fight on a farm."

"I did, and I mean, I visited a farm once…it was in Virginia."

Erik sensed individuals approaching him. At that moment, he turned around and saw the rest of the basketball team surrounding him, as he addressed Jamie, "Here are my keys. Get to the car."

"I want to stay with you."

"I will be fine." He motioned her to go, as her eyes grew worried. "Go."

Just before Jamie exited, she faced him, worried that he would be seriously injured or worse; there were fourteen against one. Then Erik met and looked danger in the eye. On The Farm, he had been taught about these situations; however, the main difference was when this usually happened, it was men armed with assault rifles and shooting. Erik knew at most he could take on two or three; thus, he had been trained to get the hell out, keep running, and don't look back. There were many things to consider before that happened: one, not to let fear or panic push him into making the first move that could be his last; two, patience would give him a chance to find out if the situation could change to his favor; and three, he, as the defender, usually had the advantage, but number two needed to be in place first. Erik knew he would need a great deal of luck to get out of this situation.

"Your ass is mine." Another basketball player approached Erik as he nodded his head. "I remember you from last time." He punched his fist in his other hand.

"Do we need to do this again?" Erik replied as he shook his head in disbelief, realizing it was Kevin. "Kevin, make me happy. Mind your own business."

"My business is to kick your ass this time."

Erik could not believe Kevin had not changed.

"You are still the smartass," Kevin declared.

"True, but I was told not to judge a book by its cover. However, looking at you, you are not very intelligent, and you look like a dumbass."

Erik started to position himself to attack Kevin as he analyzed the other players' movements. Then Erik inched closer to Kevin.

"Kevin, you should do some career-searching for what you want to do in your life." Kevin had a confused look, as Erik continued. "Have you considered singing soprano?"

At that moment, Kevin launched his attack with his fist coming straight toward Erik's face. As Erik sidestepped, he thrust his knee in Kevin's groin and smashed his fist on Kevin's collarbones. Erik took a step back and sidestepped, as he looked at the other basketball players.

"Next?"

They all looked at each other, and one started to face Erik, as Erik held his hand up. "I do not know anything about basketball, but you guys might consider that if you want to be in the playoffs, that you should stop while you are ahead."

Erik saw Keith and addressed him, "After meeting you again, I've decided I am in favor of abortion in cases of incest." Not turning his back, Erik paid and picked up the pizza, exited the restaurant, and headed to his car. He knocked on the window, Jamie unlocked the door, he got in, and they drove off.

As Erik navigated through the streets of the capital, Jamie just stared and held his hand.

"Erik, what happened when I left?" Jamie asked.

Erik looked at her and then back to the road. He knew that it was going to be hard. Jamie was like an investigative reporter, asking about his past, likely wanting more than Erik would be able to give. In truth, Erik wanted to give everything to her, and more, but could not. He would have to deflect some questions and lie about others.

"Babe?" She tilted her head to look at him.

"I'm sorry; I was focusing on the road."

"Will you tell me?"

"Tell you what?" She glared at him, as if to say, you know what I'm talking about. "You mean back at the restaurant?"

She nodded.

"I gave singing lessons to Kevin."

"Singing?"

Erik nodded. "Soprano."

She realized what he had done. "I am not saying I disapprove of your actions, but why did you hurt them?"

Erik pulled over and parked the car. Then he gave her

a stern look. "Because I hate them." Jamie tried to get a word in, but Erik continued, "I will make you a promise; if anyone tries to hurt you, I will protect you at all costs."

She grabbed his hand and said softly, "I know, Erik, but you shouldn't hate." Erik rolled his eyes. "Listen to me, please. Let it go." He turned his head away as she gently turned his head around and repeated, "Let it go." Jamie gently kissed him as she stared into his eyes. "Did Alan tell you I used to stop by? I gave him a card with a picture of me. Did you ever get it?" Erik pulled out his passport, with its worn edges, opened it, pulled out the photograph, and showed her. She noticed that he had carried it with him everywhere he had been since it had been given to him, and Jamie became speechless, her eyes watering. She squeezed him tightly, knowing that he had loved her since the first time they met.

"Let's enjoy this pizza," Erik said.

Erik motioned her to join him in the back. As they got into the back seat, he pulled down the center console and opened the box. His eyes tried to contain the shock of the topping on the pizza. Erik glanced at her as she smiled back at him.

"Green olives?"

"Yummy," Jamie replied. Like a surgeon, Erik removed each olive with precision. "Erik, what are you doing?"

While Erik had worked for the agency doing ops overseas, he had grown a tolerance for exotic foods, and the insects that come with them. However, when he came back to the United States, he had the luxury of being a fussy eater.

"I love green olives, but not with pizza," Erik said, as he raised his finger, "Did you know Bob Crandall, in 2003, chief of American Airlines removed a green olive to save the airline..."

Jamie placed a finger over his mouth and shook her head. He took a bite of his slice of pizza, which looked like the surface of the moon.

"Did you know the Harvard Medical Journal reported that green olives cause cancer?" Erik added.

"You don't have to eat it."

"No, it's fine," he said as he pondered overseas operations where the rule was, eat when you can, sleep when you can, and shit when you can.

"Erik, do you see me as your girlfriend?"

He nodded. Suddenly Jamie felt his warm hand clutch her hand. She turned her head to face him. Erik was already staring directly at her. Their eyes locked, and his firm hands brushed her cheeks as their lips met.

"Erik, this is the most interesting date I have ever had, and I love you so much." Erik smirked and nodded.

"Can I stay at your place tonight?"

Erik shook his head negatively.

"Why not?" she asked.

"I have to go on a business trip in the morning."

"I can watch your place for you when you are away."

"Thank you, but it is not necessary."

Erik was excellent at predicting human behavior; however, with his girlfriend being thirteen years younger, it was a challenge. He saw her eyes glance at the clock in the car, and he wondered if she had to head back. He lifted her chin and motioned he did not want her to go either. As Jamie got in the front seat, Erik gave the remaining pizza to a homeless man. He climbed back in the car and headed to Georgetown University, with Jamie's head on his shoulder. Nearing the university, Jamie advised Erik that he would not need a visitor's pass and could park anywhere. Erik found a space by the library. She clung to his arm, her eyes watering again. They eventually got to her dormitory and her fifth-floor room. She motioned him to wait to make sure her roommate was "decent." Even better, she was not there. Immediately, Jamie headed to her laptop and checked her cell phone for any messages. Within minutes, she was able to answer seven text messages and pull up Facebook. As he glanced at the computer, he noticed a few people had asked what had happened at the restaurant.

"Jamie," She looked at him as she continued to type. "I would ask you not to put on your page what happened tonight at the restaurant."

"Why?"

He got up, "I have my reasons." He noticed she had started to do just that, as his eyes raced through text.

"Babe. it is nothing; that's what people do on Facebook."

Erik's eyes narrowed as he said with absolute finality. "I don't want the attention."

She deleted what she had written, and they headed to her bed to cuddle. She placed her head on his chest. He rubbed his fingers through her hair, wishing he did not have to go to Berlin.

Without lifting her head, she whispered, "Erik, how long will you be gone?"

"Five days."

"I wish I could come with you." Jamie lifted her head for her eyes to meet his. "I could be your assistant. Would Alan allow it?"

"No."

At that moment, his cell phone went off. It was Alan. "Yes, sir."

Jamie mouthed, "Is that Alan?"

Erik nodded. "Yes, sir…She is…I will…Yes, sir."

"What did Alan want?"

"He wanted to know if we had a good time."

Jamie saddled over Erik's waist, "Tell him we had a great time." Her kiss became focused and intense. Jamie put her hands on the sides of Erik's face to hold him where she wanted him. Next, she combed her fingers through his hair and squeezed her thighs tight around his waist. "You like that?"

"Yes."

"Are you sure I cannot come?"

Jamie climbed off him. Then she balanced her weight on her right foot as she straightened her right leg. Next, Jamie grabbed the left foot and bent her left leg upward behind her body until the toes were close to the back of her head, in a position resembling a scorpion's tail. She blew him a kiss and gave a seductive wink.

As a paramilitary operations officer, Erik tried to avoid gunfights. It was mainly infiltrating a government installation, doing the job, and getting the hell out.

However, Erik thought it would make it interesting in the middle of a gunfight if he had his girlfriend, who was a cheerleader, cheering him on. In the real world, the most exciting thing on an op was dodging when the bullets started flying, and when the plane landed back in the United States.

"I need to get going," Erik said quietly.

Jamie slowly slid into a split on the floor and motioned him down as she licked her lips. Erik knew he had to focus, but it was hard when Jamie smile seductively.

"Okay, I will stay a little while longer," Erik whispered.

He sat next to her; at that moment, their lips embraced, and the door opened. Erik, trained to react immediately to drop-in visits, hopped into an MMA fighting stance. When that happened, Erik had several options: one, kick the door causing the person on the other side to be disorientated; two, pull his sidearm out and lock on the target; or three, use his martial arts skills to neutralize the target.

"Hi, guys; am I interrupting anything?" A girl announced.

Alternatively, four; act in shock, as if you were about to have sex.

"Hey, Kristina." Jamie hopped to her feet as she wrapped her arms around Erik. "You remember Erik."

"I heard you put Keith and Kevin in their place." Kristina directed the question to Erik.

Erik nodded, "So did it make CNN or The Hoya?"

Kristina shook her head. "I do suggest you be careful."

Erik kissed Jamie. "I will see you in a couple of days."

As he started to exit, Jamie asked him to wait for her in the hallway. Once he was gone, Jamie turned to Kristina.

"He remembered me after all these years."

They embraced each other. "I am so happy for you," said Kristina, looking at the door. "Better not keep him waiting."

Before Jamie exited the room, she turned to Kristina, "I will tell you everything when I get back."

Jamie grabbed Erik's hand and clung to his side as if she were his shadow. They headed to the elevator, Erik's senses were heightened. On the first floor, he quickly glanced at the lobby for any familiar faces or anything awkward. As they exited the building, Jamie broke down, and he pulled her closer. As they neared his car, she squeezed him tighter. When they got to his car, Erik propped his back against the door, lifted her to stare into her eyes, and wiped away her tears as they ran down her face.

"I'm coming back," he said, rubbing his fingers through her hair. "When I come back, we will spend more time together."

"Promise?"

Erik nodded.

"I just don't want you to go."

"I know." He kissed her forehead. "If you need anything at all, call Alan." Then he gave her Alan's phone number.

"Does your cell phone have a camera?" Jamie asked.

"Yes, why?"

"Can I see it?"

Erik shook his head.

"For me?"

"No." Erik's eyes begin to narrow, as his voice became firm.

"I just want you to have a picture of us on your phone."

Again, Erik shook his head.

"Are you going to take a picture of me when you go away?"

Erik nodded, even though it was against protocol.

"Could you stay a little longer?"

"I can't; I have to be up in a few hours." He saw the disappointed look in her eyes. "You have nothing to worry about. I will walk you back to your dorm."

"No, because if you do that, I am not going to let you go. Will you call me before you leave?"

Erik nodded. Again, their lips embraced, and they squeezed each other tighter. Jamie took a few steps back, pulled out her cell phone, and took Erik's picture. Then he whispered, "I love you."

"I love you more, Erik." As Erik got in the car, Jamie grabbed his attention and asked if he wanted her number.

Erik shook his head. "I don't need it."

"Then how are you going to contact me when you come back?"

"I will always find you."

Jamie walked to her dorm, sobbing all the way. She cried herself to sleep, thinking of him. Meanwhile, Erik thought that though the op was necessary, he did not want to go. Even though it was his idea, Erik did not know what he was hoping to find. He pulled out his cell phone, called Alan, and asked when he wanted to go out for breakfast. At home, Erik packed, showered, shaved, and changed his voice mail and email at the museum to cover his absence. It was nearly one in the morning before he got to bed. He eventually fell into a restless sleep.

20. THE NEW ARRIVAL BEGINS AFTER THE NEXT DEPARTURE

*"You only live twice, or so it seems. One life
for yourself, and one for your dreams."*

—Nancy Sinatra, You Only Live Twice

The time was 0530, when Erik climbed into Alan's car, and they headed to the compound. He closed his eyes and thought about Jamie.

"You awake, kid?" Alan probed.

Erik nodded.

"How was last night?"

"Fine."

Alan tilted his head to look at Erik. "You two have not seen each other in two years, and all you say is fine?"

Erik nodded.

"Do you care to elaborate?"

Erik shook his head.

They pulled up to the entrance of the compound and did the procedures to get in. Once out of the car, Alan

continued, "You didn't bore her by telling her history?"
Erik looked as if to say, 'Would I do that?'

"I love her, Alan, and we are a couple."

Alan placed his arm around Erik and said, "Good. I'm
happy for you."

"I also gave her your cell phone number just in case
she needs to get in touch with you."

"That's fine."

They eventually made it to the O.G.D.S. teams' floor.
Alan checked with Erik to see if he had changed his voice
mail and email. Erik checked his email and asked Alan
to pull up Jamie's Facebook page. He motioned him to
come over. Erik saw her latest post about her date last
night. Alan quickly read the comments, and with his
arms crossed, he stared at Erik.

"What happened last night?" Alan ordered.

"In regards to what?"

Pointing at a comment that said, Is it true what he did
to Keith and Kevin? Alan replied. "What did you do?"

"Nothing serious."

Alan gave the you-don't-expect-me-to-believe-that
look.

"I broke two of Keith's fingers in three places and gave
Kevin soprano lessons."

Just under a whisper, Alan stated, "You kicked him in
the balls?"

Erik nodded.

"Oh, Jesus!" Alan shook his head. "I told you, you need
to control that."

"I was protecting her and myself."

Alan cupped his hand on Erik's shoulder. "I know. I will put this fire out for you." He looked at his watch. "You better get ready."

Erik hovered over Carly's work station. She was finishing the final touches of the false flag; Gary downloaded Burdon Hautenfaust's file to the Bundeswehr's database. Once again, Erik would be doing a deep cover assignment. Erik knew one thing: O.G.D.S. Team 42 was the best at what they did. Erik knew he wanted to come back alive, and he had an excellent support team he could trust. Out of the corner of his eye, Erik saw John approach the simulator room. He waved to Erik to follow.

"Time for work," John chirped.

They swiped their ID badges and put in security codes.

Inside, John moved to the workstation, and Erik moved to the center of the room. John began his debriefing while Erik took deep breaths and focused. Erik knew he was going to a warehouse that contained documents of the Third Reich; however, in any undercover situation, it could quickly become a combat situation. Thus, he needed to pay attention to little things. For example, how tall is the fence, does it have barbed wire on top, are there any other entrances, or where are the exits, how many guard dogs are used. Once the little things had been done, he would need to focus on the bigger things.

"There won't be any retina scan here, but the guards will analyze your ID a little more, but you don't have to worry, because Carly made it," John noted. "Once you move through the checkpoint, proceed to the main entrance. Act normal and casual, and everything will be fine."The screen that showed the simulation was as if Erik were there and walking. Then he advised there would be guards walking around the perimeter and some were K-9 patrols. "Once in the structure, go down the hallway leading to the stairs. Head up the stairs. You will encounter more guards, but they should not bother you once you reach the second floor. Take a left and walk down that hallway until you see a black door." John informed.

"Will it have a number or identification on it?"

"No, but there will be a guard there, and he will ask for your identification and maybe ask your business. This room should have whatever you are looking for. It is a huge library. Imagine one of the old libraries with ten-foot-high bookcases and rolling ladders. That is what this room is like."

"Wonderful. I hope what I'm looking for is still there and on a lower shelf."

"Yeah, that would be helpful."

"I would like to let you know there is only one way in and one way out. However, if you need to escape the building, several ladders lead to the roof. Also, once the alarm goes off, the lockdown process begins, and speed is key." John paused so Erik could absorb everything he was saying. "You have one slight advantage."

Erik nodded and focused.

"Since this is an older building, there's a small amount of time when the guards coordinate their efforts, and they have to enter at one entrance." As John talked, Erik knew he usually could take advantage of windows. However, there was a drawback. When the guards were locking down the building, they would understand that windows would be an exit strategy and close that opportunity. "If you make it to the roof," said John as he pulled up an aero shot of the building, walked to the screen, and pointed, "head to this part of the building."

Erik walked to the screen.

"There is a dumpster, and you can use that as a cushion to fall on," John continued.

"Any hard surface items?" Erik asked.

John shook his head, "That's your best alternative. Next, run to the fence, scale it, and get the hell out of Dodge."

"Anything else?"

"There is good news and bad news on this op. The good news is there are going to be approximately 50 soldiers versus a couple hundred."

"And the bad?"

"The bad news is the intensity will be the same. They still want to kill you."

"Thanks for the tip."

"Anything that will keep you out of a body bag."

"Seriously?"

"It is not that I am worried, but anything can happen."

"I am aware of that."

"Well, then, I will see you when you get back."

21. WHAT AND WHO WILL BE THE ANSWER IN BETWEEN LIVING AND DYING

"Before you start some work, always ask yourself three questions — Why am I doing it, what the results might be, and will I be successful. Only when you think deeply and find satisfactory answers to these questions, go ahead."

— Chanakya

BERLIN, GERMANY

September 2005: It had been three months since Erik was reassigned to department 463 and doing historical research on Field Marshal Erwin Rommel. Unlike other paramilitary operations officers, Erik occasionally needed to wear uniforms from different countries. This time he would be wearing the uniform of the Heer (Army), and he would be impersonating an officer, Captain Burnon Hautenfaust. Erik's objectives were to infiltrate a warehouse; obtain information on Project Bell, also known as Die Glocke; and get the hell out. Erik did not have much to go on except that an SS Obergruppenführer named Hans Kammler was in command of Project Bell, and, whatever Project Bell was, it must have dealt with very sensitive information that was still highly classified. Gary was able to assist Erik because he had hacked into the Bundeswehr's database, and it gave the location inside the warehouse, of all information on Project Bell. However, there was one problem; even though the Germans would have everything neatly organized inside the warehouse, that did not mean the information would be there. Doing an op like this would be similar to parachuting out of a plane. One needs to pull the cord to deploy the parachute. Until the cord was pulled, there was no way of knowing if it worked. Then, of course, if he pulled it and it did not work, it would be too late.

The civilian world phrase "work smarter, not harder" also applied to Erik's world of a paramilitary operations officer on an op. For example, in the movies, the operative either sneaked in a uniform or stole one. Sneaking one is tricky. It is downright stupid, a great way to be compromised, and never be heard from again. Even though stealing was a better option, it was not smart and had a huge drawback.

When an op stole the uniform, there was a good chance it might not fit, meaning the operative would be comprised and never seen again. So, the best option was to mail, express delivery, the uniform to a UPS store or a museum. Erik preferred a museum. It fit with his cover, a historian, and he had contacts to help him. Another reason was that Erik could mail all his false flags, equipment, and sometimes weapons. However, the challenge of getting a military vehicle when needed. As an operative, Erik knew stealing a vehicle was not an option because it would be reported, and if caught, he would be compromised. In short, Erik's museum contact in Berlin would have to get one. It was like renting a car; when he was done with it, he would return it. In extreme situations, if he was not able to return it, both parties could deny everything and walk away.

Like Erik had done in Russia and so many times before, he prepared himself by getting into character as he drove down Friedrich-Olbricht-Damm. At the moment he pulled up to the gate, uniformed armed guards surrounded the vehicle. One guard asked Erik for his identification, and another asked the routine questions as he examined the ID. After the guards were satisfied, Erik was allowed to enter. As he entered the warehouse, Erik's nostrils were assaulted by a smell that was like clothes left in the wash for a week, but his eyes analyzed everything. Erik noticed the warehouse was divided into two levels, and most people inside were unarmed. He went down the hallway leading to a set of stairs and ascended to the second level. A few guards were on their routine patrols, but nothing to be concerned about yet. Erik made a left and went down the hallway until he saw a black door, with an armed sentry who asked for Erik's ID.

He entered a vast room with row upon row of bookcases, at least ten feet high, filled with files that were once the property of the Third Reich. The good thing was that each bookcase was neatly organized and labeled. Erik looked for a diagram of the room; however, no such luck. Each time he passed a bookcase, he read the labels and shook his head, overwhelmed. He finally came to the row about which Gary had advised him, and now he had to find the correct file number and see how the Dewey Decimal System was arranged. Titles were ascending from the top, and according to his file, it should be close to eye level. His eyes danced around the shelves, reading everything that they came in contact with. It was enough to make an average person go crazy, but for an operative, it was just doing the job.

Grinning, Erik pulled a box off the shelf and opened it. The files were separated by tabbed dividers and neatly organized, with no papers sticking out. On the tabs were neatly handwritten, in black ink, file identifications that were a combination of letters and numbers. He flipped through the files and eventually came to the words, Die Glocke. Immediately pulling the file out, he opened it, quickly scanned it, and reclosed it. He noticed there was another one-inch-thick folder, containing a highly classified collection of draft cables and memoranda on the Die Glocke. Erik knew in any covert operation; the closer one got to the goal did not mean that he was in the clear. At that moment, the alarm blared off, and in a panic, he glanced around. Erik quickly removed his tunic, tucked the folders in the back of his pants, put the tunic back on, and threw random folders into his attaché case as he pulled out his Heckler & Koch USP and cocked it.

Erik heard the door being thrown open, Heckler & Koch HK416's being cocked, footsteps advancing, and orders were given. Erik knew his life might be in the balance, and he was expecting a firefight. Erik got on his feet and quickly moved to the ladder, which led to the roof, located at the far end of the room. Erik's only advantage was that they did not know what he looked like, but at the same time, he could not take a gamble. As he walked, his eyes scanned for soldiers. Unfortunately, he was out-numbered. Erik knew he would have multiple attackers coming at him with a coordinated assault. With that in mind, he had only one option, defending himself while running and firing, but mainly running as Erik headed down the corridor, occasionally looking back, sweat from his armpits like rain. The ladder neared.

"Du da! Stop! You there! Stop!"

In the corner of Erik's eye, he saw a soldier lift his weapon and fire. At that moment, he ducked behind a bookcase as the bullets made thud-like noises hitting the bookcase and the boxes. When Erik heard the soldier reloading, he revealed himself and fired his weapon, killing him, did an about-face, and ran. His 9mm pistol sounded weak compared to the assault rifles that roared simultaneously when they fired. The rounds from the assault rifles sent splinters flying, shredded papers, and infected the air with more dust. The areas where the bullets wedged in the bookcases and boxes filled with documents mixed with sawdust would have irritated anyone's lungs. The concrete walls of the warehouse room took the thundering of sound and batted it around until there was silence; however, only for a moment. Erik fell on one knee, again drew his gun and squeezed off five more rounds, making an ear-shattering roar. Two more were down, as the others took cover. Erik looked up, grabbed his attaché case, dashed and leaped to the ladder, and began his climb. Once on the rooftop, Erik raced to the edge and looked down where the dumpster would be. He would use this for his escape.

As he was about to jump, Erik placed his weapon in his front tunic pocket, and a thundering voice came from behind, "Frieren! Freeze!" Erik looked over his shoulder and saw a man pointing his gun directly at Erik's back. "Drehen Sie sich langsam um. Oder sollen wir sprechen Englisch Dr. Függer? Or shall we speak English, Dr. Függer?"

Erik knew when a cover was compromised; it was never a good thing, and usually, the last thing the agent would hear and or see is the gun used to kill him. However, there was a slim chance he would be given thirty seconds to explain himself; however, when he heard the hammer of a pistol being pulled back, that would be the beginning of the end. Then in a flash, Erik thought, how did this person know his name?

"Put your hands behind your head … and turn around slowly."

"My hands are full." Erik raised both hands. One was empty, but on the other, he was holding his attaché case.

"In that case, turn around slowly and don't make any sudden movements."

Knowing the truth of who he was and what he was doing, there was not much time to think. Erik was out of moves. The only thing he could do was test fate and turn around.

"It's not Halloween. Take it off." The individual referred to Erik's mask. "Where is your weapon?"

"I dropped it." A lie.

The man gave you don't expect me to believe that glare.

Erik responded: "I don't think I am in a position to lie."

Motioning Erik to hand over the attaché case, the man replied. "You are not in a position to do anything."

Erik nodded in agreement, as the man demanded. "The case ... now." Erik tossed it. "Dr. Függer, what were you expecting to find here?"

"The original copy of Anne Frank's diary."

"Cute."

Erik inched himself to the edge of the building and prepared to jump, his heart pounding against his chest.

"It's time to die."

Immediately, Erik leaped backward and pulled out his gun and aimed. At that moment, the man dashed to the edge, set to fire, but Erik squeezed off several rounds, grazing the man's forehead. The man stumbled back, attempting to shake off the injury. Erik landed in the dumpster, which broke his fall, jumped out, and headed to the fence. Without looking back, he scaled the fence, kept on running, discarding his uniform and gun along the way. The adrenaline had caused his blood pressure to rise, and he was losing focus. It was difficult to think clearly. Training at The Farm told him he needed to clear his head. He took several deep breaths and used his will power to pull himself back from the brink. The next step was to pray for a window of opportunity to leave the country immediately.

22. LIES AND THE TRUTH ARE PAINTED BLACK

"There's a reason they call the spy trade the hall of mirrors. You can never know for sure whether you're in control or you're being played, but if you do it long enough, you learn to trust your instincts."

— *Burn Notice*, episode "Good Soldier," voiceover of Michael Weston

WASHINGTON, D.C.

"Ladies and gentlemen, as we start our descent, please make sure your seat backs and tray tables are in their full upright position. Make sure your seatbelt is securely fastened, and all carry-on luggage is stowed underneath the seat in front of you or the overhead bins. Please turn off all electronic devices until we are safely parked at the gate. Also, please fill out the customs forms. Thank you," The captain of the Lufthansa's Boeing 747 announced.

The flight attendants walked up and down the aisle assisting passengers and handing out the customs forms as the aircraft slowly descended. Erik peered out of the window, seeing Washington D.C.'s monuments becoming more defined as they drew closer. The high pitch sound with the FASTEN SEATBELT light came on.

Again, it was the captain, "Flight attendants, prepare for landing, please. Cabin crew, please take your seats for landing."

Unlike other jobs, as a CIA paramilitary operations officer, Erik could not go straight home and go to the office the following day. Erik would be picked up, driven to the Compound, given a debriefing, and would tie up any loose ends, and then maybe he could go home and rest. It didn't help when he had been stuck on a plane for nearly ten hours, even though first-class seats were comfortable, with lots of legroom.

"Ladies and gentlemen, we have just been cleared to land at Dulles International Airport. Please make sure one last time your seat belt is securely fastened."

The metallic sound of the landing gear being lowered engulfed the cabin as the plane continued to descend. Most passengers would have the joy of coming back to America and relaxing because it is one's home. As a member of the Intelligence Community, Erik had the same pleasure, but it was reinforced by surviving another op, and he wouldn't be able to relax just yet. Still, most of all, he no longer had to worry about being shot at or killed. The screeching of rubber against the tarmac was a great feeling. The aircraft raced down the runway—the whining of the engines and air brakes filling the ears of the passengers. Within seconds, the bumpy landing was over, and the aircraft was turning off the active runway and taxiing to the gate.

A flight attendant grabbed the microphone. "Ladies and gentlemen, welcome to Dulles International Airport. Local time is 9:56 am, and the temperature is 85 degrees. For your safety and comfort, we ask that you please remain seated with your seat belt fastened until the captain turns off the 'Fasten Seat Belt' sign. This will indicate that we have parked at the gate and that it is safe for you to move about."

Erik, like the others, was getting restless and stretching in his seat. He began filling out his CBP Declaration Form. As an operative working overseas, Erik could not tell anyone, so he didn't have to worry about buying any gifts. He broke that rule when he told Jamie, but Erik didn't tell her where he was going. If that were going to be a problem, he would already know.

"Please check around your seat for any personal belongings you may have brought on board with you, and please use caution when opening the overhead bins, as articles may have shifted around during the flight. If you require deplaning assistance, please remain in your seat until all other passengers have deplaned. One of our crew members will then be pleased to assist you." Erik closed his eyes and stretched as the captain continued.

Erik got his passport and pulled out Jamie's photograph, the one of her in her Georgetown cheerleader uniform, crop top with a pleated mini skirt, doing the scorpion position. He wondered what she had been doing and if she did truly love him. Most of all, he wondered if it was safe to be in a relationship with her.

A man, possibly an international banker or someone in that line of work, peered over Erik's shoulder. "You got to love them cheerleaders. They are hot in those uniforms. How were you able to tap that?"

Erik glared at him. He had spent his entire career in covert ops, and he sometimes knew it was hard to adjust back into civilian life, especially when coming back from a hostile op that was almost compromised. When in the field, Erik could take one shot to kill even before the person had a fix on him. Or he could hit someone to get information or to intimidate him. In the civilian world, Erik could not practice those techniques because he would end up in prison. However, intimidating threats were just as effective. He had to make sure he chose the right words and tone that would make the individual wish he had never opened his mouth.

"I sent two individuals who were harassing and making rude comments to her to the hospital." With a satisfied grin, he tucked the photo back in the passport.

The man gulped and fumbled to get himself organized and Erik excused himself, grabbed his belongings from the overhead bin, and exited the plane. Every time he went overseas, Erik still had to go through U.S. Customs, which was like getting a cavity filled. It took several steps to get it done, it could take a while, and lastly, it was mandatory. Erik did have the advantage of being a part of the Global Entry Program, which enabled him to bypass long lines and go to an automated kiosk and have his passport and fingerprints scanned. Next, an officer checked his luggage. The last step was to be questioned by another U.S. Customs officer, and then he was allowed to pass through a set of double doors and leave the airport. Immediately upon exiting, Erik saw Alan, waiting patiently. Alan studied Erik's behavior and had worked with Erik long enough to know when something was wrong and to approach cautiously.

"How was your flight?" Alan questioned.

"Long."

Erik leaned back in his seat and closed his eyes, mentally preparing himself for the debriefing. The drive seemed to last only a few minutes before Alan told Erik to get his ID ready. They turned down an unnamed street that was sheltered by large oak trees and prepared to do the morning ritual of getting into the compound. They came to the speaker box, and a deep authoritarian voice stated, "Identify yourselves."

"Zero-eight-zero-three-one-nine-five-three."

"One-zero-zero-three-one-nine-seven-one."

Silence.

"You are cleared to proceed."

Alan drove forward, with his headlights off, and they prepared to hand over their IDs. Two uniformed guards with assault rifles stared in Erik's direction, studying his every movement. Another appeared from a tollbooth-like station and ordered Alan to stop.

"Identifications." The guard held out his hand, and Alan gave him the IDs. "Look at the camera and state your first and last names."

"Alan James."

"Erik Függer."

The guard stared at the back seat. "What is in the bag?"

"Clothes, toiletries, and personal items. I just came from the airport."

"Open it."

"Would you like me to get out?"

"No, sir. Stay in the vehicle." He glanced at Alan and ordered, "Unlock the back door."

The guard checked the contents and closed the door. Then he went to the office. Thirty seconds later, Alan and Erik were cleared to proceed. Alan navigated to the parking lot, and they made their way to the entrance and headed to Bonesteiner's office, where he motioned them to take a seat around the table and poured coffee.

As Bonesteiner took his seat, he stared at Erik and asked, "What happened?"

"I was compromised. Someone alerted them I was coming."

"That is a rash statement. No one knew you were going except your old team, Alan, and myself."

Erik took a deep sigh. "One knew my name and asked me what I was expecting to find here. Also, he was an American."

"Did you tell Jamie you were going?" Alan interjected.

"No, sir."

The admiral leaned back in his chair as he rubbed his chin and removed his glasses., looking at both Erik and Bonesteiner.

Alan asked openly between sips of coffee, "Who would want to compromise you? Most importantly, why?"

Erik shrugged his shoulders. "I did see Paul speaking to a brigadier general when I was at Camp Swampy."

Bonesteiner glanced at Alan, who leaned forward and asked, "Erik, what did he look like?"

"Who? The guy in …"

Alan finished Erik's statement, "No, the brigadier general."

Erik closed his eyes, trying to get a mental image, "He was short, about five feet-ten but stocky. His uniform seemed to be stretched over his body. He had brown, al-most black eyes behind steel-framed glasses."

Alan stared at Bonesteiner, "Plackett."

The admiral nodded.

"Who is Plackett?" Erik asked.

"Erik, that is not important, but we need to find out why someone would try to compromise you."

Erik nodded. "The day I helped you with the tour at the museum, I was at the NSA speaking to one of my contacts."

"Scott Boone, in cyber warfare?" Bonesteiner's question. Erik nodded.

"He was trying to find any projects that Rommel was working on that were not mentioned in our databases. So, he hacked into the German database to see if there were any old files from the Third Reich. He stumbled on the name Obergruppenführer Hans Kammler."

"I never heard of that name," Alan said, as Bonestein-er gave a baffled look.

Erik continued. "He was a civil engineer between the wars, and once the war began, he became a high-ranking officer of the SS. The only information on what he did was that he was superintendent of the SS construction projects, and toward the end of the war, Hitler put him in charge of the V-2 missile and jet programs. Rommel and Kammler's names were mentioned once." Erik raised his finger to emphasize a point. "He had over a million people working for him, including slave labor. He and all his research disappeared in 1945. Oddly, his name was never mentioned at the Nuremberg Trials."

"How in the hell can a high-ranking Nazi who worked on highly classified projects disappear? There has to be some trace of him after the war," Bonesteiner objected. Erik shook his head.

"However, when I left Scott, he gave me a five-dollar bill, and hidden in it were the words Project Bell."

Bonesteiner leaned forward, "Erik, Scott was killed in a car accident three days ago." Erik's eyes widened and became speechless.

"What? How?"

"The report I got was that someone stole a car and struck Boone while he was riding his bike, killing him instantly." The admiral paused. "The driver left the scene, was never found, and when the cops did an investigation, nothing came up."

Alan added, "Admiral, I am not one to believe in conspiracy theories, but with Erik almost being compromised, Scott's death, and Plackett showing up unannounced, that is a little too convenient."

Bonesteiner nodded, "I will try to look into the matter very delicately. Were you able to retrieve any information on Kammler or Project Bell?"

"Yes, Sir." Erik pulled out two, one-inch thick folders, containing highly classified collections of draft cables and memoranda from the Third Reich, and placed them on the table.

Erik began, "Project Bell, also known as Die Glocke, has high-security status in the Third Reich, Top Secret Command Matter."

"Who would have that clearance?" Bonesteiner bounced the question off Erik.

"Hitler, Kammler, maybe Albert Speer. I cannot tell you how many, but I know only a handful and the individuals within Hitler's inner circle, but that is an educated guess."

"How does Rommel fit in all of this?"

"As I said before, Rommel and Kammler's names were mentioned once. That was on June 16 and 17, 1944, when Hitler met with Field Marshals Rommel and von Rundstedt in Margival, also known as Wolfsschlucht Two, approximately 10 km northeast of Soissons in the department of Aisne in France. This Führer Headquarters was used only one time, and this was the one time. The first meeting was between Rommel and von Rundstedt to discuss the situation on the Western front. However, at the second meeting, only Hitler, Rommel, and Kammler met." Both Alan and Bonesteiner were drawn in with curiosity. "What was discussed was not recorded, but the pieces I have put together indicate that Rommel was briefed about Project Bell." Bonesteiner gestured to get to the point. "Project Bell is speculated to be the German's attempt to do time travel. And, yes, if Hitler had to choose a Field Marshal, it would have been Rommel."

"Oh, dear God, am I glad we defeated them before they could send him back!" Alan gasped.

"Do you have any solid proof of what you just said? Also, who else knows about these folders?"

"Not yet, but I'm working on it. I am reaching out to some contacts. As for the folders, everyone in this room and very possibly those who were trying to compromise me."

Bonesteiner ordered, "I want you to take those home with you and secure them in a safe place."

"Admiral, wouldn't it be better if those folders are kept here in his Vault?"

Bonesteiner shook his head. "If they know Erik has the documents, they will be able to infiltrate the compound." He stared at Erik, "Do not leave those documents unattended." Now in a more relaxed tone, he continued, "Do you need anything else?"

Erik nodded. "I also need to speak to someone in the Navy who knows Project Rainbow."

Bonesteiner leaned back in his chair, rubbed his chin, and inquired. "Project Rainbow?" Erik bobbed his head. "Why?"

"Because in the documentation I acquired, the Germans mentioned Project Rainbow."

Bonesteiner headed to his desk and picked up the phone and motioned to Erik to hold his thought.

"Cole, Bonesteiner here...I am well, thank you, and yourself?...I know, me too. Cole, I am going to send one of my people to you; he needs some information. Help him out...He will be there within the hour...Thanks." Bonesteiner grabbed Erik's attention. "Be careful when you ask about that." Then he jotted down a few things and headed back to the table.

Handing the piece of paper to Erik, he continued, "Here is all of Cole's information." Erik nodded in appreciation. "I know you have been through a lot this last week, but when you speak to Cole, I need you to be objective."

"I will be."

"Are you sure?"

"Yes, sir."

"After you see Admiral Cole, I want you to take off the rest of the day and the weekend so you can clear your head and get a fresh start when you come back on Monday. So, you know how to use the APP on your phone to locate her by using Jamie's phone number?"

"Yes, sir."

"Erik, I will text her number to you. She called while you were away," Alan added.

Erik nodded.

"Spend time with Jamie. Dismissed." Bonesteiner replied.

"Yes, sir."

Erik grabbed the folders, placed them in his bag, and started to leave, but Bonesteiner caught his attention. "You are going to have a tough time starting your car without these." Bonesteiner tossed Erik his car keys. "Lastly, try not to break any more fingers or give singing lessons."

"Yes, sir."

After Erik closed the door, Alan asked bitterly, "What in the hell is going on here, Admiral? Do you think it is wise to send him to Cole?"

"Let us test the waters."

"This could put Erik in a precarious situation."

"Let it play out. The next move will be Cole's."

Erik exited the building, headed to his car, and drove to the Pentagon. He pulled up to one of the entrances where guards, enlisted men of the U.S. Army, stood their ground with their fingers on the triggers of their assault weapons. Erik stopped and rolled down his window as a guard approached with his hand extended, asking for identification.

"State your business, who you are, and who you are with?"

"I have an appointment with Admiral Cole, Dr. Erik Függer, and CIA."

The sentry went to the guard booth and ran his information through a computer-generated database, and ran Erik's face through a facial-recognition database. A K-9 unit was sniffing for explosives, and another was scanning underneath the car with a hand-held mirror. The sentry returned with Erik's ID, and a visitor pass and instructed him to the visitor parking area. Erik headed to the visitor parking lot, parked, and proceeded to an entrance. Once inside, Erik inserted his ID into the turnstile and continued to Admiral Cole's office, on the first floor-West, room number 1250W. He pulled out a micro tape recorder and hit "record." The hallways were filled with defense department workers from every armed service branch, as well as others in suits who were with military and government agencies. Once in a while, Erik looked at a map or asked someone directions to make sure he was headed in the right direction. He finally got to the office, took a deep breath, and entered. The office was cramped; it had a lobby with just enough space for two individuals and a secretary.

"Can I help you?" the secretary questioned firmly.

"I have an appointment with Admiral Cole."

"Your name, and is he expecting you?"

"Dr. Erik Függer, and yes, he is."

She motioned him to take a seat, as she picked up the receiver. Erik didn't know what to expect from the meeting. He did know he would be looking for the truth about Project Rainbow. Would he be given the answers he was looking for, or would he have to probe deeper, which could cause some friction? Most people knew that all five branches of the military and the members of the intelligence community work together for the greater safety of the United States. However, the reality of it is that these two parties don't see eye-to-eye; thus, when it didn't deal with national security matters, the two were like oil and water. The office door opened, and a Navy admiral and a U.S. Army brigadier general appeared, each with a large number of ribbons on their chest. The brigadier general was short and stocky. His uniform seemed to be stretched tight over well-developed muscles. Erik remembered his brown, almost black eyes, behind the steel-framed glasses, showing no emotion as if they were hiding an inner evil. The Admiral stood six feet tall, with a small but solid frame. He had relaxed blue eyes, but not to be fooled, they always stayed alert, checking his surroundings. Before the Brigadier General left, he gave a subtle nod to the Navy Admiral. When the Brigadier General walked by, Erik read his nameplate: Plackett.

Then the Navy admiral peered at Erik with cold, blue eyes, "Can I help you?"

"Yes, Sir. My name is Dr. Függer, the one Admiral Bonesteiner called about."

Erik extended his hand, and the admiral met him, introducing himself with a superficial grin, "Yes, he did. I'm Admiral Cole." Cole gestured Erik to come in and take a seat. "So, how can I assist you?" Before Erik could answer, Cole leaned back in his chair and asked, "How long have you worked for Bonesteiner?"

"I am looking into information about Project Rainbow, and I have been working for the admiral for seven years."

As he took himself around his desk, Cole's devilish blue eyes analyzed Erik, as if he were a cell under a microscope. Cole leaned back in his chair and rubbed his chin. In his baritone voice, he replied, "You look very familiar; what did you do before you were at the agency?"

"Sir, can we get to why I am here?"

Cole leaned forward, as if he were a rattlesnake striking, "No, we cannot. I want my question answered," Cole snapped. "I think I deserve a little common courtesy since you came to me for help. Wouldn't you agree, since you are just a CIA analyst working in a cubicle?"

Erik nodded and replied, "Yes, sir."

"Good. Now, Dr. Függer, what did you do before you were at the agency?"

"I was a history teacher."

"A history teacher…now isn't that a noble profession!" Cole said mockingly, "What is your first name?"

"Erik."

"So, Erik, how can I help you?"

"I am inquiring about information on Project Rainbow."

"Oh, that's right." Cole nodded his head, and his voice trailed off. Then he made an apologetic gesture with his hand. "What is Project Rainbow? I have never heard of it."

Erik and Cole studied each other's body language, change in pitch or tone, and many different ways to tell if someone is lying. Erik knew when trying to get sensitive information and going up against someone that has similar training or better, and it came down to judgment calls. If he gave too little information, Cole would deny everything. If too much information were provided, Cole would either deny everything or give out the same information Erik already knew or tell him procedures Erik would need to take before getting that information. Each case would end in the same way: Erik would have nothing. On the flip side, if Cole knew that Erik possessed more knowledge than he let on to, he might consider that a threat, making it harder to get the information needed.

"It is also known as The Philadelphia Experiment. Are you familiar with that?"

Cole nodded and smirked. "Oh, yes, I know what you are talking about." Erik's hearing was focused and ready to digest any information shared.

"But before I give you any information, Dr. Függer, do you have the proper paperwork? Also, is your security clearance high enough?" Cole raised his finger in the air to emphasize his point, "I remember you now; you gave the briefing on the Seawolf Class Submarine in Hawaii in 1994."

"Excuse me, sir? Can we address the issue at hand, sir? I am a CIA senior analyst, and my security clearance is Top Secret—Sensitive Compartmented Information/Special Intelligence."

"Don't have an attitude with me." Cole pointed at Erik. "I will address the issue. Since you do not have the proper documentation, and I was not given authority to release that information to you, you are going to have to follow the correct procedures or protocol."

"Sir, I work with Admiral Bonesteiner. If you call him, we can clear this matter up."

"Dr. Függer, until you have the proper paperwork, there is nothing more I can do or say." Cole got up and gave Erik a dismissive gesture, as Erik did what was instructed of him. They shook hands.

Erik knew it was pointless to argue and knew Admiral Cole was playing the bureaucracy game, and the game had specific rules one must follow. He also knew that to get the information, he must play the game or get nowhere.

"Then I will come back with paperwork and pick up where we left off," Erik stated.

As Erik was leaving the office, he saw Brigadier General Plackett waiting in the lobby.

Erik remarked, "Nice to see you again. I hope you are doing well. I remember you when I went to The Farm in 1997. Tell Paul McLaughlin I said hi."

"Do I know you?" Plackett replied as Erik walked by grinning.

"Yes, you should. If you choose not to remember me, that is your choice; but I will never forget you."

"Dr. Függer, explain yourself," Cole demanded.

"Admiral Cole, since you do not have the proper documentation, and I was not given authority to release that information to you, you are going have to follow the correct procedures or protocol. I am sure you understand."

"Admiral Bonesteiner will hear about this," Cole said with his teeth clenched, his cold eyes staring at Erik.

Erik turned to face Cole, his own eyes cold. "Make sure you ask him about the proper paperwork."

Erik walked off, leaving Cole and Plackett in their thoughts. He also knew he would be getting a call from Bonesteiner. The only question was how many seconds or minutes it would take. By the time he stepped outside and headed to his car, he got the call. Erik's new position was the closest thing to a civilian office job. He went to meetings, returned phone calls, and if it was the Deputy

Director of Intelligence, Admiral Bonesteiner, it could be excellent news, terrible news, or he was about to be chewed out.

"Yes, sir," Erik answered.

"What in the hell do you think you are doing? I told you to be objective." Bonesteiner demanded, and then he paused and then barked., "Well?"

"I was ..." Erik stated, as he got in his car and headed toward the University of Georgetown.

"He said you started demanding information."

"That is such bullshit."

"Erik, you forget. I know you."

"I asked him about Project Rainbow, and he said he never heard of it. I have it all on tape."

"He knows about Project Rainbow. I don't know why he would say that. Did he know he was being recorded?"

"Why would he lie, and no, sir."

"I am not sure. You make sure that tape is not lost; it might save your ass."

"He was playing the bureaucracy game; also, saying I do not have the proper documentation, and he was not given authority to release that information to me."

"Something is not right. I will get your proper documentation, but not today."

"What about the tape?"

"I will get it from you. Just try to get some rest and spend time with Jamie. I will take care of the situation."

23. I ONLY HAVE EYES FOR YOU

"When you operate in the field you expect your cover to be tested. To stay alive, you keep your facts straight, your lies simple, and try not to come face-to-face with someone you've never met but are already supposed to know. But, when that's unavoidable, you stare the stranger in the eyes and sell your relationship with everything you've got."

— *Burn Notice*, episode "No Good Deed," voiceover of Michael Weston

GEORGETOWN UNIVERSITY, WASHINGTON, D.C.

While waiting for a visitor parking pass, issued by OTM, Erik pulled out his cell phone and pulled up his GPS, Global Positioning System, and application. The upside to being a paramilitary operations officer as long as Erik had is getting the newest technology. The public was introduced to GPS nearly five years ago, and most people thought it was the greatest thing since sliced bread. The government had more advanced technology. For the version Erik was using, he could put a cell phone number in, relay it to a satellite, and back to Erik's phone. Granted, this took a few minutes, but it was the easiest way to find someone, especially his girlfriend.

"Can I help you?" Asked the man within a toll-booth-like structure.

"I need a visitor parking pass."

"Are you a student?"

Erik glared at the individual and wished he could say that he had just robbed a bank and both local and federal agencies were on his tail and wondering if he could ditch his car here? "No, I'm not."

The man handed over the permit.

"Please park in lots where the permit is issued. Those who park in unauthorized lots will be cited. The pass is only good for three hours."

"Thank you."

Navigating through the campus was like going through a labyrinth. Parking was not much better. It was about as difficult as getting on a lifeboat on the R.M.S. Titanic. Erik came upon Lot 9, located adjacent to Lauinger Library, saw a vacant space, and slipped in. Once he was out of the car, he looked at his cell phone and headed in the direction where Jamie was. Within a few minutes, he was in front of O'Donovan Dining Hall. Inside O'Donovan Dining Hall was an oversized cafeteria with several food stations and two dining levels; it was also loud and crowded with people.

"Nice hat, man," someone said.

"Thanks; by the way, do you know where the cheer-leaders sit?" Even though Erik thought college was like high school with ashtrays, he figured college cafeteria seating arrangements would be similar.

"Yeah, they sit over there with the jocks."

Erik nodded in appreciation and headed in that direction. Ever since joining the CIA and being a part of the O.G.D.S. team, he had traveled to many undesirable and hostile locations. However, showing up at Georgetown University, knowing that a week before, the entire basketball team had wanted to kill him, he could count Georgetown University as one of those locations. Even though they would not be carrying assault weapons, Erik would still need to be on his guard. On The Farm, Erik had been taught to blend in with his surroundings, which was a crucial skill in a covert operation as well; wearing a three-piece suit and a fedora did not help. However, he was trained for situations like this. He had been taught to think and evaluate quickly and move fast because things could change within seconds. Nearby, Erik recognized Jamie from her thick curly brown hair, and he also knew the other cheerleaders' faces. As he approached, the conversations became apparent, and, to make things worse, they were about him.

"Jamie, have you heard from your boyfriend, or is he too scared to show his face after what he did to Keith and Kevin?"

"He is on a business trip, and, no, he is not. Why are you defending what Keith and Kevin did? Erik was protecting me."

"Maybe so, but he broke two of Keith's fingers and kicked Kevin in the balls. That was so uncool. He better watch himself when he shows up."

Another girl mocked, as others giggled, "You mean if he shows up."

"There's no if about it; I am here," Erik replied with a sly look.

All heads faced in Erik's direction; some girls rolled their eyes, and some shook their heads in disbelief. Jamie used her incredible thigh muscles to leap toward Erik with her arms open and squeezed him tight.

She exclaimed in a jubilant, but surprised, tone, "Erik!"

As Erik wrapped his arm around Jamie, another girl jumped in Erik's face. "You have some nerve showing up here, and what you did to Keith and Kevin was totally not cool."

"I deemed that force necessary."

Erik could see that their conversation was getting more attention, as the girl retorted, "Well, you sent them to the hospital."

"Would it make things better if I sent them flowers and a card?" Erik replied in a bantering tone.

"Well, you will be the next one to go to the hospital." Then with squinting eyes, a condescending grin and arms crossed, she continued, "You might be going to your funeral."

Jamie rubbed Erik's arm nervously, as Erik replied in a quizzical tone, "Do I have time to call my lawyer and make sure my will is up-to-date?"

"You are so funny," she answered harshly, her nostrils flaring.

"You have no idea what you got yourself into." She turned to Jamie, "I hope it was good while it lasted." Erik snapped in front of the girl's face as she snapped back, "That was rude."

"No, that was getting your attention. If I had wanted to be rude, I would have told you to fuck off."

Jamie's eyes widened. "Erik, that wasn't polite."

He turned to Jamie, "You're right." Then he turned to the girl, who had her hands on her hips. "Please fuck off."

"I'm going to enjoy seeing your ass kicked," the girl blurted out.

Erik continued. "So, you have told me." Rubbing his chin and bobbed his head as if he were calculating, "So would a lot of people," Erik squinted and corrected himself. "Sorry, I was incorrect, they would like to kill me." He smiled, as Jamie and others stared at him dumbfounded, and continued, "But that's not important."

The girl said as a sadistic grin transformed her face, "You can add another two hundred."

Jamie's eyes showed signs of stress as she gulped and pulled herself closer to Erik.

He shrugged off the intimidation. "Is that it?" He rubbed his chin. "By any chance, will they be carrying Kalashnikovs?"

"Carrying what?"

"You know, AK…" Erik gave a dismissive gesture, "Never mind."

"Whatever, asshole."

Erik quickly glanced around the cafeteria, as he retraced his steps, remembering how he got here. He also knew that on Mondays, Wednesdays, and Fridays, classes at universities were fifty minutes long. The clock showed five minutes of class time left. He knew that if he, and a high possibility, Jamie also, were being chased, the chasers would have a tough time maintaining visual contact because there would be hundreds of students filling the walkways. This advantage would allow Erik and Jamie to get to his car and escape. Then, the next big challenge would be getting off the campus, but, with Jamie's help, it wouldn't be so bad.

"I could stoop to your level; however, my IQ can't go down that level," Erik replied and raised his raised a finger as he finished his last thought. "Lastly, if I did try to insult you, I would have to use small words that you would understand." Jamie's eyes scanned the cafeteria for anyone who would want to hurt him, with others doing a mocking laugh.

"Matter-of-fact, I can easily handle your pathetic two hundred who want to kill me," Erik chuckled, as his listeners revealed blank expressions. Jamie's eyes enlarged, and she pulled on his shirt, hinting she wanted to leave.

"Is that so? I don't believe you." The girl placed her hands on her hips and said mockingly, "This is not a video game."

"I never said it was a video game," Erik replied.

There were many times in Erik's career when people had tried unsuccessfully to figure him out. He knew they would fail every time. He was trained, so when others did not believe anything he was saying, they were not smart enough to know if he was telling the truth or lying. The result was that they had nothing, and they left confused.

"Hey, man, you are talking about Rainbow Six: Lockdown, right?" An individual blared out.

Erik raised an eyebrow, trying to see who had just addressed to him.

The individual continued, "I have that game too. What level are you talking about?"

"Rainbow Six: Lockdown?" Erik looked to Jamie for some explanation. She shrugged her shoulders. "What are you talking about?" Erik asked inquisitively.

"You know, you go up against worldwide terrorist organizations. You are a CIA black ops dude, and you infiltrate enemy installations and kill the enemy. It's a cool game. By the way, what level are you talking about?"

"A Game?" The individual gestured affirmatively. "I have no clue what you are talking about."

"So, is the last level where you infiltrate a secret Russian nuclear submarine base?"

"On that note, I'm leaving."

"You better, because they are coming to get you," the girl stated with a grin.

Jamie cut in before Erik had a chance to get a word in. "They will need to speak to his secretary to make an appointment."

As the girl looked like a deer in headlights, Erik replied, "Jamie is correct. I am a little busy this week. Next week might be better."

Erik and Jamie walked hand in hand as they headed to her dorm room. She flashed him a smile every time their eyes met. Erik knew people were naturally curious, especially his girlfriend. However, when his girlfriend was curious about the stories he told or his career, the best thing to do was deny everything and make her think his story was an exaggeration of the truth; thus, she would think he was joking or lying. Either way, it would diffuse the situation.

"Babe, you were silly back there."

Erik grinned, "How so?"

Jamie stopped him and turned him around as she used her eyes to try to read his thoughts.

"When you told Amber that you had people that wanted to kill you. I knew you were joking; my boyfriend would never have that many enemies, or, much less, people that wanted to kill him."

Erik had been trained in events like this to give his best poker face and lie. "You know it. I work in a museum. I am no James Bond."

"Nor do you infiltrate a secret Russian base?"

They both smiled as Erik shook his head, "It is amazing what kids think of today."

"Kids today?" Erik nodded as she continued, "Am I a kid to you?"

"No, you are my girlfriend."

She hugged him tightly as he kept his eyes alert.

"Babe, you are too nice for anyone to want to hurt or kill you," Jamie replied as she looked at him. Erik gave her a blank stare. "Did you have a good business trip?" she asked.

"A lot of running around, and the paperwork almost killed me."

"Well, you have to do historical research for the

museum; that's part of your job, right?" Erik grinned and nodded as they headed to her dorm.

"That's where I sleep at night and dream of you," Jamie pointed to a five-story neo-gothic gray stone building known as Copley Hall. Erik had been there before when Jamie took him to her dorm, he just didn't know the name of the building.

Erik tried to find out where her finger was pointing and took a guess, "The fifth floor?"

Jamie nodded and explained that she had moved here in her junior year. Even though he should be at ease, he could not relax because, at any moment, two hundred people may arrive that wanted to make his life a living hell. So, as Erik was taught on The Farm, he analyzed the structure, both internally and externally, and its surroundings. For the exterior, the things he looked for were windows; could they be breached, and how far would one need to jump if necessary. Once inside, he analyzed the hallways, how wide and long, how many doors within the hall, the locations of stairs, service closets (what is inside could be used as weapons), and finally where exits are located. In all reality, when escaping a building, it is not just about getting out alive, but what you are willing to do to survive that those pursuing you are not willing to do, like jumping through a window or something more extreme like jumping off the roof. However, when doing that, it had to be done without breaking his leg or any part of his body. If he could, great, if not, he would be in much pain, and, to make matters worse, he would be caught and get a beat-down.

As they entered through the arched doorways, she explained that the Copley Formal Lounge was used for formal receptions and as a dining room for student and university gatherings. They made it to the elevators and headed to the fifth floor. They came out of the elevator and headed to her room. Immediately upon entering, she pushed him against the door and kissed him passionately and then placed her head on his shoulder.

"I missed you so much." She held him tight and rubbed his broad shoulders and arms. "I'm glad you are back from your trip?"

"Me, too."

"So, when do you have to go back to work."

"Monday."

"So, we have today and the weekend together?" Erik nodded as a smile emerged on Jamie's face. "So, can I stay at your place?" Erik nodded again, "What are we going to do today?"

"I was thinking about lunch and just relax."

"You sit on my bed while I get ready."

She grabbed her underwear and headed to the bathroom. He fought to keep his eyes open since he had been up for nearly thirty-six hours. After experiencing several catastrophic events, it was hard for Erik to sleep, even in his place. However, being in a new place made it worse because all of his senses were heightened. Thus, the chances of his getting a cat nap were low, and he wouldn't get any shut-eye at all. Jamie stepped out of the bathroom and saw Erik asleep. She quickly got dressed and packed a few of her belongings.

She leaned over him, like a cat about to attack its prey, and she whispered seductively, "Time to wake up, professor."

Erik's eyes slowly opened, as the stiff hint of perfume drifted in his nostrils, and things become focused. There, right before his eyes, was the woman he loved, and she was amazing looking. He eyed her from head to toe and scanned her again. Jamie stared at him with her soft brown, crescent eyes that were enhanced by her eye shadow and mascara. Her makeup was perfectly blended with her natural caramel complexion, and her lipstick glistened on her lips in the light. Her wonderfully thick brown hair lay on her shoulders. She wore a white, form-fitted, button-down blouse with the sleeves at her elbows. She balanced out her top with a knee-length blue and white horizontal striped skirt, complemented by four-inch navy pumps.

"You like?"

Erik nodded. He stood up and couldn't keep his eyes off her. Trying to get some words out, Jamie giggled, knowing she had him tongue-tied. He got his wits together and grabbed her belongings. They left Copley Hall and headed toward Erik's car. After placing her belongings in the car, they got in, left the campus, and drove to downtown Washington, D.C. Both Erik and Jamie eyed each side of the street, their options becoming more limited with each passing minute. Washington, D.C. has tons of great places to have lunch, but parking is limited, and some restaurants are only for high profile people, like politicians. At the traffic light, Erik stared at Jamie, and she stared back. As they got lost in each other's eyes and their animal instincts took over, they kissed again. Car horns disrupted their passion.

"So, what are you hungry for?" Erik questioned as Jamie licked her lips and winked, as he clarified, "I mean food-wise."

"How about Italian?"

Erik nodded as he realized a car had been following him for ten minutes. Like Hollywood, Washington, D.C. has many limousines, the difference being the individuals inside and the vehicle itself. The individuals inside were members of the U.S. Congress or foreign dignitaries and bodyguards, and the limousine was armed, had bulletproof glass, and small arms weapons, from pistols to assault weapons. In downtown traffic, it was hard to lose someone tailing him. So, the best thing to do was get as much distance as he could between himself and the followers, but it made it hard when trying to appear as though he were driving normally while his girlfriend was making plans for future dates.

"What would you like to do tonight?" Jamie bounced the question to Erik.

"I don't know. I'm up for anything."

She pondered for a few moments, and then her eyes brightened, "Let's go see the KGB."

All the blood drained from his head, "What?"

"Let's go see the KGB."

Erik shook his head as he tried to form a sentence, "Yeah, I don't know about that. I try to avoid those guys." He wondered how he was going to explain this to Bonesteiner.

"Erik, you are silly; the KGB are great and very talented."

"Seriously? You like them that much?"

"Yes, and you will love them too."

Erik turned on the radio with the disc-jockey announcing, "Welcome back! This is Brian The Hammer Jackson on 96.7 and let's get back to music from the eighties, and I'm sure many of us felt the same way as Nik Kershaw in the song 'Wouldn't It Be Good.'"

It was like the disc-jockey knew something Erik didn't. Erik glanced in the rearview mirror and caught a glimpse of the front license plate of the limousine. He tried to keep calm as he realized who was in the car, President Vladimir Putin, who was in the KGB and held the rank of Lieutenant Colonel. He pulled out his cell phone, called the number to the compound, were on the other side. They listened to keywords: names, places, dates, and times. From that, the operator, like a 911 operator, sent back up or sent a shadow unit to observe the operative. After dialing, Erik placed the phone in his inner suit pocket. The limousine driver made an aggressive move, putting Erik on the left and blocking the right lane and his ability to pass since there was another consulate car. Erik immediately slammed on his brakes as Jamie screamed his name. While he made sure Jamie was okay, he rolled down the window and analyzed his surroundings as men emerged from the limousine.

"Erik, who are those men, and what do they want from us." Her voice and hands trembled.

He rubbed his hands through her hair, "Those men are from the Russian Secret Service."

"How do you know?"

Erik pointed to the upper chest bulges, "They are carrying either the GSh-18, which is a 9mm semi-automatic pistol or the PP-2000, which is a submachine gun."

"Erik, how do you know that?"

"I read it in a book." Then Erik pointed to a man who was shorter than the rest, saying, "He is President Vladimir Putin." He looked in her terrified eyes and said in a calm, soothing voice, "They don't want you; they want me. Everything will be fine. Okay?"

"Do you know President Putin?"

"Yes, of course, I know him; he and I are good acquaintances." She squeezed his hand tightly as she shook her head.

"Jamie, everything is going be okay; he likes history. No need to be scared. I love you."

Erik opened the door and exited. Putin drew closer with his bodyguards surrounding him as they analyzed their surroundings and people.

Putin extended his hand to meet Erik's hand, "Добрый день, доктор Фуггеров. Как ты? Good afternoon, Dr. Fugger. How are you?"

"Я хорошо спасибо. Как вы делаете Владимир? Что я обязан удовольствием этого необъявленным визитом? I am good; thank you. How are you doing, Vladimir? To what do I owe the pleasure of this unannounced visit?"

"Они сказали мне, в музее вы имели выходной день.

They told me at the museum you had the day off." Erik nodded as Putin glanced over Erik's shoulder. "Я не понимаю, что вы имели компанию. I didn't realize you had company.

Что я могу сделать для вас, Владимире? Является ли это социальная или деловой звонок? What can I do for you, Vladimir? Is this a social or business call?"

"Просто социальный. Ваш друг говорит на русском языке? Merely social. Does your friend speak Russian?"

"No. To be blunt, what do you want, Vladimir?"

"I would like to invite you and your friend to hear the Russian Quartet at our embassy."

"I'm honored, but when is it?"

"Tonight, at eight o'clock."

"That's short notice, and I think we have plans."

Erik glanced at Jamie, hoping she would go along with what he was saying. "Jamie, we have plans tonight, right?" He discretely nodded his head.

"No, Erik. We have nothing planned." She smiled and waved to Vladimir.

Erik turned to face Putin and stated, "Looks like we can go."

Putin reached into his suit jacket, pulled out a sealed envelope, and handed it to Erik, "I am so glad you are going to be able to make it, my good friend." Then in a half whisper, he continued, "Can you introduce me to your friend?"

"Vladimir, this is my girlfriend, Jamie Anderson." He waved as she returned the gesture. "Jamie, this is Russian President Vladimir Putin."

"It's nice to meet you, President Putin, and thank you for inviting us."

"You are very welcome, Ms. Anderson. Your boyfriend is a smart man. He knows a lot about history." Vladimir waved good-bye.

"Yes, he is," she replied, waving good-bye.

"Erik, it was good to see you again." They shook hands. "See you tonight."

They both headed to their cars and got in. Erik and Putin stared at each other like two alpha wolves, as their cold blue eyes hid their mysterious past. Jamie stared in silence and felt the tension in the car.

Once in the car, Erik gave an unemotional glance as he inquired, pausing first to make his point clear, "Jamie, I need you to be straight with me. What is this obsession with the KGB?"

"Erik, they are one of the local bands I like to go see." She flashed a smile as it transformed his stone face into one of confusion. "Babe, what were you thinking?"

"A band?" She kissed him and nodded as he leaned back in his seat and gave a huge sigh. "Oh, thank you, God."

"Is everything okay?"

"Yes." He turned and grinned, as he kissed her and thought, I have found since I work with the CIA that there are some things in life that I know and only a few people know about, and there are some things that I don't know, but a majority of people do know about. One happens to be learning the KGB is a rock group and not the agency that would kill me if they knew what I did.

"I didn't know you spoke Russian."

Erik nodded as his cell phone rang. He shook his head and thought aloud, "Seriously?"

"Who is it?"

"The Pope."

"Really?"

"Hold on." Erik shook his head as he answered his cell phone, "Guten Tag Bundeskanzler Schröder, wie geht es dir? Good day, Chancellor Schröder, how are you?"

Erik glanced at Jamie, as she mouthed, you speak German, too?

"Sehr gut danke. Wie kann ich Ihnen helfen? Very good, thank you. How can I help you?"

Jamie was mesmerized, and she just smiled at Erik as he continued, "Wann? Jetzt? Können wir zu einem anderen Zeitpunkt zu treffen? ...Ich habe mir jemand...meine Freundin. When? Now? Can we meet at another time? I have someone...my girlfriend."

Jamie acted silly by placing two fingers, as if they were Hitler's mustache, under her nose, as Erik grinned and rolled his eyes. "Danke Kanzlerin. Hört sich gut an, werden wir Sie in ein paar Minuten zu sehen. Auf Wiedersehen. Thank you, Chancellor. Sounds good; we'll see you in a few minutes. Goodbye."

"Guten Tag...ya. ya.ya." Jamie mimicked Erik as he rolled his eyes. "How is my German?"

"I recommend sticking with English." They stared at each other, as Erik realized how much he loved her.

He announced that he was going for lunch, but she could not come with him.

"Erik, why not?" Jamie frowned as if her happiness had been drained from her.

"Sorry. Where I am going, you have to be over thirty years old. I can drop you off at a McDonalds." Then he stared at her, "There is something else I have to tell you."

"You mad at me for what I did."

"No…I am joking. You can come with me to lunch."

At that moment, she punched his arm, "I never can tell if you are joking or if you are serious." Then she placed her head on his shoulder.

Erik glanced at Jamie as he turned the ignition. "I know." Jamie gave a puzzled look as Erik continued, "You were thinking, are you happy we are together."

She looked as if to say, how did you know that?

"Magic."

Erik navigated through the streets of the capital. Once again, he prepared himself for another meeting, and this time he hoped there were no surprises.

Turning on to Prospect St., NW, Erik said to Jamie, "Get your things; we are almost there."

"Am I dressed well enough for a place like this?"

Erik nodded.

"What kind of people go to this restaurant?" She queried.

"All kinds. You have nothing to worry about; you are with me." He pointed to the Cafe Milano.

He pulled into a parking lot across from the restaurant, as one valet opened Jamie's door, and the other raced to Erik's side and opened his door.

"Good afternoon, sir," the valet said.

Erik nodded, turned off the ignition, and headed to the trunk.

"Sir, I am going to need your key."

Erik gave a glance as if to say; you don't think I know that. He quickly removed the documents on Project Bell and placed them in his attaché case and carried it with him. Then Erik placed something strategically in his and Jamie's luggage so he would know if someone was looking. Then he handed the key to the valet and locked the trunk. The valet gave him a ticket and then parked his car. Erik walked to Jamie and escorted her to the restaurant.

As Erik and Jamie walked in, they were greeted by the maître d' with, "May I help you?"

"Dr. Függer and Ms. Anderson here to have lunch with Chancellor Schröder."

The maître d' checked his list, grabbed two menus, and motioned them to follow.

"Chancellor Schröder is dining in the Garden Room," The maître d' said.

As Jamie walked, she felt eyes upon her, and with each step she took, her focus was to avoid stumbling or tripping. They were guided to a room directly adjacent to the main dining room. Before entering, Erik was greeted by a distinguished older gentleman.

"Erik, is that you?" the gentleman asked with hand extended. As Erik turned around, the gentleman smiled, recognizing Erik. "Erik, how are you doing, and are you still working at the National Museum of American History?"

"John, I am great! How are you doing? Yes, I am."

298 | Erik Foge

"I'm good; just up here giving a lecture at the National Air and Space Museum," John said, glancing at Jamie. "Erik, who is this young lady?"

"John, may I introduce my girlfriend, Jamie Anderson." John reached out to shake her hand. "Jamie, this is John Glenn. He was one of the first American astronauts and became the first American to orbit the Earth."

"Nice to meet you, Mr. Glenn."

John gave a dismissive gesture, saying, "Please call me John." Then in a whisper, he asked, "Has Erik talked any history to you?"

Jamie nodded and smiled. "He amazes me how much history he has stored up in that brain of his." Jamie looked at Erik and smiled again.

"How did you meet Erik?" Jamie inquired.

"Five years ago, some other astronauts, our families, other distinguished guests, and I were all invited to a dinner at NASA, and your boyfriend sat next to me." John looked at his watch. "Well, I have to go. It was nice meeting you. Make sure he doesn't bore you to death about history."

Then, looking at Erik, he said, "Take care, Erik. Let's do lunch soon."

"Yes, sir, we will. Tell Annie I said hi."

John waved good-bye as the maître d' continued to escort them to their table in the Garden Room. One of Washington's premier private dining spaces, the Garden Room was directly adjacent to the main dining room and sectioned off by folding French glass doors. It was a glass-enclosed space that faced onto Prospect Street.

As the French doors opened, Jamie was taken away by the elegance of the room, the crystal ware, fine china, and everything else her eyes were absorbing. At the same time, the people there stared at her and looked away. She squeezed Erik's hand to release some of her nervous tension.

"Erik?" A voice with an English accent drifted in Erik's direction. "Erik, how are you doing?" Erik did recognize the voice and the face; It was Gordon Brown. He got up from his table with his hand extended.

"Gordon, I am well, thank you. How are things?"

"Things are wonderful. I see you have a young lady with you."

Erik glanced at Jamie, who was smiling and looked back at Gordon. "I do apologize; Gordon, this is my girlfriend, Jamie Anderson."

They shook hands as Erik continued, "Jamie, this is Gordon Brown, Chancellor of the Exchequer of England."

Then Gordon turned to his wife, who got up from the table. "Sarah," he said, "you remember Dr. Erik Függer, the gentleman that gave us the private tour at the National Museum of American History."

"Yes, of course. Hello, Dr. Függer; how are you?" She extended her hand to meet Erik's.

"Very well, Mrs. Brown. You can call me Erik."

She continued the polite conversation by advising him that he could call her Sarah. Then Gordon introduced the ladies to each other.

Gordon addressed Jamie, "I have not met a single

individual who knows the different views of history as well as Erik. You are fortunate to have him as your boyfriend. Not only is he intelligent but also a gentleman."

His wife added, "I would agree with Gordon. I remember, ever since I met him in 2002, I have been trying to set him up with a date, but he always says there is someone special in his life."

Sarah, as well as Jamie, glanced at Erik as she resumed, "Erik, is this the young lady that you were talking about?"

"Yes," He answered, glancing first at Jamie, then at her, "She is all that I am. She is the one who makes me complete. I am delighted she is in my life, and I believe she is the one." Jamie was left speechless as she tried to contain her tears of joy and moved closer to him.

"Well, I am very happy for you both," Sarah said.

Erik and Jamie nodded in appreciation and said their goodbyes. Immediately after that introduction was over, the maître d motioned that they were at their assigned table, as an older gentleman got up and approached Erik.

"Dr. Függer, wie geht es dir, mein freund? Dr. Függer, how are you, my friend?" Then he looks at Jamie with a smile. "Sie haben einen guten geschmack. You have good taste."

"Schröder, ich bin gut und danke. Schroeder, I am well, and thank you."

"Hat sie Deutsch sprechen? Does she speak German?" Erik shook his head as Schröder glanced at Jamie.

"I apologize for speaking German in front of you," said Schröder, extending his hand to shakes Jamie's hand. "I am Chancellor Schröder. "

"It's okay. I am Jamie Anderson. I can speak French."

"Donc ce que je peux, Erik ne sait pas ce que nous disons. Cependant sa connaissance de l'histoire est incroyable. So, can I; Erik doesn't know what we are saying. However, his knowledge in history is amazing," Schröder replied kindly.

"Oui, j'aime quand il me parle de l'histoire. Je parle couramment le français. Yes, I love when he tells me about history," Jamie responded.

"Vous avez un bel accent. You have a beautiful accent. Peut-être que vous pouvez lui apprendre. Maybe you can teach him."

"Merci. Thank you."

"My friend," Chancellor Schröder motioned to Erik and Jamie to sit, as the server took their drink orders. "How are you doing?"

"Good, thank you, yourself?"

"My health is good." Chancellor Schröder pointed to the menus. "Order anything you want; it's on me."

Erik nodded in appreciation as the server took their orders. "What is going to be your next exhibit?"

Erik had learned one thing about Schröder: that he was an excellent two-way communicator who was always straightforward, polite, and, most importantly, integrity-filled. "World War Two," he answered.

"Rommel? He was a good man." Erik nodded as the server brought lunch to the table.

"I would not disagree."

Over the course of an hour, Schröder and Erik talked about old times and their friendship, as Jamie listened.

Her eyes drifted around the room to see whom she could recognize; even though she might not know their names, she figured they had great importance. Every few minutes, Erik glanced at her to make sure she was okay and extended his hand out, as she mouthed, I love you. What most people did not know was places like this were excellent for meetings of essential people. That is why the Garden Room was private, and only specific people were allowed in. There were ears and eyes everywhere.

Schröder and a few members of his security detail got up, and Erik and Jamie followed. As they exited, Schröder turned to Erik. "My friend, I almost forgot." He handed Erik a bag. "Enjoy."

"Thank you." In Erik's line of work, it was hard to know whom to trust, but when he did, those who trusted him would help him fill in the gaps of information. Erik pulled out a box that contained a plastic model kit of Field Marshal Rommel's half-track.

24. PREPARING AND DISCOVERING

"All truths are easy to understand once they are discovered. The point is to discover them."

— Galileo Galilei

As Erik and Jamie walked over to the valet, Erik received a text from Bonesteiner instructing him to go to Diana's Couture & Bridal, at 1624 Wisconsin Ave. NW in Georgetown. There Jamie would be fitted for a gown, and once done, he was to proceed to the Haagen-Dazs Ice Cream Shop at 3120 M St NW. The car pulled, up, valets opened the doors, Erik and Jamie got in, and he drove to the bridal shop. Jamie looked at the German half-track model; all writing on the outside of the box was in Japanese. Erik studied the box and made mental notes of the image. He eventually placed it in the back seat.

Without looking at Jamie, Erik asked, "What do you want to know about it?"

"Do you read Japanese?" Erik shook his head.

"Erik, you know it is written in Japanese?" Erik nodded.

"Ready to learn?" Erik asked.

Jamie smirked and nodded her head. Erik began by telling her the basics. "This is a German half-track, used during World War Two, and it was one of Rommel's personal vehicles." He explained SdKfz stood for Sonderkraftfahrzeug, which meant in English, special motor vehicle, and the 250 was the vehicle class, and 3 was a variant, one of twelve variants. The SdKfz 250/3 was a command vehicle equipped with long-range radio equipment for communications and used by high-level commanders. The distinguishing feature of this variant was the unique frame-type radio antenna mounted on the roof of the half-track known as the "bedstead" aerial frame. Rommel's personal vehicle was named "GREIF." Named after the mythical creature known as the Griffin. Rommel, like the Griffin, was all-powerful on the land and air in Africa, even though only briefly.

Jamie shook her head in amazement. "How do you remember all that?"

Erik shrugged his shoulders. "I just remember certain things." It was true that he did have a good memory; however, while at The Farm, he had an armored fighting vehicle (AFV) and aircraft identification class that dealt with various nations' military equipment.

Jamie's eyes looked straight into Erik's. "When you were away, I saw the most amazing movie with the girls." Erik focused on the road. "It was Mr. and Mrs. Smith, have you seen it?"

Erik shook his head. She explained that John and Jane Smith were an average married couple, living a normal life in a typical suburb and working routine jobs, too. However, in reality, they were both skilled assassins working for different government agencies, both the best in their field, each concealing their real professions from the other. Neither John nor Jane knew about their spouse's secret until they were surprised to find they were targeting each other.

"Isn't that amazing that they could hide that from each other?" Jamie stated.

"Absolutely; I mean, they must have been very good at what they did."

"I know, right? If you want to see it, I will see it with you."

As Erik came to a stop, He turned to face Jamie. Her eyes were waiting to meet his and Erik's voice lowered and became dramatic. "Ms. Anderson, are you a spy?"

Jamie tried to get into character by tilting her head and lowering her voice. "Yes, and my mission is to watch Dr. Erik Függer."

In a cold, sadistic tone, and squinting eyes, Erik replied, "Is that so, Ms. Anderson?" He paused to make it more dramatic. "Who do you work for?"

Jamie bit her lower lip, as Erik's eyes never lost focus. Jamie did not realize that he was using the Reid technique, which is the trademark interrogation technique widely used by law enforcement agencies. Erik watched her body language to detect deceit. She tried to think of an answer.

"Answer me!" Erik demanded.

"The FBI." A chill ran up her spine, as Erik's eyes grew cold. "My name is Agent Anderson."

"Oh, really?" Erik leaned his forehead against hers. "What is your objective?"

She broke character, tilted her head, smiled, and kissed him. "To give him all my loving...do, you think he can handle that?"

"Oh, yeah, bring it on."

A horn broke the mood, and the conversation continued.

"That was amazing. Have you ever taken acting classes?" He shook his head. "You were like a character in a spy thriller."

"Well, I guess I have a natural talent."

"What's your favorite movie?"

Erik shrugged his shoulders.

"Just pick one," she insisted.

"Raiders of the Lost Ark...heard of it?"

"I think so..." Her eyes rolled up as she placed a finger on her chin. "Yeah, he wore the same hat as you. What is it about?"

Erik explained that the story took place before World War Two, 1936, and the main character was an archeology professor and archeologist, Dr. Indiana Jones. "One could say he had two separate lives that were very different from each other. Dr. Jones was a simple, well-mannered man who was book smart; however, in the field, he was a ruthless man who knew firearms and faced danger head-on, which could have resulted in his death at any time. Nevertheless, as a lone hero, he overcame many obstacles and always got the job done."

"You sound like him; the only difference is that people don't try to kill you," Jamie replied.

"Yeah, it wouldn't be fun being shot at."

Moments later, Erik slid into a parking spot. They both got out and headed to the small boutique. Immediately upon stepping in, they were welcomed by a short but energetic Southeast Asian woman as Jamie's eyes feasted on the gowns.

"Erik, how have you been?" The woman questioned with a thick Vietnamese accent. "James told me you were coming." She stared at Jamie and extended her hand to greet her. "Will this be a black-tie event?" Erik nodded affirmatively; the woman faced Jamie continued, "My name is Diana. Follow me."

Diana was from Vietnam. During the Vietnam War, she had been a tailor, and in 1968 she was recruited by the CIA for counterintelligence. For her services, Diana and her husband were brought to the United States after the war. She opened her shop in Georgetown. Now, Diana helped the agencies' employees and spouses on their special occasions and rush jobs like this one. Not only was Diana capable of doing quality work and fast service, but also, she could create her designs from scratch; if one had an idea, she could turn it into a reality.

She ordered Jamie to stop and stand up straight as she walked around her. Diana had perfect eyes for proportions. "You are a size four."

She turned to Erik, asking, "Will she need shoes?" Erik nodded, and then Diana led Jamie toward the racks of gowns.

Jamie turned to Erik, "Want to help me pick one?"

While Jamie was distracted, Diana discretely motioned

to Erik to see how much time he needed, and she winked, acknowledging his response.

"I need to make a call. I will be back. I promise."

Erik walked out to his car, got in, opened the model box, and pulled out a file from the Third Reich, filled with secret documents dealing with Field Marshal Erwin Rommel after his car was strafed, 17 July 1944. Knowing he was pressed for time, Erik quickly churned through the data, flipping through the pages with great speed. When skimming the pages, he looked for crucial information that had never been seen by public eyes, and once found, he deposited it in his memory. Erik closed the file, rubbed his eyes, and placed it in the attaché case. He composed himself, and then he went back to the shop.

Jamie came happily out of the dressing room wearing a black evening gown that had a sexy low back and halter design. Diana paired the gown with beautiful black heels, simple jewelry, and a small beaded clutch with silver threads. After giving Jamie the items to try on, she approached Erik and showed him the total on a calculator. Moments later, Jamie modeled her gown with the accessories, as she looked for and got Erik's approval. Afterward, Diana brought Jamie back to finish the final measurements. Jamie daydreamed about the evening and pictured herself moving through a crowd of people on a marble floor in the elegant ballroom with Erik by her side.

Diana noticed Jamie trembling and gently touched her shoulder, "Erik will be by your side. You have nothing to worry about."

"Were there others before me?" Jamie asked.

Diana shook her head as she made chalk lines. "How long, Erik?" asked Diana.

"Seven years," he replied.

Diana looked up. "Okay, you are all set; you can change now." Diana walked out; Erik followed her.

"How much time do you need?" Erik questioned as he handed over his credit card.

"Ninety minutes. How is Al..." Diana answered, motioning that Jamie was coming. Acting natural, she continued, "You can pick up her gown in ninety minutes." She handed Erik a bag that contained Jamie's accessories.

"Thank you, Diana."

Jamie glanced at Erik's credit card and asked, "Erik, how many frequent flyer miles do you have?"

A baffled look came on Erik's face. "Frequent flyer miles?"

She pointed to the credit card. "Northwest Airlines."

Erik did a forced grin. Ironically, Jamie was wrong; even though the credit card said Northwest, it was the name of the credit union CIA employees used. Then he turned to her and asked, "Ready?"

In the car, Jamie moved close to Erik and put her head against his shoulder as she held his hand. Erik drove to his next location, the Haagen-Dazs Ice Cream shop. His gut told him that he would be meeting someone from the compound; however, Erik did not know why. Jamie was so interested in how much the gown cost, at the same time trying to choose the right words to say.

"Erik, have you ever seen the movie Pretty Woman?" He nodded. "You remind me of Edward."

Erik rolled his eyes and shook his head. "I don't think so."

"Was my gown and the other things expensive? Erik said nothing. "Hello?"

"Don't worry about it."

As Erik pulled up to the ice cream shop, he recognized a man leaning against the storefront. It was Mike. Mike, like Erik, worked for the CIA, and he was a part of the Directorate of Science and Technology (DS&T). He was assigned to the Operations Tradecraft and Technical Development departments. Mike had attended MIT; he got his bachelor's in information technology and had two master's degrees as well. The first one was in Information Technology Information Assurance and Cyber Security, and the second one was in Information Technology Software Engineering. His job consisted of applying creative solutions to solve complicated and challenging technical and operational problems. Mike also analyzed requirements, proposed solutions, conducted engineering analyses, managed development activities, and transitioned systems to full operation.

As Erik got out and walked around the car, Mike discretely gestured that he needed Erik's car keys. He approached Erik with his hand extended to meet Erik's hand. The exchange was made. Erik made the introductions brief, knowing Mike had to do something with the car. The only question was, what. Whatever it was, it would only take a few moments to do, while they were eating ice cream. Erik figured it was necessary because usually individuals in the DS&T do not leave the compound.

For Erik, it was instinctive to go through a mental checklist every time he entered a building. He looked for all available exits, take a corner table, and looked for things to use as a weapon. Lastly, Erik checked out every individual and always had an exit strategy. There was one person already placing his order in front of them.

Erik turned to Jamie, "What kind do you want?"

Looking over the menu board and eyeing the flavors behind the glass, she replied, "Pistachio."

Erik glanced at her as if she had to be kidding, but he nodded and grinned.

"What?" Jamie said.

Erik shook his head and shrugged his shoulders. "Well, I also like coffee and rainbow sherbet."

"I bet the nerd with the stupid hat likes chocolate," the man in front of them said without looking back.

"Well, I bet people think you're smart until you open your mouth."

The clerk behind the counter replied, "Guys, take it outside."

The man turned around and immediately took a fighting stance, while Erik opened his arms and welcomed a friend he hadn't seen in years. Then they embraced. "How are you, brother, man?" The man asked.

Erik answered, "I'm alive."

"In your profession, it certainly is a good thing."

"But they need to catch you first."

"Exactly. Are you dining in?"

Erik nodded and placed his order, paid for it, located where Rusch was, and Erik and Jamie joined him. "Jamie, here is a great friend of mine, Rusch."

"Nice to meet you," Rusch said while eating his ice cream. "How long have you known this bum?"

"I met him when I was 18, but we just started dating."

"You need to keep him in line…just kidding; he is a great guy and one of the smartest I know." Rusch saw Erik shaking his head. "Stop shaking your head."

Jamie added, "He doesn't like comments on how smart he is."

Rusch pondered and shook his head in disbelief. "He acts the same way as the first time I met him," he added as he pointed to Erik. "He is the strangest mother fucker I have known, but he's like a brother to me."

"How long have you known each other?" Jamie questioned Rusch.

"Since 1997, before he started working at the museum."

"So, you've known Erik ever since he moved to Washington?" Rusch nodded. "I bet you've got some great stories about him."

"You have no idea."

Rusch explained how they had met. However, to Jamie and others who might be listening, it probably sounded as if they had met at a survivor camp. He told stories about Erik's tenacity in everything he did, how, unlike others who thought outside the box, Erik didn't see a box, and how he was always reading a book. Erik explained that Rusch was the glue that had bonded the men together at camp, and because of that, he commanded respect. Rusch could appear arrogant, but he had satirical humor, and it took time to understand it. Most importantly, Erik said that Rusch had a deep capacity for friendship and remained very loyal to those he considered friends.

"Sounds like camp was fun," Jamie stated, staring at Erik and Rusch. "Can anyone go?"

Rusch shook his head. "You have to be invited."

"Did you guys skydive at the camp?" Jamie asked. Erik and Rusch looked at each other and knew precisely what the other was thinking. Then they stared back at her. "You know, it is where you jump from a plane."

"He jumped from 10,000 feet." Rusch pointed at Erik. "That was Erik's first jump."

"Were you scared, Erik?" Erik shook his head as Jamie realized what Rusch had just said. "How many times have you done it?"

Erik looked at the ceiling and tried to recall, as he counted the number of times on his hand.

"Babe?" She noticed how many fingers were up ... nine. "You must be an adrenaline junkie. What's the highest been?"

"Not at all." Both Erik and Rusch ate a scoop of ice cream.

"Fifteen thousand feet?" Jamie inquired as she looked around the table as though inviting a discussion that never came. "I know you cannot go higher than that," Erik said nothing and glanced at Rusch, who mimicked Erik's mannerisms. They both knew Erik had jumped at 35,000 feet. Jamie looked at Rusch questioningly. "Am I right?" She studied them, and then she shook her head.

"What's wrong?" Erik asked.

"He acts the same way as you when you avoid a question."

Without thinking, Erik and Rusch answered in unison, "I would disagree. I don't even act like him."

They stared at each other, and Jamie as she replied, "You even talk the same way."

Rusch mocked. "No, that's not true," as they both laughed. Rusch smacked the table as he turned to Erik. "Hey, when are we going to see The Final Countdown again?" He turned to Jamie. "Have you seen that movie?" He paused for a moment and continued, "That is an amazing movie."

Erik added, "Should I bring the ice cream?"

Rusch nodded as Erik shook his head and replied, "Asshole."

Rusch looked at his watch. "Well, I have to go." He stared at Jamie. "It was nice to meet you."

Then he stared at Erik, "Walk me out?"

They left Jamie with her thoughts. Once outside, Mike approached them. His facial expression revealed that there was something wrong. Their eyes focused on their surroundings, as Mike gave his debriefing.

"I have some good news, bad news, terrible news, and disturbing news." Rusch motioned him to continue since time was of the essence. "Good is that I did find a bug. The bad is, not only can they hear you, but it has a GPS built in it."

"Did you remove it?" Erik demanded as Mike shook his head. "Why in the bloody hell not?"

"Because I figured you could use it against them. They will monitor your car, not you. Thus, you can take another car, and it will not raise a red flag."

"Good point; what's the other news?" asked Erik.

"The very bad news is that there is no electronic signature on it, so I cannot tell you who made it."

"What's the disturbing news?" Erik replied with his arms crossed against his chest.

Mike held up Erik's keys with a valet ticket attached to it. He turned the ticket so both could see the handwriting that read, We Know Your Name. "This is the disturbing news…someone is making it personal…I think this is a warning."

Rusch told Mike to meet him at the car and then addressed Erik.

"You need to be on your guard tonight. Putin is up to something." Rusch advised. He handed Erik a box as Erik handed over the tape. The box had cufflinks that contained micro transmitters. Rusch informed him that they would remain off, so they would not be detected until Erik said the sentence, "The thought has occurred to me." Erik remembered in training the sentence, "There are only solutions, not problems." Rusch told Erik that while in the Russian Embassy, he must always ask himself these questions: Who and what am I around? Who and what will affect me? And what will be the outcome? Lastly, Erik knew that opportunities do not come often, but when they do, it is good to know there is someone out there looking after you. Before Rusch left, he turned to Erik. "Putin is very good at reading people, especially operatives like you. So, remember to put discipline over emotions, or they will be your downfall."

25. LOOKING THROUGH THE EYES OF MY LOVE

"In the end it's not the years in your life that count. It's the life in your years."

—Abraham Lincoln

Erik slipped on his tuxedo jacket, adjusted it, and his bow tie while he modeled himself in the mirror to make sure everything was perfect. Next, he turned his head to the right and left to make sure his hair was styled to his liking. Then he realized that Jamie, who was poised by the bathroom door, had caught him in his private act. Jamie looked radiant in her black evening gown, which had a sexy low back and halter design. She paired it with beautiful black heels, simple jewelry, and a small beaded clutch. She added to her elegant look by wearing her brunette locks down in a beautifully blow-dried style with a slight wave and keeping her make-up to a minimum. Together, they could be mistaken for a diplomatic couple.

Minutes later, they were on the way to the Russian Embassy, as Jamie continued to role-play scenarios on how to act and what to say. Her biggest fear was being afraid of saying something stupid and embarrassing him.

"Take several deep breaths," Erik cautioned as he glanced at Jamie. "You will be fine."

Jamie gently sighed, "What kind of people will be attending?"

"Politicians and ambassadors and their wives."

"Do you get invited to these a lot?"

Erik gestured and replied, "Sometimes."

"Will I come with you when you are invited?"

Erik nodded.

The car came to a halt as he rolled down his window and handed over his invitation. Embassy guards with assault rifles surrounded his vehicle. Jamie tried not to look unintelligent and acted complacent, knowing there would be this kind of protection at the embassy. However, she felt quite safe with the extra guns, but never as safe as she felt with Erik on her arm. A few minutes went by before they could proceed. The driveway and motor court were filled with limousines and other large high-end sedans. White-gloved security staffers helped guests in formal dress exit their vehicles, and then they were escorted through the enormous front doors. Once through the doors, they offed their overcoats. Before guests could continue, security staffers politely scanned them with hand-held metal detectors.

The decorations on the grand ballroom's ceiling were in Soviet-Era dedication to political events and military victories. The marble floors shined like mirrors. A world immediately engulfed Jamie that she had only heard about and seen on documentaries. Her eyes focused intensely on the ballroom as if a new world was revealed to her. Individuals from countries all over the world, socializing, drinking, and enjoying themselves filled the room. She stuck very close to Erik as he moved through the crowd. The pace in the room made her mind and heart collide with emotions, but she appeared as if she had it all together, even though her world was chaotic. Jamie focused on not tripping and smiled at everyone; she made eye connect within the room.

A member of the catering staff approached, with champagne and offered Erik and Jamie a glass. Out of the corner of his eye, Erik saw a man with a warm smile, dressed in formal Arab dress with a turban approaching him.

"Erik…" The man waved and extended his hand to meet Erik's hand. "Erik, my friend, how are you doing?"

"Jaber, I am doing well," Erik grinned. "How are you and your family?"

"Very well. My oldest is attending the university here in Washington, D.C." Erik nodded and showed he was pleased with the news. Then Jaber's eyes focused on Jamie. In a whisper, Jaber asked, "Who is the young lady?"

"Jaber, I would like you to meet my girlfriend, Jamie Anderson." He turned to Jamie and could not keep his eyes off her figure.

"Very nice to meet you, Ms. Anderson," Jaber replied.

Jamie curled up her toes, smiled, and responded with a few kind words. Then they continued to make their way through the room. As they did, others approached Erik, said a few words, and continued. She felt a little intimidated, but with Erik by her side, she slowly built her confidence. Once she was able, Jamie whispered, "Do you know all these people, and are they your friends?"

He shook his head and informed her that very few were friends, but most were acquaintances or people he had met. Jamie became speechless as the President of the United States approached Erik.

"Dr. Függer, it's nice to see you again." He turned his head to the right and continued, "Laura, you remember Dr. Függer from the National Museum of American History."

"Of course, how are you? Is Alan here?" Then with a wide bright smile, the First Lady inquired, "Who is this young lady?"

"I am well, and I haven't seen him around. This is Jamie Anderson, my girlfriend."

They exchanged handshakes, as Laura asked, "What do you do for a living?"

Jamie hesitated to answer, as Erik gave her a subtle nod to reassure her, it was okay, "I am a senior at Georgetown."

Laura became speechless momentarily as she realized Jamie was younger than she thought, and she forced a smile. "That's nice. What is your major?"

"Public relations, with a minor in French." The President and Laura smiled, said their good-byes, and left.

Jamie grabbed Erik's hand and looked at him, "I'm sorry."

Erik pulled Jamie closer and gently held both of her hands, "What for?"

"I embarrassed you."

"You didn't embarrass me. You are with me, and you have nothing to worry about." Erik pulled Jamie even closer. "You are the youngest here, but that doesn't mean you do not belong here." He paused to let the words soak in. "I want you to be a part of my world, and when I go overseas, I will see if you can come with me."

Jamie's eyes enlarged with joy. "Really?" she said as her smile radiated the room. Erik nodded, even though he knew the chances were slim. "I am the luckiest girl in the world." She wished she could hug and kiss him passionately.

Erik saw Gordon and Sarah over Jamie's shoulder, and at the moment he turned Jamie around, they waved. Erik whispered, "Do you remember their names?"

Jamie bit her lower lip as she waved and tried to recall the names. As if a light bulb over her head had suddenly come on, she replied. "Gordon and Sarah."

Erik nodded and added, "They want to meet you again. They think you are an amazing person and don't judge you for your age."

Erik and Jamie headed toward them. She felt more relaxed and confident. Gordon and Sarah welcomed her with warm smiles and hugs, and that brought the old Jamie back.

"Erik, good to see you again," Gordon said warmly and turned to Jamie. "Jamie, how are you doing? Is this your first time at an embassy?"

"I am great, thank you, and, yes. I am just a little overwhelmed."

"Jamie, I was the same way when Gordon took me for the first time," said Sarah, giving her support and adding, "Do not worry about what others think. You are with Erik, and you can sit by us during the performance." Jamie nodded in appreciation.

"Erik, may I speak to you in private?" Gordon asked, and Erik nodded. "Excuse us, ladies."

Once they were a fair distance away, Gordon whispered to Erik. "I have not seen Putin all night."

Gordon could read Erik's expression. "I would agree that it is unorthodox. He is up to something or waiting for someone," Erik threw out a suggestion.

"Like who?"

Erik casually tapped his chest.

"Why in the bloody hell, would he?"

"I don't know."

Both Gordon and Erik glanced at their surroundings before Gordon continued, "When did this information arrive and from whom?"

"A couple of hours..."

Gordon cut Erik's last words off. "Why didn't you call me?"

"It had to be done this way."

Gordon shook his head in bewilderment. "Is your source accurate?"

Erik nodded as his eyes scanned the room.

"My friend, what have you gotten yourself into?"

Erik gestured that he could not talk about it.

"What can I do to help?" asked Gordon.

"If I do not get out before the performance is done, I want you to take Jamie with you to the British Embassy and call Alan. He will know what to do."

"The gray cardinal has just entered the room."

Erik turned to see Putin making his way through the room as Gordon motioned them to rejoin the ladies.

Jamie whispered, "I love you," as Erik nodded and kept his eyes fixed on Putin, who slowly proceeded toward him. Jamie grabbed Erik's hand to release some nervous tension, as she took deep breaths. Erik knew the goal was to control as many variables as possible when his target showed up. Also, he needed to know the situation he was going to be in and about the person who was placing him in that situation. After saying hello to Gordon and his wife, Putin's shark-like eyes focused on Erik.

"Dr. Függer, I am so glad you were able to come." Then his eyes became relaxed, "Ms. Anderson, how are you doing this evening?"

"I am well. Thank you for inviting us."

"Oh, it is no problem at all," Putin made an elaborate gesture of charm. "Is this your first time at a function like this?"

Jamie smiled and nodded.

"That is lovely. I hope you enjoy your evening."

"Thank you."

"Dr. Függer, may I speak to you about a matter in private?" Putin glared at Erik. Then he addressed Jamie and the others. "Excuse us."

Before Erik disappeared with Putin into the crowd,

Erik turned around, winked and grinned at Jamie, as she mouthed, "I love you." She was overwhelmed with thoughts about what had just happened. Her curiosity grew and wondered what they were going to be talking about. Jamie was worried that it was something she did or if she had made Erik look bad. However, she was un-aware of the danger Erik was always in and how close to death he was. Ironically, Erik did not know if he had gone too far and didn't realize how close he was.

26. THE WRONG MESSAGE COULD END YOU

"Spies and politicians tend not to get along very well. Politicians see spies as vitally important in the national interest, right up to the point where they deny ever meeting them and abandon them entirely. It makes for a tough working relationship."

— *Burn Notice*, episode "Last Stand,"
voiceover of Michael Weston

The elevator doors closed, and the elevator ascended.

"So, Vladimir, can I ask where we are going?" Erik questioned, as Putin smirked and shook his head.

Erik knew to be in another country's embassy in Washington, D.C. could be as bad as an op going wrong and getting stuck behind enemy lines. Inside the embassy, anything could be done to a person; they could make people disappear, and the agent couldn't call 911 or his team to help. While stuck in a foreign embassy, Erik knew it would be difficult to hide in the shadows and escape. If Erik was going to be held in the Russian embassy, he could wait to be killed or march into danger and face it head-on. Erik knew there was nothing he could do but move on and make the best of the situation. Even though it was a suicide mission, he could not call it off. He had been taught in situations like these that it was crucial to stay focused and be aware of his surroundings. Also, Erik knew there were high risks and he knew he must be prepared for anything. However, if things went smoothly, he might survive.

Erik and Vladimir reached the assigned floor, exited, and walked down a hallway. In the near distance, two armed men in suits were a part of the FSB. One was holding a hand-held device. Once Erik got closer, he realized the device was used to pick up any electronic surveillance equipment, such as RF transmitters. Vladimir motioned the men to do their jobs. Most people would find this awkward and start asking too many questions or complain, but to trained individuals like Vladimir, that would be a red flag. However, if Erik said nothing at all, that would be another red flag, and Vladimir might think Erik was an operative. Therefore, he had to find a balance of the two. All the while, Vladimir was studying him. In short, Vladimir would be playing a mental chess game trying to outmaneuver Erik, trying to make Erik falter under pressure.

Entering the office, Erik recognized Nikolai Patrushev, Director of the FSB and a few nameless others, who very likely worked in the Russian intelligence community. Erik was offered a seat and something to drink, which he turned down.

Vladimir took a seat next to Erik and said, "I am glad

you could make it, Erik." Erik nodded in appreciation as Putin grabbed a folder off the desk. "You are curious why I asked you up here?"

Vladimir, who was intellectually curious, loved complex problems, and he was analyzing Erik's body language. Patrushev weighed his reaction with a critical squint. From this, Vladimir would try to come up with unique solutions, driven more by concepts and abstract ideas, to test Erik.

"The thought has occurred to me," Erik replied.

Erik took everything seriously, as seriously as he did his causes and their global outlook and the big-picture focus. Thus, he was going to make it difficult for his observers to get on his wavelength because he was going to withdraw into himself.

Vladimir pulled out a photograph and handed it to Erik.

Patrushev stated, "Do you know anything about this?"

It was a picture of the Virginia class, also known as the SSN-774 class, the nuclear-powered fast attack submarine. Erik shook his head.

Patrushev continues, "It is your country's new fast attack submarine, the Virginia Class."

"Okay, and?" Erik replied in a contemplative tone, as he quickly connected the dots.

Vladimir cut in, "Can your sources get information on this submarine?"

Vladimir's mind was full of complexity, ideas, and possibilities. He was hoping he would move Erik towards a conclusion. Also, he saw if there would be any conflict that could be a part of the process. Then Vladimir would act on that information, and he would know it was time to move on. Ever since Erik had met Putin, he had found himself always being tested by him. Each new test could be immediate and unexpected. He also knew that both men were watching his eyes. For example, Erik knew if he looked to the left, this would indicate a made-up answer, and looking to the right would indicate a voice or image, and thus, he would be telling the truth.

Erik answered in an obsequious tone, "Yes, they can."

Patrushev added, "Once we get the information, we will pay you one-hundred thousand American dollars."

There was silence in the room, until Patrushev pulled out a lighter, struck the spark wheel, and a flame emerged. He took a puff of his cigarette, and blue smoke dissipated.

Then Patrushev spoke again between puffs. "Would you prefer that in cash or your offshore account?"

"The ability to compromise is not a diplomatic politeness toward a partner but rather taking into account and respecting your partner's legitimate interests," Vladimir stated.

Vladimir gave a wicked smirk as he glanced at Patrushev, then back at Erik.

Vladimir pointed at Erik in order to get his point across and stated in a haughty tone, "Nobody should have any illusion about the possibility of gaining military superiority over Russia. We will never allow this to happen."

"Do you believe that, Vladimir?"

"The FSB has reliable documented evidence of active

attempts by British intelligence to learn Russian military secrets. The arrest of two special agents exposed by military counter-intelligence proves this." Patrushev replied.

Both Erik and Vladimir were capable of reading each other's body language; however, they were always cautious of the various things that could mislead them from the truth when they searched for it. They usually had each other's backs, but they were looking to expose the other's self-deception. Putin's intuition was based on gathered information that was focused, and he was looking for validation in Erik, whom Putin was not confident he could trust. Still, Putin knew Erik was capable of getting the information he needed. As for Erik, his intuition was based on experiences and feelings; however, he was intelligent and decided that he could make them useful tools. They were both playing a mental and verbal game of chess to find each other's strengths and weaknesses.

"Dr. Függer," Patrushev paused to collect his thoughts. "Efforts to boost the defense capability, in particular, to develop new weaponry, as well as plans for reorganizing the Russian Armed Forces have sparked unprecedented interest and activity from foreign intelligence services."

Patrushev's cold blue eyes peered down at Erik as he waited for his reply.

As a paramilitary operations officer assigned to an OGDS team, Erik was used to dealing with his enemies face to face. He knew Putin was looking for intelligence, this time on the Virginia Class nuclear submarine. However, when the director of the FSB and Putin were in the same room, they were looking for something more.

Another reason was they were looking to set him up to compromise him — or both. In that case, Erik knew he needed to be alert for danger, but it was not always obvious. It could be as subtle as a comment to test you. So. while they suddenly seemed to have a little more interest in him, and not the information he could provide, Erik also knew the wrong message could end him. So, he said nothing.

Vladimir started to get up from his seat, with Erik getting up slowly; at that moment, it was as if a light bulb had gone off in Vladimir's head as he motioned Erik to take his seat. Vladimir rubbed his chin while looking at Erik. "Does SMERSH mean anything to you?"

Erik nodded and knew in his line of work that when he had worked with specific individuals long enough, they dropped subtle clues. From that, he was able to predict human behavior and know where a conversation would lead. Vladimir motioned Erik to speak.

"They were a department with the NKVD and formed in April 1943."

Vladimir nodded and grinned at Patrushev and then glanced back at Erik. "So, you know about them."

Erik shook his head. "Just heard."

"So, what have you heard about SMERSH?"

"They are not to be dealt with lightly."

"Correct, do you know their motto?

This was the part of the conversation when Erik knew that he could have seconds, minutes, or even hours, and if he was lucky, maybe days left to live. "No, I do not." However, Erik did know the answer, but he also knew that how the answer would be said would determine the outcome of this meeting.

"Death to Spies." He said with disdain and looked like he enjoyed saying those words.

"Thank you for the history lesson."

Vladimir raised his hand to let Erik know to stay seated.

"Well, I am not done."

Vladimir sat back in his chair and squared his shoulders as the temperature in the room seemed to drop, and his facial expression turned colder.

"I hope what I heard is not true…I heard a rumor you are an analyst for the Central Intelligence Agency."

He let those words sink into Erik's soul as he studied Erik's facial expressions, and Patrushev handed a set of photographs to Erik. The pictures were of Jamie in front of her dorm, with her cheerleading squad, and walking around the campus. Erik flipped through the photographs.

Vladimir continued, "I would not want anything to happen to Jamie like your other girlfriend, Jackie." As Erik placed the photographs on the desk, he gave a hostile glance at Vladimir. "Oh yes, I know about that and more."

Since Erik had been with the CIA, he had learned the ability to operate anonymously, which was his greatest weapon. He lied to individuals, like Putin, to gain their trust, then exploited it to achieve his objective. Erik put his country's national security over his. Erik had been allowed to do his job as a paramilitary operations officer anywhere, to deceive his enemies and even loved ones. When he finished an op, he slipped back into the world of anonymity. However, when individuals like Putin got in his face and threatened his girlfriend, his options got a lot more limited. At that point, all he could do was an attack, no matter who they were. The real catch was that only Erik would live or die, but it didn't matter to Erik. He reached into his pocket, pulled out the valet ticket that had the words, we know your name, and tossed it to Putin, as the bodyguards pulled out their GSh-18s.

Erik stated in a forthright tone, "You can stop playing your childish games."

Putin glanced at the ticket and handed it to Patrushev, who, in turn, placed it on the desk.

Putin replied, "You know I was with the KGB, and I do not play games." He pointed to Erik to get his point across. "If I wanted to kill you, I would not give you a warning ... I would just put a fucking bullet in your skull."

Erik leaned forward and replied in a whisper. "If you have Jamie followed, talk to her, or even touch her, many of your operatives will be on the FSB's memorial wall." Erik was applying the unwritten code of the CIA, you fuck with us, and we will fuck you harder.

"Is that so?" Patrushev asked sarcastically.

Erik nodded and continued. "And another thing, if anything happens to her, I will make sure this will be your last term as president."

Both Erik and Putin jumped to their feet and faced off.

Putin replied, "Are you sure you want to threaten me?"

"No, just stating the fact that I want you to think about every minute of the day."

"You are just an analyst and nothing more."

"Are you willing to take that chance, Vladimir?" Erik replied in an indignant tone and continued. "If I were you and Patrushev, I would highly recommend getting in your Ilyushin Il-96-300PU and get the fuck out of my country and head back to Russia."

"You better watch your back and not sleep."

"Keep this in the back of your mind when you fly over the Atlantic; anything can happen. Moreover, when you are relaxing in your seat, I would hate it if you had an engine problem. However, that wouldn't be the worst of your problems. The radio, black box, and other things that would determine your location would not be operational. On a final note, your country would have to prepare for your state funeral."

In a convincing face-off with the President, Erik gave a stern, cold 'fuck you' look to Putin, and the rest of the Barynya sitting at the table and walked out of the president's conference room, with security following him. A line of aggression was effectively established, and all Erik could think of was checking on Jamie. Upon his arrival back in the ballroom, he excused himself to Gordon and his wife. Then Erik locked eyes with Jamie and promptly escorted her out of the embassy for more suitable discrete surroundings where he could remind himself why he had just threatened the President of Russia, and the consequences that would follow.

27. WILL YOU EVER BE YOURSELF?

Sam: Are you saying I don't know how to have fun?
Al: Well, it's a relative term. Fun for you is
ancient languages, quantum physics.

— Sam and Al, *Quantum Leap*, "Animal Frat"

"Babe, are you coming?"

"Yeah, give me a second." Erik tucked in his oxford shirt, pulled out a vest from the closet, and started to button it.

Jamie walked into the bedroom and shook him with a warm smile. "Come here."

"What are you doing?"

She gently grabbed his hands, and she gestured that she was going to make him more fashionable. "I just want to do this." Jamie started to remove his vest and then roll up his sleeves.

"Oh."

She turned him around to face the mirror and straightened his shirt. Looking over his shoulder, she replied, "It's better like that."

"Yeah?"

Jamie smiled at him, nodded her head, and gave him a peck on the cheek.

"One more thing." She unbuttoned one top button. "Your shirt looked too tight, and now you look more relaxed."

"Yeah."

"Now, you are ready to go, but no Fedora."

"Okay."

Moments later, Erik and Jamie were in his car driving to a bar in the Washington, D.C. area. This time he was going to be exposed to her world. Every hour, every day, when Erik was in public, especially when he was with Jamie, he had to live the life of an ordinary man. Erik looked in his rearview mirror and thought to himself, will you ever be yourself? However, even he was claiming to be someone he wasn't, and his real self, a CIA paramilitary operations officer, lingered in his soul forever.

"Babe, is everything okay?"

"I think so."

As a paramilitary operations officer, Erik had developed a sixth sense, especially when people like Putin knew his cover. The only things Erik could trust were his instincts and always being alert. However, it didn't help knowing someone was watching him who, given the opportunity, would shoot him and ask questions later.

It was early evening when they reached the bar, Erik strategically parked his car, and they headed to the entrance of the Rhino Bar & Pumphouse. Erik and Jamie were going to meet some of her friends from the university. Jamie was in form-fitting jeans, a black and blue sweater, and low-cut black boots with heels; she looked casually glamorous. She felt entirely at home with this affluent crowd of young professionals and college students in their early 20s to early 30s wearing athletic to preppy dress from sports jerseys and polos to khakis and button-downs. As for Erik, he could adapt to any environment. However, as a paramilitary operations officer in close quarters with strangers, any one of whom could be an FSB operative who could easily bump into him and inject a biohazard poison that would kill him in hours. He had to be constantly aware of his surroundings and the individuals around him. Thus, a crowded bar did not seem like much fun. Consequently, he would have to fake it.

Jamie's friends occupied a table in a corner, and as she got closer to the table, her friends waved and called her name. Jamie introduced Erik to everyone, and they took their seats. Erik quickly analyzed his surroundings. He concluded that the Rhino Bar & Pumphouse had that traditional sports bar feel. Friendly groups of neighborhood sports lovers who wore their team jerseys for such teams as Red Sox, Eagles, Hoyas, Buckeyes, and Nittany Lions sat glued to a couple of dozen T.V.s and rooted for their teams. Erik noticed that small groups of preppy Georgetown boys, fashionable girls, and college kids continued to trickle in. Some stayed on the ground floor, while others headed upstairs. The ground floor saloon filled up quickly, with hordes of individuals huddling around high-top tables devouring wings and pitchers of beer. Then the giant rhino hanging over the bar caught Erik's eyes as he located the exits. Once he was done with that, he could devote some of his attention to the conversations at the table. Erik's job required him to lie, which he had been doing for the national security of the United States. He had to deceive its enemies. However, when he was on a date with his girlfriend in a sports bar with her friends, he had to keep reminding himself that lying was to protect him and the one he loved.

"So, Erik, Jamie tells us you guys met in a museum," Jason asked as he poured himself a beer.

Erik replied, "That's correct."

Erik raised his finger to Jason to hold his next thought as he turned to Jamie and asked, "What would you like, Jamie?"

Jamie pointed to the menu.

"Wings? What kind?" Erik asked her to clarify.

"We can do boneless and mild," Jamie replied, and Erik nodded. "Oh, their fries are amazing here, but we have to get them extra crispy, and, Erik, I want you to have fun."

Erik grinned and nodded.

"Relax, okay?" Jamie rubbed Erik's arm innocently as she kissed him on the cheek.

"Okay."

Erik motioned the server that he was ready to place his order, but Jamie got his full attention.

The server came to the table, hovered, and stated in Erik's direction, "Welcome to the Rhino Bar & Pumphouse; I am Rihanna. May I start with our drink specials?"

"Yes, the lady would like a pitcher of beer."

"Can I see your ID?" Jamie handed her I.D. over, and the server returned it, continuing, "Miller Lite or Coors Light?"

"Miller Lite," Jamie answered.

"As for myself, I will take ..." Erik tried to locate vodkas and gave up. "What kind of vodkas do you have?"

"Absolut, Grey Goose, and Skyy."

There was another thing about being in paramilitary operations: he could travel to different places of the world and get spoiled by great-tasting wines and vodkas. However, when he came back to the States, it became hard to pick a vodka that did not taste like cough syrup.

"I will take a Coke with no ice and a piece of lemon."

At that moment, Jamie placed her arm around Erik and whispered, "Babe, what's wrong?"

"I have never had any of those,"

"Vodkas," Jamie mouthed, and Erik nodded.

"Which one is better?" Erik questioned.

"Ask her."

Erik nodded and looked up to the server. "Excuse me; I have never had any of those. Which would you recommend?"

She glanced at him as if she were wondering what rock he lived under. Erik, using his keen sense of picking up on what she was feeling, addressed the issue.

Erik barked, "Yes, I know you think it is odd, so I'm asking you again, which one you would recommend?"

"Grey Goose. Would you like to make that a single or a double?"

"A single, and I will still take the Coke with no ice and a piece of lemon."

At that, as she was about to turn around, Erik raised his hand, indicating he was not finished. "We will take twenty boneless Buffalo wings, mild, and a basket of freedom fries, and can you make sure they are extra crispy?"

She nodded, turned around, and disappeared.

Erik directed his attention to Jason. "So, what were you saying before?"

Jason picked up where the conversation left off, "You are a fortunate guy to have her. The whole basketball and football teams, not to mention the frat guys, wanted to date her." A psych major, he studied Erik's behavior; however, what he didn't know was that Erik had picked up his vibe. "I confess I was interested in dating her, too, and, to be honest, I thought you two would never see each other again. Since you are here, I have to admit I see something different from the other guys." Erik gave a blank emotion as Jason continued to probe. "I am interested in people's dark corners and try to shed light on them." He tilted his head and leaned forward. "I feel you have one, and I would love to know about it."

"It's a little more complicated than you think."

"I have heard and read a lot of case studies."

"Not this one."

"Completely honest, yet avoiding the heart of the matter?"

"Maybe it's you who is not being completely honest

and avoiding the heart of the matter." Erik saw a single drop of sweat trickle-down Jason's brow and gave a malicious grin. "I thought so."

Jason quickly changed the topic. "What did you do to make Jamie fall for you?"

"You would have to ask her yourself."

"Ask me what?" Jamie cut in.

Erik was amazed that with the volume of noise in the bar, she was having two conversations going on at the same time, not including this one, and she still could hear her name. He thought she would be an excellent NSA communications operative with hearing skills like that.

"I asked your boyfriend what made you want to date him?"

"A lot of things."

Jason motioned her to continue, and Erik was intrigued to know this also. The server dropped off their drinks. Erik poured her a glass of beer; Jamie continued with the entire table listening.

"His honesty and his humor, the fact that he is down to earth, opens a door for me, and teaches me things I don't know anything about, and he is a gentleman and my knight in shining armor." At that moment, Jamie turned to Erik, smiled, and kissed him. "Oh, and he is amazingly smart. Lastly, his soul speaks to me."

One of her friends added, "Don't forget no one was good enough, spontaneous enough, or adventurous enough for Jamie."

Erik turned to Jamie. "Is that true?"

Jamie smiled and nodded.

Another of Jamie's friends addressed Erik. "We heard you have a Ph.D."

At that moment, the server brought Erik and Jamie's drinks. Erik, avoiding the question, immediately gulped his vodka as he tried to hide that he hated the taste.

"What is it in?"

"History."

A few minutes went by, and the server brought Erik and Jamie's food. "Would you like another shot?" Rihanna asked.

Erik shook his head.

It was still hard for Erik to relax; he was still on edge from last night and wondered what the outcome would be. He knew that in the world of intelligence, when threatened by a world leader, it opened not just one but many cans of worms. Not only did Erik have to worry about his own life, but now Jamie's life as well. Erik knew it was not something he could do alone. What he did not know was that everyone in the agency, including the director, had heard what had happened. They were using every resource of the agency to back and protect him and his girlfriend. Also, they had a half dozen men, all of them hiding in plain sight, all of them having the resources and skills to stop the FSB. It was a gigantic game of Stratego with each piece moving with information passed on. Each side would use analysis to determine what target would be neutralized. With each piece slowly being exposed, the CIA and FSB found themselves trying to understand their enemy more clearly and what would lead to the next phase. Erik's job was to make sure he and Jamie stayed alive.

Jason grabbed Erik's attention. "Erik, when you were an undergrad, you ate Ramen, right?"

Usually, Erik could sound educated on any topic thrown his way; however, this time, he knew the subject dealt with food, but what kind was the question. He nodded and smirked as they waited for his answer. He leaned over and whispered in Jamie's ear.

"What's Ramen?"

"It's soup."

Erik continued to bob his head.

Jamie explained further, "You know, the noodle soup."

Erik tried to make a mental image, but he came up blank as he turned to Jason and the others who were still waiting for him to answer. "No, I have not."

"Seriously?"

Erik nodded.

"How about Chef Boyardee?"

Again, Erik shook his head.

Jason changed the topic. "Erik, what is one thing you have done?"

Erik pondered as he flipped through the events he had experienced, of which there were plenty. However, the ironic thing was that there are many things he could not talk about because he had signed the National Secrecy Act. His eyes rolled in his head, and then his eyes enlarged as he recalled one.

"I was invited to a ceremonial dinner at John F.

Kennedy Space Center, where thirty astronauts and their families were attending. I sat next to John Glenn."

Erik grinned as the rest of the table just had blank expressions. He added, "It was an amazing night."

Erik felt a tug on his shirtsleeve. It was Jamie.

"They do not know who that is."

Erik tossed his hands up and shook his head in frustration.

Jamie rubbed his back to relax him. "It's okay; relax. So, you never had Ramen?"

He nodded his head.

"I still love you," Jamie said jokingly with a smile. "Next, you will tell me you never had a PBJ."

A confused look overcame Erik's face as the only thing that came to his mind was the U.S. Navy version of the World War Two B-25 Bomber. However, he knew she was not referring to that. "What is a PBJ?"

"Peanut Butter and Jelly Sandwich."

He shook his head.

"Babe, really?"

"Yes, I never had one."

"I will introduce you to one, okay?"

Erik shook his head. "If you make it, I won't eat it," he laughed.

Nearly ninety minutes had gone by, and Erik was still trying to engage in the conversation, at least when he could; however, even when he was their age, he had a difficult time associating with his peers. Because Erik was always on guard, it was hard for him to adjust and talk to those who were not in the intelligence community.

Especially when they brought up current and historical events, he knew the real classified information.

"Erik, we have started talking about the Cuban Missile Crisis in my lower-division history class. What are your thoughts on that?" Jason asked.

"Jason, what did your history teacher say about it?"

"Just the basics."

In Erik's world of the Intelligence Community, there were many ways to answer a question. One could explain it directly or encrypted. Without him thinking about it, he usually answered encrypted. "What do you mean by the basics?"

"You know, Russia trying to give missiles to Cuba and stuff."

Erik took a deep breath, collected his thoughts, and replied., "The reason the U.S.S.R. put the R-12, a theatre ballistic nuclear missile, that had a 2.3 megaton warhead, in Cuba was a direct response to the U.S. placing the PGM-19 Jupiter, a medium-range ballistic nuclear missile, which had a 1.45 megaton warhead, in Turkey and Italy. Their assigned target was Moscow." All listeners were mesmerized, including Jamie, as Erik talked; however, she remembered reading something very familiar. "During the 1960s, Russia and the United States had two different launch facilities, L.F.s, better known as missile silos, where nuclear missiles were stored and launched." Then Jamie realized where she had heard this before. It was two years ago when she was eating pizza, and a server brought her a placemat and written on it were the causes and effects of the Cuban Missile Crisis. "The Russians had their nuclear arsenal either on trains or MAZ-535 trucks which carried a missile on a flatbed. On the other hand, in the United States, their nuclear arsenal was in silos."

Jason raised his hand for Erik to stop. "Man, that is more information than I need to know."

Erik paused, looked around the table, and saw that everyone had a glazed look, except for Jamie, who had her chin on his shoulder.

"Thanks for the history lesson, but let's talk about something a little more exciting." Jason looked directly at Erik, "No offense." Erik waved it off as he excused himself.

Jamie got up and ran after Erik. Once in reach, she grabbed his hand and turned him around.

"Erik, what's wrong?"

He sighed. "I don't belong here."

"Yes, you do." She gestured him to look around the room. Jamie advised, "There is the same amount of people in this room as there was at the embassy. The only differences are that they are not in tuxedos and evening gowns, and they are not foreign diplomats." He shrugged off what she was saying, but she continued, "You told me last night not to worry what people think because I was with you, and now, I'm asking you to do the same."

"I just do not want to make you feel uncomfortable in front of your friends, and I don't fit in this crowd."

Jamie stepped closer to Erik and looked into his eyes. "Don't worry about that."

"You know when I was younger, I wanted to be like everyone else so I could fit in ... but I was not able to. I

was always different from everyone else. I am still that
way now, and it will never change."

"I am glad you are different and not like every guy out
there."

"Jamie, I am a nerd with a Ph.D."

She quickly raised her finger against his lips as she
shook her head.

"No, you are not," Jamie said firmly. He tried to get a
word in but failed as she continued, "Erik, listen to me,"
She paused until she had his total and undivided attention. "I love you for who you are."

"You could have any guy you want, so why did you
pick me."

"You're right; I could have, but I didn't."

Again, Erik tried to get a word in, but Jamie gestured
she wasn't finished. "The two years I didn't see you, I did
have a lot of guys ask me out. One happened to be a professional basketball player who played for the Washington
Wizards, and I had a celebrity actor take me to dinner."

"What was his name?"

Jamie shook her head. "That's not important."

"I am sure he was better looking than me?"

Jamie placed her hands on her hips, her eyes narrowed,
and she said bitterly. "Erik, stop."

"Did he take you to an amazing restaurant?"

"You want to know?"

Erik nodded his head.

"He was arrogant, and it was the worst date ever.
All he did was talk about himself the entire time, and I
couldn't get a word in. Erik, I wanted to die."

"You would have been better off with him than me. he could have given you everything you ever wanted and more. Unlike me…"

Jamie grabbed his shoulders. "Are you listening to me?"

Erik nodded his head.

"Yes, that might be true, but he thought his money and fame could win me over, but it didn't. Erik, you are the most amazing guy I ever met."

Erik shook his head.

"She grabbed his head and stared into his eyes. "Yes, you are. And unlike other girls, I am not attracted to the bad boys."

Erik rolled his eyes in his head in disbelief.

"Why don't you believe me?"

"I have my reasons."

"Because you think every girl wants a bad boy, and the good guys always finish last, right?"

Erik nodded his head again.

"Well, I would like to inform you, I love this amazing good guy. I have been waiting for him for two years, and now since I'm with him, I don't want to lose him. Also, I am attracted to him because he is super smart and funny, and most of all, he can teach me something I didn't know about, like the Cuban Missile Crisis." She paused as she gently rubbed Erik's cheek. "Yes, Erik, I'm talking about you."

A server walked by Jamie, and she asked for a pen and paper and handed them to Erik.

"Erik, write the word missile."

"Why?"

During training, Erik was taught to know that when someone, even his girlfriend, wanted to know something about who he was, the way they could do this was by small tests. Thus, the tests could tell them a lot about who he was. Erik knew if he refused to take the test, Jamie would automatically assume who he was if she was able to connect the dots. If he took it, there could be several outcomes. It could expose who he is and threaten his life. It could open a can of worms, and she would ask even more questions. It could be both or neither. Finally, its possible Jamie would love him even more for being honest with her.

"Please. I just need to know something." He gave her the what-are you-up-to look. "Please."

He sighed and shook his head as he quickly wrote down the word and handed the paper and pen back to her.

Jamie asked, "Who discovered the missiles in Cuba?"

"The Defense Intelligence Agency," Erik replied.

She glanced at the paper, grinned, and then looked at him.

"It was you who gave the server the placemat with the causes and effects of the Cuban Missile Crisis."

"Excuse me?"

Jamie placed her hands on her hips.

"Two years ago, at Pizza Milano, a server told me a young, handsome, blue-eyed, naval officer gave me the placemat with information on that historical event." She paused to study Erik's body language, which did not show anything. "I know it was not Alan because I had a picture of you on my phone and showed him."

"Jamie, I would like to say I am flattered, but I have asthma, and I cannot join the service. I would have liked it if I could have joined."

"I know it was you." Jamie held off the fact that she remembered an individual who raised fingers outside a car window that night.

Erik knew a general conversation about the past could quickly become very personal when his girlfriend wanted to know everything about him and certain places he had been. Thus, he knew he could be compromised and prayed no one was listening.

Jamie continued, "Okay, I am going to give you a hypothetical situation, and you tell me how you would act?"

Jamie waited for an answer, and he finally agreed.

She continued, "If you were in disguise, like wearing a mask, and you could not tell me it was you because Alan was by you, what is one thing you would say to me to let me know it was you. For example, your lucky number."

Erik shook his head. "Jamie, is this necessary?"

"Yes, it is. Erik, please. I need to know."

He glanced around him. Then he pulled her closer, and when Erik's lips touched her ear, he whispered on the exhalation, almost soundlessly, "Yes, it was me who gave the server that."

"And the other?" Jamie questioned, as her eyes began to water.

"Eins-Vier-Drei."

Jamie failed to understand him.

Erik repeated it in English: "One-Four-Three."

Tears of joy ran down her cheeks as she realized Erik was the German Officer who had protected her from Keith at the basketball game. "Why could you not tell me?"

"I was not allowed to see you or talk to you."

"Why not?"

Erik glanced around the restaurant and back into Jamie's eyes as he wiped her tears.

"Please answer my questions." Jamie pleaded.

Erik sighed profoundly and knew that he could be fired if he gave out sensitive information about himself. "Ask your questions."

"How long were you not allowed to see me or talk to me? Was it just for that night or the two years?"

"The two years."

"Where have you been?"

"Lots of places and everywhere you can imagine."

"Can you tell me?"

Erik shook his head.

"Erik, why not."

"Because when I go away for the museum, I go to some very undesirable places in this world. I cannot even tell you now because it is for my safety."

"Your work sounds very dangerous." She tried to make a joke. "Are you a sp ..." Jamie's voice trailed off as Erik crossed his arms against his chest, tilted his head down, and narrowed his eyes n as if they were penetrating her soul.

"I am sorry," Erik just nodded.

"Are you running away from something? I see your pain. Like the first day, I met you."

Erik said nothing as she stepped closer to him and saw the hurt in his eyes. "You keep it so close to you." Erik tried to pull away, but she held him close and leaned forward. "You don't have to run because I love you and I accept you for you."

Erik nodded his head and firmly expressed, "Please do not ask me anymore. This conversation cannot ever be repeated to Alan or brought up in public or private. Understand that I love you very much. I have always wanted to be with you since the first day we met."

She kissed him passionately, as people said, "Get a room."

Erik continued. "If my job asks me not to see you again, I will quit."

"What would Alan say? Could you give up your career, the prestige, and everything that goes with it just to be with me?"

"Yes."

"But Erik, you worked so hard to be where you are today."

"I don't care."

"You would give it all up for me?"

Erik nodded.

Jamie tried to find the words to say. "I . . . I don't know what to say."

"Say you love me."

"I love you, Erik." Tears continued slowly down her cheeks. "I love you, Erik."

Erik had a blank expression on his face as he slowly realized she was telling him the truth.

"Erik, how many more times do I have to say it?"

Erik raised his finger. "One more time."

"I love you, Erik."

Their lips touched, and they kissed passionately. Afterward, Erik put his arm around Jamie, and she slipped her arms around him and lay her head on his shoulder. The sweet smell of her perfumed hair, her warm touch, and feeling her heartbeat against his chest put him in a relaxed state, something he had not felt since Jackie was alive. Erik knew now he never wanted this feeling to go away, and the emptiness in his heart was now full. After holding her for a few minutes, Erik excused himself to go to the restroom.

Erik walked from a urinal to the sink and washed his hands. Another man left the restroom. Erik bent down and rinsed his face, then got up and dried it. He saw in the mirror a man standing behind him. Erik turned to face him.

"You think the CIA will just let you quit and let you and Jamie live a fairy tale life?" The individual said mockingly.

"Who are you? Who do you work for?" Erik noticed the door was locked from the inside and got in the MMA stance.

The individual shook his head. "Erik, you do not need to know who I am or who I work for." He paused to let Erik soak that in. As Erik tried to respond, the man raised his hand for Erik to let him finish. The man continued,

"If you continue the path you are on, you are going to expose yourself to unnecessary risk. I advise you to watch your back, and if you continue going down the road you are on, then you will need to know that you are digging your own grave."

"Is that so? I can fend for myself."

"You might be a CIA paramilitary operations officer, and you might be able to protect yourself; however, things can look like accidents...for example, Scott's death."

Erik thrust the man against the door and stated, "You killed him, or your agency. Why? He did nothing wrong."

With his back against the door, the man was able to maneuver himself around Erik.

Then the man declared, "I did not kill your friend. However, you have crossed paths with some people, and now they want to harm you and maybe those you know, like Jamie." The man raised his hand so he could finish. "I will tell you this; there is an agency out there who considers you a threat." Then he pointed at Erik to emphasize his point. "Your choices, and yours alone, killed your friend."

"My choices?" Erik stepped forward. "How would you know what I'm working on, much less the information I have obtained?"

"Well, let us just say that I'm in a position to know quite a lot of things about our government and, more importantly, I know about you and Project Sunflower. I am here at great peril to show you your path is deadlier with each passing moment and decision."

"When I find out who killed my friend, I will kill

them. I would like to see them, no matter what agency or individuals. If they try to kill my girlfriend or me, I will kill them." Erik raised a finger to make his next point clear. "I will find the answers to what I am working on." Erik pointed to the man. "You and your agency cannot stop me because I am fighting for what I believe is right."

"Erik, this shitty banter in the bathroom is not about me, your friend, or Jamie." He pointed to Erik. "It is about you, you son of a bitch. You are correct. The agency nor I can stop you." The man chuckled, then got serious, "You had no idea you were a threat until I said something. That is why you got a note on your valet ticket and why your car was bugged. Dr. Függer, you have much work to do on Project Sunflower, so don't jeopardize the future of your efforts."

The man unlocked the door as he ended with this note: "I will leave this final bit of information. I stand here telling you death is chasing you around every corner and behind every door, so open your eyes and use the skills you learned at The Farm, and maybe you will survive."

The man quickly left as Erik rushed out after him; however, another man trying to come into the restroom obstructed him. Erik pushed past the man and dashed out into the bar. When he looked around, he saw no sign of the man he was talking to.

Jamie noticed Erik's curious look and approached. "Babe, are you okay?" She rubbed his arm to get his attention. "Babe?"

He turned to her. "Yeah, I'm fine."

When a good friend is killed in the field, it was hard to deal with; however, it was worse knowing an agency in his government caused it, and there was nothing Erik could do. Mourning the death of someone who was a trusted colleague or friend was something he had to get used to because it was part of the job, but it was still hard to get over the loss.

After just spending a few days with him, Jamie was starting to learn Erik's different tones and facial expressions to determine the mood he was in. This was one time she did not push the issue. She was in a trance over how Erik's eyes were like that of a wolf's. His eyes narrowed and focused on every foot of the bar as if he were looking for his prey. Erik sighed in frustration as he placed his arm around her and pulled her close. Then he saw something in the near distance. Erik's analytical eyes focused instantly on something. Jamie tried to see what he was staring at but could not see anything.

"Erik, let's go back to the table." Erik shook his head negatively. "That's okay," she continued, "What do you want to do?"

"I was thinking about using infiltration tactics to bypass enemy front-line defenses, and then destroy his secure locations and strongholds from within, thus, causing destabilization and confusion to the enemy forces. If I can do that, then I can move onto targets, such as important enemy production facilities. Then after that, I would have accomplished my objective. In short, I will: Find, Fix, Flank, and Finish."

Jamie gulped, as worried wrinkles formed on her

forehead, and she replied, "Erik, maybe we should go home."

"No, I'm fine; never better."

"What you said sounds very creepy and disturbing."

"No, I'm fine. I want to play a video game." He pointed to Time Crisis 3.

Jamie released a huge sigh as she followed Erik to the game. Her only hope was that no one had heard him. Ironically, he was thinking the same thing. Erik started analyzing everything about the game.

While observing, he noticed there were several kinds of troops the enemy was deploying. Also, each troop had its unique strengths, weaknesses, and differences. Foot soldiers in green uniforms had low accuracy. Ammunition troopers wearing yellow or white uniforms carry the sub-weapon ammo, sharpshooters wearing red uniforms are the most accurate and had a higher percentage of hits. When they fired their first shot, it appeared as a red bullet.

Elite Troopers, Machine Gunners, wore yellow and orange uniforms with distinctive headgear. They continuously fired their rounds. There were approximately five seconds between each spurt that Erik could exploit as their weakness. Their strength was that it took five handgun bullets to kill them. Heavy Weaponry Troopers wore blue uniforms, and they are armed with either grenades, hand axes, rocket launchers, or flamethrowers. The flamethrowers were the most dangerous of this group. This troop took four bullets to be defeated.

Ground Infantry Troopers, also known as Clawmen,

wore light blue and white bodysuits and yellow and black bodysuits. Their strengths included agility, unpredictability in their attacking patterns, and there was great difficulty hitting them. Erik realized he would be able to get two or three rounds off, once they were stationary, which was not long. Also, he noticed these troops had life bars. He would need to make each shot count because it would take three bullets to kill the ones in the light blue bodysuits and ten rounds to kill the ones in the yellow and black bodysuits.

Last were the Maritime Infantry Troopers, also known as Scuba Slashers. Their strengths and agility made them unpredictable and hard-to-hit enemies, and they are armed with sharp blades on their arms. Again, Erik knew every shot counted because it took three bullets to kill them. In conclusion, Erik would need to be conscious of his surroundings and take advantage of what was around him so that he could kill these troops. In short, Erik knew he would have to focus, aim, and make every shot count.

Two burly guys, maybe football players from Georgetown, slammed their guns in their assigned holsters as they balled up their fists in frustration. They peered in their wallets to find any bills, but they had spent the last of their cash. One turned to face Erik but recognized Jamie.

"Hey Jamie, how are you?"

"I am great, Rob. How are you?"

"I am good. The guys are looking forward to seeing you on the sidelines." He paused as if he were building up his courage. "I take it you still won't go out with me?"

She shook her head. "Rob, I said before you are not my type of guy." Jamie wrapped her arm around Erik and pulled him close. "Also, I am taken."

"Him?" Rob pointed at Erik and shook his head as he rolled his eyes and motioned Jamie over.

"Jamie, you cannot be serious if that is your boyfriend. He looks like a geek," Rob stated, as he shot a glance at Erik.

Jamie replied. "Rob, he is more of a man then you are now or will ever be."

Erik walked toward the game, with Rob's scolding eyes staring at him.

Erik whispered to Rob, "Looks like she told you, but you quickly picked yourself up and carried on as if nothing had happened. On the other hand, this geek will be dating her."

"Fuck you."

"No, thank you; I have Jamie for that," Erik pointed to the gun. "I will be taking that from you."

Rob slammed the gun in Erik's palm, hoping it would sting. It didn't. Erik nodded as he pulled out his wallet and removed a single dollar bill.

Both guys chuckled and pointed as Rob stated, "Hey, geek, you are going to need more than a dollar."

Putting away his wallet, Erik replied with the utmost confidence. "No, I won't."

Jamie grabbed the dollar and got Erik four quarters. When she came back, Erik walked up to the machine, placed the quarters in, took several deep breaths as he closed his eyes and focused, and recalled what Senior

Instructor Rusch had said. "You will have hundreds if not thousands of enemies, in every part of the world. When they catch you, they will kill you ... but first, they need to catch you." He opened his eyes and focused on the screen, his pupils shrinking as he peered down the barrel, and he hit start as Jamie kissed him and wished him good luck.

Erik knew that even though it was just a video game, he would need to do his best with the equipment he had for an unknown tactical situation. In a real special assignment, he would have been wearing a lightweight Kevlar vest, which would have been concealed under clothing, but in the game, he had four life points until he was dead. A surprise attack had its advantages, but as in both real life and the game, no guarantee he would survive, but there was only one way to find out: just do it. Then the game alerted Erik when the fighting began with bold letters, and the computer announced ACTION!

Erik quickly realized that the narrative of the game was that he was one of two agents sent to what appeared to be a small Mediterranean nation to beat back an invasion. From the start, Erik realized the game had a predetermined path set for him, and his objective was to shoot his way past enemy lines, killing all enemy combatants. While he proceeded through enemy territory, Erik found a foot pedal that allowed him to duck and reload his weapon, which was some high-caliber pistol that held nine rounds with unlimited rounds in the magazine. Thus, if enemy combatants were firing their weapons at him, Erik could duck and avoid taking any damage. The drawback was that Erik couldn't hide forever because he had a timer continually counting down. To make it worse, he could not call in Quick Response Forces.

With that in mind, Erik knew it was similar to a real combat situation, and he would have to be aware of his surroundings: left, right, up, and down. By stage two, area two, he realized the game had many explosions, falling rocks, and other corporeal hazards to spice up the mundane, predictable process of shooting enemy combatants. However, now the enemy combatants slid out of doorways and popped up behind rocks. Also, at each new stage, the environment around Erik changed dramatically, creating some thrilling action-movie moments. Thus, Erik started to predict enemy combatants' tactics and applied what he had learned from the past stages to the new stage.

When Erik was at The Farm, he had been taught that when fighting in any environment, dehydration, exhaustion, and nerves were all equally deadly. But when playing the game, the one he was focusing on was dehydration. He motioned Jamie to get him something to drink and eat. Erik saw Rob approach him to his left, in the corner of his eye.

"Hey, man, what do you do for a living?" Rob demanded.

With his right eye, Erik saw he was coming upon a waterfall, and the enemy was using mini-subs that had automatic weapons. Using his left eye, he focused on Rob.

"I work at the National Museum of American History," Erik took out a mini-sub.

"You ever play this game before?"

"No. Rob, I would love to have this chat," said Erik while taking out another sub. "However, I'm a little busy now, and the last thing I want to do is beat your score and game. But it's still on the list."

Erik saw Jamie nearing, bringing his soda and buffalo wings. Just as the second to the last stage of level three ended, Erik quickly took a few gulps of drink. Jamie rubbed his back to relax Erik as she kissed him passionately. Coming into Stage three, Area three, Missile command, he had three life bars left. Seconds before the game started again, he closed his eyes and recalled the last thing Rosch had said to him, "Remember, you don't hide in the darkness; you are the darkness." Then Erik began attacking.

Unlike the other areas, the boss showed up first and launched a blitzkrieg attack, one after another. However, once Erik learned his pattern of attack, he attacked with the swords; once he was done attacking, Erik would need to aim and shoot him repeatedly to get his health down. As if that were not enough, it appeared many of the enemy troops had health bars and were aiming better. He knew their strategy, so it made things easier, but not really. Erik shook his head in disbelief when the enemy deployed three AFVs whose primary weapon was some kind of electricity gun.

Then it was the last duel between Erik and the boss. The boss's last act of defiance was attacking with two M202A1 FLASHES, which was the 4-barreled rocket launcher. Erik fired his final rounds at the boss. At that moment, the boss fell over backward, he was dead, and the game had finished. Erik had finished the area with two life bars left.

CONGRATULATIONS, TOTAL: 1704280, TIME: 0:30:37:90, ACCURACY: 90%

Jamie ran with her arms open, hugged, and kissed him. "You were amazing!"

"Beginners luck," Rob barked.

At that moment, the gun was ripped away from his hand with Rob standing in front of him. Jamie moved behind Erik.

"You are trying to show off in front of Jamie."

Erik shook his head.

"It's not like that in real life."

"You are right because, in real life, one cannot carry that much ammo." Erik rubbed his chin and raised his finger as a thought came to him. "There is another difference between you and me when it comes to this game."

"And that is?" Rob inquired.

"Just reminding you there is succeeding, trying, and sucking at something. I was succeeding at the game, and you were sucking." Erik saw Rob balling his hand in a fist. "You might want to think before you do that."

Erik turned to face the small crowd that had formed behind him. A few clapped and congratulated him, and others shook his hand. Ironically, when he came back from an op, this never happened. What happened would be hours of debriefing and analyzing every part of the operation, both good, bad, and what could have been done better, and then looking for the next national security threat.

He had done many ops and just recently got three medals for his service; however, they never would be talked about or shown to anyone. That was the life of a paramilitary operations officer: travel to amazing places, sleep in less desirable locations, and have people wanting to kill him. When he came home, he had to act as if he had a normal life. Erik could handle this; he just wished he did not always have to be on guard and, for once, be himself. However, this would not happen any day soon. Until that day came, Erik would face the question, will you ever be yourself?

28. WHAT YOU DON'T KNOW I KNOW

"To become another man for months or years, it's impossible to go through and not be affected at the most basic level. In a way, that's the point."

— *Burn Notice*, episode "New Deal,"
voiceover of Michael Weston

KENNEDY WARREN APARTMENTS, WASHINGTON, D.C.

The subtle vibration of Erik's cell phone from an incoming call woke him up. He felt naked not having his right hand tucked under his pillow until it rested on the grip of his Heckler & Koch MK 23, and he wondered why Alan was calling at this early hour. All in one movement, he got out of bed, unplugged his phone, and was out of the bedroom without waking Jamie. As Erik walked to his office, he mentally prepared himself. As a paramilitary operations officer, Erik hardly got calls like this, but when he did, it was usually bad news.

"Hello…okay…" Erik replied as he listened to Alan.

Erik walked over to a framed photograph on the wall and removed it. "When?" Erik questioned.

The most natural part of Erik's job was doing the overseas ops or even being shot at because he knew what needed to be done. The hardest part was the quiet hours when all he did was think about the unknown future and when he got calls like this—calls to tell him a fellow operative had been killed or a situation had developed. Unlike other graduations, when he graduated from The Farm, as a paramilitary operations officer, he had been told never to keep in touch with those who went through the fifty-two weeks of training. Every operative got a dagger and photograph of those who made it. Keepsakes like this were a reminder that a paramilitary operation officer should never bond in friendships with his classmates because others in the class could be killed, and he might be the only one left. In short, they were told that most operatives die before they are 35. Also, he could not have his friends' deaths as a distraction but needed to focus on his job. Erik heard sounds from the bedroom as the conversation was ending. "Yes, Sir...thank you...I will...roger that...zero out."

When Erik mourned the death of a friend, it was complicated because he was a paramilitary operation officer or a trusted colleague, and he could not share that information with anyone, especially his girlfriend. Therefore, he had to find another way to release his anger. At the moment, he threw the framed photograph and cell phone across the room. They struck his office chair and bounced onto the seat. Erik felt Jamie's presence, and he balled his hand in a fist and punched the bookcase. Jamie reached out to touch him.

Before she could get a word out, he stated in a cold, harsh voice, "What?"

"Babe, are you okay?"

"Yes, I'm fine." He turned around, locking his eyes on her. "Excuse me." He sidestepped her and headed to the living room.

"Erik," She replied, "Let me in." He glanced at her as if to say, do not go there. "If you want to make this relationship work, we have to share our feelings?"

"Not this one."

At the same time, Erik went to the kitchen, grabbed the Gomi Vodka and glass, and sat on the sofa; Jamie entered his office, grabbed the framed photograph and his phone, and sat by him. He poured some in a glass, took a huge gulp, clenched his teeth, and let the clean, clear, and near tasteless vodka slide down his throat. He slammed the glass and poured himself some more. Erik felt a soft touch on the back of his neck as her fingers combed through his hair. She placed the picture and his phone on the table. He slammed down another drink. Erik started to lie down, and Jamie positioned herself so he could put his head on her lap. He closed his eyes and remembered when he and Felix had gone through training together. Staring at the picture of the other five members of the forty-six Paramilitary Operations Class, Erik shook his head in disbelief that he was the last one alive.

"Erik…" He gave her the silent treatment, but she kept trying to break his shell as she turned his head to face her so she could look into his eyes. "Can you tell me who called?"

"Alan." She motioned for him to continue and mouthed, please. "He told me a friend had died." Then he turned his head away.

"Erik, I'm sorry. I had a friend who died when I was in high school. I know how you feel."

Erik jumped to his feet, with his eyes hiding all his emotions, of hate, anger, and grief all balled up into one, wanting to avenge his friend's death. He shook his head in disbelief about what Jamie had said.

Erik pointed to Jamie. "You think you know how I feel?" She nodded her head.

Erik pointed to himself and replied bitterly, "You don't have a clue how I feel."

"Erik, tell me how you feel."

Erik's nostrils flared up. "Really? Do you want to hear how I feel? That I had two friends die in the same damn week? Is that what you want to hear?"

"Yes, Erik. I didn't know that."

"No, you didn't."

"Erik, I do now. Open up to me…please." As Jamie started to stand, Erik motioned her to sit down. "Erik, did you ever think that maybe I could help you with your pain?"

"Help me? Seriously?"

"Yes, I love you. I am always here for you."

He grabbed and stared at the photograph, closed his eyes, opened them and looked into her soft, loving brown eyes, and said nothing. Like other paramilitary operations officers, Erik was always using his long-term cover, which was a part of him twenty-four hours a day, seven days a week, both domestically and internationally. He lived among his enemies and performed unethical duties for the greater good. However, Erik knew he would have to meet Jamie halfway even though she would have a tough time digesting what he was about to say. Erik knew that if he did not do this, the darkness would consume him.

Erik turned the photograph around for Jamie. "You see all these guys?" Jamie nodded her head. "They are all fucking dead!" He slammed the photo down, shattering the glass. "All of them!"

"I am sorry…"

"Sorry?"

Jamie nodded her head again.

Erik paced back and forth, and he thought out loud as if Jamie were not there. "Well, they were right, and I am the last one," referring to his job's short life expectancy.

"Who is 'they' and what were they right about?" Jamie inquired.

Erik pointed to Jamie with his eyes narrowing, as he explained, "Don't ask me anything; just listen and never speak about this." Jamie gulped and nodded. "I have lost over thirty friends." Erik pointed to the photo. "Those guys were like brothers to me. We went through hell and back. I am not the man I used to be…"

Jamie looked through his eyes and saw the years of loneliness and pain. She gasped and realized what Erik was saying. Erik fell to the floor, balled up, began to cry, and replied, "I have given up everything. I have nothing. I should be used to it, but it is so hard."

Jamie immediately joined him, wrapped her arms around him, and said softly, "No, don't say that. You don't need to be in so much pain. I will always be by your side."

"Promise?"

"Yes, Erik. I am so proud of you, and I love you so much." Jamie lifted his head, stared into his swollen, bloodshot eyes, and kissed him passionately. Erik recalled what Eagle Eyes had said, that he would travel in darkness, and along the way, there would be roses. Jamie was a whole bouquet of those roses. Jamie said softly, "Let's go back to bed."

As Jamie tried to stand, Erik pulled her down, and then there was a mad moment of hesitation, and Erik and Jamie smashed into each other's arms. Erik and Jamie kissed madly again as they rolled on the floor. Saddling him, Jamie stared at Erik. She knew that this day would come, and she was glad she had waited for Erik to take her virginity away. He stood up and picked her up as she wrapped her legs around his waist.

They looked into each other's eyes, as Erik stated, "There is something else. I want you to move in with me."

She couldn't find the words to say as she smiled and held him tight. What Jamie did not know was that when she graduated from Georgetown University, she would be offered a position from the Department of Defense as an administrative support assistant, working at the Pentagon in the Records Department on the third sub-level. This had all been set up by Admiral Bonesteiner to ensure her safety, at least for eight hours of the day until she saw Erik, since Vladimir Putin and members of the FSB, who were stationed in and around Washington, D.C., were watching them.

In the meantime, she would be watched when she left Erik's residence, and throughout the day when she was at the university. Orders were simple; if there were any attempts by an FSB operative to apprehend her, they were to be killed. Also, this meant Erik needed to carry his sidearm with him. Jamie looked into Erik's eyes with a bright smile as she realized her dream had finally come true.

"Are you sure?" He nodded. "You don't think it's too early?" He shook his head.

"When would you like me to move in?"

Erik tilted his head over his shoulder, glancing at the clock on the stove, and turned to face her, "Now."

"Erik, it's three in the morning." He shrugged his shoulders. "We will do it after breakfast," Jamie stated.

"Okay, what do you want me to make you?" Jamie shook her head. "You want breakfast later?"

She nodded as she kissed him with passion. Erik carefully carried her back to the bedroom, where they fulfilled each other's lustful desires that had been building up for the last two years. It was a new chapter in both their lives. To Jamie, it was a fairy tale that had come true. For Erik, it was a happy time again. Now he needed to remain even more focused and not distracted. That was one reason he had wanted to stay detached from Jamie. When she was around, he got distracted. That kind of distraction could be dangerous. Erik stared into her soft, adoring brown eyes before they both went to sleep and thought, *What you don't know I know.*

29. YOU COULD DIE CHASING THIS FEELING

"For a spy, compartmentalizing is second nature. Information is given on a need-to-know basis. In your professional life, this approach keeps you safe. In your personal life, it can be dangerous."

— *Burn Notice*, episode "Sins of Omission," voiceover of Michael Weston

CIA HEADQUARTERS, LANGLEY VIRGINIA

This brightly lit room had approximately 125,000 books and subscribed to about 1,700 periodicals that were divided among its three distinct collection areas: Reference, Circulating, and Historical Intelligence. It is the CIA Library, and only the agency personnel can use its resources that were selected around current intelligence objectives and priorities. The reference collection included the most up-to-date core reference collection. The research tools, either hardcopy or CD-ROMs, were encyclopedias, dictionaries, commercial directories, atlases, diplomatic lists, and foreign and domestic phone books.

The circulating collection, either hard or soft copy, consisted of monographs, newspapers, and journals from all over the world, always current. Lastly was the Historical Intelligence Collection, dedicated to the collection, retention, and exploitation of material dealing with foreign and domestic intelligence. This collection included more than 25,000 books and extensive press clippings. Hours upon hours could be spent here to find or research information, but not Erik.

Hunched over a computer, Erik rubbed his bloodshot eyes as he tried to find any information on Project Rainbow, also known as The Philadelphia Experiment. It was like finding a needle in a haystack of information. How were the Nazis to know about the project that happened in 1943, and not the Department of the Navy? Then, after hours of looking, something came up on his latest search, he hit print, logged off, grabbed the printout, and headed to the Historical Intelligence Collection.

He walked between the stacks with its neatly organized books and press clippings. Erik's sharp analytical eyes scanned each section up and down and left to right. His focus came upon the file he was looking for; he opened it and shook his head in frustration. The file contained a single letter from the Department of the Navy, dated July 23, 1976. It read:

"As for the Philadelphia Experiment itself, ONR (Office of Naval Research) has never conducted any investigations on invisibility, either in 1943 or at any other time. In view of present scientific knowledge, our scientists do not believe that such an experiment could be possible except in the realm of science fiction. A scientific discovery of such importance, if it had occurred, could hardly remain secret for such a long time."

He tossed the folder back on the shelf.

At that moment, Erik recognized a voice which he had encountered only once, at the Rhino Bar and Pumphouse. "You must be pretty desperate if you are looking in here for information."

"How in the hell did you get here?" Erik replied as the man lifted his ID. "So how did you acquire that, or was it made?"

Erik did not wait for his answer and walked past the man.

"We need to talk," the man stated.

Erik did an about-face and pointed as he emphasized his point. "We have nothing to talk about, you son of a bitch."

"Admiral Cole knows how resourceful you are, and he will make sure you never obtain the information you are looking for."

In a half-whisper, Erik replied, "Project Rainbow?"

The man nodded his head as he passed Erik and answered, "Follow me; we cannot talk here."

They walked by the courtyard that had an all-encompassing grassy lawn, fishpond, and flowering plants and trees. This area was a popular area for the employees during lunch, a chat with a colleague, or a short break in the fresh air.

"At least it is nicer here than where I work." The man's eyes glanced around casually; however, he was analyzing everyone and his surroundings. "They say you are very outspoken." He glanced at Erik. "But you are not saying much."

Erik stopped, looked around, and looked directly at the man as if to say why are you here?

"Erik, within the continental United States, there are storage areas, some as big as 15,000 square feet, that store classified documents." Erik mouthed Project Rainbow. The man nodded his head and continued, "This morning at 0100, Operation Umbrella went into effect, led by Admiral Cole—he was the Navy's offensive counterintelligence premier expert. During the Cold War, his job was to feed Soviet operatives false information when they reported home."

"He is going to destroy the information in the files."

"Mm-Hmm." He looked down, then directly into Erik's eyes. "Quick response. I would say you have…72 hours before all the information is sanitized." He walked by Erik and stared at him. "After that, it will be like nothing has happened." Then he pointed at Erik, "Your life is in danger."

"Why?"

"When you were in Berlin, you saw things that weren't to be seen. Care and discretion are now imperative."

"Project Bell?"

The man nodded. "This will be the last time I can provide you with information, but I am doing it because it's in my best interest to do so." The man handed Erik an envelope.

"What is your interest?" The man said nothing. "I did

find something in Berlin; they tried to kill me. You have to tell me why?"

"Erik, why do you always risk putting yourself in danger to find the truth? Why are you not dissuaded by all the evidence to the contrary while others accept the given answer and do not question authority?"

"Because I need the evidence, even though it is not entirely dissuasive, to make the best answer."

"Precisely."

"Will they continue to make things difficult for me and still try to kill me if I continue."

The man nodded his head, "You could die chasing this feeling."

Then he walked to the nearest door, opened it, and disappeared. Erik opened the envelope, pulled out the paper and a brass key, and read the contents of the paper. "Location: Pentagon Sub-Level 5, Clearance Top Secret Majestic, Military Identification Code: 14.1AEG-9906753, Combination, 10-28-19-43, Alphanumeric Tracking Code: 37104:AA920435:GTVKNJ37, Special Access Program Code Name: Cold Sunshine."

Erik placed the paper in the envelope, headed to his old O.G.D.S. team, and thought, it's not much, but it's a start.

30. EVERYBODY KNOWS THIS PLACE AS ...

"Human intelligence can often be collected with a cover identity. There are times, though, when a cover ID has more to do with who you are than how you act."

— *Burn Notice*, episode "A Dark Road," voiceover of Michael Weston

FORTY-EIGHT HOURS LATER:

As Erik descended by escalator, he took deep breaths and started mentally preparing himself to get in character, like so many times before. This time he was Lieutenant Commander Laurence Justinian. Unlike the other times, he would be infiltrating the Pentagon, and in a short period, he had his old O.G.D.S. team do what they do best. Carly made a latex mask and his false flag. Gary and John hacked, uploaded his false flag information, and established pin numbers so he would be able to get past security.

However, Gary and John advised him the only way they were able to do that and not get caught was to bounce the trace through twenty relay stations around the world and off four satellites. They said it would be the hardest trace the DOD (Department of Defense) had, but it had to be completed within ten minutes. That was the easy part, and now it was up to Erik to do his job, which was also illegal.

He strolled down the atrium of the New Headquarters Building, filled with potted palms. He looked up at the four-story arched skylight of green-tinted glass enclosing the atrium that allowed Erik to enjoy the outdoors and to see if the weather was good or bad. This area Erik enjoyed most because suspended from the ceiling on exhibit were models of the U-2, SR-71, and D-21 Drone. These models were there to remind people of intelligence history. These models, donated by Lockheed Martin Corporation, were the one-sixth scale of the real planes, and all three had photographic capabilities. He was filled with pride every time he walked into the atrium.

The moment Erik stepped out of the atrium and headed to his car, a black sedan with dark tinted windows and government plates prevented him from continuing. The passenger front window slid down for Erik to see a 9mm pistol was pointing at him, and a voice demanded that he get in. The individual pulled the hammer back. Once he was in, the driver immediately headed to the nearest exit.

Erik turned his head to face the driver. "So, are you here to stop me?"

"No, I am trying to prevent you from becoming a star on the memorial wall and give you some tips, so you do not get charged for treason," Alan replied as he pointed to the back seat. "Grab the attaché case." Alan waited for a few seconds and continued. "Inside, you will find a folder with forged documents on Project Rainbow." He pointed to Erik as he got off at the Columbia Pike exit, and continued, "You will replace the originals with these."

Alan explained that planting false information would be necessary because Admiral Cole or someone would be coming for it. He also knew this was a subtle art, and there needed to be enough reliable information to make it seem credible; but, not so much that it could be verified. There were two options. Do it right, and he could get away with it, or do it wrong, and he would be held, polygraphed, questioned, and lose his job and maybe his life.

He also advised Erik of the fastest way to get to elevators that would lead him to sub-level five and that he will have at most forty minutes to get in and out because Cole and Plackett had just landed at Dulles. They pulled up to the security gate at the Pentagon, showed their identifications, and proceeded to the entrance. Alan turned to Erik.

"Is Laurence Justinian a saint?' Erik nodded. "Why did you pick him?"

"Because when he was nineteen, he was granted a vision of eternal wisdom. When I was nineteen, I was exposed to the intelligence community."

Alan nodded. "Be careful not to run into Jamie."

"Roger that."

Erik saw the Pentagon from a different view and noticed things from analyzing them closer. As Erik walked up to the stairs, he thought of the Pentagon looking more like a fortress, with no marble or no ornamentation on its exterior. One could classify it as a no-nonsense structure, and not a building one would think of as a national headquarters. After going through the first security checkpoint, Erik proceeded down a hallway that led to the A-E Drive and took a left. What most people did not know about the Pentagon was that because of its design, it could take an average person seven to eight minutes to get to any part of the building. With that in mind, Erik had fourteen minutes to get to and leave sub-level five, two minutes for the elevator and checkpoints, and from fourteen to twenty-four minutes to find the file and replace it.

Well, that was the best-case scenario. The Pentagon had numerous stairways, two-way escalators, and passenger elevators; however, none of these would benefit Erik. He finally reached A Ring, the most inner ring of the five rings, and walked down a narrow corridor. In the near distance, Erik saw a pair of turnstiles and several armed Marines. One of the Marines by a monitor watched him with curious eyes, as he pulled out and inserted his identification and punched in his security code. Erik knew that if he made an error, he could be detained and questioned. After going through, he entered the elevator, inserted a brass key, and turned it clockwise, and at that moment, the elevator descended to sub-level five.

In the US Intelligence Community, the entire covert network, Erik had the resources of an entire intelligence agency; however, when he was doing an op, there would be no one behind him. He had reliable intelligence that pointed him in the right direction. That was his starting point in trying to put that last piece of the puzzle into place in a gigantic jigsaw puzzle of information that required months of research and analysis. However, he was warned that his life was in danger, and certain agencies would kill him if they saw him as a threat. They did. The government agencies not known to the American public specialized in surgical operations when dealing with such threats. They were done by discrete individuals or teams that no one ever heard about, and they would make a death look like a common accident or suicide.

This would make most people stop. However, it pushed Erik with his tenacity. With each piece of the puzzle, Erik found he understood that the enemy would get closer to him. He was penetrating the secrecy that shielded the people behind the scenes. He would keep fighting, trying to put that last piece of the puzzle in place, the one that would give him the answers he was looking for.

Stepping out of the elevator, Erik was immediately confronted by armed Marine guards and one at a podium. Erik knew as a paramilitary operation officer; no amount of experience or planning could help in situations like this. That's why he always had to be ready to adjust.

"Your identification, Sir." Erik handed it over. It was swiped and run through a facial recognition database. Once that had been confirmed, the ID was given back, and he was asked to sign in. "Thank you, Sir."

One advantage of being in high-classified areas was that the guards didn't ask about his business. Erik came to the door, swiped his ID, punched in his code, waited for the buzzer, and entered. The room was a large structure, divided into three major areas, from the ASCII map. Erik quickly analyzed the map and his surroundings, and he could tell this area was used to store documents and items that were highly classified. Erik made his way to Area B, an active environmental protection area, maintained at a constant temperature of 60°F, and a consistent humidity of 10 percent to preserve the documents properly. All crates and cabinets in the room bore no markings other than a standard military identification code scheme. The military identification code was made up of a three-letter code, an item number, up to seven numbers, and PP, part number, optional, for items that had been disassembled and stored in several crates. A few containers had warnings such as fragile, do not bend, or this item must be placed up. In summary, the documents and items here were only known by a few select individuals or were to be forgotten and never to be seen again.

Erik came to the GSA Class 6 — filing cabinet. The US General Services Administration set standards for locks and containers used for the storage of classified material for the entire federal government. This heavy-duty file cabinet had four drawers with a combination lock in the middle of one drawer. The mechanical combination lock had a limit to the number of times a combination could be attempted. After a certain number of failed tries, this lock would be permanently locked, requiring a locksmith to reset it. The third drawer had the military identification code, 14.1AEG-9906753. Again, it was like finding a needle in a bureaucracy haystack of information. However, Erik knew the lower the area and the tighter the security, the more valuable the information it was protecting, and it was going to be worth it. He opened the fourth drawer and quickly flipped through file folders until his eyes stumbled upon Tracking Code: 37104:AA920435: GTVKNJ3. He pulled out the folder, which was approximately two inches thick and had the words stamped on it: PROJECT COLD SUNSHINE. Below that, it said UL-TRA and the date 28 October 1943. He quickly replaced the original file with the duplicate, closed the drawer, and headed to the exit. Erik knew there was a chance he could be compromised, so his option was to take what he could on his way out. Like doing an op overseas, he needed to keep calm and collected and get the hell out.

He proceeded to the elevator, signed out, and continued. He ascended to ground level. As he moved and exited the turnstiles, he saw two individuals approaching him. Then Erik realized who they were: Cole and Plackett. He overheard Plackett speaking.

"His car is at Langley."

"Any updated transcripts?" Cole questioned. Plackett shook his head. "I do not want him to have any information on Project Rainbow."

"Do you think he will attempt to come here?"

"He might have some field experience in Russia, but their security is primitive. He is just an analyst, and we know his every step since his car has a tracker, and we have his car bugged."

"We found some more information on him," Plackett added, as Cole motioned him to continue. "He has a girlfriend. We do not know her name, but we are working on that."

Erik glared at them with scolding eyes, and then he disappeared around the corner and quickly headed to the exit. Calculating how much time had gone by during the distance he had walked, he knew Cole would be nearing the safe or opening it. At the moment Erik walked out, Alan pulled up with the passenger door swinging open, Erik slid in, and Alan accelerated to the exit. Alan bashed his hand against the steering wheel, as he looked at his watch and rolled down his window.

"We are out of time," Alan stated, watching a guard picking a phone. "Hang on, kid." At that moment, Alan pushed the accelerator to the floor, barely missing the guard. Erik looked back, as Alan said, "The Pentagon is shut down."

31. NO QUESTIONS ASKED

"The most dangerous time in any operation is just as everything is coming together. You never know whether you're about to get a pat on the back or a bullet to the back of the head. Of course, there's not much you can do but act like everything is fine."

— *Burn Notice*, episode "Lesser Evil,"
voiceover of Michael Weston

While Carly and Erik were in Hollywood Room One destroying all physical evidence of Lieutenant Commander Laurence Justinian, Gary and John were eliminating all computer files of the same person. Erik stepped out of the Hollywood Room and headed toward Alan, then to the exit, as Gary gave a thumbs up, indicating that the task was completed. Alan and Erik agreed they would leave separately, three minutes apart, with Erik going first and Alan holding the documents. Erik did not know what was going to happen next or when it would happen, but either way, he knew he trusted his team, Alan, and, most importantly, his gut. He was trained to stay calm and collected in all kinds of situations, especially when two black SUVs with dark tinted windows were blocking his car, and seven men armed with semiautomatic weapons were getting out. Among them, he recognized Admiral Cole and Brigadier General Plackett.

"We need to talk," Cole announced with an accusing finger pointing and motioning the security detail to surround Erik. At that moment, Erik dropped his attaché case and pulled out his service weapon and aimed it at Cole while the security detail aimed their assault rifles. "Lower your weapon and get in the vehicle ... now."

"And if I refuse?"

Cole stepped forward. "Then, I will do it for ..."

"Put down your weapons now!" A voice ordered.

The Central Intelligence Agency's Security Protective Service (SPS) surrounded Erik and the others. Their job was the protection of agency personnel and facilities, and they would use lethal force if necessary. The SPS would rank with the best SWAT team, both in tactics and in firepower. Erik took a glance around him as Cole's eyes narrowed. Erik noticed the SPS control officer, executing the plan for contacting suspects, by considering the elements of his team's surroundings, such as areas of cover and factors that may affect sight and hearing.

"Sergeant, I am Admiral Cole ..."

"Sir, I am ordering you and your men to place your weapons on the ground and put your hands up. Do it now!"

He glanced at Erik. "Dr. Függer, lower your weapon. We have this under control." The control officer's eyes and other members of the SPS were reading the body language of Cole's men while calling in additional units to establish a perimeter as they approached the suspects. The support officers kept the appropriate distance between themselves and the other individuals and stayed alert to identify potential resistance or threats, as they backed each other. "I am not ordering you again. Lower your weapons and place your hands behind your heads!" Cole looked around and noticed more SPS officers arriving, surrounding, and inching forward. The officer in charge coordinated the cover officers, who had just arrived as the initial officers detained Cole and his men. The officer in charge was handling all communication, commands, and interviews. Once the men had been detained, the officer in charge approached Erik. "Dr. Függer, are you okay?"

Erik nodded and asked that one of the vehicles be moved so he could be permitted to leave. Erik rubbed his chin and grinned maliciously. "Excuse me, officer; what is your name?"

"Officer Yates."

"Officer Yates, I am ordering you to detain them as long as you can and shoot the tires of the SUV's."

"Why, sir?

"They are a threat to the National Security of the United States until they are identified. Now order your men to do what I said."

"Yes, sir."

Erik approached Cole as shots were fired, immobilizing each vehicle. "I hope you have roadside assistance because flat tires are such a pain in the ass."

Cole responded, "This is far from being over, and we will meet again."

"If you have a problem with me, write it on a piece of paper, fold it, and stick it up your ass."

As Erik drove off, he texted Alan to let him know he was on his way. He took a deep breath and thought to himself, *I wake up every morning, and I have more enemies. One day I will have to face that my enemies will know who I am. I believe that day has come. Now I will always have to be on my guard and be looking over my shoulder.*

32. CONFESSIONS OF THE FORGOTTEN

"For a spy, compartmentalizing is second nature.
Information is given on a need-to-know basis. In
your professional life, this approach keeps you safe.
In your personal life, it can be dangerous."

— *Burn Notice*, episode "Sins of Omission,"
voiceover of Michael Weston

Alan glanced at his watch, and his eyes narrowed as they focused on Erik. "You do know now there is no turning back, and now you are sailing in uncharted waters."

Erik's eyes rose above the file as he nodded, "I know." Then he went back to reading.

August 12, 1943, Second Test: Onboard the Eldridge, DE 173, there was a voluntary crew made up of 33 sailors and officers. The signal was given to turn on the equipment that was made up of some 3,000 6L6 tubes in a hedgerow, one pulse generator system, and other exotic equipment. It was a manned operation. The first seventy seconds went according to plan, and the USS Eldridge, a destroyer escort, became invisible to radar. However, it was possible to see the shape of

Eldridge's hull through a greenish mist. Then suddenly, the ship disappeared entirely from the harbor without a trace.

"Have you read this?" At the moment Erik looked up, Alan tapped his watch. Alan knew they were running out of time until they could be compromised by having this file. Erik continued reading. *Once that happened, panic spread like fire on the observer ships. Radio operators repeatedly tried, with no avail, to communicate with the Eldridge. The Eldridge reappeared four hours later, in the same place, but something was not right. A boarding party was sent to investigate. As they neared, they saw the superstructure was damaged, including the antenna built by T. Townsend. Once onboard, what they saw was devastating; In a count later, four men were buried, two on deck—their bodies stuck in steel—and two in walls. A fifth man had his hand stuck in a steel wall; he lived but had his hand amputated. Also, some of the crew suffered from fourth-degree burns that went through entire skin and into underlying fat, muscle, and bone. Their skin was black charred with eschar. Once a headcount was done, it was clear that many of the crew had disappeared. Those few who survived were classified as insane. After the second test, all records and crew disappeared, never to see the light of day again.*

"Dear God, that is so fucked up." Erik tossed the folder on Alan's desk, shaking his head in disbelief.

Alan glared at Erik as if to say, are you done now, and Erik nodded. "You need to focus on the here and now."

"Alan, how can you ignore what's in this folder?"

Alan gave a blank expression and replied, "That's the way it is."

"In 1943, at that moment before the experiment, the Navy knew who they were and the next, after the experiment, the Navy had no memory of them, and all you can say is, 'That's the way it is?'"

"'That's the way it is' can sometimes be the best explanation."

"Not for me."

"I'm not sure you're ready for more."

"Try me."

"Erik, can you accept what you see and what you are going through as your reality?"

"Which reality do I accept?" Erik raised his eyebrow. "That one? The one the CIA created, or my real life that hardly exists?"

"Haven't you accepted both, looking into all those mirrors?"

Erik rubbed his fingers through his hair. "I am tired of looking at them."

Alan leaned over his desk and stared into Erik's bloodshot eyes. "Erik, you've done a lot of good for the agency. Bonesteiner and I know you can do a lot more."

"More? I don't want more. I want to be myself and quit."

"Then why haven't you?"

"Because I want to serve my country and make the world a better place."

"Erik, you are like a cop."

Erik shook his head. "No, no! I am nowhere close to being like a cop."

"Kid, you just contradicted yourself." Alan raised his

hand so he could finish his thought. "You know how cops can't turn off the job? Their shift ends, but they take one more call and then one more."

Erik pointed to himself, "That's not me." Then he pointed at Alan. "You know that."

"That's bullshit, and we both know it. Erik, you can do this as long as you want to."

"I can quit anytime I want?"

"Technically, yes."

"Technically? What's the catch?"

"There is no catch." Alan pointed at Erik, "You control your destiny."

"I just wish I could share the things I know or even vent about days like this to Jamie."

Alan shook his head as he lifted the folder, "Who can you share this with?" Erik shook his head, knowing the answer was no one.

"Exactly. This will get you killed or make you disappear."

Erik glanced at his cell phone and looked up. "I just got a text message, and the number is blocked."

"It's Admiral Cole. What did he say?"

"He wants me to meet him at the Lincoln Memorial. Should I meet him?"

"You are going to have to meet him sooner or later." As Erik left Alan's office, Alan warned. "If you are not careful, you are two steps from your death."

33. TWO STEPS FROM YOUR DEATH

"Every normal man must be tempted at times to spit on his hands, hoist the black flag, and begin to slit throats."

—H. L. Mencken.

LINCOLN MEMORIAL, WASHINGTON, D.C.

Erik knew meetings were never fun, especially with someone compelling in the IC who hated him, but of course, if Admiral Cole wanted him dead, that was a different story. Erik decided to show up early because he never knew what Cole was planning. The hardest part was knowing when to show up. If Erik showed up too much earlier, eventually, he would get bored, and then he would have to force himself to stay alert. If he showed up near the meeting time, Cole could have surveillance set up and be watching his every move. So, the lesser of the two evils was learning how to wait. However, there was a definite advantage of being early: he could prepare an exit strategy and map out in his head an escape route or two, just in case things went south.

Most people would think it was an advantage to have law enforcement walking around so the other person would not pull out his weapon; however, that would be a wrong assumption because if the person worked for a dark agency, he could kill a cop and walk away. That was why it was hard to act natural and be prepared to use his weapon. Lastly, Erik had to beware while he was talking to Cole because several things could happen. Cole could have someone hook up a C4 detonator to his car, or force him to a vehicle, then have a bag put over his head and be taken to a remote location to be questioned. Either way, it was not a good ending, but he would have to wait and see the hand that was dealt him.

Erik had his back facing the statue and watched the individuals coming in, which were very few in the early evening. Then wooden heel dress shoes echoed throughout the chamber, as Erik recognized the men from Cole's security detail who spread out to secure the perimeter. Admiral Cole appeared and made his way into the blinding light of the memorial. Cole was in his service dress blue uniform that showed the rank of admiral as noted by the four stars on his shoulder boards and the gold sleeve stripes, making all those inside instinctively back away or leave because of his commanding presence. Then a deathly quiet swept throughout the memorial, as Cole and Erik approached each other.

Once in hearing distance, Cole ordered Erik, "Follow me." Erik complied, and they proceeded to the exit and headed to the Reflecting Pool, as the security detail followed closely behind.

As they descended the flight of stairs, Cole pulled out a BlackBerry. Unbeknownst to those that might be a witness, this small black box was able to detect and scramble listening devices. He calmly pressed a series of buttons, then held the device between them. Both men were in the deadly, mysterious, and treacherous world of international espionage, where neither could be trusted, each always looks over his shoulder, knowing that each breath could be his last. Cole was hoping there would be fewer people out this evening as the moon played peek-a-boo between the clouds and, when out, it made the tranquil water of the reflecting pool look like mercury. Cole was not able to follow his original plan. Even though Cole had sent Erik a text message to meet, what would be discussed could not be addressed over the phone, no matter how secure the communication lines were. Both men also knew that to underestimate each other was a tactical mistake, and if exploited, one could take advantage.

"Dr. Erik Függer, an analyst for the Central Intelligence Agency?"

"You already know who I am," Erik declared.

Cole smirked, "I was making sure I was talking to the right person."

Erik glared back, "Oh, were you afraid someone could be listening?"

Erik looked into Cole's cold blue eyes and replied, "Admiral Dean Cole, when you were in the Navy, you did offensive counterintelligence." Cole just listened with a blank expression. "Your job was to feed Soviet operatives false information that they then would report home."

"I see you have been asking around or digging where your nose does not belong."

They continued walking, as they played chess mine games, attempting to outwit the other into checkmate.

"Maybe I am better at getting information than you are."

Cole attempted to read Erik's body language, his eyes penetrating. "Like in the Pentagon?"

Erik knew Cole was using different interrogation techniques: first, don't ask questions directly and study the person's body language; second, ask for exactly what you want and listen to the tone in his answer. Both were very effective; however, Erik knew it was like a game of poker, and one must not show his cards. In training, it was ground into his brain that as a paramilitary operations officer, he would have many enemies. However, when an individual or agency from his own country saw him as a threat to them or national security, everything changed. He found out who his friends were, knowing every breath could be his last. Erik said nothing and stared at the reflecting pool.

"You are just an analyst, and you do not have a clue whom you are fucking with."

Erik nodded, "You are maybe a director or something for a dark agency who thinks they can get away with anything with no jurisdiction."

"You are crazy. Listening to too much of that early morning radio show that talks about government cover-ups and conspiracies."

"Am I?" Erik looked into Cole's eyes and knew he was

hiding something. "Then, why are you so quick to answer?"

"What makes you so sure there are such agencies out
there?"

"Because the other side believes it too." Cole just listened. "You and I know that."

"You are walking on thin ice, and you stick your nose
where it does not belong, one day you will regret it."

"Are you threatening me?" Erik pointed an accusing
finger at Cole.

"You are a poor, dumb son of a bitch." Cole looked
around and then back to Erik. "You have done more
damage than you know."

"Good."

"It didn't have to end this way. You don't know when
to stop."

"Of course, it did. I was doing my job."

Cole leaned forward, and in a half whisper, he replied,
"You're about to be a very lonely man."

"If you kill my girlfriend, I will find you and kill you."
Cole did not seem fazed by Erik's threat. "If you try to kill
me...you better not miss."

"Are you done?" Cole mocked. "I will tell you something...next time you go on an op, you will be remembered as a star on the memorial wall."

"Another threat?"

Cole shook his head, his eyes narrowing. "I am letting
you know that you are two steps away from your death."

34. MAKE YOUR OWN FATE

"Things are not always what they seem; the first appearance deceives many. The intelligence of a few, perceives what has been carefully hidden."

— Phaedrus

Thirteen minutes later, Erik cautiously walked to his car, his analytical eyes glancing at everything they made contact with. Erik knew FSB and other government agencies, including ones in the community, had assassins. There were several problems when dealing with them. First and most importantly, they were hard to spot, even for trained individuals. Second, there were many different ways to kill a person besides shooting, such as C4 hooked up to the car starter, injection with poison, and more. Third, nine percent of an assassin's job was preparation for the assassination, one percent was the assassination itself, and 90 percent was forestalling moves, formulating approaches, and finding the perfect opportunity to execute the murder. Lastly, for the target, the job had only one criterion, 100 percent waiting. Unfortunately, there was nothing Erik could do in this situation because the assassin very likely had been watching him, so the assassin had the upper hand.

However, Erik knew there was often a fine line when he thought someone was following him and when to act on it. When this happened, there would be one of three possible results: one, the assassin would win; two, Erik would win; or three, he would scare the hell out of an innocent bystander and possibly kill him and be arrested. Of course, there was only one way to find out, and that was when it happened.

As Erik did an about-face, he pulled and aimed his service weapon at the individual behind him, who had a parcel. Erik's eyes narrowed as the individual's eyes widened, and sweat trickled down his forehead.

"Give me one reason I shouldn't kill you," said Erik, who usually would not hesitate, but he knew that either this was not the assassin, or he could be a decoy, or neither of the above.

"I was instructed to give this to you."

"Open it." Again, Erik was taking a risk because even though the parcel did not appear to contain a pistol, it could carry a biological weapon. However, he figured whoever wanted him dead would not risk others. Then again, maybe they would. Erik noticed the individual's eyes looking over his shoulder. "Whoever is behind me, I will advise, I will take one maybe both of you." Sweat built between Erik's palm and the grip of the gun, as he was about to pull the trigger. Then a familiar voice came from behind him.

"Erik, he means no harm. Take the parcel."

"I thought we were not going to meet again?"

"Something came up; we need to talk. Let him go."

"What's his name?"

"That is not important." The man saw Erik's actions as he demanded an answer, so he replied, "Craig."

Erik grabbed the parcel, turned around, holstered his weapon, and demanded, "What do you want?"

"In the near future, you will be called to Admiral Bonesteiner's office, and there will be two gentlemen you have met already. They are from a dark agency and will ask about your historical theory on Field Marshall Rommel."

"Who? What dark agency?" Erik asked as the man sighed. "Why do you play these games? Just tell me. Is it Admiral Cole and Brigadier General Plackett?"

The man gave a blank stare and nodded affirmatively.

"Whom do they work for?" asked Erik.

"Harry Nilsson was with us in 1968."

A blank expression came over Erik's face. "I fear you've relied on me way too much."

Erik pointed to himself and back at the man. "You are the one that came to me." He gave a theatrical gesture. "Who is Harry Nilsson?"

"Admiral Bonesteiner knows."

"You know the admiral?"

The man nods.

"How?"

"I served under him. When I need his help, he gives it, and vice versa. Especially when it comes to you and Cole."

404 | Erik Foge

"I see," said, Erik rubbing his chin as he read the body language of the man. "Did Bonesteiner ask you to assist me?"

The man gave a blank stare as if he were a corpse.

"Then tell me who is Harry Nilsson?" inquired Erik.

"You are resourceful; look him up." The man pointed to the parcel. "You will need that."

Erik pulled out a German Officer's ID book. As he flipped through it, he saw a photo of himself in a major's uniform of the Heer. "What in the hell is going on?"

"As I tried to tell you, in the near future, you will be called to Bonesteiner's office. You will discuss Rommel with two other gentlemen, and then you will be told you will be sent back in time." Erik shook his head in disbelief as he rubbed his forehead. "You might not believe me, but two others you know went back in time already."

"Who is that, or can't you tell me?" Erik mocked.

"Knight and Mulder." Erik gave the I-don't-believe-you look. The man continued, "Make sure you sign in proper locations and bring that back, or you will be compromised. You have made some powerful enemies, and they are making plans for you."

Erik waved him off and headed to his car.

"Plans? Do you mean, plans to kill me?"

"I don't know."

Erik motions him to continue talking.

"You have become too high-profile, and killing you could expose them."

"Expose who?" asked Erik.

The man shook his head.

Erik continued probing for answers. "I don't know who you are. I know nothing about you."

"I'm a friend, and my friends call me Greg."

Erik crossed his arms against his chest and asked, "Why won't you tell me?"

"There are some things you do not need to know."

"Can you tell me anything?"

The man motioned Erik to walk with him. "You are a man that has made many enemies, both overseas and in the intelligence community. Your enemies in the community see you as a crusader." He glanced to read Erik's body language, which revealed nothing.

Erik finished his thought. "And those individuals do not like the crusader and the crusade I am on."

The man nodded his head.

"Then why help the crusader?" asked Erik.

"Because you cannot do this alone."

35. WHAT COMES NEXT

Higgins: You never complained 'til yesterday
Joe Turner: You didn't start killing
my friends until yesterday!

—Joe Turner and Higgins, *Three Days of the Condor*

CIA HEADQUARTERS, LANGLEY, VIRGINIA

July 21, 2008: Erik's eyes focused on every aspect of Route 123; his thoughts focused on the most important day since he had been assigned to Project Sunflower nearly three years ago. He was prepared to give his briefing in front of Admiral Bonesteiner and two people from another agency. Erik knew he had to play dumb and act like he did not know what agency or the people were represented.

Erik was not afraid to present what he found, knowing that he had been warned last year when he was digging for his information that he should just let it be. Erik brushed it off as if it were nothing. The headlights from his car illuminated that old familiar sign that he passed every day going to work, "WARNING, RESTRICTED. U.S. GOVERNMENT INSTALLATION EMPLOYEES AND OFFICIAL VISITORS ONLY". Then he headed down the unnamed street that was sheltered by large oak trees and prepared to do the morning rituals of getting into the compound as he slowly neared the guarded entrance. He came to the speaker box, and a deep authoritarian voice stated: "Identify yourself."

"one-zero-zero-three-one-nine-seven-one."

Silence.

"You are clear to proceed."

Erik drove forward, turned his headlights off, and pulled out his ID. Two uniformed guards with assault rifles stared in Erik's direction, studying his every movement. Another appeared from a tollbooth-like station. He ordered Erik to stop.

"Identification." The guard held his hand out, and Erik placed it in his hand. He ordered, "Look at the camera and state your first and last name."

"Dr. Erik Függer."

Approximately thirty seconds went by, and Erik was cleared to enter. He navigated to the parking lot and parked in his usual spot and made his way to the entrance. It was a raw day with an overcast sky that hovered over the 258 acres. Nearing the doors of the Original Headquarters Building, he pulled out his ID again. Once in the building, he crossed the seal of the agency. He paused and paid his respects to all those who were remembered on the Memorial Wall. The stars symbolized all those CIA officers, analysts, and field operatives, who had given their lives for the United States and its government. He glanced above the stars and read the inscription: "In honor of those members of the Central Intelligence Agency who gave their lives in service of their country."

He continued to walk, stared at the south wall that had a Biblical quotation fixed in stone. The verse — "And Ye Shall Know the Truth and the Truth Shall Make You Free, John 8:32" — which stood as the agency's motto. He thought out loud. "Let us hope that will hold true today." Then he got to the last security check, entered his ID, and then was allowed to proceed to the elevators. He descended to the sublevel where his office was. The elevator came to an abrupt stop. He exited, and strolled along, staring in the distance down the poorly lit walkway. He stopped and saw a group of people clearing out two offices. They worked in the same department as Erik.

Erik cleared his throat. "Excuse me. May I ask why you are clearing out Mulder and Knight's Vaults?"

"They are no longer with the agency," the individual stated as he continued working.

Looking for an explanation, Erik pushed, "What do you mean by that? Were they relieved of their duties or …" He paused before continuing, "Did they die?"

The worker stopped and stomped in Erik's direction. "Let me make it clear for you. They are no longer with the agency. Is that clear?"

"No, it's not. We were friends, and we worked in the same department."

"Well, you are not at liberty to know. Move along."

Erik continued to his office, with his thoughts racing

in his head, trying to make sense of what he heard. He pulled out his keys, unlocked the door, placed his attaché case down, and took a seat at his desk. The office was damp and dark with a musty old paper odor from old newspapers and books which consumed the room. The air conditioning struggled to push out the cold air through a rusted air vent layered with dust. A single light on the desk broke the darkness as the light dissipated over books and classified documents.

Erik was behind the desk, hunched over, with his curious eyes reading and analyzing. After every couple of seconds, he wrote down detailed notes. The sound of graphite scratching the surface of the paper was the only noise. He occasionally glanced at a computer screen, the glare reflecting on his face. Surrounding him were bookcases filled with both historical and reference books covering the European Theater of World War II and Field Marshal Erwin Rommel. Directly behind him was a poster of a duck, sitting in a chair, staring over his shoulder at a wall that had two bullet holes by his head, with the caption, "Sitting Duck."

He turned his head away from the computer screen and glanced at the framed photograph of the love of his life. He grinned as he drifted into a daydream. The ringing of the phone broke the silence and awakened him.

"This is Dr. Függer. Yes, sir. I am on my way."